DESERT
DESTINY

MILLS & BOON

Dear Reader

Summer is here at last...! And what better way to enjoy these long, long days and warm romantic evenings than in the company of a gorgeous Mills & Boon hero? Even if you can't jet away to an unknown destination with the man of your dreams, our authors can take you there through the power of their storytelling. So pour yourself a long, cool drink, relax, and let your imagination take flight...

The Editor

DESERT DESTINY

THE SHEIKH'S REVENGE
by
EMMA DARCY

HOSTAGE OF THE HAWK
by
SANDRA MARTON

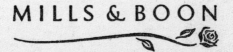

MILLS & BOON LIMITED
ETON HOUSE, 18-24 PARADISE ROAD
RICHMOND, SURREY TW9 1SR

CONTENTS

THE SHEIKH'S REVENGE

BY
EMMA DARCY

HOSTAGE OF THE HAWK

BY
SANDRA MARTON

Emma Darcy nearly became an actress until her fiancé declared he preferred to attend the theatre *with* her. She became a wife and mother. Later, she took up oil painting—unsuccessfully, she remarks. Then she tried architecture, designing the family home in New South Wales. Next came romance writing—'the hardest and most challenging of all the activities,' she confesses.

Recent titles by the same author:

DARK HERITAGE
HEART OF THE OUTBACK
THE UPSTAIRS LOVER
AN IMPOSSIBLE DREAM

THE SHEIKH'S REVENGE

BY

EMMA DARCY

*MILLS & BOON and the Rose Device
are trademarks of the publisher.*

*First published in Great Britain in 1994
by Mills & Boon Limited*

© Emma Darcy 1993

Australian copyright 1994

ISBN 0 263 78588 2

*Set in Times Roman 10 on 12pt.
49-9408-46078 C*

*Printed in Great Britain by
BPC Paperbacks Ltd
A member of
The British Printing Company Ltd*

CHAPTER ONE

LEAH HAD the uncomfortable feeling of being watched. It was a strange, prickly sense of some strong presence menacing her peaceful solitude.

Absurd, she told herself. It was one of the perks of her job that this walled garden was completely private to her, a safe retreat where she could enjoy herself in her own way, without interruption or interference.

Nevertheless, she sat absolutely still for several moments, listening. There was no sound other than the soft splash of water bubbling from the fountain, supplying a cool tranquillity that blocked out the rest of the world. She ruefully decided her nerves were still on edge from all the emotional dramas of the morning. The whole palace was in a ferment in preparation for the month-long wedding celebrations. It was a welcome relief to get away from it for a while.

Perhaps the lingering feeling of something being wrong was still unsettling her. Samira had been so tense and agitated, natural enough for a bride-to-be who had never met her groom, Leah thought, but Leah had expected her to be more happily resigned, even excited about her imminent and highly prestigious marriage.

She heaved a dismissive sigh. If there was something wrong, there was nothing she could do about it. As an Arab princess, Samira had always been destined for this kind of marriage. It was not as though she was unprepared for it. She had been raised to it from birth. And the royal families certainly looked after their own.

Leah had learnt a long time ago to stand back from palace politics. She might be treated as one of the family, but she knew the indulgence depended on their approval of her behaviour and the way she carried out her job. Some self-protective instinct had urged her to distance herself from Samira this afternoon. If something went wrong... But it wouldn't, Leah assured herself. Everyone was hyped up, anxious everything be as perfect as it should be. That was all.

Beside her was a small table on which lay rows of the coloured wools she needed. In front of her stood the frame on which her tapestry was stretched tight. Having firmly put aside her concern for Samira, Leah worked the needle through the stiff fabric with nimble eagerness, wanting to complete the last remaining section of dark foreground so that she could begin on the more interesting flesh tones of the naked woman.

"Miss Leah Marlow?"

The softly spoken inquiry startled Leah. It was a male voice asking for her, and it was not the voice of her brother. No other man had the right to be admitted here. She jerked her hand up from the tapestry as her head spun towards the archway, the only entrance to the garden.

Her heart kicked in shock as she recognised the man who stood there, flanked by two fierce-looking soldiers, automatic rifles in their hands, the loose flow of their Arab robes disrupted by bandoliers.

Leah had seen his picture in the newspapers, watched him on television. The charisma of the man made him unforgettable. It was easy to understand why he had been the one to replace his uncle, who was shifted aside as 'not fit to govern.' Despite the simplicity of his plain brown robe and a soft white headpiece held down by black cording, there was no doubting his identity.

Sharif al Kader.

The Sheikh of Zubani.

The man Samira was to marry tomorrow.

Leah's brain clicked through these facts, yet stopped short of dictating some response to this unexpected and totally unheralded visitation. She stared at him, strangely unable to do anything else. Perhaps it was his utter stillness or the shimmering heat of the afternoon that made her feel he was a mirage, a representation of all man had been since the world had begun, hunter, warrior, zealot determined to conquer whatever needed to be conquered in forging the destiny of his choice.

A weird, fluttery sensation swept through Leah. It was as though the intense vitality of his life force had invaded her own, playing havoc with the inner serenity she had cultivated over the years. It was both exciting and unnerving, making her a stranger to herself. No man had ever had such an effect on her. After the messy and bitter divorce of her parents, Leah had developed an instinctive practice of blocking men out of her life. Except for her brother, of course.

"Miss Leah Marlow?"

The softly repeated question seeped slowly into her consciousness, then abruptly snapped the odd sense of unreality that had gripped her. "Yes, Your Excellency," she replied, automatically using the normal mode of address to a man of his status. She half rose to her feet before the tug of fixed thread reminded her of the tapestry needle in her fingers.

"Do not be disturbed, Miss Marlow. Resume your seat. Be at ease," he commanded as he stepped towards her, away from his bodyguards.

Leah was glad to comply. Her fingers trembled slightly as she slid the threaded needle into the spare fabric at the edge of the tapestry. It was good to subside into the safe comfort of her chair. She was acutely aware of the power emanating from this man, and it made her feel intensely vulnerable.

The sense of being watched was now explained. It was said that his eyes were like searchlights. Nothing escaped them.

She had not heard his approach and had no idea how long he had been watching her or what it portended. The silence of his arrival and the lack of any warning of it had to be deliberate. Yet why the sheikh of Zubani should intrude on her privacy like this was totally incomprehensible, completely outside normal protocol.

He was a man who made his own rules. He was also the type of man whose world was immovably centred on himself and his people. Since she was a Western woman, her personal rights were probably discounted in his mind.

Leah struggled to ignore her agitation, the rocketing beat of her heart. She folded her hands in her lap and kept her eyes lowered as he walked past the fountain. She could not imagine what he wanted with her, and it was not her place to ask, but her sense of danger was immeasurably heightened when he came to a halt beside her chair, apparently interested in viewing what she was working on.

"The rape of the Sabine women," he observed in a slightly mocking drawl, naming the famous Rubens painting imprinted on the fabric.

He moved behind Leah, picked up one of the garden seats and positioned it beyond the small table that held her wools. He sat down facing her, emitting an air of patient purpose, his lean brown fingers idly interlocking in his lap.

"Does such a subject interest you, Miss Marlow?"

"I enjoy doing tapestries, Your Excellency," Leah replied evenly, ignoring the silky taunt in his voice.

"You chose that one yourself?"

"Yes."

"Does it excite you? The idea of women being carried off and ravished by men of strange and foreign lands?"

The contemptuous sting in his words goaded Leah into meeting his eyes, dark, riveting eyes that impaled her with their sharp intelligence. His face was one of those that defy the ravages of time, austere in its beauty yet enticing in its refinement, the kind of face one wanted to touch or trace or hold. There was a stamp of hard, immutable strength on it, but it was the power of his eyes that made him a leader of men.

Sharif al Kader was both daunting and compelling, but Leah was not about to be intimidated into letting him nurse some undeserved contempt for her. "I find the idea absolutely revolting, Your Excellency. I have no desire to be ravished by any man. I couldn't imagine anything worse."

He raised his eyebrows quizzically.

"Rubens was a great artist," she continued coolly. "I was more interested in the composition of colour and shape than in the actual subject he chose to paint."

He smiled as though in approval, but his eyes gleamed cynical disbelief. His gaze drifted to the pale gold of her hair and travelled slowly down its shiny length. Leah had not bothered pinning it up since the thick mass was still drying from its recent wash when she had come out to the garden. She had simply rolled back swathes from each side of her face, clipped them together at the back of her head and left the rest to flow loosely over her shoulders.

Leah was aware that her fair colouring excited more than a passing curiosity and interest in the males of the Middle East. When she went out in public she wore a veil to protect herself from unwanted and unwelcome attention, but this *was* her own private garden, and not even the sheikh of Zubani should be viewing her appearance as less than modest. Her long-sleeved white caftan covered her from neck to toe, yet that didn't escape from critical appraisal, either.

It was all Leah could do to hold herself completely immobile as he virtually undressed her with his eyes, lingering on the high, firm roundness of her breasts before slowly following the curve of hip and thigh where the long garment was tucked under her. She told herself it was the feeling of helplessness that made her want to squirm. Impossible to get up and walk away.

When he began what felt like an insultingly intent study of the shape of her mouth, a surge of rebellious anger tilted Leah's chin higher and sent splashes of hot colour into her cheeks. It made the blue of her eyes more vivid as they defied the common judgement on Western women whose supposedly loose morals made them fair prey for Arab men who desired them. To Leah's mind, if any censure was deserved for *loose* behaviour, then both sides were equally at fault.

Sharif al Kader was reported to have been educated in England and France, and Leah was willing to bet he had not been celibate throughout all those youthful years in a more liberal culture. Yet, she had to admit that apart from his flawless English accent, the Western world did not appear to have scratched the surface of this man. Perhaps he had always held himself aloof from it.

"I do not know that you are at all suitable," he finally declared. "Indeed, my first impression is that you are entirely unsuitable."

Unsuitable for what? Leah wondered angrily. Pride in her self-worth was beamed straight at him, but she held her tongue, waiting for him to elaborate on his contentious statement.

He frowned in brooding disapproval. "I was expecting a woman who had put aside any hope of attracting a husband. A woman of no feminine allure whatsoever. You do not fit that image, Miss Marlow."

Leah remained silent, disdaining any reply to his prejudiced opinion that the only goal of an attractive woman had to be marriage. It might be so in his world, but she had other options. Attracting a husband was not on her wish list. A marriage certificate promising forever love and loyalty and fidelity was nothing more than dispensable paper, in Leah's experience. Having been through that disillusionment as a child, she had no intention of inviting more of it as an adult.

"I was informed that you have been both teacher and companion to Princess Samira since she was eleven years of age," the sheikh continued, still with that air of brooding disapproval.

"That is so, Your Excellency," Leah answered with cool dignity. "But as you must know, Princess Samira was sent to England for her formal education, then to a finishing school in Paris. My responsibility here is to supervise the learning of all the royal children and prepare them for schooling in other countries. For the most part, I have only been a companion to Princess Samira during her vacations."

"I know all this," he said in curt dismissal. "What I find disquieting, Miss Marlow, is that you were given this position when you were only eighteen."

"My brother sponsored me. He is King Rashid's personal pilot."

"A surprisingly high position for so young a man."

Leah bridled at his critical tone. "Glen has been here for ten years, Your Excellency," she pointed out.

"Against all normal procedure." The dark eyes stabbed some underlying accusation at her. "Few foreigners are granted more than a two- or three-year contract. Yet your brother has been here for ten years. And you for eight. Your contracts renewed again and again and again," he emphasised. "To me it adds up to one thing, and one thing only."

"What is that, Your Excellency?" Leah asked, struggling to keep calm under what felt like an attack on her probity.

"Someone of high royal blood wants to keep you here."

"I do my job with the children very satisfactorily," Leah said, reacting to the disturbing sense that she had to justify the longevity of her employment.

A flare of angry frustration burst from him. His hand slammed down on the table, scattering the neat rows of wools. "Whose concubine are you?" he demanded. "Do you have the king himself?"

Leah was shocked out of any guard on her tongue or manners. "I am not a concubine!" she retorted fiercely. "And never will be one! No man will ever get me to surrender myself to his pleasure!"

The sheikh threw his head back and laughed in utter disbelief. "You are a simple minder of children?"

"That is what I choose to be," Leah bit out, seething under his open derision and cursing herself for having revealed her deeply entrenched hatred of sex-

ual desire that overrode every other caring consideration.

"Has no man satisfied you?"

"None seems likely to."

Her eyes furiously defied the challenge in his, the
intensely male challenge that asserted he could do it
with his hands tied behind his back if he wanted to,
teaching her a pleasure that would have her begging
for more. He was, at that moment, the most sexual
man Leah had ever met, and the feelings he aroused in
her were quite frightening.

"And the Princess Samira. Have you corrupted her
mind with fanciful stories of how you believe love and
passion should be?" he mocked.

"Certainly not!"

"You have not talked to her of your frustration with
all the lovers you have tried and found wanting?"

"I have never once mentioned lovers to her."

"She has not asked?"

"It is not a subject I care to discuss. With anyone,
Your Excellency," Leah shot at him, bitterly resent-
ing his outrageous assumptions about her.

He eyed her wildly flushed cheeks with an air of
weighing her truthfulness, then relaxed in his chair,
apparently satisfied. He gave her a thin smile. "Your
discretion does you credit, Miss Marlow."

Leah glared, rejecting any credit from him. If he
expected her to thank him for the grudging compliment, he could wait until Doomsday. Perversely, her
stubbornly rebellious silence provoked a gleam of
amusement in his eyes.

"The Princess Samira...tell me your impression of her," he commanded.

Leah took a deep breath to calm her turbulent feelings. Common sense dictated that she reply to a direct command, however improper she felt the question was. "I'm sure you will find the princess a suitable wife, Your Excellency. She has been brought up to accept the duties of state."

"Meek and mild and resigned to her fate, Miss Marlow? Is that what you are giving me to understand?" he mocked.

It stung Leah into a further reply. "Princess Samira has the natural high spirits of her young age. I would not call her meek."

"So, she is a shrew."

"I didn't say that," Leah hotly denied. "It's only natural that a young woman of her broad education and lively intelligence should form opinions of her own."

"I hope the princess has not picked up your independent attitudes, Miss Marlow. It would not lead to domestic harmony."

"I'm sure your authority will hold sway, Your Excellency." Leah gave him a thin little smile.

His gaze flicked to her mouth, then back to the clear blueness of her eyes. "Perhaps you should have chosen a tapestry depicting a Leonardo da Vinci painting, Miss Marlow. It would seem that *Mona Lisa* is more your style. I always felt her smile deceptive."

"No doubt you are a greater expert on such matters than I am, Your Excellency."

He was amused by her tactic of agreeing with him with the same silky contempt he had used on her. Leah dimly recognised she was on dangerous ground, but he had riled her into a wild recklessness that demanded she give him back tit for tat.

"I like to make my own judgement of people, Miss Marlow, particularly where a position of trust and influence is involved."

"A judgement reflects the prejudices of the judge," Leah said tartly, still smarting from his distasteful cross-examination.

He raised an eyebrow. "You expect me to accept at face value that a woman of your beauty and intelligence is content to spend her life being a minder of other women's children?" He shook his head. "Something is wrong."

"I happen to *like* children, Your Excellency."

"Perhaps you mean you feel safe with them, Miss Marlow, because you are in control of the situation," he said with an insidious softness, slicing too close to an uncomfortable truth.

"I care about them," she defended.

"Then it will be no burden for you to care for mine. I have two daughters from my first marriage. They will be staying in the children's wing for the month of the wedding celebrations."

He paused, watching Leah intently as she absorbed the shock of this announcement. She had not been informed of any such arrangement for the sheikh's children, and while the reason behind this extraordinary meeting was now clear, the idea of being in any way responsible for this man's daughters had no appeal for her.

The manner in which he had inspected and cross-examined her demonstrated a lack of respect and trust that Leah found extremely offensive. And should any mishap occur with the children while they were in her care, Leah had no doubt the consequences would be equally unpalatable.

"Naturally I will do my best to make their stay here a happy one," she said, hating the fact that she had no choice in the matter.

"They will not be completely in your charge, Miss Marlow. My daughters are very close to my heart, and I would not leave them with a stranger. Their nanny, Tayi, will be looking after them for the most part. Tayi is a loyal and highly valued member of my household, and I place the utmost confidence in her."

"I see," Leah said dryly.

"I, also, shall see. You may teach my daughters some English while they are here, and I shall monitor their progress under your guidance. Nothing you do over the next month will escape my notice, Miss Marlow."

It was both a promise and a threat, and it was no pleasure for Leah to discover that the sense of her peaceful privacy being menaced was deadly accurate. While she had nothing to fear in being spied upon, Leah bristled at the thought of being constantly under this man's distrustful scrutiny.

He raised his hand, and one of his bodyguards instantly bowed then disappeared from the archway.

"You will now meet my daughters. Please remember, Miss Marlow, that from this moment on, I will be watching you with the eyes of a hawk. Whatever is wrong, I will know of it."

Something was wrong, all right, Leah thought with grim irony. It was suddenly clear to her why everyone had been in a state of nervous agitation this morning. It all sprung from the coming of this man. He had swooped in like a desert hawk, bringing all the uneasiness of a force that acknowledged only his way and his will.

Leah took another deep breath in an attempt to calm the storm he had stirred in her. One month and Sharif al Kader would be gone. Surely she could withstand whatever small pressures he might bring to bear on her. After all, her conscience was clear of any wrongdoing.

She sternly told herself she had nothing to fear from the sheikh of Zubani. Nothing at all!

CHAPTER TWO

AS THEY WAITED for his children, Leah watched Sharif al Kader's fingers drumming lightly on the armrest of his chair. They should look like talons, she thought, but they didn't. They looked strong and sensual, and the steady beat of their touch had a relentless rhythm. She wondered how Samira would feel tomorrow night when...

Leah swiftly repressed the uncharacteristic speculation. She did not want to think of Sharif al Kader as a lover. She did not want to think of lovers at all. Besides which, love didn't enter into this marriage. The sheikh of Zubani was simply taking a new wife to warm his bed and cement a political friendship with the royal family of Qatamah. The latter purpose was undoubtedly more important to him, since his rise to power was relatively recent.

It was said that one of the reasons he had moved against his uncle's rule in Zubani was the old man's refusal to use the oil wealth pouring into the country for the welfare of its people. His uncle's belief that their traditional way of life would be destroyed by too much too soon was not shared by Sharif al Kader.

His first wife had died from an infection after the birth of their second child. He had laid the blame for it on the ill-equipped and inadequately staffed hospital his uncle had done nothing to improve. Less than perfect medical facilities no longer existed in Zubani. Any problem that touched this sheikh's heart was obviously dealt with in a ruthless and very thorough fashion.

His fingers stopped drumming. Leah flicked a glance at his face and saw his whole demeanour change. The man of relentless purpose was transformed by a smile that radiated warm and loving indulgence. He rose to his feet and turned towards the archway. "My daughters," he said with deep paternal pride.

Leah rose more slowly from her chair, stunned not only by the change in her powerful antagonist, but also by the sheer magnificence of the woman who held the two little girls by the hand. A descendant of the highly valued Ethiopian slaves from the last century, Leah surmised. She stood at least six feet tall, her majestic figure enhanced by a silk robe coloured in vivid yellow and orange. A matching turban was wound around her head. The fine delicacy of her features was dominated by the striking beauty of large, velvety eyes.

"Thank you, Tayi." The sheikh spoke in Arabic. "Send them forward to meet Miss Marlow."

The little girls were released and given a gentle push. They walked forward shyly, staring at Leah with huge, wondering eyes. It seemed that she was as much a figure of awe to them as their nanny had been to Leah.

"My daughters have never met a woman of your fair colouring before," the sheikh explained with dry

irony as he moved to line them up for a formal intro-
duction to Leah. "This is Nadia. She is five years old.
And this is Jazmin. She is three years old."

He touched them with love and there was love in his,
voice. For a moment Leah's mind spun to her own
childhood, when she had been close to her father's
heart. It had hurt so much when he had betrayed that
love and withdrawn the security of his caring, leaving
her and Glen with their mother who cared far more for
her new husband than she did for them.

She looked sadly at Sharif al Kader's daughters. As
beloved as they undoubtedly were now, they also
would be passed into the care of strangers when the
sheikh married them to men of his choice. But at least
they would be raised to accept that, and they would be
spared the feelings of betrayal.

They were beautiful children, and their innocent
appeal tugged at Leah's heart. She crouched to meet
them on their level, smiling to put them at ease. She
spoke the Arabic greeting that would be most familiar to them, and the elder girl replied in a rush of relief and pleasure. The younger appeared to be totally
tongue-tied. She tentatively reached out and touched
Leah's hair.

"Jazmin," her father reproved. "Where are your
manners?"

She looked up at him in wide-eyed confusion.

Leah smoothed over the awkward moment, speaking soothingly in Arabic. "It is strange to meet someone who looks different, but you will soon get used to
me, Jazmin."

"I wanted to know if your hair was real," the little girl said apologetically.

Leah gently caressed the child's soft black curls. "As real as yours."

"Can I touch it again?" she asked eagerly.

"Jazmin!" The pained patience in her father's voice held her in check. "You have not yet greeted Miss Marlow."

She rattled out the required greeting with somewhat irreverent obedience to her father, then breathlessly added, "How did you get blue eyes?"

"Enough!" the sheikh cut in brusquely. "Go off with Tayi now. You will see Miss Marlow again tomorrow."

They went, glancing over their shoulders at Leah, who smiled after them as she straightened up.

Sharif al Kader heaved an exasperated sigh. "Perhaps I have indulged Jazmin too much."

"Her curiosity is only natural, Your Excellency," Leah replied, amused at the thought there was one little female who was undaunted by the authority of this formidable man.

"Miss Marlow . . ."

The steely edge in his voice commanded her full attention. She turned to face him. Any trace of warm indulgence had been wiped from his expression. There was a gleam of mocking resignation in his eyes.

"I am a fair man. It is clear that you do have an empathy with children."

Leah's eyes scorned the concessionary nature of this statement. To her mind, he owed her an apology, not a grudging concession. There had been no reason for him to judge her differently in the first place. An apology, however, was obviously not forthcoming, and her silence evoked a thin little smile.

"I am told that Princess Samira is very fond of you, Miss Marlow."

"As I am of her," Leah replied, wondering how Samira would fare with him and feeling oddly ambivalent about the marriage. It might be right politically, but she hated the thought of Sharif al Kader's dominant personality crushing the sparkle out of Samira's lively nature.

"It is against my inclination to employ you, but I wish to make the Princess Samira happy in our marriage. Therefore, should you prove satisfactory to me, I will permit you to be some kind of minor companion for her. And you can make yourself useful by looking after my children and teaching them the English language."

The sheer blazing arrogance of this speech raised Leah's hackles. Did he expect her to thank him for such condescending beneficence? "I don't think I understand, Your Excellency," she bit out with barely controlled anger. "My position here..."

"Will be continued in my palace, Miss Marlow. You will accompany Princess Samira's retinue when we return to Zubani," he stated as though the decision had nothing at all to do with Leah.

Despite her fondness for Samira, everything in Leah recoiled from being in any way connected to this man's domestic affairs, let alone receiving confidences from the young bride about her new husband. She didn't want to hear, didn't want to know anything more of

Sharif al Kader, particularly not the kind of intimate details Arab women bandied around between themselves. Just the thought of hearing about him in that way made Leah feel sick.

Apart from which, to be in his employ, and therefore in his power, was only asking for trouble. He didn't like her, and she certainly did not like him.

"Please pardon me for declining your generous offer, Your Excellency," Leah said strongly. "Thank you very much, but I am happy here. I am also bound by contract—"

"Your contract will be terminated."

"On what grounds?" she demanded.

His eyes glittered with amusement at her apparent naivety. "Perhaps you forget you are not in your country, Miss Marlow. You stay here at our will, not your own. It is a simple matter to find you unsatisfactory. As an example, being rebellious against well-meant advice is quite pertinent. Your contract would be handsomely paid off, and you would be expelled, never to return."

"The royal family has been pleased with my service," she argued. "King Rashid—"

"King Rashid will be more concerned for his daughter's happiness than yours, Miss Marlow. Unless there is some personal reason for him to keep you here?"

Leah flushed at the pointed implication. "The welfare of the children—"

"Can be attended to. Easing Princess Samira through a period of adjustment is of more urgent consideration."

"So I have no choice but to accept your offer."

"That's correct."

Oh, no it's not! Leah promised him. The sheikh of Zubani was dead wrong if he imagined she would submit to his power. She had suffered from a total lack of choice when her parents had divorced. She was not a helpless child now.

"Perhaps I have already stayed too long in the Middle East," she said in icy disdain of *his* plan for her.

He raised one eyebrow in derisive challenge to her show of defiance. "Perhaps your brother has also, Miss Marlow. You wish to cause his fall from favour?"

Leah seethed at the shameless blackmail, yet knew the Arab culture automatically linked family members together. Favour or displeasure flowed to all and affected all. It was because of Glen that she had been welcomed and treated so well. Because of her, Glen could be summarily dismissed from a job he loved.

"I shall consult with my brother," Leah said stiffly.

"Do that, Miss Marlow."

He gave her a cruel little smile then strode away, having shattered her peace and menaced not only her future, but Glen's, as well.

Leah stood staring at the empty archway for a long time, fighting a paralysing sense of disbelief that the secure world she had constructed for herself could be taken away from her with a mere snap of the fingers. Or more accurately, by an act of will. Sharif al Kader's will.

This was her home, she kept thinking. She had made it her home. What right did the sheikh of Zubani have to uproot her from it?

She would ask for an audience with the king. King Rashid liked her. Though not in the way Sharif al Kader had intimated.

But what if the king did put his daughter's happiness first? Samira had to leave *her* home. The only home she had known. Not an adopted home, as it was for Leah. Would the king argue that Leah would be made just as comfortable in Zubani as she had been made here?

Despite the heat of the afternoon, Leah shivered. Impossible for her ever to feel comfortable in Sharif al Kader's household. His manner towards her was not indulgently paternal, like King Rashid's. He made her feel . . .

Leah instinctively shied away from examining what he made her feel. She simply wanted nothing more to do with him.

Glen would intercede with the king for her. The Arab respect for family would surely hold weight if Glen invoked it on her behalf. It would be all right, Leah assured herself over and over again. It had to be all right. After all, Glen's skill as a pilot had saved King Rashid's life when they had been forced to crash-land due to engine problems. King Rashid wouldn't want to lose Glen's services. Her brother's nerves of steel were legendary.

A rueful smile flitted over Leah's lips. She doubted anyone understood her brother as she did. Glen was more wedded to an airplane than he would be to any

woman. Women didn't figure in Glen's life any more
than men figured in Leah's. The hurt and betrayal of
their mother's many infidelities had left him with little regard for the female sex. Except for Leah, who
had shared that miserable time with him.

Flying gave Glen all the satisfaction he wanted in
life. He shared an intimate relationship with whatever aircraft he was piloting, and was instinctively
aware of what it could do in response to his handling
of it. If truth be told, he had probably been more at-
tuned to saving the plane than saving his own life or
King Rashid's.

Nevertheless, the incident had raised Glen to hero
status in Qatamah. Did Sharif al Kader know that?
Could he really override the king's favour with his demands?

Leah shook off the lingering influence of the power
that had emanated from him. Since there was nothing
she could do about this situation until she talked to
Glen, there was no point in churning over it or standing around in a daze. Yet she could not dispel the fear
that clung around her heart, despite making a determined effort to get on with what she'd been doing before the sheikh of Zubani had invaded her life.

She picked up the wools that had fallen from the
table when he had slammed his hand on it. The idea of
her being a concubine made Leah burn all over again.
She sat down in front of her tapestry and fiercely
wished she had chosen some other print. But the
Rubens was a fine dramatic picture, with definite lines
and areas to it. Since her last tapestry had been an im-
pressionist print by Manet, Leah had wanted a sub-

ject that was more clearly defined this time. Just because it was naked women being carried off by men on horseback did not mean she fancied such a fate for herself.

Men, she thought in disgust, had only one thing on their minds when it came to women. It had been more important to her father to give himself the pleasure of having a new wife than to take custody of the daughter of his first marriage. And her mother had been no better. She hadn't stood up for Leah against the mean little cruelties of her new husband.

Sharif al Kader was right about one thing. Leah did have an empathy with children. If it turned out she had to leave her job here, Leah knew what she would do. Go back to Australia and find work in a child-care centre.

Calmed with these thoughts, Leah picked up her tapestry needle and resumed stitching with a dogged determination not to think of Sharif al Kader again. At least, not until she had to. She finished off the section of dark foreground and was threading the lighter wool to begin on the woman's foot when she heard her brother's voice calling out for her from her apartment.

"I'm in the garden, Glen," she called back, leaping to her feet in pleasure and relief at his timely visit.

She ran to greet him and they almost collided in the archway. He grabbed her upper arms to steady her and spoke with urgent haste. "Leah, I haven't much time. Come inside with me quickly."

"What's the matter?" she cried, alarmed to find her unflappable big brother in a state of tense anxiety.

His handsome face wore none of the easygoing confidence she was accustomed to. It was tight and strained, with no trace of the sunny, carefree disposition that was as much a part of Glen as his sky-blue eyes and his gold-streaked hair. He had vowed at the time of their parents' divorce he was never going to let anything touch him deeply again. Roll with the punches and keep coming up roses was his philosophy.

But something had got to him today. He ignored Leah's question, virtually bundled her into her living room, swiftly closed the door behind them, then began pulling his shirt out of his trousers.

"Glen!" she protested. "What on earth are you doing?"

"Taking off this money belt." His eyes fastened on Leah's with a sharp intensity that commanded her attention. "It holds ten thousand American dollars, Leah. I'm leaving it with you."

"What for? What do you want me to do with it?" she asked, bewildered and deeply disturbed by his manner and actions.

His gaze dropped from hers as he unbuckled the belt and slid it from his waist. "Put it in your bank account."

"I don't understand. Why don't you put it in yours?"

"Taxation purposes," he said as he headed for her bedroom.

Leah followed him, her agitation increasing as she watched him put the belt under the pillows on her bed.

"Have you been doing something wrong, Glen? Flying in contraband or—"

"No." He straightened and gave her a fleeting smile that was supposed to be reassuring, but wasn't. "It's all legitimate money, Leah. Don't worry about that."

"Then why—"

"Haven't got time to explain. The king has ordered an unscheduled flight. I've got to get going." He busied himself tucking his shirt in again as he strode to where Leah stood in the bedroom doorway. He moved her aside and dropped a kiss on her forehead. "Wish me luck, Leah," he said thickly, then attempted a devil-may-care smile.

Something was terribly wrong. "Glen, does this flight have anything to do with all the unease there's been in the palace today?"

The smile froze on his lips. His hands curled tightly around her shoulders. His eyes flickered with... Could it be despair? "What unease, Leah?" he demanded in an urgent rasp. "What's been going on? What's happened?"

"Don't yell at me, Glen."

His fingers dug bruisingly into her soft flesh. "Tell me. It's important!"

"Nothing that I could put my finger on," she said. "Just a feeling. I thought it had to do with the sheikh of Zubani coming. He appears to unsettle everyone."

"Nothing substantial then?"

"No."

His relief was palpable. As much as she wanted to unload her troubles on him, Leah realised this wasn't the right time to tell him about Sharif al Kader's threatening visit to her.

"I truly need to talk to you, Glen," she said fervently. "As soon as you get back."

"Leah..." A pained look crossed his face. Then suddenly he swept her into a hug that clamped her body to his so fiercely she could feel his heart thumping madly against the wall of his chest. He rubbed his cheek over her hair with a ragged tenderness that twisted Leah up inside. Glen had never shown affection like this. Usually it was a kiss on her nose or cheek or forehead, a fond hug of the shoulders, a squeeze of her hand. Leah had the frightening sense he was taking some last farewell of her.

"Stay in this apartment tonight, Leah," he ordered huskily. "If there's unrest in the palace, keep well away from it."

"Glen—" panic swirled through her mind "—this flight. Is it dangerous?"

He drew back enough to chuck her under the chin and give her a crooked smile. "Is there any flying job I can't handle?" His arm slid away from her as he planted a last kiss on her nose. "Got to go. Be a good girl and do as I say."

She trailed him out to the living room, desperately wanting to stop him from leaving her yet feeling helpless to do so. There was resolution in the rigidity of his squared shoulders, driven purpose in his step. He reached the door, opened it.

"Glen." It was a desperate little cry, an appeal not to leave her alone.

He turned reluctantly, her golden big brother who was father and mother as well as brother to her, all the family she had. But he had already said goodbye to her. There was a faraway look in his blue eyes, as though his mind was already set on his mission. "I have to go, Leah," he said flatly.

Her heart squeezed tight at the finality in his voice. "You said to wish you good luck."

A wisp of a smile. "*Inshallah,*" he said softly.

He left her with that word, the Arab word for "I hope." It held out no guarantee for tomorrow. It expressed the desert philosophy of uncertainty, where man is not governor of his own fate. He has only a loose hold on the reins.

Leah was riven by the terrible feeling she would never see Glen again. What would she do if he didn't come back? How would she survive on her own? She had lived in the warm cocoon of his protection for so long. Without him . . .

A dreadful sense of isolation closed around her. The dark image of Sharif al Kader supplanted Glen's in her mind. How could she fight *him* without Glen at her side?

Why was everything happening today?

It felt so wrong, wrong, wrong!

Then a dreadful thought struck her. This unscheduled flight that had been ordered . . . was the sheikh of Zubani behind it?

CHAPTER THREE

LEAH FELT TOO CHURNED UP to settle to anything. She brought her tapestry in from the garden but could not pluck up the interest to continue with it. She needed some distraction to take her mind off worrying about Glen. She could find it easily enough in the children's wing, but Glen had told her to stay in her apartment tonight. As harmless as the company of children surely was, Leah could not bring herself to ignore his protective warning.

She played a video of her favourite movie, but it failed to captivate her.

She fixed herself a light meal but didn't have the appetite to enjoy it.

Her restlessness was so pervasive that it was a relief when a knock came on her door, providing her with some brief but definite direction. She opened the door, only to be plunged into more perturbation. The nanny to the sheikh's children, the majestic Ethiopian, stood in the corridor, her beautiful face expressionless, her dark, velvety eyes staring unblinkingly at Leah.

"Can I be of help?" Leah asked, prompted into speech by the other woman's silence.

Without uttering a word, the woman turned and moved off down the corridor, walking with a slow, swaying grace that was almost hypnotic. Leah roused herself to try to find some sense in the woman's actions.

"Tayi? Do you want me to follow you?" she called after her.

There was no response. The woman kept walking away. Was she deaf? Unable to speak? No, that couldn't be right, Leah reasoned. Tayi had responded to the sheikh's command this afternoon. In any event, she could have tried some gesture to make herself understood. So why had she knocked on Leah's door?

The answer that leapt into Leah's mind sent a wave of fury through her. She slammed the door shut and raged around her living room. Sharif al Kader was using Tayi to check up on her, finding out if Leah was in her apartment and whether she was alone.

He was an abominable man! No way in the world would Leah consent to being part of his household. Not for Samira's sake! Not for the children's sake! Not for anyone's sake! Glen had to come back and sort this out for her.

But what if he didn't come back?

She was standing in the middle of her living room, in an agony of uncertainty when a more peremptory knock came on her door. Perhaps she had misunderstood Tayi, she thought hopefully, and the Ethiopian nanny had come back to make herself more clearly understood this time. Since the idea of being spied upon was intolerable, Leah again felt a surge of relief as she went to answer the summons.

It was short-lived.

Two guards stood in the corridor. Their faces were stern, their bodies stiffly alert. One of them spoke in harsh, clipped tones.

"The king commands your presence, Miss Marlow. We are to escort you to the throne room."

Alarm skittered through Leah's heart. She was accustomed to seeing the king in the children's wing or the women's apartments, but never had she received an official royal summons to the throne room. She had been there only once, the day Glen had presented her to King Rashid, eight years ago. It was where the king held his morning *majlis* for the men of Qatamah to put their petitions to their ruler or tell him of problems. It was the place of government. It was not a place for women.

Yet a royal summons was a royal summons and could not be denied or ignored. Mindful of proper courtesy and custom, Leah swiftly said, "If you'll excuse me for a moment, I must put on an *abba*."

As she turned, a strong male hand grabbed her arm, detaining her. "Come now."

The curt command allowed no argument. There was a look in their eyes that promised she would be taken by force if necessary. She chose the more dignified path of submitting to their orders, her trepidation growing with every step she took. To appear before the king in his throne room with her head uncovered and her face unveiled was tantamount to showing disrespect. For such a consideration to be swept aside had to mean that something terrible had happened.

Glen, she thought in sickening panic.

The moment she entered the throne room Leah found herself the cynosure of all eyes. Conversation stopped. The groups of men who lined the long room stiffened into silent observation. The attendants around the king drew back, revealing his regal presence on the throne. Seated prominently beside him was the sheikh of Zubani.

There was no smile of welcome from either man as Leah was ushered forward, and she was acutely aware that the atmosphere around her was not one of friendly sympathy. Something was very badly wrong, and Leah had never felt so frightened in her life. She kept her eyes trained on the grave face of the king, afraid that her shaky legs might falter if she so much as glanced at Sharif al Kader. Whatever this crisis was, every quivering instinct told her that the sheikh of Zubani was at the centre of it.

She managed a deep curtsey.

"It is with deep sadness that I see you here, Leah," King Rashid said solemnly. "Until a few minutes ago, it was thought you had accompanied your brother on his flight out of Qatamah."

"I don't understand, Your Majesty," Leah replied in bewilderment. "I have been in my apartment since my brother visited me this afternoon."

"So! He did come to see you."

"Yes."

His dark, liquid eyes filled with sorrowful hurt and accusation. "After all these years of being amongst us, you felt no loyalty to this household? You conspired with your brother to bring shame upon us?"

"What shame, Your Majesty?" Leah cried. "My brother informed me he was to take an unscheduled flight for you. He gave me no details of it. As far as I know, we have both been completely loyal to you and your family."

There was a mutter around the room. The king's long, noble face remained impassive. The sheikh of Zubani leaned over and murmured something to him. King Rashid nodded and signalled an attendant forward. The man leaned down and received some whispered instruction, then hurried from the room.

Leah watched all this with intense agitation. Was there some plot to discredit her and Glen? What had Sharif al Kader suggested to the king? Whatever was happening had to be his fault, she wildly decided, trying to drown her fear with a wave of righteous anger.

The king addressed her again. "Once it was confirmed that you were still in the palace—"

Confirmed by the Ethiopian nanny, Leah thought in bitter resentment. *His* loyal servant!

"There was only one course to be taken, Leah, and I have taken it."

The grim authority on the king's face engendered a presentiment of doom. Leah desperately clung to the idea that justice had to prevail in the end.

"I have ordered out the air force with instructions to intercept your brother's plane. If he does not respond to the command to turn back, he will be shot down."

Shock paralysed Leah for several moments. Her premonition of dire danger, of seeing Glen for the last time, was coming true. Before she knew it her arms stretched out in frantic appeal.

"But why? Why would you do that? What has Glen done for you t—" she swallowed hard as bile rose in her throat "—to order him shot down?"

The king's face could have been carved from stone for all the impact her plea had on it.

"He has betrayed the trust I placed in him."

"How?" Leah begged.

The king's face tightened. A muscle contracted in his cheek. He looked past her as though her question deeply affronted him and he would not reply to it.

Leah waited for long, agonising moments for the king to acknowledge her presence again. She was left standing in unbearable tension. No-one spoke. No-one looked at her.

Except Sharif al Kader.

Leah could feel his eyes boring into her.

She could feel his powerful aura swirling around her, drawing on her like a magnet. She grimly fought the insidious force that commanded her to meet his eyes. She would not give him the satisfaction of any acknowledgement he had been proved right about her and her brother.

He wasn't right.

There had to be some dreadful mistake. Glen would never betray the king's trust.

Yet Leah could not dismiss the anguished feeling that had poured from her brother this afternoon in his farewell hug. Glen must have known he was flirting with death in what he planned to do. And King Rashid did not make impetuous decisions. She frantically searched her mind for some reason that might drive her brother to put aside all normal considerations, to risk this fatal condemnation from the king.

Had he felt his life was under threat anyway? But if that was the case, why not take her with him? Why leave her behind? He must have known she wouldn't want to stay here if he was never to return. From the king's earlier words, it had been assumed that Leah *was* with her brother. And from other implications made, it would seem Glen might have been safe if she had gone with him.

Try as she might, Leah could make no sense out of the sequence of events. She was still floundering through improbable possibilities when the nerve-tearing silence was broken by the return of the attendant who had been sent off earlier. Leah barely withstood another shock wave as she recognised what he held out to the king. It was the money belt Glen had shoved under the pillows on her bed.

A sense of outrage billowed over her shock. Her private apartment had been searched. That was what the sheikh of Zubani had suggested to the king. Leah seethed in impotent fury as King Rashid stared at the money belt and listened to his whispering attendant. Finally the king returned his gaze to her, and there was condemnation in his eyes.

"You still protest your innocence, Leah?" he scorned in a harsh voice.

"Of what am I guilty, Your Majesty?" she replied, her chin lifting defensively, her eyes defying any false judgement.

"This money belt was found hidden in your apartment. It is your brother's. The amount of money it contains is proof of your complicity in his treachery."

"Is it a crime for a brother to give his sister money?" Leah argued strongly. "I have no knowledge of any treachery, Your Majesty, and I cannot believe—"

"Enough! You will wait here for your brother's return, dead or alive." His eyes blazed a fierce denial of any further defence on her part. "There is no more to be said. You were party to the abduction of my daughter, the Princess Samira."

The accusation thumped into Leah's heart, shattering the spirit to keep on fighting for her own and her brother's integrity. Her mind grappled weakly with all the things that had been wrong today. Slowly, inexorably, they fell into a straight, inevitable line.

Samira, so tense and agitated this morning.

The wedding tomorrow.

The arrival of the sheikh, her designated bridegroom, who set about imposing his will on what he considered suitable for their marriage.

Glen saying goodbye, making what provision he could for Leah against the consequences of his mad, quixotic decision to fly away with Samira.

Not an abduction. Leah didn't believe that for one moment. It was the king's pride insisting his daughter had been abducted. To admit anything else would be an intolerable humiliation in front of the sheikh of Zubani.

No way in the world would Glen abduct Samira, or do anything to hurt or harm her. Rescue her, yes. If

Samira had pleaded with him for help, begging him to save her from being married to a man she had never met and didn't want as her husband, Glen would have felt deeply touched by that plea, whether he liked it or not. Not only did he have a strong protective streak, but Samira had always been his favourite amongst the royal children.

He had flown her away to school and home again over the years, shown big-brotherly interest in her progress from childhood to adolescence to womanhood, treated her hero-worship of him with indulgent kindness. Leah understood only too well that Samira would see Glen as her white knight, the one person in Qatamah she could turn to who could effect her escape and set her free of a future she did not want.

When had she made her decision?

When had she contacted Glen?

Leah shook her head at her futile musing. Sometime today the die had been cast, and Leah knew in her heart neither Glen nor Samira would turn back now. The runaway princess and her white knight would fly to their death rather than concede defeat.

A fierce pride in her brother's abilities battled the fear that his plane would be shot down. Glen was the best pilot in Qatamah. He would give the whole air force a run for their money. She wondered which plane he had chosen. Was it fast enough to outfly his pursuers? Or had he gone for manoeuvrability? The Harrier, perhaps.

The waiting played havoc with Leah's nerves, but she kept telling herself that each passing minute meant Glen and Samira were closer to safety. There was only so far to go before the pursuing air force would be intruding on some other country's airspace. Impossible then to shoot down a plane without creating an international incident, and that would be anathema to the king. The last thing he would want was worldwide publicity about his daughter's defection.

Leah called on every last fibre of pride to hold herself erect throughout the long ordeal of standing before the king until the final outcome of Glen's flight was known. She would not bow her head in any supposed guilt. She was innocent of any wrongdoing, and she was not ashamed of what Glen had done.

Nevertheless, when the king's eldest son, Prince Youssef, strode past her to hold counsel with his father, Leah felt herself sway from the strain of holding herself together.

Please, God, let it be good news, she prayed with desperate fervour. Glen had taught Prince Youssef to fly. They had been the best of friends. He couldn't shoot his best friend and his own sister out of the sky, could he? Surely his father would not have asked it of him. Yet he was in his airman's uniform.

The message he delivered was spoken in low tones, impossible for Leah to make out. The king slumped forward, covering his face with his cloak. A collective moan ran around the room. Youssef stepped back and swung around, his handsome face drawn with grief. He looked at Leah with such pain that she cried out in anguished protest.

"No, Youssef. No..."

"Neither of them will ever return, Leah."

Her knees startled to buckle, and she half stumbled towards him. Youssef caught her and held her upright, giving her the support she needed.

"Why?" he rasped, his eyes begging hers for an explanation. "Why?"

"Samira must have asked him. Glen wouldn't..." The defensive words trailed into silent desolation as she felt some vital part of her dying inside. Her brother, her beloved big brother, shot down.

"It's done," Youssef said in bleak resignation. "All that we shared...it's over."

He withdrew the support he had impulsively given her and strode away, leaving her to his father's mercy. Or rage.

Leah felt so numb that nothing mattered. With Glen gone out of her life, lost to her forever, it was totally irrelevant what the king might decide to do with her. Somehow she remained standing upright, suspended in a vacuum of nothingness. All she could think of was that she hadn't hugged Glen back, hadn't kissed him goodbye, and it was too late now to tell him how much he meant to her.

At the first sign of movement from King Rashid, Leah instinctively straightened her shoulders and lifted her head high. She was innocent of any treachery, and she would wear the badge of innocence to her grave, if it came to that. Her own life held no significance to her now, and she would not shame her brother's memory by acting like some snivelling coward.

Very slowly the king drew his cloak back, uncovering a face that had sternly put sorrow aside. He rose to his feet with regal dignity and swept his gaze around the room.

"Be it known," he proclaimed, "that my daughter, the Princess Samira, is dead."

There was a rippling murmur of agreement.

The king turned to the attendant who held Glen's money belt. He took it from him and tossed it contemptuously at Leah's feet. "Take your blood money and go, Leah Marlow. I expel you from Qatamar. You will be taken from this palace within the hour and flown beyond our borders. You will take no farewell of anyone, and you are never to return. Go now and pack whatever possessions you wish to take with you."

The sentence of expulsion reminded Leah of the sheikh of Zubani's earlier threat to her. A sense of bitter irony penetrated the numbness in her heart. Glen was out of Sharif al Kader's reach. Samira was out of his reach. And now she was out of his reach. Forever.

She felt a savage desire to scorn his power, and turned her gaze to the man sitting beside the king. Their eyes clashed in a challenge that sizzled with deeply primitive emotions. Sharif al Kader acknowledged no defeat. Leah found herself shaken by the searing force of his will. She tore her gaze away, but burned into her mind was the impression that he meant to exact payment for this loss of public face. He had no intention of ending up a loser.

She did not pick up the money belt. As much as she might need the ready funds, to take the belt with her was tantamount to admitting guilt, on her own part and on Glen's. She would not give anyone the satisfaction of that implicit confirmation.

She did not curtsey to the king. Nor did she bow her head to his judgement. Leah walked down the long throne room with slow, determined dignity, acutely aware of everyone's eyes watching her. There was one gaze she felt burning into her back. It could burn as much as it liked, Leah thought vehemently. The sheikh of Zubani would never see her again.

He might make many demands in compensation for what had been done to him, but he could make no demand regarding Leah.

The king had spoken.

She was free to go.

CHAPTER FOUR

LEAH WAS FLOWN from Qatamah to Dubai, the closest international airport. A car was waiting to take her to the passenger terminal. It was a courtesy she had not expected, given the circumstances of her leaving, but her mind was too laden with grief to question it. The king probably meant to have her seen onto a flight that took her to some other part of the world, far away from the Middle East.

Leah had travelled the route to the terminal many times. When the Mercedes deviated from it and turned towards the city she felt a niggle of disquiet. "Is there some repair work being done to the road?" she asked, since that was the most obvious explanation.

The driver said nothing. The guard in the front passenger seat replied, "A slight detour. No problem. We will get you to your destination."

Leah began to feel more disturbed when the car kept heading into the city. "Where is my destination?" she asked, wondering if she was to spend the night in a hotel.

Perhaps she had been booked onto a flight with a specific destination. An air ticket to Australia, she hoped. But would King Rashid give her that much consideration when he had expelled her with such towering condemnation? Unlikely.

She frowned when she received no reply. "Where are you taking me?" she asked more sharply.

"The sheikh of Zubani desires your presence. We are taking you to him."

Dear heaven! Leah thought in dazed horror. Would this terrible day never end?

"You can't do that!" she cried in frightened protest. "King Rashid ordered that I be—"

"You are no longer under the jurisdiction of Qatamar," came the cutting reply. "That border was crossed some time ago."

"I'm not under the jurisdiction of Zubani, either," Leah argued. "We're in Dubai."

"And we will very soon be out of it." The man in the passenger seat turned hard, impassive eyes on her. "May I suggest you relax. We have a long journey ahead of us. If you look, you will see a similar car to this in front of us, and another behind us. We are now travelling in convoy. There is no hope of escape."

The underlying threat was not lost on Leah. Whatever she said or did would have no effect on the final outcome. Sharif al Kader had her neatly and securely trapped in his power, and there was no-one to rescue her. No-one who knew where she was.

She slumped back in her seat and closed her eyes. *Oh, Glen!* she thought in abject despair. *What have you left me to?*

Yet she could not blame her brother for what he had not known. Glen had gambled that the king would let her go, and he had been right about that. He had gambled that Leah would understand the choice he had made to set Samira free, and she did understand, however deeply that choice grieved her now.

The mistake had been hers. She had not told him about the wild card in the pack, the outside force that could break any predictable outcome. She had underestimated the will of Sharif al Kader.

She was now his prisoner, and the only question was . . . what form would his revenge take?

Wearily she opened her eyes and found they were speeding out into the desert on the four-lane highway that linked the United Arab Emirates. How far was it to Zubani, she wondered, but couldn't find the spirit to bother asking. As inexorable as the sands of time, so, too, was her eventual arrival there.

Meanwhile, she had already exhausted all her reserves of energy. She told herself she didn't care what Sharif al Kader wanted with her. Nothing could hurt more than Glen's death. She wished she had been in the plane with him. Since that oblivion had been denied her, she settled herself more comfortably into the cushioned leather seat and invited the oblivion of sleep.

It was dawn when she awoke, and they were still travelling through desert. The vast stretch of sand looked strangely luminous in the half-light. Large dunes rose above the road, their flanks falling sheer on one side, on the other shaped and scalloped by ripples of wind. A visual eternity of subtly moving desert.

Was it moving over Glen's plane—somewhere out there—already covering up the evidence of two lives linked together in death? Leah shivered and quickly closed her eyes again, trying to wipe the painful image from her mind.

The voices of the men in the front seat woke her the second time. She sat up and found they had left the desert behind. There were date plantations on either side of the road. Irrigation ditches divided the land into squares. Beneath the date palms were fruit trees and crops of market garden vegetables. Pomegranates and bananas and oleanders and vines grew among them. Pigeons fluttered around the big clay dovecots beside the occasional flat-topped dwelling. Leah looked ahead and saw that they were approaching a village.

"Where are we?" she asked.

"The oasis of Shalaan," came the obliging reply. "It is the sheikh's birthplace and spiritual home."

Had the sheikh retreated here for some spiritual re-boosting after his wedding fiasco in Qatamah? Leah frowned as she saw nothing that remotely looked like a palace. The only large building was the mosque, dominating the centre of the village. Despite the many new concrete constructions, the place was clearly a quiet backwater where goats and hens roamed the streets.

"Is this our destination?" she asked.

"Soon," was the unhelpful reply.

Once they were through the village, Leah did not need any assistance in identifying their destination. The road led nowhere else, and her heart quailed at what she saw at the end of it. A massive stone fortress stood at the edge of the desert, looking as bleak and unwelcoming and impregnable as any prison could be.

It was a huge square creation, the high and heavily blocked walls supported at each corner by round towers. It had clearly been built to withstand attack against marauding forces in the days of warring tribes, and it was still rock solid, despite the ravages of war and time and natural elements.

It suited him, Leah thought, this birthplace and spiritual home. Born and bred to survival of the fittest. It had been her first impression of him, a man finely honed by poverty, heat, hardship and desert loneliness, rising above every test of his mettle to lead his people into the world of the future. Daunting, intimidating, formidable and invincible.

But he was wrong about her.

A bitter pride rose out of her desolation over Glen's death. Sharif al Kader could imprison her beyond any possibility of escape, but she would prove him wrong in his judgement of her. And she would fight any judgement he made against Glen. She would not have her brother denigrated in any shape or form. He was a hero to her and always would be.

The entrance to the fortress was guarded by two massive iron doors, standing open for them to drive straight into the paved courtyard. Within the walls was a continuous building running around all four sides, fronted by an arcade, which opened onto the courtyard and provided ready shade from the sun. Tubs of fruit trees at regular intervals provided some colour, but did little to break the grimly austere look of the place.

In the centre of the courtyard was an ancient well, undoubtedly drawing on underground water from the oasis, ensuring a constant supply to last through the longest siege. The cars slowly skirted it before coming to a halt in front of a large arch in the far wall.

The men poured out of their cars and were met by other men emerging from inside the building. There was a short conference. Leah remained seated in the back of her car, mentally steeling herself for the inevitable confrontation with Sharif al Kader. Eventually her travelling companion from the front seat stepped back and opened her door, signalling her to alight.

Leah gathered up her courage and stepped out, glad she was wearing the traditional long robe and *abba*, since she was once more the cynosure of all eyes. She had planned to change into Western dress at the international airport, but since her kidnap, there had been no opportunity to do anything. She was in considerable discomfort from the need for a bathroom, but she grimly maintained control of herself as she was ushered through an avenue of men.

Two black-robed women waited at the main entrance to the building. "Your servants," her guide informed her. "They will take you to your apartment and see to your needs."

Leah breathed a sigh of relief. Perhaps the sheikh had not yet arrived from Qatamah. In any event, she had a reprieve from an immediate meeting with him, as well as time to refresh herself and become oriented to her surroundings.

The women led her along the arcade to the adjoining side of the square, then up a narrow staircase to the next floor. They went along a corridor, and at the end of it Leah was ushered into an amazingly rich and luxurious sitting room, Oriental in its furnishings and with a heavy use of red and gold. The room was all the more exotic for being circular, and Leah realised this was part of one of the corner towers.

Astonished to find such contrast to the outer austerity of the fortress, Leah was more prepared for the equally lush and exotic furnishings of the adjoining bedroom. She might be in a prison, Leah thought, but it was certainly gilded with every creature comfort.

"Is there a bathroom?" she asked.

She was shown into a spacious en suite. The plumbing left nothing to be desired, either. When she emerged ten minutes later, she felt considerably better and tidier. The women had begun unpacking her luggage, which had been delivered to the apartment. Their movements were arrested by the sound of an approaching helicopter.

"The sheikh comes!" one of them murmured, and gave Leah a hard, searching look. Then they herded her into the sitting room before scuttling away. This must be the appointed waiting place, Leah thought, fighting against the tension that knotted her empty stomach.

The beat of the helicopter blades grew louder and louder. Leah moved over to the long, narrow windows. They were barred and looked out to a chain of mountains beyond the desert. Wherever the helicopter was landing it was out of her sight, but she heard the engine cut off and the blades gradually whine to a halt.

She wondered if she should sit on one of the silk brocade sofas, but decided she preferred to stand until Sharif al Kader sat. The behaviour of the servants left little doubt he was on his way to see her right now.

She remained at the window, staring out at the distant mountains. They rose up mistily over the horizon, their peaks hazy and insubstantial, stretching away as far as the eye could see. She heard a door open and knew he had entered the room. There was nothing hazy or insubstantial about the presence of Sharif al Kader. He emitted a force that jolted Leah's heart into nervous palpitation. Her hands clenched as she fought his effect on her, but she made no other movement, flouting his power with her stillness.

"Turn around!" he commanded.

She stubbornly defied him.

"Rebellious to the bitter end?" he softly mocked.

"Why have you brought me here?" she asked, her back rigidly maintaining her scorn of his authority.

He came up behind her, his nearness stirring a turbulence inside her that was impossible to control. It took an intense act of will not to shrink away, to resist every shrieking impulse to put some defensive distance between them. Her skin crawled with awareness of his greater physical strength, the hard maleness that sought to dominate her softer femininity.

But he did not touch her.

He made no attempt to enforce a submission to his command.

He raised an arm, pointing past her to direct her gaze. "See the pigeons down there," he said, his voice low and resonating intimately in her ear. "Many times when I was a youth, I captured them with my bare hands. At first, there's a sense of exultation in holding them, stroking the softness of their feathers, feeling their helpless fluttering—''

''Does it give you pleasure to take even a bird captive?'' Leah bit out, fighting the fear clutching at her heart.

His arm lifted, and as though deliberately enforcing the image he had conjured up, he gently slid his fingers through the fine silkiness of her hair, a sensual caress mesmerising in its underlying threat.

She felt her pulse quicken, and to her horror, knew it was more from excitement than fear. What was it about this man that mixed up her feelings in such an alien fashion?

''I always let them go,'' he said softly. ''When one has the power, there is more pleasure in setting them free.''

It snapped the hypnotic spell he had been weaving with his touch. Leah turned to him in surprise. ''Does that mean you captured me only to let me go? Purely to feel your power?''

His dark, compelling eyes glittered with triumphant satisfaction, and Leah knew before he replied that she had been trapped again, drawn into facing him whether she wanted to or not.

His mouth curled into a cruel little smile. ''Your case is different. The pigeon did no harm to me.''

''But I—'' She cut off the futile protest. No point in arguing. To his mind, to every Arab mind, Glen had done this man an injury, and it was only right that his family pay the price. Her innocence was totally irrelevant.

"Your brother stole my bride," came the flat indictment.

"No. Samira went with him of her own free will," Leah retorted, denying the false charge of abduction.

"She was promised to me."

"A promise her father made for her."

"She agreed."

"Under family pressure."

"There is no excuse for what was done, Leah Marlow. Your brother took the woman who in all good faith was promised to me. But I shall not go to a cold empty bed tonight. There will be a woman in it. From whom I shall take my pleasure."

He paused, and there was unbending ruthlessness in his eyes when he added, "And that woman will be Glen Marlow's sister."

"No," Leah whispered, unable to believe he would think of taking his revenge so far.

"Yes," he hissed, a deep, deadly anger searing her with its intensity.

"You can't—"

"I shall."

"Have you no decency?" Tears welled into her eyes, grief mixing with a burgeoning rage. "My brother was shot down because of you! Glen and Samira are dead because of you! Isn't that payment enough to soothe your damned pride?"

"Dead?" He gave a harsh laugh. "At this very moment they are probably in each other's arms, making love with all the passion of illicit lovers."

She stared at him in wild confusion, hope taking a soaring leap through every other emotion. "What are you saying? King Rashid announced—"

"The Princess Samira is dead in Qatamah. What else can she be, in the circumstances?" he savagely mocked. "But your brother owns the sky. Isn't that what is said of him by those who aspire to be his peer in the air?"

"Yes. Yes, it is," Leah whispered, hardly daring to believe what the words implied.

"That he goes where no other pilot dares to go. That he and his plane are one. And no-one could catch him. Or shoot him down. He was master of everything sent after him. Even supposedly unbeatable rockets. So it was said in Qatamah. In excuse to me."

"Oh, thank God!" Leah breathed, uncaring of the sheikh's rage or revenge. Glen was alive! Both he and Samira were alive, home free!

"I see you rejoice in your brother's escape. I hope you rejoice in my bed tonight," the sheikh drawled, jolting her out of the sweet elation that had replaced her leaden grief.

"You don't understand," she said impulsively. "Glen and Samira aren't lovers. He's like a big brother to her."

"Her knight in shining armour?" he mocked. "Saving her from the beast?"

Yes, Leah thought, but caution held her tongue in the face of Sharif al Kader's burning fury. Of course, he would not think of himself as a man from whom women had to be rescued. The offence went soul deep. Particularly when he had gone so far as to accept Leah into his household, against his better judgement, for the sake of making his bride as happy as he could.

The humiliation of Samira's rejection was personal as well as public, and Leah sensed that the personal hurt was far greater than the public one. "I'm sorry," she said quietly. "But I swear to you I did not know what they planned, and I played no part in it."

His eyes swept hers in cynical disbelief. "Your brother exchanged one sister for another," he said harshly. "He left you to me. Remember that when you exult over his freedom. Because you will never be free of me, Leah Marlow. Never!"

She suddenly realised his purpose in telling her Glen was alive. "You can't destroy the love I have for my brother," she shot at him.

He laughed. "You think I care what you feel for him?"

"If it's revenge you want, why not let me go on thinking Glen was dead?"

"Perhaps I didn't want a mourning martyr in my bed. A fiery spirit is much more exciting."

Leah flushed under the hot glitter of his eyes. "Glen didn't know what kind of man you are," she said, hating the strong sexuality he exuded, aware that it stirred something in her she did not want to acknowledge.

"What kind of man am I?" he asked with sardonic amusement.

Her eyes hotly challenged the primitive purpose in his. "I guess I'll find out tonight, won't I?"

"Resigned to your fate?"

"I'll fight you every inch of the way," she vowed vehemently.

"I shall enjoy that. Believe me—" his eyes gleamed with unholy anticipation "—I shall enjoy every moment of your surrender to me."

"You can undoubtedly take me by force," Leah fired at him with bitter contempt, "but believe me, Sharif al Kader, I shall never surrender to you. Never!"

"We shall see," he said with such arrogant self-assurance Leah wanted to hit out at him with a violence of feeling she had never experienced before. Again she clenched her hands, struggling for the self-control that continued to elude her in his presence.

"You left your tapestry behind in the royal palace at Qatamah. I had it packed for you." His smile taunted her unmercifully. "Perhaps you would like to spend the hours of waiting working on it, since the composition of colour and shape is so much to your liking. I'll have it sent up to you."

He turned and walked away from her.

"I left it behind because it reminded me of you!" she fired after him.

It was a bad mistake.

He paused in his step long enough to cast her a glinting look of satisfaction. "Yes. I thought it would. Until tonight, Leah."

CHAPTER FIVE

LEAH SEETHED over Sharif al Kader's interpretation of the Rubens tapestry. If he had thought she fancied being carried off and ravished by him, he would find out differently tonight.

She remembered his taunt about all the lovers she had tried and found wanting, a taunt she had angrily dismissed at the time, but perhaps she should have positively refuted his insulting insinuation. It might have saved her from this form of revenge.

If she told him she'd never had a serious lover, would it change anything?

He wouldn't believe her, came the swift answer.

And she wasn't about to explain the various events in her life that had shaped her attitudes towards that final act of intimacy.

Besides, to advance another argument about innocence would sound like pleading, and Leah was through with pleading. She would only demean herself in begging his forbearance. His mind was set, and nothing was going to change it. The philosophy of an eye for an eye and a tooth for a tooth was the order of the day. And night.

The heat of anger was banished by the chill of reality. There was no chance of escape for her. Not before tonight. But at least Glen was alive, she consoled herself. He would make inquiries about her, come after her in due course. Her brother would not leave her to rot in a desert fortress. Somehow he would find out where she was and rescue her. She knew he would.

Meanwhile... Her glance skated around the lavishly decorated sitting room, and this time Leah was struck by the sensuality of the furnishings, silks and satins and velvets, gold tassels on the cushions, smoothly polished wood, richly veined marble. This room, the whole apartment, shrieked of one purpose, an indulgence of the senses. And suddenly Leah knew where she was. These were the quarters set aside for a concubine whose duty it was to pleasure the sheikh.

Leah closed her eyes and took a deep breath as a wave of panic churned through her. She knew nothing about pleasuring a man, and she didn't intend to learn, either. She fiercely resolved to be the most unsatisfactory concubine the sheikh of Zubani had ever had. He might let her go once his taste for revenge proved too unpalatable to bother with any more.

A flock of servants interrupted Leah's bitter reverie. They brought a tray of fresh fruit, coffee, a plate of sweet biscuits and her tapestry on its custom-made stand with the accompanying box of wools. The manic impulse to tear the tapestry from its frame and hurl it out one of the barred windows was very strong. Common sense and a spark of proud defiance persuaded her she would very quickly regret such an action.

Firstly, she needed something to occupy her in this sumptuously sexual prison or she would probably go mad. Secondly, why should she let Sharif al Kader's twisted mind spoil her pleasure in an activity she enjoyed? She would mark off a section to do each day, and it would become a secret way of counting the days until Glen came to rescue her. Knowing that, she could laugh at whatever Sharif al Kader made of her interest in the tapestry.

It was a long day for Leah. She tried to block out what she had to face tonight by sleeping through most of the afternoon. It was not a highly successful ploy since fearful dreams chased through her mind. She was woken by a servant who had prepared a bath for her.

The water was scented. Leah momentarily rebelled at the thought of being *prepared* for the sheikh, but some of her muscles were stiff from the long journey in the car, and the idea of a soothing bath was attractive.

She was acutely aware of her body as she lowered herself into the water. She remembered Sharif al Kader undressing her with his eyes. Was it only yesterday? She hated the thought of him seeing her naked. She had spent most of her life covering up her femininity, and having it all bared to *his* eyes would be more a violation than anything else. Maybe she could avoid it. Maybe he would only want to *do that* with her, and it would all be over quickly.

Hope springs eternal, Leah thought with bitter irony. There was probably no hope Sharif al Kader would spare her anything.

It wasn't until she was dressed again and the servants had left that Leah found the knife. She was roaming the sitting room, trying to work off a bad case of nervous agitation when she spotted the ornamental *agal* on a side table. It had a gem-encrusted handle and a wickedly curved blade. She tested the latter for sharpness and realised she had a deadly weapon in her hands.

Her heart thumped madly as her mind leapt through the possibilities.

Could she protect herself with it?

Was she prepared to wound Sharif al Kader... kill him?

He had no right to take what he intended to take, yet was what he intended to do a fate worse than death? She would be facing certain death if she attacked the sheikh of Zubani with such a weapon.

Of course, she could always kill herself.

But while there was life, there was hope of being rescued.

Could she escape if the sheikh wasn't around to give orders? Were the cars still in the courtyard? In the dead of night when everyone was asleep, could she creep out and get away? Or were there sentries posted when the sheikh was in residence at the fortress?

So many things she didn't know and had no means of finding out. Unless she asked Sharif al Kader himself. She could pretend curiosity. But he would be suspicious. No, he would simply mock her curiosity, arrogantly confident she could not escape him.

She had to hide the knife.

Not in the sitting room. If she showed it there, he had the strength to overpower her. If it was to be done at all, it could only be done when he was fully distracted by... other things. Leah shuddered as she looked at the murderous blade again. Could she do it? If he was doing dreadful things to her, it would be self-defence. At least it gave her a choice. She could use it or not, as circumstances dictated.

She hurried into the bedroom and thrust the knife under the pillows on the bed where he meant to take her. She had to give herself a chance to stop him. He had no right to wreak such a terrible revenge on her. She was innocent of doing him any wrong whatso-ever.

She found that her hands were trembling, and hurried into the sitting room. She went straight to the window where she had stood this morning, curling her fingers tightly around the bars to steady herself. Her mind kept seeing the knife under the pillows. Madness, she thought, yet it took away the helpless feeling that had been eating at her all day.

Beware the claws of this pigeon, Sharif al Kader, she mentally hurled at him, then was startled when a door opened behind her, as though he had come to challenge her menacing thought. She swung around in wild defiance, only to find a stream of servants bringing in a sumptuous feast. Apparently the sheikh was intent on satisfying every appetite tonight.

The lamps were lit. The scene was set. But only one of the players was on stage as yet. The servants cast surreptitious glances at Leah, and she stared right back at them, uncaring what they thought. She wasn't here by her own free will and she would not thank them for following the sheikh's orders.

They no sooner left than their lord and master made his entrance. He was all in white save for the gold-and-scarlet cord around his headdress. Leah was supposed to be in white, too. The women had laid out a special robe for her, but she had scorned to wear what *he* had designated. She had chosen one of the plain black robes she had always worn when going outside the palace at Qatamah. It was as sexless and unfeminine as any robe could be.

She glared at Sharif al Kader, defying his critical appraisal of her apparel. His mouth quirked into a mocking smile.

"What are you mourning, Leah? Your lost virtue?"

"I'm not your bride," she retorted, and gave him a scathing head-to-toe look before adding, "I have nothing but contempt for the action you're taking."

He laughed and strolled towards her, his dark eyes sparkling with devilish amusement. "Do you think you are cheating me of pleasure with that unbecoming garment? Hiding something I shouldn't see?"

He paused at the low central table where his vengeful wedding feast had been set out, picked up a bunch of grapes, then took a circular route towards her, around the sofas.

Leah tensed as she realised he would pass right by the table where the ornamental *agal* had lain. She watched him step-by-step, fiercely willing him not to look, not to see the empty space that should not be empty. His attention seemed to be fixed on the bunch of grapes, his fingers idly picking through the cluster as though intent on finding the most perfect specimen. She could detect no sideways glance as he passed the danger area.

Leah almost sagged with relief. She was still collecting her distracted wits when the sheikh came to a halt in front of her.

"Have a grape," he said, holding one up to pop into her mouth. His eyes gleamed a teasing challenge.

Leah kept her lips closed, her eyes deriding the invitation.

"I can't tempt you?" he asked, popping it into his own mouth.

She disdained a reply.

"A hunger strike hurts you, Leah. Not me." He tossed the words at her carelessly, moving to examine the tapestry, which had been set up by the window for her. "Not a stitch done today," he observed. "Too unsettled? Or too excited?"

"I know you'll find this difficult to believe, but the decisions I make do not spin around you," Leah said acidly. "I shall eat when I want to eat, and I shall do as I please regarding everything else."

"Ah, yes!" he drawled. "The proudly independent Miss Marlow who will not bend to anyone's will."

He set the bunch of grapes on the windowsill, gave her a smile that sent danger signals down her spine, then moved on in what seemed to be a continuation of his walk around the room. Leah remained where she was, pretending to ignore his progress, pretending she didn't care where he went or what he did. Yet she was acutely aware of his prowling presence, and every nerve in her body was waiting for him to pounce.

Suddenly she felt fingers grazing down the sides of her face, scooping her hair back, lifting it up. The action happened so quickly, Leah simply froze in shock.

She was totally unprepared for the touch of warm lips on the exposed nape of her neck, the soft, sensual kisses that made her skin tingle with unbearable eroticism. She ducked her head in an instinctive bid to escape the sensation. An arm slid around her waist, pulling her against a hard, unyielding male body, and his lips moved to her ear, arousing such an electric feeling that she jerked her head aside.

"Your head bends to my touch," he murmured.

"Only to get away from it."

"I can feel your body tremble against mine."

"In indignation at being manhandled!"

It was a lie, and she knew it. She was frightened by the havoc he was stirring inside her. She pushed at his restraining arm, but it tightened around her. He trailed his lips down the outstretched curve of her neck, then back to her ear, softly nuzzling the lobe as he whispered, "Your skin is so soft, so fine, I think I shall find pleasure in tasting it all night."

"Stop it, damn you!" Leah cried, shaking her head violently to deter any further kissing. "I don't want this."

The caressing whisper roughened to a rasp. "What do you want? Pleasure or pain? It can be done either way."

"You can't give me pleasure," she declared vehemently.

"You think I don't feel your response to me?" He released her hair and softly stroked it to one side, splaying it over her shoulder. "It's yourself you're fighting, not me. And that's a fool's playground, Leah. Make your choice. Put on a martyr's mask and suffer my desire. Or be honest and let yourself relax and enjoy."

Her mind shied away from whatever truth was in his words. She thought of the knife. But it was too soon. She didn't know the things she needed to know.

"I'd like to eat first," she said. That would give her time to think, defer the moment that was coming and have the immediate effect of stopping him from doing these intensely disturbing things to her.

There was a moment of taut stillness from him, then he relaxed into a low laugh. "By all means, let us eat first." He smoothly spun her around to face him, and while Leah was still off balance, he tilted her chin, compelling her to meet the glittering mockery in his eyes. "Shall we start with an appetiser?"

His mouth closed on hers with a devastating swiftness and sureness. Her body was swept against his, allowing her none of the personal space she had clung to for so long. She felt unbelievably weak and helpless against the power of his invasion. Shields that she had erected against all men were smashed to smithereens. Her whole body was suffused with sensitivity, absorbing the imprint of his.

The wild, reckless passion of his kiss stirred sensations both frightening and fascinating. Frightening because she had no control over the feelings induced by what he was doing to her, fascinating because they weren't unpleasant. Leah was conscious of a desire to know more, a curiosity mixed with a strange yearning for a fulfilment she had never known. He aroused some deep feminine need in her that had never been aroused by any man before, something primitive that urged her to savour this new inner world of swirling excitement, to feel all there was to feel in the mating of a man and a woman. But years of deeply ingrained inhibitions made her fight against the tantalising temptation. She could not let herself be dominated by this rampant sexuality.

She twisted her head and shoulders away from him, breathing in hard to sober the seductive turbulence that had shredded her dearly held convictions. She would not be like her mother. Or her father. Never would she let the treacherous need for physical satisfaction rule her heart and mind! And that she could feel such things with a man who intended taking her in place of his wife was the ultimate in madness!

"You're vile!" she spat, her mouth still throbbing with the taste of his.

"But you tremble."

"From weakness. I haven't eaten since this morning."

"You have a reason for everything. But is it what you feel?"

"You're drunk with your own power, Sharif al Kader."

"I'm intoxicated with the thought of setting you free."

It snapped her head up. She searched his eyes, not wanting to be fooled. "You're just playing with me? You mean to set me free?"

There was a flash of irony. "There are many kinds of prisons, Leah. Freedom can be a state of mind. If you mean physically... yes, eventually. After the bride price has been paid."

Bitterness rose from that swiftly crushed illusion. "You know what you're doing to me will be found out. Your name will be denounced throughout the world."

His eyes hardened. "It will be feared."

"Is that what you want?"

"It is better than being laughed at. I shall command respect. What has to be done to achieve that purpose will be done."

"But it doesn't have to be," Leah argued, trying one last desperate plea. "If you think it's necessary to have it known that I was taken in Samira's place, I don't mind going along with the story."

"And give you the chance to betray my trust, as your brother betrayed King Rashid's?"

"But—"

He placed silencing fingers on her lips. "There is no argument that will change my mind." The grim set of his mouth slowly softened into an indulgent smile. "But I shall feed you first."

Leah was once more stunned by the way his face could be transformed by a smile. What was the power that lit this man's soul, that could make him a figure of dark menace or a man of compelling attraction?

While she was still staring at him in bedevilled confusion, he stooped and swept her off her feet, cradling her against his chest with alarming possessiveness.

"Put me down!" Leah cried in panicky protest.

He grinned at her. "You said you were weak from hunger. If I remove my support you might faint from lack of strength. So being a kind and considerate host, I shall carry you to a sofa."

"Oh!" Leah gulped, and as he carried out his declared purpose, she found she was mad enough to wonder what it would be like to be married to such a man. And if Samira had been a fool to run away from him.

Which meant things were going from bad to worse, and she had better straighten out her muddled mind and firmly ignore treacherous feelings or she would end up being the spineless victim! And how could she hold her head high after that?

CHAPTER SIX

LEAH WORKED HARD on restoring an appropriate simmer of justifiable hatred for Sharif al Kader's treatment of her. Her whole body burned with it. Or so she sternly told herself. She was certainly considerably heated from the way he held her around her thighs and pressed her to his chest.

He leaned over a chaise longue and as he set Leah down on it he swept the decorative cushions onto the floor. Having seen to her comfort, and with a casual air of pleasing himself, he proceeded to toss every cushion from every sofa onto the floor between Leah and the round table.

It was just as well she hadn't chosen to hide the knife behind them, Leah thought. He would be laughing at her now, his dark eyes mocking her futile attempt to change the course of this night. Despite the reassuring knowledge she still had a card up her sleeve, Leah's heart fluttered nervously as he sank down on the cushions beside her.

"Let me make you more comfortable," he said, and before Leah could guess his intention he deftly slid the light sandals off her feet.

She instantly curled her legs up away from him.

His eyes danced teasingly at her. "Cast aside your fears, Leah. This is a night for loving."

"There's no love involved in what you're doing," Leah retorted hotly.

"What is love?" he countered, raising a quizzical eyebrow.

"It's caring about what the other person feels."

"But I do care what you feel, Leah." He reached out, picked up a dish of perfect melon balls and offered it to her. "Here I am, catering to your needs."

She had to fight the impulse to throw the whole dish in his tauntingly handsome face. Sanity prevailed. She ate some melon and worked on getting her mind straight. She was wasting precious time reacting to him instead of steering her own course.

"How old is this fortress?" she asked, hoping to lead him into answering more pertinent questions.

"It has stood for over a thousand years, protecting the oasis of Shalaan from those who wanted to seize control of the ancient caravan routes from the mountains to the sea."

"The men who brought me here said it was your birthplace and spiritual home."

"It is true. My family has ruled this land for many centuries. This is our ancestral holding."

Leah wondered what it would be like to belong to a family and tradition that had continued unbroken for centuries. She had no sense of roots at all. Glen had been her only mainstay in a life marked by shifting loyalties and relationships. It was one of the things she had admired about the Arab way of life, the security of closely knit family where doubts about one's position were never harboured.

Samira would miss that. The probability was that Samira would feel more lost and lonely than Leah had ever felt, and end up bitterly regretting the choice she had made. It was so easy to overlook what one took for granted until it was no longer there. Did Glen realise the enormity of what he'd done in taking Samira away from all that had been dear and familiar to her? Why had marriage to the sheikh of Zubani been so repugnant to her?

Leah looked searchingly at him as he returned the dish of melon to the table. Handsome, intelligent, powerful. He might not have made the most comfortable of husbands, but if one were to choose a man to have children by, Sharif al Kader was certainly not without many attractive qualities. To all intents and purposes, he had been a very good match for Samira.

Leah was jolted out of her introspection when he offered her a finger bowl to wash away the melon juice. He threw her into more internal turmoil when he made a slow, sensual ceremony of wiping her fingers dry, one at a time, with a soft hand towel. Why did his touch affect her in so many disturbing ways? *I mustn't think about it,* Leah swiftly cautioned herself.

"There can't have been any practical need for this fortress for a long time now," she remarked.

He lifted his head, pausing in his playful task to give her an ironic smile, creating more internal havoc for Leah. "I do find a practical use for it now and then."

"But you don't post guards or anything like that, do you?"

His smile grew wider and he lifted her hand to his lips. "Looking to escape me, Leah?"

She watched in fascination as he slid one of her fingers into his mouth. She felt her stomach clench in some wild anticipation.

Stop it! her mind screamed. She wrenched her gaze up to his, saw a smouldering satisfaction in his eyes and tore her hand out of his grasp before he could entrap her any further with his potent brand of sexuality.

He laughed and turned to the table to select another dish. "The chicken salad looks tasty," he mused. "Would you like to try some?"

"Yes," she said huskily, then swallowed hard to get more self-assertion into her voice. "The gates to the fortress were open when I arrived this morning. Can they still be closed?"

"Of course. We would never let this fortress fall into disrepair. The doors are always closed during a sandstorm."

"At no other time?"

His eyes twinkled amusement as he handed her a small plate of salad. "There is no need," he answered. "I can hold you without sealing the fortress, Leah."

She could not control the flush that swept into her cheeks. "Do you make a habit of locking up your concubines in this apartment?" she shot at him in fiery contempt.

His amusement slid into something far more dangerous and heart twisting. "I have never been tempted that far by a woman. I was satisfied with my first wife.

And I anticipated being satisfied with my second. This apartment was prepared for her pleasure. Not for any concubine."

No wonder the servants had acted as they had! She was wrong for their sheikh, wrong in every way, since she was not his wife and never would be.

Despite her antagonism towards him, she could not doubt what he said, and it forced her to reevaluate the man. He had looked forward to his new marriage, prepared for it, sought ways to make his bride happy, even to employing Leah against his personal inclination, purely to give Samira a familiar companion. That kind of dedication to making a marriage work evoked respect.

But Sharif al Kader was still a menacing force, Leah reminded herself, and it was sheer stupidity to feel any sympathy or compassion for him. He allowed none for her.

She forced herself to eat the light helping of chicken salad, a mixture of chopped meat and cucumber and celery, blended together with a sweet mayonnaise.

At least now she knew the way out of the fortress was open. If she could keep spinning out the time before he took his satisfaction from her, she might have a chance of getting away.

If she could bring herself to use the knife!

"Why did you accuse me of being a concubine if you don't have them yourself?" she asked resentfully.

He gave her a searing look that completely undermined her hard-won composure. "Perhaps I found you too desirable to imagine anything else."

"Well, you were wrong," she snapped. "And this is wrong."

"On the contrary, never have I felt anything so right."

Leah berated herself for making another useless protest. She thrust her empty plate at him, desperate for more distraction.

He supplied her with a variety of delicacies, infinitely patient in pleasing her appetite yet subtly making her more and more aware of what was coming. He idly stroked the soles of her feet, caressed her hair away from her face, wiped a pastry crumb from her lips, a light, gentle, seductive, touching, relentless in arousing a constant and acute sensitivity. If she pulled away, he simply moved his hand to somewhere else, to touch again where she least expected it. And always the predatory look in his eyes, waiting, watching her resistance dwindle into helplessness.

What could she do?

There was no evading him.

He had a countermove to any move she made.

If she tried to fight him, he would revel in subduing her with his superior physical strength. She knew he would. And she hated the thought of letting him feel that kind of power over her. Yet was submission to his insidious touching any better? It was more dignified, she argued to herself. And it lulled him into being off guard. She still had the knife to stop him from taking his ultimate revenge.

But could she do it?

And where would it lead?

Leah found it harder and harder to keep any train of thought in her mind. The sense of there being no escape from Sharif al Kader, no matter what she did, became more and more pervasive. Eating became a mechanical exercise, purely defensive. She tried asking questions to promote conversation, but somehow words became meaningless. She drank what he gave her to drink, and he sipped from the same golden goblet, making an intimate ceremony of it, his lips replacing hers, his eyes compelling her to watch, to feel the bond he was forging with everything he did.

She felt she was drowning in his eyes. When he leaned over and kissed her she did nothing to stop him, even though he did not storm her mouth as he had before. It was the gentlest of pressures, his lips grazing softly over hers, slowly, hypnotically, drawing her into a response. Her lips moved, clung to his, parted, and then she was whirling into an ever-increasing spiral of sensation, lost to any outside reality.

She felt strangely weightless when he lifted her from the chaise longue. As he carried her in the protective warmth of his arms, her whole body seemed to pulse to the beat of his movements, a drumming of inevitability that could not be turned aside. It was only when he set her on her feet and disrobed her that a frisson of horror ran through Leah, yet it did not have the power to drive any resolution into her mind. Her hands fumbled in agitated protest as he removed her underclothes, but before the chill of her nakedness could permeate the swirling chaos inside her, he was naked, as well, and pressing her to his warmth again.

The shock of feeling his flesh against hers was intense. Her thighs quivered against the hard strength of his. Her stomach contracted, shrinking from the threat of his fully aroused virility, yet clenching with excitement at the same time. Darts of piercing sensitivity exploded through her breasts. His mouth ravished hers with a sweet violence as his hands roamed her back, caressing, moulding her softness with a possessive desire to have and to hold all that she was.

Her hands moved, drawn by a need that could no longer be denied, sliding up the powerful muscles of his thighs, over the taut mound of his buttocks, discovering the pit of his back and travelling on in their blind quest of fascination with his maleness.

He swung her onto the bed and rolled with her, their bodies entangled in a mesh of limbs, his face buried in the silky flow of her hair, her hands finding the fascination of soft curls at the back of his neck. He trailed burning kisses over her shoulder, moving with devastating passion to the swell of her breasts. Leah arched in a paroxysm of wild feeling as he kissed them, sucked on them, swirled his tongue around nipples hardened to fierce arousal.

Her body was a mass of writhing nerves when he moved lower. She clutched at his head but was hopelessly distracted by the stirring caress on her inner thighs. It drove her beyond control. She didn't know what was happening to her. It was frightening, as though she was undergoing some metamorphosis, everything inside her breaking down and flowing into some other form. She ached for it to be finished.

She was barely aware of the movement that at last provided focus for the torment inside her—Sharif's arms under her, lifting her, and the welcome pressure of his body entering hers, a solidity that she craved. She was totally uncaring of the tearing pain of his penetration. A sigh of relief whispered from her lips as her body found form again, convulsing in exquisite pleasure around a firmness that was wonderful. She cried out in anguished protest when he started to withdraw what he had given her, then moaned with satisfaction when he surged more deeply to fulfil her need again.

Slowly her body began to hum to the rhythm of his movement, to sing exultantly to each inward beat, to soar with wild elation then swoop to throbbing anticipation, only to soar higher and higher with every sweet thrust of his possession. She felt herself melting around him, a strange, warm flooding on which she floated into blissful contentment. And the movement stopped, as though their togetherness was sealed forever.

She was vaguely aware of Sharif carrying her with him as he rolled onto his side. She could hear his heart thumping madly and idly wondered why. Her heart was at peace. Everything had slowed down. Her limbs felt limp and heavy, although tingling in the aftermath of such extreme turbulence. It felt good when Sharif began to stroke her back, softly soothing. She shivered with pleasure, her skin still alive with sensitivity.

"Leah..." There was a strained note in his voice, as though it pained him to say her name. His arms came around her in an enveloping sweep, holding her more firmly to him. She felt his chest rise and fall in a deep sigh. Then, in flat murmur, he said, "It is done."

It is done.

The words echoed in Leah's emptied mind, gathering a force that shattered her peace. Her heart hammered an agonised protest at what he meant, but there was no denying the truth of those pitiless words. He had done what he had set out to do, avenging the wrong that had been done to him. That was all this meant to him.

Revenge!

And she had shamed herself in letting him have it, becoming a willing party, an avid, completely wanton party to the lovemaking that had nothing to do with making love. Humiliation swept through her from head to toe. She had let herself be seduced and deceived by a sexual expertise he had wielded like a weapon against her, totally careless of what wounds it left. If he had knifed her heart it couldn't be worse.

The knife!

A surge of bitter hatred fired her blood. She pushed out of his arms, scrabbled under the pillows for the *agal* she had hidden there. Her fingers found the gemencrusted handle, curled around it. A savage satisfaction gripped her. She could deliver vengeance as ruthlessly as he.

He had turned on his side, was looming over her, dark and menacing again. No more, she thought in violent mutiny. The knife did not even clear the pillow. She knocked the obstruction aside as her hand swept up and stabbed down.

A rock-hard palm stopped the killing arc, jarring the bones of her arm. Steel fingers closed around her wrist like a vise.

"Let me go!" she screamed at him.

He pried her fingers from the handle and flung the *agal* across the room. She flailed at him with her free hand, wanting to punch and claw and bite in her furious frustration. He captured it, pinning it down with the same viselike grip as he moved his body over hers, defeating her fierce struggle against him with his superior weight. She lay helplessly beneath him, heaving her rebellion until the last shred of mad strength drained away.

"Even now, after what we shared, I cannot trust you."

He breathed the words with harsh feeling, and to Leah's ears the accusation held the most bitter irony. "From the moment I first set eyes on you, I knew you couldn't be trusted," she spat at him.

"Yet there was one thing you did tell the truth about," he acknowledged. "You have never been with another man."

She glared at him, hating all his judgements of her, hating all he had made her feel. Everything false! "You were the first. And as God is my witness, you'll also be the last!"

He shook his head. "Why are you so embittered?"

"Because people tell you that they love you, but they don't care about you. It's all lies!"

"And if you were to find someone with whom it could be different?" he asked with insidious softness.

"I wouldn't believe it," she retorted with vehement passion.

"Who hurt you so badly, Leah?"

She couldn't say her mother or her father. In the Arab culture that would be unthinkable. "People like you who only care for what they want."

"Is that all you have known?"

No, there was Glen. Glen had always cared. But he had left her to this man, left her to be taken and... Tears welled into her eyes.

"Leave me. Let me go," she choked out, her throat thickening with an uncontrollable swell of painful emotion. "You've had your revenge."

But he did not let her go or leave her. He moved to one side and gathered her into his arms, holding her tightly to him as she wept out her grief for all the faith and trust and love that had been taken away from her.

CHAPTER SEVEN

LEAH AWOKE SLUGGISHLY. Her eyelids felt too heavy
to open. Better to go back to sleep, her mind said. She
moved to settle her head more comfortably on the pillow and instantly felt the alien sense of nakedness. She
froze as the memory of last night burst into full consciousness.

Was he still in the bed with her?

She held her breath and listened.

No detectable sound.

Her nerves screaming caution, she slowly raised her
eyelids.

The dark eyes of Sharif al Kader looked down at her
with indulgence. He was propped on his side, and a
long tress of her hair was woven through his fingers.
He smiled. "You slept long and well."

Leah's heart clenched. She closed her eyes and
fiercely wished she had never woken. She didn't want
to face another day with him in it. He did things to her
that she had no answer to.

What manner of man was he?

He should have spurned her after she had struck at
him with the knife. If he had called up his guards and
had her dragged off to some vile dungeon, that would

have been in keeping with what she had thought him to be.

Why had he held onto her? And the gentleness with which he had settled her for sleep when she had exhausted herself with weeping, the tender way he'd stroked her hair as though she was a troubled child, comforting, soothing... It didn't fit the other things he'd done.

Although it did, in a way. He hadn't taken her roughly, as she had dreaded he might. But that only made it worse in the end. A spasm of anguish twisted through her at the memory of what she had felt, lifted to incredible heights of ecstasy, then crushed by the horror of knowing all the wonderful intimacy was a lie.

Some of her feeling must have shown on her face. He tenderly cupped her cheek and asked, "Do you hurt, Leah?"

She glared at him, rejecting his concern, which only disturbed her further. "I don't want you here."

"As you wish," he said surprisingly, and bent to brush his lips over hers, leaving them tingling.

She watched him roll away from her, then stride around the bed to where their clothes had been dropped on the floor. She could not help thinking he was beautifully made, his body sleekly muscled, firmly fleshed and perfectly proportioned. He moved with the grace and assurance of an athlete who knew precisely what his body could do.

He walked past the clothes, and Leah shuddered with revulsion when she saw him pick up the *agal*. Whatever her fate with Sharif al Kader, she was glad his reflexes had been quick enough to check that utterly crazed attack.

She tensed as he straightened, expecting him to make some critical comment on her extreme action. He gave her a sardonic look. "It was a good stroke. Straight at the heart."

Leah stared at him in helpless confusion. Could he shrug off a threat to his life so easily? Was he without fear?

He moved to the heap of clothes and scooped them over his arm, including her black robe.

"That's mine," she said.

"Yes, I know." His eyes glittered some deep satisfaction at her. Then he crossed to the ornately carved wardrobe, opened the door, found her other black robe and threw it over his arm, as well. "I do not want you to wear black," he said.

"Why? Because it would make you feel guilty?" she shot at him.

He raised a mocking eyebrow at her. "Of what should I feel guilty, Leah?"

She flushed, painfully aware that her vengeance had been far more grievous than his. But he had driven her to it.

His eyes burned into hers. "It was right, Leah. Never have I felt it so right. No matter the reason it was done, or why you are the way you are, you cannot say you did not feel it was right between us. And I will not let you devalue what we felt together."

The arrogance of certain knowledge was stamped on his face, and Leah's denial stuck in her throat. No other man had even come close to stirring her into the responses he had drawn. Would there ever be another man who could? And Sharif had felt the same.

She stared wonderingly at him as he walked to the door to the sitting room. Was that why he had forgiven her the knife? Had he understood what she felt because he also had felt something beyond his experience?

He opened the door and paused to look at her. "Will you be ready for breakfast in half an hour?"

"Yes." A cup of coffee was precisely what she needed.

"I'll join you in the sitting room and we shall have it together."

Leah frowned, not having expected another session of togetherness so soon.

"Did you really think I would leave you alone, Leah?" he asked softly.

"Why not?" she flashed at him. "Isn't your revenge complete?"

His smile mocked her reasoning. "Have you forgotten that a month was scheduled for wedding celebrations?" His eyes gleamed with determined purpose. "I think I shall find it a very interesting month with you."

He left her with that thought, and to Leah's intense displeasure with herself, her sense of outrage was considerably depleted by a treacherous feeling of lively anticipation. She couldn't *want* to spend a month with him.

But he was the most intriguing person she had ever met.

That didn't mean she wanted to stay with him. Not at all. It simply meant that since she didn't have any apparent choice about it, she might as well spend her captivity trying to satisfy the curiosity Sharif al Kader aroused in her.

She needed something to lift her mind off the terrible storm of sexuality he had the power to invoke. And she would certainly fight that next time. She had to. It could never be right to her. Not in these circumstances.

She was not going to succumb to such dreadful mindlessness again. He might force a surrender of her body until such time as she *could* get away from him, but she would never let herself forget she was here to satisfy his sense of revenge. Whatever other satisfactions he got from her were incidental to that. She would not let him delude her into thinking there was something *right* in anything they shared together.

Half an hour later Leah was washed, groomed and dressed in blue. Her captor might have prevented her from wearing black again, but be damned if she would wear white for him!

When she entered the sitting room, the remnants of last night's feast had been cleared away and the cushions replaced. As she wondered when the cleaning up had been done, servants started bringing in the breakfast their sheikh had ordered. The sound of an approaching helicopter caused them to pause in their work. They looked at Leah, as though it had to be connected to her.

Leah wished it was, but knew it was far too soon for Glen to know of her predicament, and there was no-one else who cared enough to rescue her. Nevertheless, she soon realised that the arrival of the helicopter carried some import. The servants left, several minutes ticked by, and the sheikh of Zubani did not make an appearance.

Since it was unlike him not to do what he said he was going to do, Leah could only conclude he had been unavoidably delayed by matters that demanded his urgent attention. She decided there was no point in letting the hot croissants get cold. She poured herself a cup of coffee and sat down to eat, telling herself what she felt at being left alone was definitely relief, not disappointment.

She had finished her breakfast when he made his entrance, perversely enough wearing a plain black robe and a black cord around his white headdress. His dark eyes glittered with some private satisfaction as he appraised her appearance, but he made no comment on it.

"You did not wait?"

"No. Why should I? You made the appointed time," she reminded him tersely, more from the tension his presence brought than from any offence at his tardiness.

"Forgive me," he said, a smile twitching his lips. "A visitor arrived."

"Someone important?" she asked curiously.

"It should be interesting."

Again that glittering look of satisfaction.

Leah didn't know what to make of it, but she knew intuitively he was not about to elaborate.

He poured himself a cup of coffee and sat down on the sofa opposite her. He wore an air of preoccupation as he ate a light breakfast. Occasionally he cast a speculative glance at Leah but he made no attempt at conversation. She did not know why he was bothering to pass the time with her.

Pride forbade her to show any inclination for a more companionable effort from him. Having borne his silence for far longer than any normal politeness demanded, Leah stood up and walked over to her tapestry. Her sense of independence dictated that she pay him even less attention than he was paying her. She opened the box of wools and selected the colours required for the section she would do today.

"Blue becomes you."

Leah ignored the appreciative remark. She concentrated on threading a needle, which was difficult. She could feel the full force of his attention burning into her.

"Leave that, Leah," he softly commanded. "We are about to take a little walk. I want you with me."

The lure of the open air was enough to convince Leah that any rebellious stance was self-defeating. Besides, it might be to her advantage to learn everything she could about the fortress and its environs. Who knew what loophole she might find for escape in the month ahead?

She put down the needle and swung around. He was on his feet, turned towards her, the light from the window shining directly on his face. Leah was instantly reminded of her first sight of him. The aura of indomitable power forged to his will, his way, his destiny, was so strong, Leah was once more swept by a weird fluttery sensation. Like the pigeon caught in his hands, she thought, with a little stab of fear.

"Where are you taking me?" she asked, a brittle edge to her voice. *The walk* suddenly had dark menace behind it.

"To the room where I usually hold *majlis* when I am in residence."

"I thought that was for men only."

"You shall be the exception today."

"Why?"

His mouth curled into a cruel little smile. "Because a nail is driven home most effectively with a hammer." He gestured towards the door. "Come. It has been a long enough wait."

Leah could make no sense of his enigmatic words, but it was crystal clear he was in no mood to brook any disobedience to his command. She took the course of dignified compliance, but her mind warred between fear and curiosity. Something was afoot, and Leah had the sinking feeling that her part in it was not as an onlooker.

They did not go outside. He led her into a corridor that took them to a wide staircase. At the foot of this was a spacious foyer, decorated with murals made of tiny ceramic tiles. Guards stood on either side of the arched entrance to the courtyard. Another set of guards stood at the double doors at the far end of the foyer. As their sheikh and Leah approached these doors, the guards moved into place to open them at his command.

Sharif al Kader paused in front of them. He took Leah's hand and placed it on his arm, holding it there with his other hand. "So, my little captive," he said with sardonic amusement. "We shall see how the crimes are to be appeased."

Leah knew his fingers would tighten around hers like steel bands if she tried to remove her hand. She could feel the latent power there, ready to take action. Did he intend to flaunt his possession of her in front of his people? Was this the next step in his revenge?

He nodded to the guards and the doors were flung open. Leah called on all her inner resources to detach herself from whatever was planned. It had no meaning to her. A month, at most, and she would be away from here. Yet as they entered the reception room, Leah's resolve to cocoon herself against the reaction of a crowd of men was totally shattered.

There was only one man waiting for them. He rose from his chair, a startled sound breaking from his lips as he stared at Leah. His gaze jerked to Sharif al Kader, down to the hand clasp on the sheik's arm, then back to Leah. His expression changed from shock to anguished dismay as he saw the flush of shame and humiliation burn into Leah's cheeks. Her legs would have faltered if she had not had the enforced support of the man who held her captive.

Over the years of his close friendship with her brother, Prince Youssef of Qatamah had always treated Leah with the respect he gave to his own sisters, the kind of respect Sharif al Kader had ruthlessly violated. Youssef knew—it was too obvious for him not to know—why she was being paraded in front of him.

Nevertheless, it was imperative that all personal feelings about this situation be set aside. He had undoubtedly been sent by his father, King Rashid, to perform a highly delicate political mission, and that could not be jeopardised. He made a valiant attempt to recover before the sheikh of Zubani came to a halt in front of him.

Formal greetings were made and returned.

The sheikh escorted Leah to a chair that had been set beside his. He released her long enough for her to sit down, then as he settled himself he took her hand again and held it under his on the armrest of his chair.

The action was pointed enough to draw Youssef's attention. Leah saw the struggle on his face, saw it harden into resolution. He lifted his gaze to hers, silently promising all the support he could give, then with an air of proud integrity, he turned to the man he had to challenge.

"Forgive me, Your Excellency, this is not what I have come to say, but may I put to you that you have an innocent hostage in Miss Marlow."

"You surprise me, Your Royal Highness," Sharif al Kader drawled. "Believe me, Miss Marlow is not a hostage. She remains with me at my pleasure."

The deliberate emphasis on Leah's fate made Youssef flinch. Leah felt an intensely bitter hatred towards the man who held her forcibly at his side. He was sparing her nothing in his quest for revenge.

Youssef gathered himself and tried again, his voice terse with barely restrained anger on her behalf. "I knew Glen Marlow for a long time. He would never involve his sister in anything he considered dangerous. She was not directly involved, Your Excellency."

"Glen Marlow endangered his sister by abducting your sister," the sheikh pointed out with unarguable logic. "Abducting my promised bride," he added with more bite.

"No." Youssef grimaced. "As much as it pains me to say it, my father chooses to believe that, but it is not so. My sister Samira went with Glen Marlow of her own free will. I have no doubt in my mind it was also at her request. Glen would never have tried to persuade her against fulfilling a duty of state."

"But he did take her."

"Yes."

"The woman who was promised as a wife to me."

"Yes," Youssef agreed on a despairing note.

"And he left his sister."

"To be expelled from Qatama, as he had clearly anticipated, Your Excellency."

The plea was futile. Leah knew it, and Youssef must have realised it, too. She was grateful to him for trying, but her present situation did not hang on her innocence. The sheikh proceeded to clear Youssef's mind of all concern on that score.

"The balance of justice had to be redressed, Your Royal Highness. Forgive me, but I thought your father, King Rashid, left much to be desired." He paused, then drove in the point. "At my cost."

"My father appreciates that very keenly, Your Excellency, which is why I have come to bring you the offer he now makes to you. And since it is a matter of some delicacy, I would like to speak to you alone.''

"Oh, I do not think Miss Marlow will divulge my private affairs,'' the sheikh drawled. He turned to Leah with an air of indulgent consideration. "I'm sure you would like to hear what is offered to me from the royal family of Qatama. With whom you have been so intimately associated.''

Her eyes spit blue fire at him. She hated him all the more for so callously using her as a political pawn. "I am not interested in your affairs. I would rather go.''

His hand tightened around hers. "No, no, there is no need for you to be tactful. You must stay. I want you to.''

He turned to Youssef. "Miss Marlow stayed in the throne room at Qatamah to hear the end of the alliance that had been agreed upon by your family, Your Royal Highness,'' he said with silky venom. "I think it only fitting that she hear what you have to offer in its place.''

Youssef's face tightened as he comprehended the depth of the offence given to the sheikh of Zubani. Leah looked away. She was painfully acquainted with humiliation. She had suffered it at the hands of her father. She had suffered it at the hands of her mother. She had suffered it at the hands of Sharif al Kader. She did not want to watch the effect on Youssef while the sheikh made mincemeat of him.

"As you will, Your Excellency,'' Youssef said in grim resignation.

"You have my attention, Your Royal Highness.''

"My father has many daughters. The Princess Fatima is of marriageable age."

A wave of repugnance swept through Leah. Fatima was only sixteen, and no match for the man beside her. The thought of his taking Fatima as his wife, making love with her, doing all that he had done to Leah last night... It wasn't right. Couldn't be right. To Leah's mind it was obscene. Callous, she reminded herself savagely.

A shudder ran up her arm as she felt Sharif's fingers moving caressingly over hers. Only then did she realise her own had curled up, her fingernails digging into the wood of the armrest. She instantly straightened them and took a deep breath to steady her reaction to what Youssef was offering.

He was listing Fatima's attributes, painting the image of a beautiful and dutiful young woman who would quickly fit into the role of the *sheikha* of Zubani and be all the sheikh could want in his wife. He spoke with eloquent persuasion and finished by assuring the sheikh that his every requirement would be conscientiously fulfilled with this new alliance.

"It is to our mutual benefit that we conclude this affair in harmonious accord," Youssef finished on a pertinently political note.

Why should she care if Sharif al Kader married Fatima, Leah fiercely argued to herself. It was a way out for her, wasn't it? And undoubtedly Fatima would accept her fate placidly. Fatima had a placid nature. Let him agree to the marriage. Then he would have to release her.

"More," the sheikh said icily. "I want more."

Of course, Leah thought cynically. He already had a woman to warm his bed. She was the hammer to drive that nail home. Qatamah had to offer more than a wife.

Youssef stiffened. "The border village of Reza, which has been a source of dispute for over a century, and which you now control. We will cede all claims on it."

"More," said the sheikh.

"Reparation of a hundred million dollars will be paid to your state."

"More."

"I am not authorised to offer more."

This statement was greeted by stony silence.

"Your Excellency—" Youssef took a deep breath. "Whatever safeguards you require to be assured of a happy conclusion—"

The opening of the doors behind him was a distraction that could not be ignored in the middle of such an important meeting. Youssef turned to frown at the unwelcome intrusion.

The woman in the doorway galvanised all eyes. She was dressed in a striking robe of brilliantly swirling violet and turquoise. A matching turban was wound around her head. She moved with a majesty that was unique, and as she advanced down the room, the swaying grace of her walk added its mesmerising wonder to the Ethiopian's magnificent beauty.

The doors were closed behind her.

Tayi had made her entrance.

CHAPTER EIGHT

ALTHOUGH TAYI WAS visibly jolted at her first sight of Leah sitting beside the sheikh, the crack in her composure was swiftly attended to. Her large velvety eyes focussed on the man beside Leah with deep intensity as she walked forward.

Leah wondered why a nanny would be allowed to interrupt a meeting concerning critical matters of state. But she sensed no alarm in the man at her side. No tension at all. He was not disturbed by Tayi's admission to this room.

It was Youssef who reacted. He rose from his chair, his gaze riveted on the woman who approached. Whether this was an unexpected interruption or some prearranged ploy by the sheikh, Leah did not know. Perhaps it was the regality of Tayi's bearing that prompted Youssef to stand, but it was more likely he had risen in offence that a woman whose antecedents had surely been slaves was now to be given attention ahead of his mission.

Youssef's movement diverted Tayi's attention from the sheikh. Her feet stopped moving. There was a flicker of disquiet in her expression as she stared at the handsome nobility of Youssef's face. At that moment he was very much the son of his father. Youssef's body stiffened with proud dignity. Tayi quickly turned her head to the sheikh, perhaps realising she had blundered in coming into this room. Nevertheless, she resumed her approach as though it had never been broken.

"What brings you here, Tayi?" he asked when she stopped in front of him. "This is a very important meeting."

"There is one more important thing," she answered in soft, melodious tones.

It was the first time Leah had heard Tayi speak. Her voice had a velvety quality that somehow matched her eyes.

"What is it?" Sharif asked sharply.

"Jazmin is sick and calls for you."

"I will come immediately."

This reaction surprised Leah. She cynically wondered if his concern for his daughter was really so urgent, or if he simply chose to end the meeting with Youssef. She remembered the death of his first wife and what had followed from that. Perhaps the welfare of his children was of prime importance to him.

Tayi did not appear surprised by his decision. She turned and looked straight through Youssef as though he weren't there, her head tilted high in disdain of his status and his mission. She had shown that her power over the sheikh's attention was much higher than his. She made her exit with the same supreme dignity with which she had made her entrance.

The sheikh rose from his chair, drawing Leah to her feet with him, her hand firmly clasped on his arm.

"Who is that woman?" Youssef demanded.

"That is Tayi, the minder of my children."

"She is very striking," Youssef remarked, frowning over Tayi's relatively low status in the sheikh's household.

"Yes. One day I hope to marry her off advantageously to her position," Sharif said dismissively. "But we digress. And I must leave you. Tell your father I will reflect on his offer. Perhaps we shall talk more anon."

There were no formal farewells. He swept Leah from the room, leaving Youssef to make his own departure. Tayi was waiting in the arched entrance to the foyer. As soon as she saw them, she went ahead, walking along the arcade in the opposite direction to the way Leah had been taken yesterday.

This was one time Leah didn't mind being swept along with the sheikh. It gave her the opportunity to check out the courtyard. The scene with Youssef had convinced her she must do her utmost to escape from this dreadful situation.

She felt both used and abused by Sharif al Kader. Having been offered such handsome reparation by King Rashid, he had no justification in continuing his revenge. For Leah to be taken *at his pleasure* while a marriage with Fatima was being negotiated was the ultimate in degradation. Clearly he could have no feeling for her whatsoever, and she could not bear to be a victim of his powerful personality again. She had to escape!

Leah counted ten cars parked against the walls on either side of the great iron gates. Whether keys were hanging ready in ignitions she had no way of knowing. Besides, there were men everywhere, around the ancient well, next to the gates, sitting in the shade of the arcade. Some were armed with guns, some not. The sheikh's entourage was formidable. If the guards had been issued with orders to prevent her from leaving, she saw no ready way past them.

Depression weighed heavily on her heart as they mounted the staircase to what was presumably the children's quarters. If there was no way out of this fortress, what was to become of her? How could Glen stage a rescue under these conditions? It was hopeless. Hopeless!

A servant opened a door for them, and Tayi ushered them into what was obviously Jazmin's bedroom. The little girl was propped up on pillows, her face pale and tear-streaked and woebegone, although her older sister, Nadia, was sitting on the bed trying to interest her with a selection of dolls.

Both children instantly brightened at seeing their father. "Papa, Jazmin has tonsillitis again," Nadia informed him.

"Ah, yes, I can see it hurting, my poor brave little one," he said with loving sympathy. He sat on the bed and felt her forehead. "What did the doctor say?"

"That it wasn't bad, but she's got to take medicine," Nadia answered him.

"Then we will soon make it better, Jazmin," he assured her, and bent to kiss her nose. "Now, what would you like your papa to do for you?"

"You brought the lady with the golden hair," Jazmin said in a husky whisper, her eyes turning to Leah in wonderment.

"Yes. Do you remember her name?"

"Miss Marlow," Nadia said triumphantly.

"Can I talk to her, Papa?" Jazmin asked.

Sharif al Kader turned commanding eyes to Leah. It was on the tip of her tongue to refuse, to say she would have nothing to do with his daughters under the obscene terms of her captivity. But then the thought struck her that his daughters might provide a means of getting away from here. Surely they were not kept within the walls of the fortress day in and day out. If they should become eager for her company, and want her to go with them on their outings, this was a chance she would be foolish to ignore.

She smiled at the sick little girl and went to sit beside her on the opposite side of the bed to her father. "Would you like me to tell you a story, Jazmin?"

For the next hour Leah had both girls entranced with fairy stories. Their father's dark eyes sparkled amusement and approval and warm pleasure at her, as though the public flaunting of his revenge was of no consequence whatsoever. Leah silently but fiercely promised herself she was not about to forget it at *his* convenience.

Jazmin's eyelids gradually drooped lower and lower. By the time she drifted into sleep, Leah was satisfied she had achieved her purpose. Both little girls would certainly be asking to see her again. She had made allies of Sharif al Kader's daughters, but as she left the room, Leah found she had made one enemy. Tayi stood by the door to see them out. She said nothing, but her large, expressive eyes spoke volumes to Leah, and none of it good.

Jealousy? Leah wondered. But jealous of what? The liking of the children, or the way the sheikh of Zubani had reacted to her? She remembered the initial jolt of shock on Tayi's face when she had seen Leah seated beside the sheikh at the meeting with Youssef. Was there more than loyalty in Tayi's heart for her employer?

Leah shook her head. That was no concern of hers. Her major concern was to get out of this place and way beyond Sharif al Kader's reach. Unfortunately that seemed beyond the realms of possibility today.

He escorted her back to the sitting room in the tower and had the crass insensitivity to swing her straight into his embrace. "You were very good with my daughters," he said, his eyes simmering with a desire that had nothing to do with her ability to relate easily to children. "I think I shall have to make love to you."

"No!" Leah cried vehemently, curling her hands into fists against his chest.

"Why not?"

"If you're going to marry Fatima..."

"No commitment has been made. I am a free man. And I want you, Leah Marlow." A teasing smile hovered on his lips as he raised a mocking eyebrow at her persistent resistance to his embrace. "Did I not demonstrate this morning how highly I value you?"

"By humiliating me in front of Prince Youssef?" she raged.

"By refusing all he offered me. I would not exchange you for his sister, not even for the further inducement of undisputed control over Reza and a hundred million dollars. Does it not warm your heart to know I am so deeply in your power that I prefer to have you to—"

"Don't think you can fool me, Sharif al Kader!" Leah snapped. "You're holding out for more."

He laughed. "Perhaps I am. More of you. More of this..."

His mouth claimed hers with passion, and Leah's resistance fought a losing battle against the overwhelming power of his will. He gave her no time to erect defences. The blows she struck were like water off a duck's back to him while he skilfully fed the temptation to feel again what he had made her feel last night. In the end, her struggle against the inevitable only seemed to heighten the excitement of the physical intimacy he forced upon her, and the only battle she fought was to incite him out of his damnable control so she had the satisfaction of drawing a wild response from him.

"The earth moved," he murmured afterwards, giving Leah a smile that seemed to make the earth move for her.

But she would not admit it. She would not be beguiled or seduced or deceived into conceding anything more than some mad sexual compatability with him. Which was inexplicable. But undeniable. Sharif al Kader had stripped her of any choice about it, but Leah told herself if she was ever free to choose, she would never be held or swayed by such purely physical feelings. It was a trap that blinded people to the more important values of real loving and caring.

In the days that followed, Leah was invariably defeated by Sharif al Kader's will, no matter what she said or did. He not only spent every night with her, but frequently took her to bed during the day, as well. As a lover, he was overwhelming and apparently insatiable, and Leah was both shamed and exhilarated by the response he always drew from her. She railed at herself with heated disgust. She was no better than her mother, revelling in sexual pleasure, but Sharif had only to look at her with desire and a treacherous excitement seized her.

It was not all sex. Sharif would talk to her about the programs he had set up for the welfare and education of the women and children of Zubani. He would ask her opinion and draw her into a discussion on plans for the future. Leah's attempts to maintain disinterest in his affairs usually crumbled under his persuasive persistence. Besides, she enjoyed challenging his point of view, and she told herself that conversation staved off the more insidious form of intimacy.

He was only too happy for her to visit his children in their quarters, but he always came with her and stayed the whole time, as though they were playing at being a family. Jazmin was soon well again, and the little girls did have outings, but only with Tayi. Leah was never given a chance to get beyond the fortress walls.

Time started to become meaningless, the days flowing into one another, each one barely distinguishable from the last and the next. Leah clung to doing a section of her tapestry every day to mark some difference. She had bursts of rebellion, demanding to know if Sharif had made any decision about the negotiations with Qatama, but he always dismissed that issue by kissing her senseless and telling her he preferred the reparation he had chosen for himself, implying *she* satisfied him.

Leah knew this couldn't be true. The revenge he had taken might earn a fearful respect, but it did not settle the political impasse between Qatama and Zubani. Sooner or later some resolution had to be found. Alliances could be of critical importance in the Middle East. Youssef had not been speaking lightly when he said it was of mutual benefit for the two states to be in harmonious accord.

A week slid by. Two. Glen had to know she was being held by now. Was he doing anything to effect her freedom? Youssef knew where she was. Surely he would tell Glen. Or was the political situation too delicate for it to be known he had revealed her whereabouts?

There was nothing Leah could do to break her imprisonment. If Sharif wasn't with her, there was always a woman sitting outside her door. All her movements were observed. If Glen didn't come to rescue her, would Sharif let her go when the month was over? Or would she be held here at his pleasure until he no longer found pleasure in her?

Despair hung heavily on her heart at times. Sharif's pleasure in her was certainly not waning in any way whatsoever. What if he intended to keep her on as his concubine after he married Fatima? Leah couldn't bear that thought.

On the afternoon of the eighteenth day of her captivity Sharif announced that matters of state required him to he be at his palace for a day or so, but he would come back to her as soon as he could. He flew off in his helicopter.

Leah wondered if King Rashid himself had come to negotiate a settlement this time. One thing was certain. Whatever was agreed between the rulers of Qatama and Zubani, Sharif was not yet prepared to let her go.

Leah spent a miserable night alone in her bed. Sharif's absence brought home to her how very deeply enmeshed she had become in the relationship he had forced upon her, depending on him for company and the sense of intimate togetherness they shared in bed. It could only get worse, she thought, despairing of ever being free of him even if he did let her go.

The next morning, she was sitting listlessly in front of her tapestry, forcing herself to get on with it, when she received a surprise visitor. Leah had no reason to think Tayi cared about her loneliness, and she was amazed to see the nanny enter the sitting room. Tayi was carrying a basket, and Leah was even more astonished to see her draw from it the money belt that had been left on the floor in the throne room at Qatamah.

"How did you get that?" she asked.

Tayi did not reply. She walked forward to hand Leah the belt. "Put it on under your robe," she commanded.

"I don't understand." Leah rose from her chair. Despite the fact it was Glen's, she felt reluctant to take the belt. Was this some trick to get her into trouble with the sheikh? "Why are you giving it to me?"

"Do you want to stay here or go free?" Tayi demanded, her large, velvety eyes firing a hostile challenge at Leah.

"I must get away," Leah said vehemently.

"Then there is no time to waste. Do as I say."

"Why are you helping me?"

Tayi disdained a reply to that question. "Put the belt on now."

Leah took the belt, and as she hitched up her robe to fasten it around her waist, Tayi went to the central table and deliberately knocked a bowl of fruit over. Then she walked to the door and waited for Leah to join her.

As usual, a woman servant was sitting in the corridor just beyond the door. Tayi ordered her to clean up the spilled fruit in the sitting room, then swept off down the corridor with Leah fast on her heels. The moment the servant was safely out of sight, Tayi drew a black cloak and *abba* from her basket and handed them to Leah.

"Cover yourself," she commanded.

Leah made sure there was only a slit for some eyesight left uncovered as they hurried down the staircase. No-one challenged them as Tayi led the way across the courtyard to a car by the gateway.

"Get in the passenger side," she directed.

Leah did not hesitate. Why Tayi was risking the sheikh's displeasure in doing this, she did not know, but she was not about to do anything to jeopardise this chance at escape.

None of the sentries made any attempt to stop them or question where they were going as Tayi drove the

car out of the courtyard. Few women drove cars in
Arab countries, but apparently Tayi had the privilege
of complete freedom of movement, going wherever
she pleased. Again Leah wondered if the Ethiopian
woman was a simple minder of children. She had an
air of authority that seemed to go much higher than
that.

"Who are you?" she asked impulsively, as they
travelled towards the village.

Predictably enough, Tayi made no reply.

It didn't matter, Leah told herself. If this escape
worked, she would soon be out of Zubani, and Tayi
and Sharif al Kader would play no further part in her
life. The sudden wrench on her heart at that thought
was proof enough that this opportunity had come
none too soon.

"Can you drive?" Tayi asked abruptly.

"Yes."

They went through the village and stopped at the
outskirts on the other side. Tayi turned to Leah, the
light of a mission accomplished in her eyes. "The car
is yours. Go. And never come back."

"Why did you do this?" Leah asked, still not sure
it wasn't a trap of some kind. "You don't care about
me."

Again there was no reply. Tayi alighted from the car
and walked away, a majestic figure who feared nothing and no-one. Unforgettable, Leah thought, as she
quickly rounded the car to take the driver's seat.
Whether it was a trap or not, freedom beckoned.

Leah put her foot down on the accelerator and
drove as fast as she deemed safe. If she was caught, the

sheikh's revenge did not bear thinking about. She breathed a sigh of relief when at last the road joined the four-lane highway. Not far now, she told herself, anxious to have the most dangerous part of this journey over and done with. She was fifty miles short of the border when she heard the helicopter overhead.

It couldn't be him, she told herself, but her whole body churned with turbulent emotion at the thought that he had come after her and would not let her go. The helicopter seemed to hover above her for long, interminable minutes, then she saw it swooping ahead of her. Yet there was the sound of one behind her, as well.

The highway was dead straight for miles. Two helicopters, clearly belonging to the military, landed in unison, one in front of her, one behind, effectively blocking the road with her car neatly trapped between them. Armed men poured out of both and spread out in a line. There was no way past them.

Leah slowed her car to a halt, turned off the ignition and sat waiting, knowing she was captured but feeling strangely numb about it now that it was done. Two men broke from the line ahead of her and came forward to the car. One opened her door and motioned her out. Leah complied. She was asked to remove her *abba*. It made identification easy enough, she realised. The two men stared at her long, pale gold hair for several moments before one of them spoke.

''Come,'' was all he said.

There was no point in trying to disobey. Her bid for escape was comprehensively crushed. As she was escorted towards the helicopter, Leah again wondered if

it had been a trap all along. Would Tayi be rewarded
or punished for what she had done? Whatever the
outcome for the other woman, Leah knew she was
about to feel the weight of the sheikh of Zubani's displeasure. Yet what greater price could be asked than
that already paid?

She was motioned towards a seat in the helicopter
and strapped in. As the vehicle took off, Leah felt absolute despair. Undoubtedly she would be taken back
to the desert fortress from where she'd come. No-one
could save her. No-one could rescue her. As far as she
was aware, she could spend the rest of her life as the
sheikh's captive, giving him whatever pleasure he desired.

CHAPTER NINE

LEAH SUFFERED THE TRIP in total disinterest. When they landed she submitted to being helped out of the aircraft with dull resignation. Only then did she realise they were not in the desert. They had landed on a helipad within the grounds of what had to be the palace of Zubani.

While Leah was in no mood to appreciate the elegant architecture of the impressive white palace, she had to admit it looked a whole lot better to her than the fortress outside the oasis of Shalaan. It had obviously been built in recent years to reflect the new wealth and importance of the country, and the windows she could see were not barred.

It was also an unexpected pleasure to see grass, flowering shrubs and stately date palms. She had sorely missed her private garden in Qatama. Not that she expected to be allowed to roam free here. It was simply a relief to have some other view than desert and distant mountains.

She was not given much time to enjoy it. The guards marched her straight inside the palace. There she was passed to another set of guards who were apparently waiting to escort her directly to the sheikh. They crossed the huge domed foyer and entered a wide arched hallway. At the end of this was a set of double doors, which were ceremoniously opened for her.

Leah walked into a fabulous art gallery. Paintings from the Renaissance, impressionists and Fauvists virtually leapt at her from the walls, masterpieces from some of the greatest artists the world had known. No wonder Sharif was familiar with Rubens and Leonardo da Vinci if this was his private collection, Leah thought. But she had no time for more than a cursory glance at the paintings. The sheikh of Zubani compelled her full attention as he rose from the bench that ran down the centre of the room.

Whether she liked it or not, Leah felt linked to him in some unfathomable way, and she realised with a considerable jolt that it was curiously comforting to see him again, as though he added a vibrancy to her life that would be forever lost without him. The dull sense of resignation was dispersed the moment her eyes clashed with his. Her whole body was poised in a high state of awareness, ready to meet the challenge of his reaction to her flight for freedom.

"Ah! You have arrived," he said with satisfaction.

Leah waited, expecting an angry outburst for putting him to so much trouble in foiling her attempt at escape.

He frowned as he walked towards her. "Did I not say you weren't to wear black?"

Leah stared at him in disbelief. To pick on such an irrelevant detail as his first reprimand seemed totally out of keeping with the situation.

He reached her, unfastened the cloak, whipped it off her and tossed it away. His eyes glittered over the blue caftan she had put on that morning. "That is much better."

Leah was relieved he could be pleased about something, but she suspected this was the calm before the storm.

His hands started to slide around her waist, abruptly stopping when he felt the money belt. "What is this?" he demanded, his dark eyes searing hers with distinct displeasure.

Leah winced. "My brother's money belt."

He frowned in disapproval. "So! You accepted it after all."

"A matter of necessity, under the circumstances," she defended.

"Take it off. Now!" he commanded, then turned and paced halfway up the gallery while Leah removed the belt.

She placed it on top of the despised black cloak and composed herself as best she could for the diatribe that had to come.

Sharif swung around and shook an accusing finger at her. "This escape of yours. It was gratuitous ill-mannered misbehaviour. I don't find it at all becoming in you."

"I'm sorry," she said, wary of giving him more offence.

"So you should be. Have I not done everything I can to please you? Do you not yet know that we are right together? It is foolish for you to want to leave me," he declared with passion, his eyes searing hers, compelling her to feel the same desire for him as he felt for her.

Leah took a deep breath, defying the power of his undeniable charisma. "I don't like being a prisoner," she stated, her eyes flashing their accusation at him.

He gestured dismissively. "That is your own fault."

"*My* fault?" Leah echoed incredulously.

His challenge was instant and unequivocal. "How can I trust you to stay with me?"

"I want to be free, Sharif. You can hardly blame me for trying to attain what you deny me," Leah argued.

He heaved an exasperated sigh. "Well, if you must try escaping again, do me the honour of being more clever next time."

While Leah was still swallowing her astonishment at such a perverse piece of counselling, his eyes flashed sparkling admiration at her. "Now the knife," he said with relish. "*That* was worthy of you. But this plan—" He made a contemptuous sound. "Too predictable!"

"It wasn't my plan," Leah heard herself say, as though needing to defend her lack of cleverness.

He grimaced. "Tayi means well. She simply does not comprehend the situation. She sees, yet does not see."

So it hadn't been a trap, Leah thought. Tayi had acted on her own. Which made her remarkable in character, as well as in person.

"What will you do to Tayi?" she asked in concern for the other woman.

He looked surprised. "Nothing! Why on earth should I do anything to Tayi? She acted in good faith."

The machinations that were going on here made Machiavelli look like a schoolboy, Leah thought. Sharif al Kader was certainly the most *unpredictable* man she had ever met! He was not only dismissing her attempt at escape as inconsequential, he was shrugging off Tayi's part in it, as well.

"Maybe I don't see either, Sharif," she said with feeling. "Why am I here? What do you intend to do with me now?"

He frowned and kept on frowning as he paced around the far end of the bench and halfway up the other side of the room. Then he paused and shot her a hard, measuring look. "Things have changed. I shall take you into my confidence."

"Thank you. I'd like that," Leah said, quick to encourage any offer of information.

"Representations have been made on your behalf," he said, as though deeply vexed by this development. "The situation is extremely delicate, to say the least."

Glen had come forward, was Leah's immediate and exultant thought. But surely it was terribly dangerous for her brother to confront the man who had every reason to do him long and lasting damage. Perhaps Glen had contacted the Australian embassy, informing them that one of their nationals was missing and it was rumoured she was with the sheikh of Zubani. In the end, it could only be her brother prompting action on her behalf.

Rather than increase Sharif's vexation with the situation, Leah held her tongue, hoping to hear precisely who was inquiring after her and how Sharif meant to deal with it.

He glowered reproof at her as he continued. "You gave me to understand that you were unloved by any family other than your brother, who has had you under his protection for the last eight years."

"That's correct," she said, wondering why he should question it.

"No. It is not."

The emphatic rebuff startled Leah into asking, "Has the government made inquiries about me?"

"No. It is the person who it should be. Your father."

Leah could hardly believe her ears. "Why did he bother coming?" It made no sense to her. Her father had abandoned her sixteen years ago, devoting himself to his second marriage and the stepchildren who came with it.

"It is his duty," Sharif answered, too imbued in his Arab culture to comprehend a father who felt no paternal duty to his daughter. "He wishes to see you and be certain that you have been well looked after. Which you have. And to pay whatever price I ask to set you free."

"My father?" Leah felt completely bewildered.

"Of course. You are his daughter. Naturally he is concerned for you. He will pay handsomely for your release."

For several moments all the stored-up bitterness was infiltrated by sweet memories of her childhood, her father coming home from his overseas flights and swinging her up in his arms, loving her and teasing her about the doll she knew he would have for her in his suitcase. He had bought her a wonderful collection of dolls, all in national dress from the countries he had flown to in his job as a Qantas pilot. But that was before...

She looked at Sharif with pained uncertainty. "My father really has come for me? You're not just saying this?"

His eyes probed hers with sharp intensity, wanting to understand. "Why should he not, Leah?" he asked quietly.

A thousand reasons why not, she thought sadly, but gave a dismissive shrug. "It doesn't matter."

"I think it does. It was he who hurt you?"

"Things happen," she said flatly. "My parents were divorced when I was ten. My father has another family now."

"But you are still very dear to him."

She gave a rueful smile. "It seems that way. Are you going to let me see my father, Sharif?"

He slowly nodded. "Yes. There is a need." He walked up to her and drew her gently into his arms. Leah did not resist. She felt too confused by what he had told her and by the way he was acting towards her, as though he cared that she had been hurt and wanted to make things better for her.

He returned her rueful smile. "I cannot deny a father his daughter. And you will feel more free with seeing him and talking to him."

"When do I get to do that?" she pressed, as his head bent to hers. "Where is he staying?"

His lips brushed a tantalising kiss. "He is staying here in the palace." Another more sensual kiss. "And you will meet him tomorrow." A kiss that simmered with passion. "After we have made love many times."

More than that he would not say. He conducted her to a suite of rooms that guaranteed them privacy, and although it was weak of her to submit without at least some token protest, the urge to know if there would be some different quality in Sharif's lovemaking overrode every other consideration. It was crazy to wonder if there could be some lasting future with him, yet she could not stop herself from dreaming foolish dreams as he comprehensively demonstrated that his pleasure was also hers.

At first he made love to her with a fierce possessiveness, perhaps prompted by her trying to leave him, a deeply primitive male need to affirm that she belonged to him. Then there came a tender loving, as though she was truly precious to him and he cherished all she was. Leah found it utterly impossible not to respond to him. There was a side of her that craved for this intimacy to go on forever, another side that wanted to hoard the memory of it because sooner or later it had to come to an end, no matter how *right* it felt with him.

As she lay in the seductive warmth of his arms, she had to remind herself that the sense of fulfilment he gave her was only transient. To her, Sharif was a totally confusing mixture of a man, hard and ruthless in going after what he deemed would best serve him, yet there was kindness and caring and a fine understanding in much of what he did.

His plans for his people and the progress of his country were far-thinking and admirably idealistic. She wished she could stay with him and share in them, to see worthwhile goals coming to fruition. But that wasn't what Sharif wanted her for, and Leah knew she could never be happy in the role of a concubine.

For the welfare of Zubani, Sharif would have to terminate what he shared with her. It was probably that very knowledge driving him to take all he could of her now, while it was still possible, without adverse consequences to his political position.

His judgement over the issue with her father had undoubtedly been swayed by his love for his own daughters, but perhaps there had also been representations from Qatama within the past twenty-four hours. If his revenge on Leah had served its purpose, Sharif could possibly be seeing her father as an appropriate way to let her go.

She remembered him saying, "Things have changed." How much? she wondered. Was he beginning to care about her feelings, or was he simply referring to the political situation?

"Will you let me go home with my father, Sharif?" she asked, wanting some hint of what was on his mind.

He turned her onto her back and propped himself up on one elbow, eyeing her sternly as though she had earned his disfavour with that question. "What is this home you speak of?" he demanded. "Your father has another family. You said so yourself."

"I meant home to Australia," Leah swiftly corrected.

"You left it behind long ago," came the terse dismissal. "Have you not made your home amongst people like mine for the last eight years? Of your own choice?"

"I was happy in Qatama," she conceded. "But I did have my brother there, Sharif."

"And now you have me to make you happy," he argued. "You like being with me. We are right together. Do not deny it."

Leah heaved a deep sigh. She was hardly in a position to deny it right now. "You said my father would pay the price for my release," she reminded him.

"He made the offer. Which shows he cares for you. As he should."

"And what did you say to him?"

"I said *more*."

"My father isn't a rich man."

"That is irrelevant." The dark brooding disintegrated into a slow, satisfied smile that squeezed her heart. "I am thinking there is no price that could buy your release. I know that you do not want to leave me."

"I tried to leave you today," Leah said dryly.

"That was untimely. And not your plan. Tayi did not understand."

"Sharif, you must know this revenge of yours can't go on forever. The month will soon be over, and you'll have to make some settlement with Qatama. I'll only be in the way then."

"We shall see," he said, and would not be drawn any further on the matter.

But throughout the many ways and many times he made love to her, Leah kept wondering what was *timely* in Sharif's mind. Was tomorrow the day of decision? Or did he really mean there was no price that could buy her away from him?

CHAPTER TEN

IT WAS ALMOST NOON the next day when Leah received the sheikh's summons to a meeting with her father. All her belongings had been brought from the desert fortress, and she had been established in a light, airy apartment in the women's quarters of the palace. Despite the lift in her spirits from feeling less of a prisoner, she had been tense all morning, waiting for this moment, not knowing quite what to expect.

As she was led through seemingly interminable hallways, a host of inhibitions crawled around her heart. It had been too long an estrangement, with far too much water under the bridge for her to feel close to her father. He had let her down in so many hurtful ways, she could not bring herself to believe he would not do it again in front of Sharif. Which would be intensely humiliating.

It was stupid, really, to have dressed as attractively as she could. What difference would it make? None to a father who had left his daughter behind in favour of making a new life for himself. It was pride, she supposed, pride in herself that had made her select the embroidered and beaded turquoise robe that was her favourite.

Sharif would appreciate it, she thought, which was probably why her eyes went straight to him when she was ushered into the formal reception room where he and her father were seated. Both men rose to their feet at her entrance. The flash of admiration in Sharif's dark eyes, the look of pride in her that shone from his wonderfully autocratic face was precisely what Leah needed.

Her head tilted slightly higher. She didn't stop to think how strange it was for her to gather strength and self-assurance from the powerful charisma of her captor. He looked very much the sheikh of Zubani this morning, as she had first seen him in her garden at Qatama, but he no longer struck fear in her. His re-action to her escape yesterday had dissipated all fear of him. In his way he treated her well, within the framework of his revenge.

Her gaze slowly shifted to the man who had come for her, Captain Robert Ian Marlow, at her service. Glen took after him in looks, big, blond, skin that took a golden tan, handsome in the clean-cut way that invited trust. But there was uncertainty in the blue eyes that fastened on Leah's, a look of appeal that had lit-tle hope in it.

"As you can see, Captain Marlow, your daughter is in fine health," Sharif said matter-of-factly, then very personally to Leah, "and very beautiful."

"Yes. Thank you, Your Excellency." Her father's voice did not quite attain a similar aplomb. He offered her a tentative smile. "It's good to see you, Leah."

He stood stiffly, not expecting her to fly into his arms as she would have done a long time ago. Leah came to a halt several arm's lengths away from him, her mind too cluttered with question marks to think of smiling.

"It was kind of you to come," she said, her eyes searching his for the reason behind this extraordinary gesture. What did his wife think about it? His step-children?

"I had to," he answered simply, and there was a look of painful regret in his eyes. "I won't let you down this time, Leah."

A sudden well of emotion choked any possible reply. As though sensing her distress, Sharif seized the moment to take her hand and lead her to an arm-chair. "Be seated, Captain Marlow," he said to cover any awkwardness, then proceeded to seat himself where he had Leah to his right and her father to his left. Clearly he had no intention of leaving the two of them alone together.

Leah desperately cast around for something to say to her father. "Have you seen Glen?" she blurted out.

"He came straight to me." Said in a firmer voice. "He asked if I would fly the plane he had taken back to Qatama."

A wry little smile flitted over Leah's lips. Glen had always stayed close to their father. Of course, he had been much older than she at the time of the divorce, sixteen to her ten, and he had bitterly blamed their mother for the marriage break-up. Apart from which, Glen had always wanted to be a pilot, and he shared that interest with their father.

"I'm glad to hear that he's safe. Until Sharif told me otherwise, I thought he had been shot down," Leah said ruefully.

Robert Marlow frowned, his gaze flicking sharply from her to the sheikh and back again. "We waited to hear from you, Leah. Glen anticipated that you would be expelled. When there was no word, I flew the plane to Qatama and sought an audience with King Rashid."

Leah looked at him in surprise. "He saw you?"

"No. But Prince Youssef did."

"And he told you where I was?" It was a monumental indiscretion on his part with regard to such a delicate political situation between the two states.

"No. He was deeply concerned for his sister. I was able to assure him she was safe and very shortly to be married to my son."

"Married! Glen and Samira?" Leah shook her head in bewilderment. "I thought—" She shot a probing look at Sharif, but he did not appear the least bit concerned by this information, let alone offended by it. Perhaps he had already drawn these facts from her father. She turned back to him. "I didn't know...had no idea they felt like that."

"As it was told to me, Glen and Samira have loved each other for a long time," he replied quietly, "but neither had ever spoken of it. Both of them had obligations and responsibilities that precluded any expression or pursuit of what was in their hearts. It was only on the eve of her wedding that Samira broke down and told Glen how she felt, that she'd rather have any kind of life with him than without him."

There was a pained apology in his eyes as he continued. "Glen had very little time to get Samira out of Qatama, Leah. She masqueraded as you so she could leave the palace with Glen without any questions being raised. There was no other way it could be done. Glen had to ask you to remain out of sight. And leave you behind."

So that was how it happened, Leah thought in bemusement, remembering the turbulent feelings emanating from Glen that fateful afternoon. Not only worry for her, but the hidden love for Samira coursing wildly, hopefully, fearfully through him. Little things came back to her, the softening of Glen's voice when he spoke of Samira, the way Samira looked at him. Not hero-worship. Something far deeper. And desperate enough to tear asunder the long-woven fabric of both their lives.

"Glen didn't want to leave you, Leah. He had to make a choice. He did the best he could for you at the time."

The strained plea in her father's voice drew her gaze to his. Did he think she blamed Glen for what had happened to her? It was impossible for her brother to have foreseen the sheikh of Zubani's revenge. Not in the heat of the moment, anyway, not when fast and dangerous action had been called for. She didn't begrudge Glen and Samira their chance at happiness together.

"I understand, Dad," she said softly, dismissing the recriminations he thought she might be harbouring.

"Do you, Leah?" His eyes searched hers uncertainly. "You can forgive your brother?"

She flushed as she realised the question was a reflection of what he felt himself, that she had never forgiven him for the choice he had made in leaving her behind. But that was different. A whole lot different, in Leah's book.

Was it the best he could do for her to leave her with a mother who put anything her new husband wanted ahead of everything else? And what attention had her father ever given her on the visits she was allowed? Nothing special. Nothing just for her. She had had to share him with his stepchildren, and they always got the lion's share of his attention. His priority had been the same as her mother's. Pleasing his new partner. Leah was only in the way to her parents after their divorce.

"I don't understand why you came here," she said flatly. "You never put yourself out for me when I needed you before."

"Leah..." A spasm of guilty anguish crossed his face. "It was a chance for me to say I'm sorry. And, perhaps, for you to believe me."

"No." She shook her head, unable to accept that. "You did it for Glen. Not for me. My brother asked you to come in his place, didn't he?"

He sighed. "Yes. But I wanted to, Leah."

She blocked her heart to that assertion. "How did Glen find out where I was?"

Robert Marlow threw a wary look at Sharif. "Through contacts he has. As you know, Glen was well-liked and respected by many people here."

Leah felt a surge of pride in her brother. He would have tried everything in his power, and never stopped trying until he found her. "Tell him not to worry about me anymore," she said impulsively. "And please thank him for me for offering a ransom. I appreciate the—"

"I offered the ransom, Leah."

The flat statement shook Leah's perception of her father. She stared at him uncertainly. There was grim resignation on his face, but he met her gaze with a look of hard pride.

"I'm aware that I haven't done much right by you, Leah. I'm sorry you were short-changed in the choices I felt I had to make. It wasn't that I loved you any less. But after the kind of marriage I had with your mother, I needed Helen in my life. And I truly believed it was best for you to stay with your mother."

Best for you, you mean, was the bitter thought that ran through Leah's mind, but she didn't voice it. Maybe he did regret the way he had let her become the leftover baggage from a marriage he wanted to put behind him.

"What does Helen think of this offer you've made for me? Or doesn't she know about it?" Leah asked, scepticism creeping into her tone as she added, "Won't it disadvantage her and her children?"

His gaze dropped, then slowly lifted to hers again with heartbreaking sadness. "I do care about you, Leah. Very much. And Helen understands that I couldn't live with myself if I didn't do all I could for you now. However too little it is, and however too late."

The protective shell she had clung to for so long cracked open, and the bitterly repressed love for her father welled up and pricked her eyes with tears.

"I don't suppose..." Her voice failed her. She took a deep breath, offered him a wobbly little smile and tried once more. "I don't suppose you brought me a doll."

"No. I didn't think of it. I wish I had," he replied gruffly, a sheen of moisture in his eyes as they both remembered shared happier times.

"Captain Marlow," Sharif suddenly interjected, compelling their attention. "I respect your offer," he declared, giving a nod of approval. "It is worthy of your daughter."

"Does that mean you're accepting it, Your Excellency?"

Leah was instantly plunged into emotional confusion, knowing she should be feeling the same eagerness for her release from captivity that her father was expressing, yet torn by a sharp sense of loss at the thought of never being with Sharif again.

"Let it be understood, Captain Marlow, that it is not a case of too little. You have spoken well. I am impressed by your sincerity. Because of this, I shall grant you time alone with your daughter."

He rose from his chair and smiled approvingly at Leah, his dark eyes caressing her with warm respect. "The strength of your mind is matched by a heart that is good. I did not think otherwise. I shall order lunch to be served here for you and your father. You may walk in the palace grounds afterwards, if you so desire."

"Your Excellency," her father pressed. "How can I persuade you to release my daughter to me?"

Sharif turned to him, his demeanour arrogantly resolute but not unkind. "You cannot, Captain Marlow. I recommend that you do not waste your time with plots and plans. Your daughter will remain with me. Make your peace with her."

He strode towards the doors, half turning when he reached them to deliver an afterthought. Or perhaps it was a well-calculated punch line. "Captain Marlow..."

"Yes, Your Excellency?"

"Tell your son I want him here. It is his duty to come. It is not seemly that the men of Leah's family do not do right by her. That is the way of my people, and that is what I expect, Captain Marlow."

CHAPTER ELEVEN

SHE SHOULD HAVE KNOWN, Leah thought despairingly, that Sharif would exact the full price of revenge—her for the bride stolen from him. Glen for the loss of face he had suffered politically. Her brother was, of course, the coup de grâce to deliver to Qatama, the man *they* had been unable to prevent from going free with their royal princess. And Samira would pay by being deprived of the man for whom she had publicly rejected the sheikh of Zubani.

What a fool she had been to think for one moment that Sharif had begun to care for her! It shamed Leah further to remember the dreams she had indulged in last night, dreams that could never come true. All she was to Sharif al Kader was a tool in his grand plan for revenge. With the additional advantage of her service as a woman in his bed!

She turned to her father. His face was drained of all colour. He looked at her with tortured eyes. "Must I lose my son to regain my daughter?" he asked, but it was not so much a question as a cry torn from a soul that had borne too many painful choices.

"No, Dad," Leah answered, her heart torn by the love he had shown her. Words spilled from her lips in a stream of reassurance. "Glen doesn't have to come for me. I don't want him to. I'd rather stay here. Tell him I wish him and Samira every happiness, and he's not to worry about me. I'm fine. I don't have any plans for the future, anyway. It doesn't matter for me."

"Oh, Leah!" Tears swam into his eyes. He swallowed convulsively, shook his head, but he fought a losing battle against the emotion that racked him. He lifted his hands in a gesture of helplessness. "How can I let you be the one to lose out again?"

Leah moved instinctively to comfort, to close the cold distance that could no longer be upheld. She threw her arms around him in a tight hug and felt his arms enfold her with anguished tenderness. "Leah," he murmured gruffly, and slowly rubbed his cheek over her hair.

Tears filled her eyes, as well. To be held like this by her father again, knowing he cared for her, really cared, meant more than she could say. Especially with the disillusionment Sharif had just dealt her fretting through her mind.

She now knew she had been wrong to judge her father so bitterly, that the betrayal she had felt so deeply was not quite as black and white as it had seemed to her at the time. But the fact remained he did have a family to go back to, and she did not belong to it.

"It's all right, Dad," she assured him huskily. "I'm glad you came for me, but I've learnt to live with myself. And Sharif is good to me. In his own way. Besides which, he'll let me go eventually. Neither you nor Glen have to do anything."

She felt his chest rise and fall in a deep, shuddering sigh. "No, Leah. You will not be sacrificed for my happiness, or Glen's," he said heavily. "I shall ask the sheikh to take me in place of my children. Whatever penalty is to be paid in order that you and Glen go free, I will pay it."

"No. It won't work, Dad," Leah protested, her eyes lifting anxiously to his.

"It must!" he replied with desperate conviction. "I'm your father. Glen's father. If the sheikh of Zubani wants blood, let it be mine. Surely to God he'll see the justice in that!"

"Please listen to me, Dad. It's not as bad as you think."

"Leah, Glen and Samira were married the day before yesterday. Their love for each other is something I never expected to see. I thought Glen had been turned off everything to do with marriage. And you—" he gently stroked her cheek "—as the sheikh said, you are very beautiful. And you deserve to find love, too, instead of leading this...this stifled half-life in rejection of so much of what your mother and I did. The least I can do now is give my children the opportunity to fulfil their lives."

"But there's Helen," Leah argued. "And your other children."

His face tightened. "I've done my best by them for sixteen years. At your cost. And Glen's. It's time the scales were balanced, Leah."

She saw the grim determination on his face and knew there was only one way to break it. Besides, it gave her a savage satisfaction to use Sharif's revenge on her to put a stop to the rest of his grand plan. She would not let him draw Glen or Samira into his vengeful net. She would not let him use this insidious emotional pressure to get at the rest of her family.

She pasted a smile on her face and spoke with loving indulgence. "You don't understand, Dad. It's not a half-life anymore, and I don't want to leave it. I want to stay with Sharif al Kader. I love him. And I know I couldn't love any other man as I love him."

Her father's hands moved to grip her upper arms in an agitated denial of her allegiance to the man who had taken her by force. "Don't, Leah!" he begged. "You're only saying that to—"

"It's true." Her eyes held his in a steady blaze of conviction. "You forget that I've made this life mine. I don't want to go back to Australia. Sharif is the man I want. So let it be."

"Leah, you've been his prisoner for three weeks..."

"He's also made love to me for most of those three weeks," Leah countered, pouring as much warmth as she could into her voice. "Sharif is a wonderful lover."

Her father looked intensely disturbed. "He took you in place of Samira?"

"It more or less started that way," Leah said, "but things have developed between us since then. In any event, I want to see where it leads, so I'm not going to leave him until he wants me to. There's no point in either you or Glen making any sacrifice on my account. I'm perfectly happy here."

"You love your brother more than yourself," her father said gravely. "And you'd do anything, say anything, to safeguard his happiness. And his marriage. But you're not to worry about it, Leah. We will find a way."

"Dad, just let it be," she pleaded.

"No more, Leah. We will talk of other things. Come sit with me now, and tell me the happiest things that have happened in your life. I would like very much to hear them."

She wanted to argue, wanted to resolve the situation along the lines least harmful to all their lives. What did it really matter if she remained Sharif's concubine for as long as he wanted her? It wasn't as though she found him unbearably loathsome or anything like that. And she wanted, from the most primitive depths of her soul, to turn the tables on the single-minded and totally ruthless sheikh of Zubani. He would find her a worthy opponent, all right! To the death, if necessary!

But she saw that to persist with the argument of her love for him would only disturb her father more deeply. There was a need in his eyes begging the kind of response she had once given naturally to the father she had adored. She forced her mind back to the past and smiled to show her lack of concern about the present.

"The happiest times for me were when you came home from your flights, and you'd play with me, cuddle me..."

"And tease you before giving you the doll. Yes. They were happy times." He returned her smile and drew her onto a sofa with him, holding her hand as though desperately wanting to reforge the link between them. "Your mother needed a man at her side,

Leah," he said quietly. "I wouldn't give up flying. Don't blame her too much. Our marriage was a mistaken love."

His eyes pleaded for understanding and forgiveness. "But you were a joy to me, Leah. The only beautiful light in some very dark years. Please believe that."

She gave his hand a reassuring squeeze. "It's okay, Dad. Remember when..."

The hours passed all too quickly, bittersweet hours filled with love and sadness as both of them reached across the chasm of years and became father and daughter again. When it came time for them to part, Leah hoped she had said enough to undermine his resolution to put himself in jeopardy for her sake and Glen's. She planted a loving kiss on his cheek and smiled at him with warm confidence.

"Give Glen and Samira my love. And tell Helen thank you for letting me have my father back. And no-one is to worry about me. I'm fine here. Truly I am."

Her father said nothing. He hugged her tightly. Then after one last long look at her, as though imprinting all that she was on his mind, he surrendered himself to the escort that had arrived to take him away.

Leah also had an escort, back to her apartment in the women's quarters. She found her tapestry set up for her by a window in the sitting room. Despondent from saying goodbye to her father, goodbye to a lot of things, she walked to the frame and slowly ran her fingers over each section of tapestry she had worked while waiting for Glen to come.

He wouldn't come now.

She didn't want him to.

As for the tapestry, well, she might as well keep doing it, something to fill in her time until Sharif came to a decision about her. She sat down, threaded a needle, but the stitches her fingers could work so nimbly came at long intervals. Her mind kept filling with the wonder of Glen and Samira and all the other things her father had told her.

It changed her perception of so much, forcing her to rethink her life, her reactions, her responses. Perhaps if she had been different, less defensive, less critical, less prickly, not so quick to judge bitterly and hatefully, her life may well have taken a far different course. Yet regrets were pointless. Better to learn from her mistakes and move on. If that became possible.

An intense loneliness seeped through her. She told herself she was glad that Glen and Samira had each other, glad that her father had Helen and her children, even glad that her mother had found whatever contentment she craved with her second husband. It was just that she had no-one special to herself anymore, now that Glen had gone. She was going to miss her big brother. Terribly.

The slamming of a door snapped Leah out of her reverie. The accompanying swirl of tension warned her that Sharif had entered the room, yet she felt reluctant to face him right at this moment. The hours with her father had left her feeling drained and empty. Defenceless. She moved her fingers, pressing the needle through the tapestry, pretending that she was not affected by the power of his presence.

"How can you sit there, so calm and serene, when you create so much continuing trouble for me!" he hurled at her accusingly.

Leah was so stunned by this incredible statement that surprise made her turn to look at him.

Satisfied that he had her full attention, Sharif stalked around the room, glowering with discontent. "You have brought chaos into my life ever since you walked into it!" he declared.

Leah rose from her chair, spurred by the outrageousness of his claims. "It was you who walked into my life, Sharif al Kader. I had nothing to do with it. I was sitting alone in my private garden, minding my own business..."

"Doing that tapestry that made me think things I should not have thought," he shot at her.

"I did my best to correct you," she retorted hotly.

"Which made everything worse! Arousing my interest. Defying me. Challenging me. Why pretend you are meek and mild when you are patently not? Never has any other woman looked at me as you did!"

"And just what do you mean by that? It was you who undressed me with your eyes, making me feel..."

"Huh!" His finger went up in triumph. "You admit it then."

"Admit what?"

"You wanted to know what it would be like with me. So now you know. It is therefore totally capricious of you to complain about it to your father."

"I did not complain about it to my father!" Leah cried indignantly. "Quite the opposite, in fact."

"What opposite?" Sharif demanded.

"I told him I loved you. That you were a wonderful lover. And that he should go home and not worry about me because I was perfectly happy to stay here with you." Her blue eyes blazed absolute fury at him as his whole demeanour was transformed by beaming delight. "I only said that—"

"Because it was the truth," he cut in with relish.

"To stop him and Glen from doing something stupid, like putting themselves in your power for my sake," she finished in vengeful triumph.

"I knew you would come to love me," he said, arrogantly ignoring her disclaimer and apparently uncaring that she had done her best to torpedo his grand revenge. "It is good that you can now admit it to yourself."

"I do *not!*" Leah fumed at him.

"It had to be in your mind and heart, or you would not have said the words."

She stamped her foot in frustration. "Sharif, will you listen to me? I do *not* love you! How on earth could I love you when you've done what you've done to me?"

His dark eyes sparkled with amusement at her protests. "What is it I've done that you did not truly want?"

"You kidnapped me, for a start," she flung at him scornfully.

He raised a mocking eyebrow. "Did you not challenge me to do precisely that when you looked at me in the throne room at Qatama?"

"Of course not!"

"Yes, you did, Leah. You deliberately challenged me. And you would never respect a man who did not meet your strength with more strength."

His eyes burned knowingly into hers as he moved to sweep her into his embrace. Leah curled her hands against his chest, a small, instinctive rebellion that was totally ineffective in preventing his power to arouse responses in her that she could not control.

"You wanted to know me," he declared with searing certainty. "It is merely your contrary pride that denies it. And the sense of your power as a woman. You do not like to concede anything too easily."

Leah was flooded with confusion as Sharif gathered her closer to him. Was there any truth in what he said? Had she put other faces on her reactions and responses because they didn't suit her perception of herself? Everything seemed to be changing today. First her father, making her see the past in a different light. Now Sharif, making her feel . . . What did she feel? It was all so complicated and messed around with other considerations.

His lips grazed softly over hers. "Say you love me. I want to taste the words," he murmured.

"I'm still your prisoner," Leah forced out, fighting the insidious rush of warmth through her body. She would not surrender to his will. Not while his mind was still bent on revenge. But was it? He no longer seemed to care about it.

"Say you love me and I will give you more freedom," he promised, kissing her with sensual seduction.

"Without freedom, how can I know what I feel?" she argued.

He lifted his mouth from hers and heaved a rueful sigh. "Why do you make difficulties when the obvious is looking you in the face?"

Leah suddenly recollected what had brought this whole subject up in the first place. "Why were you so angry about my father?"

He shrugged dismissively. "It does not matter. All is explained. It is only natural your father should take offence. He is very stubborn. Like his daughter."

"Why do you say that? What did he do?" Then more fearfully, "What did you do?"

He grimaced. "I thought you had ruined all my good work in affecting a reconciliation between you. Which would have been very ungrateful of you, Leah. As it is, your father has made difficulties where there should have been none. I have now made sure he is on his way home."

"Unharmed?" Leah asked anxiously.

Sharif frowned. "Of course, unharmed. I do not want his life."

Leah's heart sank. Her father had clearly gone back to Sharif and tried to bargain with his own life. She desperately hoped he would give more credence to what she had told him and not upset Glen and Samira with his disbelief in her happiness with Sharif.

"While I respect his sense of paternal responsibility," Sharif continued in a somewhat vexed tone, "he must respect the reality that I also have responsibilities. The welfare of Zubani has to be considered. I cannot always do what I want, when I want. The proper steps must be taken.''

Leah's heart sank lower. She did not ask herself why the warmth Sharif had aroused suddenly chilled into misery. "You mean you must marry Fatima," she said dully.

"I have no intention whatsoever of contracting a marriage with her or any princess from Qatama," Sharif declared, sounding even more vexed. "Why should you think it?" he demanded.

She looked at him in bewilderment. "For the welfare of Zubani. Wasn't that what you meant?"

He made a contemptuous sound. "You think I would accept the terms offered by King Rashid?" His eyes glittered with vengeful pride. "No, my beautiful Leah, *they* will come to *my* negotiating table and accept *my* terms. Qatama must be humbled to Zubani's will. I shall not have it any other way."

Thus spoke Sharif al Kader, Leah thought with a wild lilt of exhilaration, hunter, warrior, zealot determined to conquer whatever needed to be conquered in forging the destiny of his choice. It was certifiable madness to think he meant to forge a future with her, but suddenly there was a smile on her lips, a gush of pleasure streaming through her veins, and her hands uncurled and slid around his neck.

"Perhaps I did want to know you, Sharif," she conceded.

Desire instantly blazed over pride. "So now you will say you love me."

"There's a little matter of my freedom."

"Can I trust you not to cause more trouble for me?" he countered, lowering his eyebrows sternly.

"Hmm...we shall see." She enjoyed using his own words back at him.

He laughed, a joyous ripple of laughter that jiggled her heart and took her breath away. His eyes danced intense pleasure in her, and Leah knew—there was no questioning it—she wanted this man to be hers. Perhaps it was the loneliness inside her prompting the need or desire, but she wanted to belong to Sharif al Kader, and she wanted him to belong to her. No matter what it led to in the future.

A knock on the door demanded attention.

Sharif's laughter faded into a sigh as he reluctantly released Leah. "There are times when it is inconvenient to be a father, but a promise is a promise. My daughters are eager to see you again. I had them flown up from Shalaan."

He opened the door, and the two little girls rushed in to greet Leah, hurtling past their father in excited anticipation.

"Miss Marlow..."

"Miss Marlow..."

"Will you tell us another story?"

"And Papa said you will teach us to speak English."

"But a story first," Jazmin appealed. "Can I sit in your lap?"

"It's my turn, Jazmin," Nadia reproved.

Sharif swooped on them and lifted them up, one daughter in each arm. "What is this? You do not even greet your father?" he chided.

"But we've already seen you today, Papa," Nadia said. .

"And we've been waiting and waiting to see Miss Marlow," Jazmin complained.

"Then I will pardon you this once. But you are to remember your manners with Miss Marlow, who may tell you a story if you ask her nicely. And may teach you to speak English if you are very good girls."

"Yes, Papa," they chorused fervently.

In the hour that followed, Leah felt very much included in a family circle of love. Surely Sharif would not encourage such a situation if he did not mean it to continue indefinitely. How he intended to resolve the political problem with Qatama Leah had no idea, but she resolved to stop worrying about the future. One way or another, Sharif al Kader would take care of it.

Two things were certain.

He was not going to marry Fatima.

And Leah did not feel lonely anymore.

CHAPTER TWELVE

SHARIF HAD NO SOONER left Leah the next morning than Tayi arrived. The two women faced each other across the sitting room, the memory of their mutual failure to effect Leah's escape weighing heavily between them. Tayi's dignified bearing did not invite any closing of the distance she maintained, but her dark, velvety eyes were no longer hostile. Leah felt she was being assessed in some enigmatic way that would have meaning only to Tayi.

"I did not think we would meet again," she offered, wanting to reach out to the woman.

The comment was ignored.

"I wish to ask your advice," Tayi said.

Leah had the impression this must be a first in Tayi's life. She had always gone her own way. Even now, in making her request, she projected an air of personal decisiveness that denied any dependency on whatever Leah replied.

Before she could stop herself, Leah asked. "Why? What do you care about how I think?"

Tayi eyed her with wary reserve. When she finally replied, her melodious voice came in short, lilting cadences, giving a hypnotic power to her speech. "You do nothing. Yet the world changes around you. You create a storm. I've watched you. Now I, too, wish to create a storm. I ask you how you do it."

Leah was nonplussed. It was clear that to Tayi the words had momentous import, but to Leah they made no sense at all. A series of contradictions. Although there was one correct observation amongst them. It was true that Leah had done nothing. Everything lately had been done to her! As for creating a storm or the world changing around her, Leah had no knowledge of either. Tayi could hardly be referring to the chaos Sharif declared she had brought into his life. That was undoubtedly a personal exaggeration.

"You will not answer?"

Leah shook her head in helpless confusion. What could she say? "I don't know how to answer," she blurted out.

The ensuing silence vibrated with tension. With the swaying grace that gave her so much regal dignity, Tayi walked to the window closest to where Leah stood. She looked out with a fixed gaze that suggested to Leah she saw nothing but her inner thoughts. Slowly her head turned, the large, dark eyes focussing directly on Leah's, searching for truth.

"Or you have decided not to answer?" she asked. "Not to help me?" There was a pained look of rejection as though she had laid herself open in a way she never did, and didn't know how to handle it.

Leah stepped forward, her hand lifting in instinctive appeal, touching Tayi's arm in a gesture of reassurance. "What is it that you want, Tayi?" she asked, trying her utmost to project sympathetic encouragement. "Tell me specifically."

Tayi instantly withdrew, guarding the reserve she kept around her. "I cannot give myself over to an enemy," she said, watching Leah with heightened intensity. "It would give you the power to destroy me."

"You're not my enemy. Nor would I ever destroy anyone."

The reply spilled naturally from Leah's lips, and Tayi slowly accepted it. "Then you will tell me how it is done. How you did it."

"Yes. Everything I can," Leah affirmed, although she still had no idea what the other woman was talking about or what was required of her. That had lost any importance. It was the reaching out and acceptance that was most needed here and now.

Tayi's tension eased. The music of her voice softened to a warmer tone. "The sheikh has always promised he will arrange a marriage for me that is advantageous to my position."

Leah's mind leapt through a range of logical possibilities, desperately trying to pick on Tayi's obscure train of thought. "You've fallen in love?" she asked.

A faraway look crept into her eyes. "I have seen a man who stands above all others."

Leah felt a sense of triumph at having finally hit on the right wavelength for this strange conversation. She wondered who had found favour with this majestic woman. A soldier? One of the sheikh's attendants? It would surely have to be someone attached to the household.

"Who is he, Tayi?" Leah asked with keen interest.

She smiled with all the magical mystique of a woman fathoms deep in love. "Prince Youssef of Qatama."

Leah's heart turned over with painful compassion. It was an impossible match. Surely Tayi had to understand that. Yet the dream in the dark velvety eyes denied any recognition of reality. Leah swallowed her shock and tentatively tried to spell out the indisputable facts.

"You realise, of course, that such a love, such an ambition, would one day lead..."

"Yes. I would be Queen of Qatama. But it is not for that reason I asked for your advice. He looked at me. I felt it. Drawing me to look at him. And it was written into my destiny."

The blissful conviction in Tayi's voice made Leah feel helpless. Her mind slowly grasped the parallel that must have worked through Tayi's mind. If a minder of children could captivate the sheikh, why should not a minder of children captivate a prince? Leah had no sooner worked this out than Tayi pressed the question.

"You will tell me how it's done. What herbs to put in his drink."

"This cannot be done with herbs," Leah said hopelessly.

"But you will help me," Tayi pressed with artless appeal. "The sheikh is angry with Qatama. You have made him happy. Happier than he has been since his wife died. If you were to suggest the marriage..."

Leah simply could not bring herself to erase the wondrous glow of anticipation in the other woman's eyes. "For what little it is worth, I will do everything in my power to help you, Tayi."

"You will not betray my secret?"

"Never."

Her beautifully sculptured lips curved into a satisfied little smile. She turned her head to the window, her long, graceful neck arching as she looked out to some distant horizon. "The winds of change howl through the desert. Nothing will ever be the same again," she said in the dreamy tone of a mystic soothsayer.

"Is that good or bad?" Leah was drawn to ask.

"Both. But change is inevitable." She slowly swung her gaze to Leah, and there was the light of sure destiny in her eyes. "I will be part of it."

Content that Leah understood and empathised with her position, Tayi departed, completely unaware of the storm of confusion and despair she left behind. Everything she had said kept revolving around Leah's mind for hours afterwards.

Why had Tayi considered her an enemy? Was it because of the children's ready affection for her? Because of Sharif's desire for her? Had she seen her world changing because of Leah, the sheikh placing her at his side where his wife had once been?

Perhaps Tayi had leapt to the conclusion the sheikh intended to marry Leah because he would not let her go. A most unlikely outcome, Leah thought with painful irony. But that idea might have seeded Tayi's unrealistic hope for a marriage with the crown prince of Qatama.

Could a single look at a man strike a woman's heart so deeply? Leah wondered. Was that how it had been for her that afternoon in the garden at Qatama, looking at Sharif and feeling the sense of destiny? She shook her head. So difficult to sort out how she felt when he held her a prisoner of his will. But Tayi and Youssef...

Youssef had definitely been struck by Tayi. He had said as much. But on being told her status in Sharif's household, he would have known a pursuit of interest was pointless. A crown prince did not marry a simple minder of children. The winds of change did not howl that fast through the desert.

Her promise of help was futile. Leah knew it in her heart, and empathised deeply with the disappointment and loss Tayi must inevitably feel. Nevertheless, when the opportunity arose to bring up Tayi's cause with the sheikh, she would do so. A promise was a promise.

As it turned out she did not see Sharif until late that evening. Nadia and Jazmin were brought to her for an English lesson that extended into the lunch hour, making the meal a lot of happy fun together. Then, to Leah's surprise, she was taken on a tour of a girls' school in the city, and had the system of education explained to her by the headmistress.

When Sharif came to her apartment after dinner, he wanted Leah to give him a critical appraisal of all she had seen and heard at the school, relating it to her Australian education. He listened, questioned, discussed possible improvements with her and smiled his pleasure and approval at her willingness to express her opinions.

"You care about my people," he declared with satisfaction.

"I care that girls be given as much opportunity to develop their capabilities as are boys," she corrected with some asperity. "And what's more, Sharif, you're going to need them to help run this country of yours, if you don't want to depend on the expertise of foreigners forever and a day."

His eyes sparkled with triumph. "You care."

"I care about a lot of things."

"Tomorrow I have arranged for you to visit the women's health centre. It will be of interest to you." He rose from his chair and drew Leah from hers, gathering her into his embrace. "You are right. It is good for you to have more freedom. I want you to be happy with me."

Her eyes ruefully mocked his idea of freedom. "I'm not exactly being given a choice, am I?"

He raised his eyebrows. "You do not want to go to the women's centre? There is also the museum to visit, and the..."

Leah sighed at the futility of arguing over the essence of freedom. "The centre is fine," she said, grateful for small mercies.

"Ah! You surrender to me."

"No, I don't," Leah flashed at him. "I will never surrender to any man. I simply decided on the centre."

His eyes challenged hers with simmering desire.
"Then I shall have to take you to bed and make you
love me."

Leah didn't have much choice about that, either, but
she did privately concede Sharif was a wonderful
lover. Which he proved once again.

It was while she was lying in his arms after being
very thoroughly made love to that she was reminded
of her promise to Tayi. With Sharif's heart beating
with slow contentment in the fulfilment of his desire
for her, Leah decided this had to be the best possible
time to approach the delicate subject of Tayi's desire.

"Remember when Prince Youssef came to the fortress, Sharif?" she started.

"Mmm..." It was a noncommittal sound. He was
weaving her long hair through his fingers, as he often
did after making love.

"And Tayi interrupted the meeting?"

"Mmm."

"You said you would arrange an advantageous
marriage for her."

"It is being done."

Leah jerked her head up, causing the long, silky
tress he had been weaving to slide through his fingers.
He smiled, enjoying the sensation.

"You're arranging a marriage for her right now?"
Leah asked, demanding his full attention.

"It is a matter of negotiation." A gleam of steely
purpose speared through the hazy contentment in his
eyes. "I shall have my way."

"But what about Tayi?" Leah asked in alarm.
"What if she doesn't love the man you've chosen?"

"I have Tayi's best interests at heart."

"Have you talked to her? Does she know?"

"There is no need. Tayi will be happy with my choice."

"How can you know that?" Leah cried despairingly. "What if she wants to choose for herself?"

Sharif frowned at her. "Why do you question it? I have made my judgement. It will stand."

"Like King Rashid's judgement with Samira?" Leah snapped in frustration.

There was a blaze of something very dangerous in his eyes. "You dare to throw that in my face, Leah?"

"Yes, I do!" she retorted recklessly. "What if Tayi loves another man? You could at least try asking her, instead of treating her as though she had no mind and heart of her own."

"Did I not know your heart and mind better than you did yourself?" he demanded.

"That's very much open to question," Leah insisted vehemently.

"The winds of change might be howling through the desert, Leah Marlow, but I shall do what I believe is right. For you. For me. For Tayi. For Zubani. Let there be no more question about it!"

And that was that, in Sharif's mind. Leah realised she was going to have an uphill battle trying to change it in any way whatsoever. Arguing was utterly useless. Maybe if she worked hard at making Sharif happy, she might bend him more to her way of thinking. Tayi apparently believed she had the power to do it.

If she created a storm by doing nothing, what could she do if she really tried?

CHAPTER THIRTEEN

LEAH DID NOT find it difficult to make Sharif absolutely delighted with her over the next few days. The places he sent her to visit were of interest to her anyway, and she applied herself to finding out all she could about them, the programs being followed and what could be initiated to improve what was already being done for his people.

She could see the difficulties in assimilating the huge technological leap the country was making, the reluctance of the older people to accept change, the fear of the unknown. She developed a new appreciation of too much, too soon. Yet the eagerness in the younger people to broaden their lives captured her imagination and lent zeal to her voice when she talked all these matters over with Sharif.

Oddly enough, in working to make Sharif happy, Leah found a happy purpose in her own life that was immensely satisfying. It was easy to forget she was a prisoner most of the time. And Sharif listened to her more and more.

When Tayi approached her after one of the children's English lessons and inquired in her shy, obscure way if Leah had spoken to the sheikh, Leah could say with considerable confidence that she was

working on it. Nevertheless, the resulting glow in
Tayi's eyes did give Leah a twinge of guilt. It was all
very well for her to want Tayi's love answered, but
what of Youssef? Was it remotely possible that a man
of his status would accept Tayi as his wife?

Perhaps it was a fool's dream. Yet somehow Leah
could not give up hope of making it come true, however unlikely it was. Soon, she promised herself, she
would bring it up with Sharif again, at least make him
see he was wrong not to consider Tayi's feelings.

In the fervour of all her planning and the pleasure
of Sharif's happy response to her more positive attitudes, Leah forgot that her month with him was coming to an end. She also forgot the deep, blinding
compulsion for revenge. When she least expected its
reemergence, Sharif totally devastated her with a display of feeling that rocked her world again.

He swept into her apartment on the heels of her return from visiting a baby health clinic. He exuded an
aura of highly fired energy. Leah had never seen his
face so animated, his eyes so brilliant, and his voice
vibrated with exultant power.

"I have them. At last. Finally."

He laughed from sheer elation as he paced to one of
the windows, looking out with the distinctive air of
being lord and master of all he surveyed. He breathed
in as though the air held the scent of the sweetest nec-
tar. "What a glorious, wonderful day to be alive!"

Then he swung around to face Leah again, emanating total exhilaration as he lifted his arms in an open-
handed gesture. "They're in my hands. The instruments of power." His fingers curled into fists. "And

they shall beat to my drum!'' he declared with intense relish.

Leah snapped out of her bemusement with him and fired an appeal. "If you'll tell me what you're talking about, I might be able to appreciate it, Sharif. What instruments?"

His smile glittered with triumph. "The Princess Samira and your brother!"

Shock splintered into fear. "What's happened? Have you had them abducted, too?"

His lips curled in mocking indulgence of her lack of understanding. "No. It was far simpler and more subtle than that. They have come to offer themselves as hostages, malefactors, in order to secure your release."

Leah barely stifled a groan of despair. Her father had not delivered the messages she had asked of him. Her revelation that she and Sharif were lovers must have made things worse, not better. "How could they be so stupid!" she cried in bitter frustration.

"Their sense of honour outweighed their self-interest," Sharif replied with intense satisfaction. "I expected it of your brother, Leah. He would not be a man if he had not come for you. But the Princess Samira... She is a bonus. The anvil to my hammer."

The dark, vengeful note in his voice struck more fear. "You won't hurt them, Sharif," Leah pleaded. "You can't."

"I shall pass the sentence of the law upon them."

The light of a zealot was in his eyes, and his face wore the hard, immutable look of a relentless and vengeful judge. Leah could feel herself shrinking from it as the pain of disillusionment withered the liking and loving he had drawn from her. Revenge had been his mission all along, the one he had nursed in his heart and soul.

She had fooled herself again. Taking her, having her, had only been incidental to the main thrust of his purpose. Perhaps an amusing little challenge on the side. A charge to his ego to get her to love him. Or better still, to surrender to him.

And she almost had.

"You've used me as a lure," she accused in her need to lash out at him.

His eyes danced with unholy amusement. "You fulfil my purpose."

Her eyes blazed with fury. "If you so much as touch a hair of their heads..."

"You will use the *agal?*"

He laughed, a joyous shout of laughter that rang around Leah's mind, inflaming her to a rage of monumental intensity. She flew at him, wanting to rake his eyes out and pummel his chest with her fists until his deceiving heart stopped beating.

"I hate you, I hate you," she cried as she rained blows at him. "You're the vilest, most despicable man I've ever come across. You are without shame. You bring dishonour upon yourself, your family, your country..."

"Stop this foolishness!" He caught her wrists and forcibly held her back from him.

Leah's eyes fiercely challenged any force he could bring to bear on her. "I will never stop!" she said with heated venom.

A wild exultation leapt into his eyes. Before Leah could catch her breath he swooped to pick her up and hoist her high in his arms. She kicked and hit out at him as he marched into her bedroom, but he might have been a rock for all the effect her blows had on him. He tossed her on the bed and stood, arms akimbo, glowering at her.

"I can have you any time I like," he declared with all the arrogance of his superior male strength.

Leah hurled herself off the other side of the bed and faced him across it, her arms planted on her hips in matching aggression. "I'd rather die than ever let you touch me again," she flung at him. "I won't talk to you. I won't eat with you. I won't sleep with you, and if you try anything I'll spit in your face."

He raised his eyebrows in haughty disdain of her threats. "I will not stay with you when you are in such an unreasonable mood."

He turned his back on her and headed for the door, denying her any more expression of the fury aroused by his perfidy. Leah would not let him get away with it. She whirled over to a side table, seized a vase of flowers and hurled it after him. It smashed against the door jamb at head level. He did not so much as pause or flinch. He passed through to the sitting room with arrogant dignity intact.

"You hurt Glen and Samira, and see what you get!" Leah yelled at his retreating back.

He strode on.

Leah charged into the sitting room, picking up and hurling whatever objects came to hand, but her moving target continued to ignore the missiles thrown at him. Her aim was frustratingly awry. As he opened the door that led out of her apartment, she only just missed him with a dish that flew over his shoulder and smashed somewhere in the corridor beyond him.

"You think I've brought chaos into your life, Sharif al Kader?" she shouted. "I'll give you chaos like you've never seen chaos before! I'm warning you!"

She groped for something more to throw and was forced to look down when nothing came to hand. When she looked back, Sharif was gone and Tayi was standing in the doorway. The woman had a look of intense interest on her face. Her eyes shone with admiration.

"I now understand the storm," she lilted.

With a sigh of deflation Leah lowered the little brass bell she had picked up. "Your sheikh is impossible, Tayi," she replied bitterly.

"He will come back," Tayi said with unshaken confidence in Leah's ability to draw him back.

"He'd better not," Leah seethed. "Unless he changes his mind."

"So, you have asked him and he has refused?"

It took Leah a moment to rearrange her mind to Tayi's wavelength. She had obviously come about Youssef again. "I'm sorry, Tayi. I tried. But he wouldn't listen."

The other woman nodded sagely. "What you have done is good. You are on my side."

"What I need is an *agal*," Leah said, more to herself than to Tayi.

"Do I need an *agal*, too?" came the serious inquiry.

Leah's eyes flared with righteous fury. "All women need *agals* against men like him!"

Tayi turned aside from the doorway and clapped her hands. Two women servants arrived in a flurry. "Go and get two *agals* and bring them to me," she commanded. "I shall be with Miss Marlow."

Leah stared in astonishment as the servants hurried off to obey. Then, with a majestic air of authority, Tayi stepped inside the sitting room and closed the door behind her. Leah couldn't help thinking Tayi was certainly made in the mould of a stately queen, and there were many questions about her that Leah wanted answered.

"I have much to learn from you," Tayi declared, a burning light of mission in her beautiful dark eyes. "It is with power that you deal with power. I am beginning to see."

"Who are you, Tayi?" Leah demanded, deciding it was well past time she had all the information she could get. "You go where you like, when you like. You give orders as though you were born to it. Everyone makes way for you."

Tayi looked surprised at Leah's ignorance. "I am of the ruling family. There is no question that I should be obeyed."

"You're part of Sharif's family?" Leah could hardly contain her shock. That was the last thing she had expected.

"I am his closest cousin," Tayi said with great dignity. "My father was the sheikh who stood aside. He had three wives. I am the daughter of the youngest wife, Shasti. My mother was of the ruling family of

Omala, but she married beneath her status, and the children of a sheikh take their status from him," Tayi explained with regal pride.

This accounted for the majestic image Tayi had invariably painted in Leah's mind, and it was more than enough to stir her simmering rage into another wild ferment. How dare Sharif call Tayi a simple minder of children! And not to consider his closest cousin's feelings on the matter of her marriage partner was totally abominable male chauvinism! He deserved to be hanged, drawn and quartered. And not only on Tayi's behalf. If he intended to harm Glen or Samira . . .

"I'll kill him," Leah muttered with venom.

Tayi looked at her in bewilderment. "How will that help? Will it solve the problem?"

"He has to know we are very serious in what we say. What we want. We have to make him see that there is a price to pay if he doesn't do as we ask."

"Ah!" The large, dark eyes glistened with approval. "That I understand. It is a good plan."

Leah wondered if a strong sense of revenge ran in the family. If so, it was far better to have Tayi on her side than against her. Which meant it was imperative to tackle the Youssef problem head-on.

A knock on the door heralded the return of the servants who had been sent to do Tayi's bidding. They handed over the two *agals* to their mistress. As though it was perfectly natural for her to carry such a weapon, Tayi slid one of the *agals* into the folds of her turban. The other she presented to Leah.

"There is not much time," she advised. "King Rashid of Qatama has been summoned. Perhaps

Prince Youssef will accompany his father. That will be a very positive sign. Do you not think?''

"Yes. Youssef will come," Leah said with certainty. For his sister's sake, if not for Glen's. It could be the last time they would ever see each other. "If my brother and the Princess Samira are to be judged by the law, Youssef will undoubtedly accompany his father.''

"There is to be a special *majlis* tomorrow morning. You think Prince Youssef will attend?''

Leah was intensely grateful to Tayi for this information. "Yes. And we must attend, as well.''

"It is forbidden. The *majlis* is only for men.''

Leah eyed her sternly. "We have to attend that *majlis*, Tayi. It is your only chance to fight for what you want. The sheikh has to know you are very serious about your desire to marry Prince Youssef.''

It might also be Leah's only chance to influence the judgement made on Glen and Samira. Or, failing any mercy granted, to take her revenge on the sheikh of Zubani.

"The sheikh will not like it," Tayi warned.

"Let the winds of change howl tomorrow morning!" Leah quoted at her. "You said you would be part of it, Tayi. If you want Prince Youssef of Qatama as your husband, the time for change has come.''

Tayi seemed to grow immeasurably taller as conviction blazed in her eyes. "I will be part of it. I will do it," she affirmed. "I thank you for your advice. Tomorrow I shall create a storm.''

So take that, Sharif al Kader! Leah thought with intense satisfaction as Tayi made her queenly way out of the apartment.

Revenge would certainly be taken tomorrow.

Chaos would reign.

CHAPTER FOURTEEN

LEAH SPENT a very restless and disturbed night alone.
It spurred her determination to break in on the morning *majlis* and make her presence felt, one way or another. Sharif al Kader would find out she could not be
overlooked or ignored.

It gave her a perverse pleasure to dress in white on
this day of ultimate decision. She strapped the *agal* to
the inner side of her left arm, carefully testing that the
long sleeve of her robe completely covered it. As usual,
breakfast was served in her sitting room, and she tried
to eat some of it in order to settle her stomach. She
was nibbling at a croissant when Sharif suddenly
stepped inside her apartment.

He stood by the doorway, eyeing her balefully. "I
trust you have recovered your temper this morning."

Leah's eyes flashed scorn at him. "No," she
snapped. "I doubt I ever will."

His face looked drawn and tired, as though he also
had spent a restless night. His dark eyes brooded over
her in turbulent discontent. "What is it that you want
from me?" he demanded. Then, as she was about to
answer, he gruffly added, "Apart from releasing the
Princess Samira and your brother."

Leah glowered her discontent right back at him. "I want to be free. I want to go to the *majlis* today. I want—"

"It is forbidden for a woman."

"I don't care if it's forbidden or not. You're the sheikh of Zubani. You make the rules. You can change them." A spark of inspiration added the silky taunt, "I would find that very becoming in you."

He frowned. "If you come to the *majlis*, it will be seen as insulting to King Rashid and Prince Youssef."

Leah disdained any reply to that excuse. She simply stared at him with steely resolve in her eyes.

An air of decision slowly gathered and stamped itself on the sheikh's face. The powerful charisma of a man of destiny shone once more. "It shall be as you wish. You may come to the *majlis*. I will send an escort for you when it is time."

He left Leah to savour her sense of triumph alone. She could hardly believe he had actually bent to her will. What did it mean? Had she become more important to him than his revenge? Had he reconsidered his judgement on Glen and Samira? Or was that hoping for too much? *Apart from their release*, Sharif had said.

But at least she now had entry to the *majlis*. She could afford to play a waiting game to see what Sharif had in mind. If his judgement did not meet her approval, she would take whatever action was warranted in the circumstances.

Having sorted this through in her mind, Leah summoned one of the servants to send a message to Tayi. Her new friend and ally had to be informed that the sheikh was allowing Leah to be present at the *majlis*. This exception to the men-only rule would undoubtedly bolster Tayi's resolution to break it. Leah had no scruples whatsoever about having encouraged Tayi to go after what she wanted. It was, after all, what Tayi's closest cousin invariably did as though it was his divine right.

Other people had rights, as well, whether they were divine or not, and it was about time the sheikh of Zubani started respecting them, Leah thought with burning conviction. And what's more, if he didn't do that, no way was Leah going to remain at his side!

She fretted through two long hours before the escort came for her. It gave her a deep appreciation of what Glen and Samira must be going through, not knowing what their fate was to be but fearing the worst at the hands of the sheikh of Zubani.

When she was ushered into the official room for the *majlis*, the scene was almost an exact replica of what she had experienced at Qatama a month ago. A line of men seated along the side walls, their murmurs to each other halting as Leah was brought in by two armed guards. Facing her at the far end were the sheikh of Zubani and King Rashid of Qatama, seated side by side on elaborately carved, high-backed chairs that denoted their status. To the left of King Rashid, and at an angle to him, sat Prince Youssef. A chair similarly placed to the right of the sheikh was empty.

A tense silence accompanied Leah's long walk down the avenue of men. Leah sensed that whatever negotiations had been discussed prior to her arrival had not gone well. Both the sheikh and the king were stern-faced. There was certainly no air of amity between them. The atmosphere in the room bristled with discord. It did not bode well for Glen and Samira, Leah thought, her heart torn between fear and a fierce, desperate courage.

She kept her head high, defying the right of both king and sheikh to have any power over her and denying them the obeisance of a bow. Her eyes clashed momentarily with Sharif's. An electric challenge vibrated between them for several long seconds. Then he gave a slight nod, and she was led to the vacant chair to his right.

Leah sat with her hands folded in her lap, surreptitiously feeling for the handle of the *agal* under her sleeve, anxious that it be easily accessible to her. Her heart was pounding so hard it seemed to be ringing in her ears. She looked across at Youssef. His eyes met hers but expressed nothing. His face was tightly closed against showing any feeling.

It's going to be bad, Leah thought in sickening panic. If Sharif had not won what he wanted from King Rashid, there would be no room for mercy in the judgement on Glen and Samira. Leah turned her head to the king. His gaze was directed at the entrance doors, but his eyes had a fixed, unseeing look that suggested to Leah he would not allow the sight of his daughter to make any impression on him. He had declared the Princess Samira dead, and dead she would remain to her father.

The doors began to open.

Leah sucked in a deep breath.

But the doors were not opening for Glen and Samira. It was Tayi who stepped into the room, Tayi in all her magnificence, robed in shimmering scarlet and gold, a matching turban wound around her head and an *agal* prominently displayed in her hand.

There was a rustle of movement amongst the men seated along the walls, murmurs of disquiet. Tayi swept a commanding gaze around them, regally defying anyone to stop her from doing as she willed. The sheikh raised his hand in a motion for everyone to be still. Tayi gave a little nod of acknowledgement to Leah, then looked directly at Prince Youssef. The dark, velvety eyes glowed with a luminous love that seemed to transfix the crown prince of Qatama.

"Who is this woman?" King Rashid demanded.

"My closest cousin, Tayi al Kader," the sheikh replied with strong emphasis on her status.

Youssef rose from his chair, as though drawn hypnotically to his feet by the power of the feeling flowing from Tayi to him.

Perhaps it was the signal Tayi had been waiting for. She started forward, moving with a slow, swaying grace that held even the king of Qatama mesmerised with her approach. She came to a halt at a respectful distance from the sheikh and the king. Her gaze fastened purposefully on her cousin's.

"I have come to speak my heart," she announced with grave dignity.

"Does that require an *agal* in your hand, Tayi?" Sharif asked with equal gravity.

"It is to show that I am serious."

Sharif flicked a hard look at Leah, who returned it with interest. He addressed Tayi in a sterner voice. "It is not seemly in this company."

The advice had no effect on Tayi. She emanated fixed and unshakeable purpose. "You will listen," she demanded.

The sheikh apparently decided he was not averse to a diversion at this point. "Speak as you will, Tayi," he said with good grace.

"It concerns the arrangement of my marriage."

"It is still to be fully negotiated."

Her gaze swung to Prince Youssef. "There is one man who stands above all others."

"I have made other plans for you," Sharif said, frowning over this new complexity in the situation.

"I shall have no other man," Tayi declared, still looking straight at Youssef, leaving no-one in any doubt as to her choice of husband.

Youssef stepped towards her, and there was certainly no lack of expression on his face now. He was utterly captivated by the woman who was openly declaring her love and desire for him.

"Completely out of the question," King Rashid snapped, glaring furious disapproval at Youssef. "I wish to marry off my daughters, not my son. I won't countenance such an alliance. It does not have my approval."

Youssef wrenched his gaze from Tayi's to shoot a glowering frown at his father. Rebellion was in the air, and Tayi was well on the way to creating the storm that would change her life. Leah watched Sharif, willing him to respond to his cousin's initiative. She saw the slight curve of his mouth as his mind grasped the possibilities of exploiting what was happening in front of him. A gleam of animal cunning brightened his eyes.

"Such a marriage has certain advantages," he said, as though musing over the idea. He turned to King Rashid with an air of weighing important factors. "It would cement the alliance between our two countries." He paused, then ruefully added, "But I had planned to marry my cousin to King Ahmed of Isha."

Tayi's head swivelled instantly to the sheikh. Her whole body arched in protest. "King Ahmed of Isha is seventy-five years old."

"I did not expect the happiness of the marriage to last forever," Sharif said dryly. "You will understand that Prince Youssef is of much lower status than King Ahmed, Tayi. Such a marriage would be quite unacceptable in comparison unless adequate compensation were to be offered."

King Rashid's long, noble face took on a grimmer expression at the sting to his pride. "A mere cousin," he began, clearly about to voice rejection of the idea.

"Father," Youssef cut in with urgent intent. "Think of the advantages. It will redress the problems caused by the desertion of duty by Samira."

The king looked at him in disgust. "The Princess Samira is dead."

Leah saw her chance to break the king's intransigence and strike a blow against any harsh judgement on Glen and Samira. "If your daughter is dead, Your Majesty," she said, her voice raised for all to hear, "then the sentence of the law cannot be passed against her."

A murmur ran around the room as that inarguable piece of logic sank in.

"A debating point," the king scorned.

"We need some clear thinking," Sharif declared with ponderous gravity. But there was a sparkle of appreciation in the glance he flashed at Leah.

"Perhaps we could bring her back to life," Tayi suggested, her melodious voice lilting with sweet reason as she added, "if she is to be my sister-in-law, I do not want her dead."

"Neither do I," Youssef pressed in fervent support. His eyes glowed pure adoration at Tayi. "You are a woman who stands above all other women."

"There is no dignity in being stoned to death in the marketplace," Tayi said. "The time for change has come."

"I couldn't agree more," Youssef said strongly. He reached out and took the *agal* Tayi held, then slowly enfolded her hand in his. "You speak my heart, as well."

The sheikh cleared his throat in a rumbling demand for their attention. "In the interests of amity and friendship . . ."

"You call this amity and friendship?" King Rashid thundered in towering disapproval.

Sharif turned to him with a greater measure of towering disapproval, his dark eyes as cutting as lasers. "Do you forget the humiliation Zubani has suffered because you did not listen to your daughter's heart? Your son speaks well. I am favourably impressed."

The king flushed, highly discomfited by the reminder of Qatama's shame at not delivering what had been promised. "Very well. We shall call this amity and friendship," he conceded tersely.

"In view of the fact that my cousin wishes this marriage," Sharif continued with unrelenting purpose, "I am willing to forgo some of the compensation that should be given for the lowering of her status."

There was a look of black fury from the king at the repeated slight to his son's status.

"But such matters as need to be negotiated can be worked out at a later time," Sharif allowed with a show of benevolence. "Are we agreed on this marriage?"

The king's mouth tightened, resisting to the bitter end.

"Father, I ask your consent." It was more a command from Youssef than an appeal. Although he was as tall as Tayi, he seemed to have gained in stature simply by having her at his side.

For a few tense moments the king's eyes warred with his son's. Then his gaze moved to Tayi in all her regal glory, and a flicker of wonderment softened his expression. It was not difficult for Leah to read the king's mind. Tayi would certainly cut an impressive figure as queen of Qatama. Besides which, he could not afford the scandal of a second runaway couple from his royal household.

"We are agreed on the marriage," he said, making it a clear and firm announcement.

Tayi smiled with happiness at Leah, her eyes glowing with gratitude for the plan that had won her heart's desire. Leah smiled back, then turned challenging eyes to Sharif al Kader, who was observing this side play with acute interest. An amused little smile twitched at his lips as he shifted his attention to Tayi again.

"You have your wish," he said with familial benevolence.

It was a dismissal, but Tayi was having none of it. "I shall sit with Prince Youssef and attend the *majlis*. It is of concern to both of us," she announced with conviction.

Youssef instantly led her to his chair, taking it upon himself to bypass any rebuff from the sheikh or the king on the matter of Tayi's right to stay. He stood at her side, ready to defy any criticism.

The king looked decidedly ruffled by this further erosion of tradition. He shot Sharif a beetling look that clearly said his patience was being sorely tried. The sheikh's shoulders lifted a fraction, then dropped in imperturbable acceptance of the changes being wrought in front of his eyes. Not a word of protest was raised by the men in the room, but after a few mumbles amongst themselves, they looked at the sheikh with an air of expectation.

"Bring in the prisoners," he commanded.

Leah tensed, her pleasure for Tayi withering as fear clutched her heart. The doors were flung wide. An escort of four armed guards marched in with Glen and Samira between them. Relief surged through Leah as she saw that no apparent injury had been done to either of them. Their hands were linked in a tight clasp, but apart from that statement of togetherness, they showed no fear of what was to come, walking with

their heads high in disdain for any judgement of what
they had done.

Leah couldn't help thinking they made a striking
couple. Her brother's tall and muscular physique was
always impressive, but it was the strong character lines
of his handsome face that drew most attention. His
sun-streaked hair and golden tan emphasised the azure
blue of his eyes, his expression hard and unwavering
with the determination to fight whatever needed to be
fought to protect his sister and his wife.

Beside him, Samira looked small and exquisitely
feminine, her beautiful face framed by a shiny cas-
cade of black curls. But there was nothing weak in her
slighter stature. There was no quiver to her sweetly
curved mouth, no dropping of her lustrous dark eyes,
no lowering of her delicately rounded chin. She walked
with her man, proud to be at his side.

Glen's eyes fastened on Leah's in a clear promise
that he was ready and willing to pay the price for her
freedom. But she didn't want him to. She desperately
didn't want him to. She looked at Samira. Her gaze
was fixed on her father, perhaps pleading for his pardon before she paid for loving a man who was not her
father's choice.

Was Sharif thinking this woman should have been
his bride? Leah darted an anxious look at him as the
prisoners were halted halfway down the room. He was
not looking at Samira. He was eyeing Glen in the
measuring way that one strong man looked at another.

Leah glanced at her brother and found him eyeing
the sheikh with belligerent anger for what had been

done to his sister. No, Leah thought helplessly. It didn't matter. Yet she felt a deep sense of pride that her brother had come to challenge Sharif al Kader over his treatment of her. It was obvious that Glen was simmering with the need to speak out and deliver his own condemnation.

Which would only make everything worse, Leah thought despairingly. Somehow she had to stop this before it got started and irrevocable things were said. As she was searching her mind for a way to intervene effectively, Youssef stepped forward with a passionate outburst against any proceeding.

"If we're all agreed Samira is dead, the sentence of the law cannot be passed upon her, Your Excellency."

"I thank you for your caring, Youssef," Samira said with loving pride. "But if my husband is to die, I wish to die with him."

"No!" Leah cried, rising to her feet and shooting a pleading look at Sharif.

"Has not the price been paid?" Tayi said, gesturing her support for Leah and giving the sheikh a knowing look.

Sharif frowned, considering the storm that could very well break out on both sides of him.

Leah seized the initiative before it was too late. "I respectfully request a private audience with you, Your Excellency. If you would call a short recess . . ."

Sharif was not slow in coming to a decision. He rose to his feet. "I declare a recess," he announced. "The prisoners are to be seated until I return."

He turned to bow to King Rashid. "You will excuse me, Your Majesty. With due weight to be given to the cementing of this new alliance, there are grave matters to be taken into consideration.''

The king nodded his acquiescence.

Sharif swung around and gestured for Leah to accompany him. He led the way to a side door that opened to a private office. No sooner was the door shut behind them than he grasped Leah's left arm and pulled her towards him, his eyes glittering with knowing mockery.

"First the *agal*. I do not care to be stabbed in the back by a woman to whom I have granted many favours. One *agal* a day is quite enough for me to cope with."

Leah surrendered her weapon with a rueful sigh of resignation. "You can't say it didn't work for Tayi."

"It worked because I let it work," he said in arrogant dismissal, tossing the knife on the large desk at the other end of the room. "Now what's on your mind, Leah?"

She took a deep breath and searched his eyes in desperate appeal. "Do I mean anything to you, Sharif? I mean personally, not as an instrument of revenge."

His mouth twisted with irony. "You mean more to me than I care to admit. Why do you think we are here, Leah? Do I not try to give you everything you ask?"

Relief flooded through her, untangling the knots of pain and fear and bitter turmoil. "Then please listen to me, Sharif," she begged. "Since Princess Samira is dead in her own country, you should take her under your protection for the advantages it will give you."

He frowned. "What advantages?"

"Prince Youssef's gratitude. He loves his sister. Surely that is clear to you?"

"Yes."

"And if you have Samira under your wing, you get my brother, as well. If Prince Youssef changes his mind about marrying Tayi and flies off in his airplane, you need Glen on your side to shoot him down. Everyone knows that no-one can handle a plane as well as Glen."

"What other advantages?" he asked with a calculating air.

"You could take Glen on as your personal pilot. That's one in the eye for King Rashid, as well," she argued. "I think this amity and friendship thing can be a bit overdone. His manner to you was quite insulting, Sharif. But if you end up with his daughter, his pilot *and* your cousin married to the prince who will make her queen of Qatama, you'll definitely be seen as the winner."

His smile caressed her with warm appreciation. "I agree. I like the way your mind thinks. I shall take your brother as my personal pilot. That will be part of the sentence I will impose. Will that please you and give me credit in your eyes?"

"Yes. Oh, yes, Sharif." She threw her arms around his neck in an exultant hug. "And you'll find him the best pilot in the world. Truly you will," she cried, her eyes shining with the love that had burst free of the constrictions forced upon it by his earlier thirst for revenge.

His arms swept around her in a fiercely possessive embrace, and he kissed her with all the hunger of a man who deeply felt the deprivation of the intimacy they had shared. "Leah," he groaned as he moved his lips to cover her face with kisses. "Do you really want to be free of me?"

"I can never be free of you, Sharif," she whispered, blissfully turning her face to the warm fervour of his desire for her. "You've become part of me, whether I want it or not."

"I want you to choose freely." He drew back a little, his eyes seeking hers, searing them with his need. "Will you marry me, Leah? Share my life with me? Be my *sheikha* who cares for my people? Or would you rather leave me?"

Leah's heart turned over. She had never once dreamed that Sharif would want her as his wife. While she was still stunned by his unexpected proposal, he quickly added another persuasion.

"It gives me good reason in the eyes of my people to pardon my brother-in-law."

"You really want to marry me?" Leah asked breathlessly, her eyes sparkling with incredulous hope and happiness.

"Yes. Very much. Say you love me, Leah," he pleaded gruffly.

"I love you, Sharif. And I'll be anything you want. Everything," she promised, and she carried the promise to his lips, to seal it there forever.

Elation sang through her mind at the wonderful future Sharif was offering. He smiled his delight in her. "This is the way marriages should be arranged.

Emotion must not be allowed to get in the way," he said, then completely disproved his argument by kissing her with more and more emotional passion.

Leah eventually became aware that a considerable amount of time had passed. "We should go back and tell the others," she murmured reluctantly.

"They can wait a little longer," Sharif said with firm authority.

And they did.

CHAPTER FIFTEEN

"YOU REALLY WANT to marry him, Leah?" Glen asked for the umpteenth time, unable to shake his concern that she was sacrificing herself for his sake and Samira's.

Leah laughed at him, her eyes happily teasing. "You think you're the only one who can fall madly in love? Let me tell you it was lucky Samira didn't have Sharif to compare with you, or you might have lost out."

"No. Never," Samira said with an adoring look at Glen. "There is no-one to compare with my husband."

"Well, Tayi thinks the same of Youssef, so I guess everyone sees from the heart," Leah said with warm pleasure in how everything had turned out.

They were sitting in the reception room where Leah had met with her father. The *majlis* was long since over, but Sharif was still closeted with King Rashid and Prince Youssef, negotiating the details of the compensation between Zubani and Qatama. Leah and Glen had been granted permission to call their father and assure him that all was well and he would be welcomed to the palace at any time he cared to visit.

"Tell me about Tayi," Samira pressed with eager curiosity. "And how did it happen that she is to marry Youssef?"

Leah related the sequence of events that culminated in the agreement made at the *majlis*. Samira was still expressing her admiration for her future sister-in-law when Sharif swept in on a wave of exuberant good humour, his eyes brilliant with the wild elation of success. They automatically rose to their feet in deference to his commanding presence.

"It is done!" he declared. "The royal family of Qatama are to be summoned to honour the celebration of our marriage, Leah. As you say, one in the eye for King Rashid!"

She laughed and giddily hurled herself into his embrace. "You are the cleverest negotiator in the world, Sharif!"

"It is merely that I have a fine appreciation for what happens around me," he said with a hopeless attempt at humility. He grinned at Glen. "I think I should thank you for your example."

"What example is that, Your Excellency?" Glen asked in puzzlement.

"Sometimes there is only one chance to have what one wants. You did well to take Princess Samira. It left me free to take Leah. So we are all happy, are we not?"

"Well, that's one way of looking at it," Glen conceded ruefully.

"I have been thinking," Sharif said with more seriousness. "As my wife's brother, you need more status than that of my personal pilot. You should be head of the air force in Zubani. Are you agreed?''

"It's a very generous offer, Your Excellency.''

"Family is family. You have proved yourself a worthy brother to your sister. Who is an exceptional woman. I have no doubt you will serve me and my people well.''

"Thank you. I appreciate your confidence,'' Glen said in some bemusement at his change of fortune.

Sharif directed a sympathetic smile at Samira. "I regret to say your father is proving obdurate over your status in Qatama. However, I leave that problem in the hands of your brother Prince Youssef and my cousin, Tayi, who together will be a formidable lobby in your cause.''

"My father would never have listened to me as you listened to Tayi,'' Samira said with a mixture of apology and admiration.

"Acceptance of change sometimes comes slowly,'' Sharif said, his arm tightening possessively around Leah. "However, with the new alliance between our countries, you will undoubtedly have ample opportunity for visits from your family.''

"Thank you, Your Excellency,'' Samira said with warm sincerity. "You are most kind.''

His eyes twinkled. "Your family will be here for a month. There is not only my marriage to celebrate, but the marriage of Youssef and Tayi, which will take place on the same day.''

A month for a month, Leah thought, imagining Sharif's relish in stipulating that length of time. There could be no doubt he had enjoyed the negotiations immensely, once she and Tayi had put him on the right track. Although, of course, she would never point that out to him. It was to his everlasting credit that Sharif al Kader had accepted change with admirable speed and aplomb.

Tayi came in, no less exuberantly triumphant than Sharif, but retaining her dignity, as always. She addressed the sheikh first. "I thank you for all you have done for me today. Have you sent messages to King Ahmed of Isha calling off the negotiation of the intended marriage to him?"

"Yes, I have. And expressed my concern that if the intended marriage with you had gone through, it would have endangered not only his heart, but also his life," Sharif said dryly. "I've also asked for compensation because he suggested the marriage in the first place, and quite clearly he is out of tune with the times. In retrospect, I find the offer provocative and insulting."

Tayi turned her shining gaze to Leah. "I have learnt much from you. I shall make Youssef very happy."

"I'm sure you will," Leah said warmly, although she couldn't help wondering how Youssef would weather the storms ahead. Tayi was extremely single-minded once she had a purpose dear to her heart. However, since Youssef's happiness was now her prime concern, Leah had no doubt nothing would be allowed to get in the way of achieving precisely that. She had a vision of the winds of change howling around King Rashid's head. Qatama was never going to be the same again.

Tayi smiled at Glen and Samira. "I have come to show you to your apartment in the palace. All has been arranged for your comfort and convenience."

"Thank you, Tayi," Samira said with glowing admiration for this remarkable woman who had given Samira entry into her family again.

Glen moved forward to offer his hand to the sheikh. "We have much to thank you for, Your Excellency. But above all else, I am glad that you care for my sister's happiness. Leah is very dear to me."

Sharif gripped Glen's hand with both of his. "And to me. We shall be good friends, you and I." His eyes sparkled at Leah. "Your sister will tell you that I listen."

"Then does what he wants," Leah said dryly.

"With due regard to your happiness," he retorted.

Leah laughed. "All right, Sharif. I surrender."

"Ah!" he said with intense satisfaction. He released Glen's hand and waved towards the door. "We shall talk more tomorrow. Be at ease in your new home."

The moment they were gone he drew Leah into his arms. "I think I need to taste this surrender of yours and make sure it is true."

"I agree. It might only be a passing surrender."

"Then there is no time to waste."

Leah gave him an inviting kiss. "I missed you last night, Sharif."

He took full advantage of the invitation. "Not as much as I missed you. Which I shall prove. Now."

The rest of the afternoon was spent in Leah's apartment. Strict orders were given that they were not to be disturbed.

"Soon I shall be your wife," Leah said dreamily as the light began to fade.

"You have been my wife from our first night together," Sharif said smugly. "I was merely waiting for your surrender to the fact."

She levered herself up from the pillows to challenge him. "You can't really mean that."

His eyes glowed with the light of destiny. "It was meant, Leah. We are right together. It could be no other way."

She smiled, knowing it was true. For Sharif al Kader, his choice was the way, and always would be, and he had made it her destiny, as well. Leah was more than content for it to be so. In surrendering to him she had found a freedom of the heart that was above all other freedoms. To share her life with the man she loved above all others was the only freedom she wanted.

Sandra Marton has always believed in the magic of storytelling and the joy of living happily ever after with that special someone. She wrote her first romantic story when she was nine and fell madly in love at sixteen with the man she would eventually marry. Today, after raising two sons and an assortment of furry, four-legged creatures, Sandra and her husband live in a house on a hilltop in a quiet corner of Connecticut.

Recent titles by the same author:

NO NEED FOR LOVE
ROMAN SPRING

HOSTAGE OF THE HAWK

BY

SANDRA MARTON

MILLS & BOON and the Rose Device are trademarks of the publisher.

First published in Great Britain in 1994 by Mills & Boon Limited

© Sandra Myles 1994

Australian copyright 1994

ISBN 0 263 78588 2

Set in Times Roman 10 on 11½pt.
49-9408-51909 C

Printed in Great Britain by BPC Paperbacks Ltd A member of The British Printing Company Ltd

CHAPTER ONE

THE cry of the *muezzin* rose in the warm evening and hung trembling over the crowded streets of Casablanca. Joanna, listening from the balcony of her hotel suite, felt a tremor of excitement dance along her skin. Not that there was really anything to get excited about. While the hotel was Moroccan in décor, it was the same as hotels everywhere.

Still, she thought as she put down her cup and leaned her crossed arms on the balcony railing, it was wonderful to be here. This part of the world was so mysteriously different from the life she knew. She felt as if she had stepped back in time.

'Jo!'

Joanna sighed. So much for stepping back in time. Her father's angry bellow was enough to bring her back to the present with a bang.

'Jo! Where in hell are you?'

And so much for the mystery of Casablanca, she thought as she straightened and turned towards the doorway. She was used to Sam Bennett's outbursts—who wouldn't be, after twenty-six years?—but she felt a twinge of sympathy for whatever poor soul had made him this angry. Jim Ellington, probably; Sam had been on the phone with his second in command, which meant that Jim must have done or said something that displeased him.

'It's about time,' he snapped when she reached the bedroom. 'I've been calling and calling. Didn't you hear me?'

'Of course I heard you.' Her father was glaring at her from the bed where he lay back against a clutch of squashed pillows, his ruddy face made even redder by the pain in his back and his bad temper. 'Half the hotel must have heard you. I take it there's a problem?'

'You're damned right there's a problem! That stupid Ellington—he screwed things up completely!'

'Well, that's no surprise,' Joanna said pleasantly. She plumped the pillows, then took a small vial from the nightstand and dumped two tablets into the palm of her hand. 'I tried to tell you not to rely on him, that he was the wrong person to deal with this idiotic Eagle of the East.'

'Hawk,' Sam said grumpily as he took the tablets from her. 'Prince Khalil is called the Hawk of the North.'

'Hawk, eagle, east, north—what's the difference? It's a stupid title for a two-bit bandit.'

Sam grimaced. 'That "two-bit bandit" can end Bennettco's mining deal with Abu Al Zouad before it starts!'

'That's ridiculous,' Joanna said. She poured some orange juice into a glass and offered it to Sam. 'Abu's the Sultan of Jandara——'

'And Khalil's been harassing him for years, stirring up unrest and trouble whenever he can.'

'Why doesn't Abu stop him?'

'He can't catch him. Khalil's as sly as a fox.' Sam smiled grimly, then gulped down the juice and handed back the glass. 'Or as swift as a hawk. He swoops down from the northern mountains——'

'The mountains Bennettco wants to mine?'

'Right. He swoops down, raises hell, then escapes back to his mountain stronghold, untouched.'

'He's more than a bandit, then,' Joanna said with a little shudder. 'He's an outlaw!'

'And he's opposed to the deal we've struck with Abu.'

'Why?'

'Abu says it's because he's opposed to our bringing in Western ways.'

'You mean, he's opposed to our bringing in the twentieth century,' Joanna said with a grimace.

'Whatever. The point is, he'll do everything he can to keep Bennettco out. Unless we can change his mind, we might as well pack up and go home.'

'I still don't understand. Why can't Abu simply have Khalil arrested and——?' Her brows lifted as her father began to chuckle. 'Did I say something funny?'

'Have him arrested!' Sam's laughter grew, even though he clutched at the small of his back. 'Have pity, Jo! It hurts when I laugh.'

'I'm not trying to amuse you, Father,' Joanna said stiffly. 'I'm just trying to understand why this man isn't in prison if he's an outlaw.'

'I told you, they can't catch him.'

Joanna's brows lifted. 'In case you haven't noticed,' she said drily, 'Khalil can be "caught" this very moment at a hotel on the other side of Casablanca.'

'Yeah, yeah, I told that to Abu.'

'Well, then——'

'He doesn't want to cause an international dispute with the Moroccan government. This is their turf, after all.' Sam sighed and fell back against the pillows. 'Which brings us back to square one and that dumb ass Ellington. If only I could get out of this bed long enough to make that dinner meeting——'

'When we left New York, you made it sound as if this meeting were pro forma.'

'Well, it is. I mean, it should have been—if I hadn't pulled my back.' Sam's mouth turned down. 'I know I

could have finessed the hell out of Khalil—and now
Ellington's managed to make a bad situation worse.'

'I'll bet Ellington obeyed you to the letter, phoned
your regrets about tonight's meeting, and said he'd dine
with Khalil in your place.'

'You're darned right he obeyed me.' Sam glared at
her. 'If he wants to keep his job, he'd better!'

'It's what everybody who works for you does,' Joanna
said mildly, 'even if your orders are wrong.'

'Now, just a minute there, Joanna! What do you
mean, my orders were wrong? I told Ellington to tell the
Prince that something had come up that I couldn't help
and——'

'You insulted him.'

'What?'

'Come on, Father! Here's this—this robber baron with
an over-inflated ego, gloating over the fact that he's got
Sam Bennett, CEO and chairman of the board of
Bennettco, over a barrel. He's probably been counting
the minutes until tonight's meeting—and then he gets a
call telling him he's being foisted off on a flunky.'

'Don't be foolish! Ellington's my policy assistant.'

'It's a title, that's all, and titles are meaningless.'
Joanna sat down on the edge of the bed. 'Who would
know that better than an outlaw who calls himself a
prince?'

'I already know we're in trouble, Jo! What I need is
a way out.'

'Take it easy, Father. You know what the doctor said
about stress being bad for your back.'

'Dammit, girl, don't fuss over me! There's a lot at
stake here—or have you been too busy playing nursemaid
to notice?'

'I am not a "girl".' Joanna got to her feet, her gaze
turning steely. 'I am your daughter, and, if you weren't

so determined to keep me from knowing the first thing about Bennettco, I wouldn't have to ask you all these questions. In fact, I might have been able to come up with some ideas that would have gotten you off the hook tonight.'

'Listen, Jo, I know you have a degree in business administration, but this is the real world, not some ivy-covered classroom. It's Ellington who let us down. He——'

'You should have told Ellington to tell Khalil the truth, that your back's gone out again.'

'What for? It's nobody's business that I'm lying here like an oversized infant, being driven crazy by you and the hotel doctor!'

'Contrary to what you think,' Joanna said coolly, 'being sick isn't a sign of weakness. Khalil would have understood that he wasn't being insulted, that you had no choice but to back out of this meeting.'

Sam glared at her, then shrugged his shoulders. 'Maybe.'

'What did you plan on accomplishing tonight?'

'For one thing, I wanted to eyeball the bastard and see for myself what Abu's been up against.'

'And what else?'

Sam grinned slyly. 'He may resent us dealing with Abu—but I bet he won't resent a deal that has some under-the-table dollars for himself in it.'

A frown creased Joanna's forehead. 'You mean, Bennettco's going to offer him a bribe?'

'*Baksheesh*,' her father said. 'That's what it's called, and you needn't give me that holier-than-thou look. It's part of doing business in this part of the world. It just has to be done delicately, so as not to offend the s.o.b.' Sam sighed deeply. 'That was the plan, anyway—until Ellington botched it.'

'Have you any idea what, exactly, he said to the big pooh-bah?'

'To Khalil?' Sam shook his head. 'Ellington didn't even talk to him. He spoke to the Prince's aide, a guy named Hassan, and——'

'His first mistake,' Joanna said with crisp self-assurance. 'He should have insisted on speaking with the Prince directly.'

'He tried, but Hassan says Khalil doesn't deal with underlings. Underlings, can you imagine?' Sam chuckled. 'The only good part of this is imagining Ellington's face when he heard that.'

'What did Ellington say then?'

'The conversation was all Hassan's after that. He made some veiled threats, said if Sam Bennett wasn't interested enough to deal with Khalil man to man, Khalil wouldn't be responsible for what might happen.'

'That's insane! He can't be fool enough to think he can ride down on our crews with his band of cut-throats—can he?'

'Maybe—and maybe not.' Sam grunted with displeasure. 'Hell, this meeting was the key to everything! I just know that if I could have met face to face with this Khalil I'd have been able to convince him that Bennettco——'

'We still can.'

'How? I just told you, Khalil won't meet with Ellington.'

'But he might meet with me,' Joanna blurted.

She hadn't planned those words, but once she'd said them her heart began to pound. Sam's prideful stubbornness, Ellington's blind adherence to orders and the arrogance of a greedy bandit with a fancy title had set in motion a series of events that might make all the difference in her life.

Sam laughed, and Joanna looked up sharply.

'Right,' he said sarcastically. 'I'm supposed to send my daughter to meet with a barbarian. Do I look like I'm crazy, Jo?'

'Come on, Father. He's not exactly a barbarian. Besides, I'd be meeting him for dinner, in a fancy restaurant. I'd be as safe as if I were dining in my suite.'

'Forget it. The great Khalil doesn't deal with underlings.'

'Maybe he'd feel differently about someone named Bennett, someone with a vested interest in Bennettco.' Joanna looked at her father, her voice strengthening as her idea took shape. 'Someone who could identify herself as not just her father's daughter but Bennettco's vice-president.'

Sam scowled darkly. 'Are we back to that?'

'We never left it. Here I am, your only offspring, somebody who grew up as much in the field as in the office——'

'My first mistake,' he grumbled.

'Here I am,' Joanna said evenly, 'the only person who knows as much about business as you do, my university degree clutched in my hand, and you absolutely refuse to let me work for you.'

'You do work for me. You've been my hostess in Dallas and New York since you were old enough to carry on a conversation.'

'That,' she said dismissively.

'Yes, that! What's wrong with "that", for lord's sake? Any girl in her right mind would grab at the chance to——' Joanna's brows lifted and Sam put his hand to his heart. 'Forgive me,' he said melodramatically. 'Any *woman* in her right mind would be perfectly happy to——'

'Stanford Mining's offered me a job,' Joanna said softly.

'They did what?'

She walked to the bureau and leaned back against it, arms folded over her breasts. She'd never meant to tell her father about the offer this way; she'd planned on working up to it, using it as the final link in a well-conceived argument designed to convince him, once and for all, that she wanted more than to be a beautifully dressed figurehead, but she knew in her bones that now was the moment.

'The manager of their Alaskan operation is leaving. They asked if I might be interested.'

Sam's face darkened. 'My own daughter, working for the competition?'

'The key word is "working", Father. I've told you and told you, I've no intention of spending the rest of my life like some—some over-age débutante.'

'And I've told you and told you, I didn't work my tail off so my daughter could get her hands dirty!'

'I'm not asking you to let me work in the field,' Joanna said quickly. 'Even I know better than to expect the impossible.'

'Joanna.' Sam's voice softened, took on the wheedling tone she knew so well. 'I need you doing just what you've been doing, baby. Public relations is important, you know that. Having your name listed on the committee for charity benefits, getting your picture in the paper along with the Whitneys, Rockefellers and Astors——'

'You're wrong about the importance of that stuff, Father, but if it matters to you so much I can hold down a job and still manage all the rest.'

Sam gave her a long, hard look. 'Are you serious about taking the job with Stanford?'

Until this moment, she had only been serious about considering it—but now she knew that she would accept the offer rather than go on playing the part her father had long ago assigned her.

Joanna nodded. 'Yes,' she said, her eyes locked with his, 'I am.'

They stared at each other while the seconds passed, Joanna's emerald gaze as unwavering as her father's pale blue one, and finally he sighed.

'Do you really think you could get this guy Khalil to agree to meet with you?'

A little thrill raced through Joanna's blood but she was careful to keep her expression neutral.

'I think I could have a good shot at it,' she said.

'By telling him you're my daughter?'

'By telling him the truth: that you're ill but that this meeting is too important to miss. By telling him I'm your second in command, that everything I say has your full support and backing.'

Sam pursed his lips. 'That simple, hmm?'

Nothing was ever that simple, Joanna knew, not in business, not in life, and surely not in this place where custom vied with progress for dominance. But this was no time to show any hesitation.

'I think so, yes.'

She waited, barely breathing, while Sam glowered at her, and then he nodded towards the phone.

'OK.'

'OK, what?' Joanna said, very calmly, as if her pulse weren't racing hard enough so she could feel the pound of it in her throat.

'Call the Prince's hotel. If you can get past that watchdog of an aide, if Khalil will talk to you and agree to meet with you in my place, you've got a deal.'

Joanna smiled. 'First let's agree on the terms.'

'I'm your father. Don't you trust me?'

'You're my father and you raised me never to sign anything without reading it twice.' She saw a glimmer of a smile in Sam's eyes as she held up her fisted hand. 'Number one,' she said, raising her index finger, 'I get a vice-presidency at Bennettco. Number two, it's a real job with real responsibilities. Number three——'

Sam threw up his hands. 'I know when I'm licked. Go on, call the man. Let's see if you're as good as you think you are.'

Joanna's smile blazed. 'Just watch me.'

Her father reached out, took a notepad from the nightstand, and held it out to her. 'Here's the phone number. It's direct to Khalil's suite.'

Joanna nodded and reached slowly for the phone. She would have preferred to make this call from the other room instead of here, with her father watching her every move, but Sam would be quick to pounce on that as a sign of weakness.

'Good evening,' she said to the operator, then read off the number on the notepad. Her stomach was knotting but Sam's gaze was unwavering and she forced a cool smile to her face as she sank into the bedside chair, leaned back, and crossed her legs. The phone rang and rang. Maybe nobody was there, she thought—and at that moment, the ringing stopped and a deep voice said something in a language she couldn't understand, except for the single word 'Hassan'.

Joanna clasped the phone more tightly. 'Good evening, Mr Hassan,' she said. 'This is Joanna Bennett. Sam Bennett's daughter.'

If Hassan was surprised, he covered it well. 'Ah, Miss Bennett,' he said in impeccable English, 'I am honoured. What may I do for you?'

'Well?' Sam said impatiently. 'What's he saying?'

Joanna frowned at him. 'How are you enjoying your stay in Casablanca?' she said into the phone.

'The city is delightful, Miss Bennett, as I'm sure you agree.'

Joanna touched the tip of her tongue to her lips. 'And the Prince? Is he enjoying his stay, as well?'

'Dammit,' Sam hissed, 'get to the point! Is Khalil there, or isn't he?'

'Indeed,' Hassan said pleasantly, 'my Lord Khalil has always had a preference for this city.'

Joanna took a deep breath. Enough pleasantries. It was time to get down to business.

'Mr Hassan,' she said, 'I should like to speak with the Prince.'

Hassan's tone hardened. 'I'm afraid that is out of the question, Miss Bennett. If you have a message for him, I shall be happy to deliver it.'

Joanna's hand began to sweat on the phone. Her father was still giving her that same steadfast look and a self-satisfied smile was beginning to form on his lips.

'Give it up, baby,' he said quietly. 'I told you you couldn't pull it off.'

'Mr Hassan,' Joanna said evenly, 'I'm afraid you don't understand. I want to assure the Prince that the only reason for the change in plans is because my father is ill. As for Mr Ellington—I'm afraid he misunderstood my father's instructions. The Prince will be dining with my father's representative, whom he trusts completely and holds in the highest esteem.' Joanna looked at Sam. 'Vice-president Jo Bennett.'

'One moment, please, Miss Bennett,' Hassan said.

Joanna felt a rush of hope. She smiled sweetly at Sam. 'He's going to put the Prince on,' she said, and hoped that her father couldn't see her crossed fingers.

* * *

Across town, in the elegant royal suite of the Hotel Casablanca, Prince Khalil glared at his prime minister.

'What sort of man is this Sam Bennett,' he growled, 'that he asks his daughter to telephone me and beg on his behalf?' He folded his arms across his chest, his dark blue eyes glinting like sapphires in his tanned, handsome face. 'Bennett is worried,' he said with satisfaction as he leaned his hard, six-foot frame against the wall.

'Precisely, my lord. He must be ready to bend to your will or he would not have ordered a woman to act as his agent.'

'Only a fool would bring his daughter on such a trip,' Khalil said with disdain. 'The woman must have thought Casablanca would be an exotic playground in which to amuse herself.'

Hassan's grizzled brows lifted. 'Of course, my lord. She is, after all, of the West.'

Khalil grunted in assent. 'What does she want?'

'To speak with you.' Khalil laughed and Hassan permitted himself a smile. 'I told her, of course, that was not possible, and then she said Sam Bennett wishes tonight's dinner meeting to take place.'

'Ah.' Khalil's hard mouth curled with the shadowy beginnings of an answering smile. 'Bennett has decided he wants to keep our appointment now?'

'He is ill, sire, or so the woman claims, and wishes to send an emissary. I suspect it is an excuse he uses to save face.'

Khalil strode forward. 'I do not meet with emissaries, Hassan.'

Hassan dipped his head in respect. 'Of course, my lord. But her offer is interesting. The emissary is Joe Bennett, a vice-president of the company.'

Khalil's eyes narrowed. 'Who? I have never heard of such a person.'

Frowning, Hassan took his hand from the telephone and spoke into it. 'We have no knowledge of this person who would meet with Prince Khalil, Miss Bennett. Is he related to your father?'

'Mr Hassan, if I could just speak with the Prince——'

'The Prince does not speak with underlings, and he surely does not meet with them,' Hassan said coldly. 'If you wish to answer my questions, I will transmit the information to my lord. Otherwise, our conversation is at an end.'

'Jo,' Sam said, 'give it up. You're not gonna get to first base with this guy.'

Joanna swung away from her father. 'Jo Bennett is hardly an underling, Mr Hassan.'

'Jo,' Sam said, his voice gaining authority, 'did you hear me? Give it up. You took a shot and you lost.'

'Miss Bennett,' the voice in her ear said sharply, 'I asked you a question. Who is Joseph Bennett? Is he Sam Bennett's son?'

Joanna swallowed, shut her eyes, then opened them. 'Yes,' she said into the telephone, praying that the Prince would forgive the deception after she convinced him that there'd be enough money in this deal to make him happy, 'yes, that's right, sir. He is.'

'A moment, please.' Hassan put his hand over the mouthpiece again and looked at the Prince. 'The man you would dine with is the son of Sam Bennett.'

Khalil glared at his minister. 'A son,' he snarled, 'a young jackal instead of the old.' He stalked across the elegant room, turned, and looked at Hassan. 'Tell the woman you will accept a meeting with her brother. Perhaps my judgement is wrong. Perhaps the son has some influence on the father. At any rate, you can convey my message clearly: that I will not be ignored in this matter!'

Hassan smiled. 'Excellent, my lord.' His smile fell away as he tilted the phone to his lips. 'Miss Bennett.'

Joanna blinked. 'Yes?'

'I, Adym Hassan, Special Minister to His Highness Prince Khalil, will meet with your brother tonight.'

Joanna clutched the cord tighter. 'But——'

'Eight o'clock, as planned, at the Oasis Restaurant. As they say in your world, take it or leave it, Miss Bennett.'

'Jo?' Sam's voice rose. 'Dammit, Jo, what's he saying? He's turning you down flat, isn't he?'

Joanna hunched over the phone. 'Of course,' she said, 'eight o'clock. That will be fine. Thank you, sir.' She hung up the phone, took a deep breath, and turned to her father. 'You see?' she said briskly. 'That wasn't so hard after all.'

'He's meeting with you?' Sam said doubtfully.

Joanna nodded. 'Sure. I told you he would.'

Sam blew out his breath. 'OK,' he said, 'OK. Now, let's figure out how to get the most mileage we can out of tonight.' He looked at his daughter and a grin spread over his face. 'Not bad, kid,' he said, 'not bad at all.'

'It's not "kid",' Joanna said with an answering smile. 'It's Vice-President Jo Bennett, if you don't mind.'

Vice-President Joseph Bennett, she thought, and gave a little shudder. Things were going to get interesting when Special Minister Adym Hassan found out he'd been lied to.

Halfway across the city, Special Minister Hassan was already thinking the same thing.

'I am suspicious of Bennett's motives, my lord,' he said to Prince Khalil as he hung up the phone. 'But we shall see what happens. The woman's brother will meet with me tonight.'

Khalil nodded. 'Good.' He turned, walked slowly across the room, and stood gazing out the window as if he could see beyond the city to the hills that marked the boundary of his kingdom. Sam Bennett was a sly, tough opponent; it was more than likely his son would be the same. Too sly and too tough for Hassan, who was loyal and wise and obedient but no longer young. How could he let the old man meet with Bennett? If he'd learned one thing these past weeks, it was that dealing with anybody named Bennett was like putting a ferret in charge of the hen house.

Khalil spun away from the window. 'Hassan!'

'Yes, my lord?'

'I have changed my mind. I will meet with Sam Bennett's son myself.'

Hassan looked startled. 'You, sir? But——'

'There are no "buts", Hassan,' Khalil said sharply. 'Call down for some coffee and lay out my clothing.' He smiled tightly, the sort of smile that chilled those who knew him well. 'I promise you this, old man. One way or another, tonight will change everything.'

It was Joanna's thought, too, as she sat beside her father, only half listening as he droned on about tonight's agenda.

One way or another, she knew in her bones that her life would not be the same after this night ended.

Afterwards, she would remember how right she'd been.

CHAPTER TWO

WHAT did you wear to a dinner meeting with a Hawk of the North?

Not that she'd be dining with the great man himself, Joanna thought wryly as she peered into the wardrobe in her bedroom. Her appointment was with Hassan, Special Minister to Prince Khalil, although what a bandit needed with a minister was beyond her to understand. Their conversation had been brief but it had been enough to give her a good idea of what he'd be like.

He'd be tall and angular and as old as the hills that lay beyond the city. The skin would be drawn across his cheekbones like ivory papyrus. His eyes, pale and rheumy with age, would glitter with distaste when he saw her and realised that she was Joanna Bennett, for he lived in a world in which female equality was unheard of.

Joanna smiled tightly as she riffled through the clothing hanging inside the wardrobe.

How would she convince him to continue the meeting, once her deceit was obvious?

'Surely, the great Khalil wishes prosperity for his people,' she'd begin, 'and would not wish you to refuse to meet with someone who can provide it.' Then, as distasteful as the prospect was, she'd dig into her purse, take out the envelope with the numbered Swiss bank account her father had established, and slide it gently across the table.

After that, Hassan wouldn't care if she were a man, a woman or a camel.

* * *

20

Joanna glanced at her watch as she stepped from her taxi. Eight o'clock. Her timing was perfect. She put her hands to her hair, checking to see if the pair of glittery combs were still holding the burnished auburn mass back from her face, then smoothed down the skirt of her short emerald silk dress. She'd hesitated, torn between a Chanel suit and this, the one cocktail dress she'd brought with her, deciding on the dress because she thought the suit might make her look too severe, that it would be enough of a shock for the minister to find himself dealing with a woman without her looking like *that* kind of woman.

The doorman was watching her enquiringly and she took a deep breath, lifted her chin, and walked briskly towards him. She was nervous but who wouldn't be? Everything she wanted—her father's approval, the vice-presidency at Bennettco—hung on the next couple of hours.

'*Masa el-kheyr*, madam.'

Joanna nodded. 'Good evening,' she said, and stepped through the door.

Soft, sybaritic darkness engulfed her, broken only by the palest glow of carefully recessed overhead lighting and flickering candlelight. Music played faintly in the background, something involving flutes and chimes that sounded more like the sigh of wind through the trees than anything recognisable to her Western ear.

'*Masa el-kheyr*, madam. Are you joining someone?'

The head waiter's smile was gracious but she wondered if he would continue smiling if she were to say no, she wasn't joining anyone, she wanted a table to herself.

'Madam?'

Joanna gave herself a little shake. The last thing she needed was to get herself into an antagonistic mood.

'Yes,' she said pleasantly. 'My name is Bennett. I believe there's a reservation in my name.'

Was it her imagination, or did the man's eyebrows lift? But he smiled again, inclined his head, and motioned her to follow him. There was an arched doorway ahead, separated from the main room by a gently swaying beaded curtain. When they reached it, he drew the curtain aside and made a little bow.

'The reservation request was for as private a table as possible,' he said.

Joanna nodded as she stepped past him. A private alcove. That would be better. At least, she and Hassan wouldn't have to deal with——

A man was rising to his feet from the banquette. Joanna's eyes widened. He was thirty, perhaps, or thirty-five, tall, with a lithe body and broad shoulders contained within a finely tailored English suit. Her gaze flew to his face. His eyes were shockingly blue against his tanned skin. His nose was straight, his mouth full and sensuous. And he was smiling.

Joanna's heart gave an unaccustomed thump. Lord, he was gorgeous!

She smiled back, flustered, then turned quickly to the head waiter.

'I'm terribly sorry, but there must be an error.'

'Yes.' The man had spoken, and she looked back at him. His smile had grown, tilting a little with intimacy and promise. 'I'm afraid the lady is right.' His voice was soft, smoky, and lightly tinged with an indefinable accent. 'If I were not expecting a gentleman to join me——'

The head waiter cleared his throat. 'Excuse me, sir. I believe you said you were waiting for a Mr Joseph Bennett.'

'Yes, that's right. I am.'

'Then there's been no error, sir. This is the gentleman—uh, the lady—you were waiting for.'

Joanna's eyes flew to the man's face. They stared at each other in silence. This was Hassan, Minister to Prince Khalil? Oh God, she thought, as she saw his expression go rapidly from surprise to disbelief to fury, and she stepped quickly forward and shot out her hand.

'Mr Hassan,' she said with a big, determinedly cheerful smile, 'what a pleasure to meet you. I'm Jo Bennett.'

He looked at her hand as if it were contaminated, then at her.

'If this is an example of Western humour,' he said coldly, 'I should warn you that I am not amused.'

Joanna swallowed, dropped her hand to her side, and fought against the desire to wipe the suddenly damp palm against her skirt.

'It's not a joke, no, sir.'

Sir? *Sir*? What was going on here? Was she really going to permit this—this arrogant minister to a greedy despot to reduce her to a deferential schoolgirl? It was one thing to be nervous, but it was quite another to let the balance of power be stripped from her without so much as a whisper. Whether Mr Hassan liked it or not, they were here on equal footing. The sooner she reminded him of that, the better.

Joanna lifted her chin and forced a cool smile to her lips.

'I am Joanna Bennett,' she said calmly. 'And I can understand that you might be a bit surprised, but——'

'Where is Sam Bennett's son?'

'I'm his son.' Joanna shook her head. 'I mean, he has no son, Mr Hassan. I am——'

'You are his daughter?'

'Yes.'

'You are Joe Bennett?'

'Joanna Bennett. That's right. And——'

He swung towards the head waiter. 'Bring me the bill,' he snapped. 'For my apéritif, and for whatever the restaurant will lose on this table for the evening.' He snatched a liqueur glass from the table, drained its contents, slammed it down, and made a mocking bow to Joanna. 'Goodnight, Miss Bennett.'

Open-mouthed, she stared after him as he strode towards the beaded curtain, still swaying delicately from the waiter's exit, and then, at the last second, she stepped out and blocked his path.

'Just a minute, Mr Hassan!'

'Step aside, please.'

It was the 'please' that was the final straw. The word was not offered politely, but was, instead, tossed negligently at the floor, as one might toss a bone to a dog. Joanna drew herself up.

'And what will you tell Prince Khalil, Mr Hassan?' Joanna slapped her hands on her hips. 'That because you were narrow-minded, old-fashioned, petty and stupid——'

The dark blue eyes narrowed. 'I advise you to watch your tongue.'

'And I advise you to use your head,' Joanna said sharply. 'Prince Khalil sent you here to meet with me.'

'I came here to meet with Sam Bennett's son.'

'You came to meet with his emissary, and that is precisely what I am!'

A muscle knotted in his cheek. 'Whose idea was this subterfuge? Ellington's? Or was it your father's?'

'There was no subterfuge meant, Mr Hassan.'

His smile was swift and chill. 'What term would you prefer? Deception? Trickery? Perhaps "fraud" has a finer ring.'

'At the worst, it's just a misunderstanding.'

He rocked back on his heels and folded his arms over his chest. 'Please, Miss Bennett, don't insult me with games of semantics.'

'I'm simply trying to explain why——'

'What sort of misunderstanding could possibly have led to your thinking I would even consider discussing your father's greedy plans for my country with you?'

His disdain, his contemptuous words, were like a bucket of iced water. Joanna met his harsh gaze with unflinching directness.

'Wrong on all counts, Mr Hassan. For starters, I did not wish to discuss anything with you. It was Prince Khalil I wished to meet this evening, remember? As for greed—it is not my father who's standing in the way of progress and betterment for the people of Jandara, it's your high and mighty ruler.'

Hassan's brows lifted. 'An interesting description of the Prince, Miss Bennett. Clearly, your father didn't send you on this errand because of your subtlety.'

Joanna knew he was right. Her words had been thoughtlessly spoken but to back down now would be a mistake.

'He sent me because I have his trust and confidence,' she said. 'And if my honesty offends you, I can only tell you that I see little value in not being as direct as possible.'

An unpleasant smile curled across his mouth. 'How readily you use the word "honesty"—and yet here you stand, having lied your way into my presence.'

'I did no such thing! I am who I said I was, Jo Bennett, the vice-president at Bennettco.'

'And we both know that if you had identified yourself properly, this meeting would not have taken place.'

'Exactly.' Joanna smiled thinly. 'I'm glad you admit it so readily. You and the Prince would have turned your noses up at the very idea of discussing business with a woman.'

'Typical Western nonsense,' he sneered. 'A woman, taking a man's name, trying to pretend she can do a man's job.'

'I haven't taken anything,' Joanna said coldly. '"Jo" is short for Joanna. As for a woman trying to pretend she can do a man's job—I don't know how to break this to you, but women don't have to "pretend" such things any more, Mr Hassan. In my country——'

'Your country is not mine,' he said, his tone rife with contempt.

'It certainly isn't. In *my* country——'

'In Jandara, those who lie do not break bread with each other.'

Joanna glared at him. 'It isn't my fault you assumed Jo Bennett was a man.'

'I don't recall you attempting to correct that assumption, Miss Bennett.'

Anger overcame her. 'If I didn't,' she said, stepping forward until they were only inches apart, 'it was because I knew your boss would react exactly the way you are at the prospect of a woman representing Bennettco. No wonder my father's gotten nowhere all these weeks! Trying to deal with a—tyrant is like—like...'

The rush of words stopped, but it was too late. He smiled slyly as she fell silent.

'Please, Miss Bennett, don't stop now. You've called Prince Khalil a tyrant, a chauvinist—I can hardly wait to hear what else you think of him.'

What was she doing? She'd come here to further her cause, to succeed in a tricky endeavour and convince Sam that she was capable of carrying her weight at Bennettco, and instead she was alienating the Hawk of the North's right-hand man with terrifying rapidity. She took a deep breath, let it out, and pasted a smile to her lips.

'Perhaps—perhaps I got carried away.'

The Prince's emissary smiled tightly. 'You may not be given to subtlety but you surely are given to understatement. Referring to m—to the Prince as a dictator is hardly——'

'I never called him that!'

His brows lifted. 'But you think it.'

'Certainly not,' she said, lying through her teeth. Of course she thought it. If this—this overbearing, arrogant, insolent pig of a man was the Prince's minister, she could only imagine what the Prince himself must be like. 'Besides, my opinion of your Prince is no more important than your opinion of me. You and I have lost sight of the facts, Mr Hassan. We are representatives, I of my father, you of Khalil. I doubt if either of them would be pleased if we reported back that we'd cancelled this meeting because we'd gotten off to a bad start.'

Her smile did nothing to erase the scowl from his face. 'Perhaps we'll simply tell them the truth, that we cancelled it because I resent having been made a fool of.'

He had a point. Much as she hated to admit it, she had twisted the facts to suit her own needs. She'd lied to him, lied to her father. And if Sam found out...

'Well?' She blinked. He was staring at her, his expression as unyielding as stone, his eyes cold. 'What do you say to that, Miss Bennett?'

'I say... I say...' Joanna swallowed hard. Go for broke, she thought, took a deep breath, and did. 'I say,' she said, her eyes meeting his, 'that you have every right to be annoyed.'

His scowl deepened. 'The start of another bit of trickery?'

Colour flared in Joanna's face but she pressed on. 'I admit I may have stretched the facts, but I haven't lied. I do represent my father. I have his every confidence and I'm fully authorised to act on his behalf. I know you have a problem dealing with me, but——'

But, he thought impatiently, his eyes on her face, but! She was good at suggesting alternatives, this Joanna Bennett. She had insulted him, apologised to him, and now she was doing her best to convince him her father had Jandara's best interests at heart—but for what reason? Why had Sam Bennett sent her? She kept insisting she was Bennettco's representative, but what man would be fool enough to believe that?

His gaze moved over her slowly, with an insolence born of command. She kept talking, although her skin took on a rosy flush, and that amused him. Why would a woman like this colour under his gaze? Surely she was not innocent? She was a beauty, though, perhaps more beautiful than any woman he'd ever seen. What she couldn't know was that her beauty meant nothing to him. Despite what Joanna Bennett thought she knew of him— or of the man she believed him to be—he had long ago wearied of beautiful faces and bodies that hid empty souls. He preferred his women with strength and character, individuals in their own right, not the pampered lapdogs Western women so often were.

The logical thing to do was to tell her that she and her father had wasted their time, that he was not Hassan but Prince Khalil, that he was not interested in whatever game it was they were playing.

But if he did that, he would not learn what game it was. And that, surely, was vital.

'I still fail to see why your father sent you to this meeting, Miss Bennett,' he said sharply, 'unless he thought you could succeed where others had failed simply through the element of surprise.'

'If it makes you feel any better,' Joanna blurted, 'I'm as surprised as you are. I thought you'd be—I thought...'

'Yes?' His eyes narrowed. 'What did you think?'

Joanna stared at him. That you'd be a million years old, she thought, that you'd be a wizened old man... His voice. His voice had sounded old on the telephone. Hadn't it? Maybe not. She could remember little of their conversation except how desperate she'd been to make him commit to this meeting—this meeting that she was on the verge of ruining, unless she used her head.

'I thought,' she said carefully, 'we'd be able to sit down and discuss our differences face to face.'

He smiled tightly. 'But not man to man.'

'The bottom line,' Joanna said, ignoring the taunt, 'is that we—that is, Prince Khalil and Bennettco—*do* have differences.'

'Yes. We do, indeed.' His voice hardened. 'Bennettco thinks it can ignore Khalil and deal only with Abu——'

'Abu Al Zouad is the King of Jandara,' Joanna said with an icy smile, 'or has your Prince forgotten that little item?'

'He is not the King, he is the Sultan,' Khalil said sharply, 'and surely not Khalil's.'

'Abu is the recognised leader of your country, and he has guaranteed Bennettco the right to mine in the northern mountains.'

Khalil's smile was wily. 'If that is the case, why has your father sent you to meet with me?'

'To talk about what is best for Khalil's people.'

He laughed, this time with such disdain that it made Joanna's spine stiffen.

'You spout nonsense, Miss Bennett. That is hardly the issue we're here to discuss.'

At least the man was blunt, Joanna thought grimly. 'Very well, then,' she said. 'My father's sent me to talk about what will most benefit Bennettco—and what will most benefit your Prince, which is why your unwillingness to listen to what I have to say surprises me, Mr Hassan. This meeting is in Khalil's best interests, but——'

'Sir?' They both spun towards the curtained doorway. The head waiter was standing just inside it, smiling nervously. 'The bill, sir.'

Khalil looked at the silver tray in the man's hand, then at Joanna. She was right. It would be foolish of him not to find out what tricks her father had up his sleeve, even if it meant enduring her company.

'Very well,' he said. 'I will give you an hour, and not a moment more.'

Joanna nodded. She was afraid to breathe or even to answer for fear this impossible man would change his mind again and walk out.

Khalil nodded, too, as if they had made a pact, then looked towards the waiter.

'Bring us the meal I ordered,' he said with a dismissive wave of his hand.

'Certainly, sir.'

'Be seated, Miss Bennett.'

Be seated, Joanna thought as she slid into the padded banquette, just like that. No 'please', no attempt at courtesy at all. It was ludicrous. He'd already ordered dinner, even though she'd reserved the table. The man was impossible, arrogant and imperious and——

'So.' She looked up. He had slid into the booth opposite her and he was watching her intently, his eyes unreadable as they met hers. He sat back, his broad shoulders straining just a bit at the jacket of his suit, and a faint smile touched his mouth. 'Why don't you start our meeting by telling me about the Bennettco project?'

She did, even though she was certain he knew all the details. It would only help her make her case at the end, when it became time to ask him for assurance that he'd not try and hinder the project. She talked through the lemon soup, through the couscous, through the chicken baked with saffron, and finally he held up his hand.

'Very interesting—but you still haven't told me why I should permit—why my Prince should permit Bennettco to mine in the mountains?'

'Well, first of all, the operation will bring money into Jandara. It will—it will . . .' Joanna frowned. 'Permit, Mr Hassan? I don't think that's quite the correct word, do you?'

'English is not my first language, Miss Bennett, but I learned it at quite an early age. "Permit" was the word I intended.'

'But the decision's not Khalil's. It's Abu's.'

'Is it?' He smiled lazily. 'If that were completely true, you wouldn't be here.' He smiled lazily. 'You're concerned that Khalil will interfere with the project, isn't that right?'

What was the sense in denying it? Joanna shrugged her shoulders.

'We think he might try, yes.'

'And have you stopped to consider why he might do that?'

'Perhaps he hasn't given enough thought to how much this project will benefit his people.'

The arrogance of the woman! Khalil forced his smile not to waver.

'He is selfish, you mean?'

Joanna looked up, caught by the man's tone. He was still smiling, but there was something in that smile that made her wary.

'Well, perhaps he doesn't see it that way,' she said cautiously, 'but——'

'But you do, and that's what matters.'

'You're twisting my words, Mr Hassan.'

'On the contrary. I'm doing my best to get to the heart of your concerns. What else am I to tell him, apart from a warning about his selfishness?'

Joanna stared at him. Was he asking her to be more direct about the bribe money? It galled her to make such an offer but reason seemed to be failing. Sam had warned her that this was the way things were done in this part of the world, but——

'Don't lose courage now,' he said coldly. 'Be blunt, Miss Bennett. It's why you came here, remember?'

'Tell him—tell him we won't tolerate any harassment of our workers.'

'I see. You worry he might have them beaten. Or shot.'

There was a lack of emotion in his words, as if having men hurt were an everyday occurrence.

'We are not "worried" about anything, Mr Hassan,' she lied, her tone as flat as his. 'This project will go ahead, no matter what your Prince does. We simply want to encourage Khalil's co-operation.'

His nostrils dilated. He yearned to take the woman's slender shoulders in his hands and shake some sense into her.

'Really?' he said, and if Joanna had not been so caught up in her own determination to succeed, if she had not already decided that the only thing that would close the deal was the enormous bribe Sam had suggested, she'd have heard the note of warning in that single word. 'And how are you going to do that, Miss Bennett?'

Joanna gave him a look laced with contempt, then unclasped her evening bag and took out the envelope her father had given her.

'With this,' she said bluntly, and slid the envelope across the table towards him.

He bent his head and looked at it. His anger made the words on the paper a meaningless blur but then, what this female Judas was offering didn't matter. She had accused him of being obstinate, selfish and despotic, and now she had sought to buy him off as if he were a common thief.

'Well?' Her voice was impatient. 'Is it enough?'

Khalil silently counted to ten, first in Arabic, then in English, and then he took the envelope and stuffed it into his pocket.

'Oh, yes,' he said, the words almost a purr, 'it is enough. It is more than enough.'

She'd done it! She'd won the co-operation of the infamous Prince Khalil—well, Bennettco's bribe had won it, which stole away most of the pleasure. Concentrate on the victory, she told herself, on what this will mean to your future...

He rose to his feet. 'Come, Miss Bennett,' he said softly.

Joanna looked up. He was holding out his hand and smiling. Or was he? His lips were drawn upwards, but would you really call what she saw on his handsome face a smile?

'Come?' she said, smiling back hesitantly. 'Come where?'

'We must celebrate our agreement with champagne. But not here. This place is for tourists. I will take you somewhere much more authentic, Joanna.'

Joanna? Joanna's heart thudded. Don't go with him, she thought suddenly, don't go.

'Joanna?'

That was ridiculous. She had done it, she had closed the deal her father thought couldn't be closed. What on earth could there possibly be to fear?

Smiling, she got to her feet and gave him her hand.

He led her through the restaurant, pausing only long enough to say something to their waiter, who bowed respectfully all the way to the front door. Outside, the night seemed to have grown darker. He was holding her elbow now, his grip firm, as he led her towards a low-slung sports car at the kerb.

Suddenly, Joanna thought of something.

'Did you say we were going to have champagne?'

He nodded as he handed her into the car, came around to the driver's side, then slipped in beside her.

'Of course. It's a celebration. Why do you sound surprised?'

Joanna frowned slightly. 'Well, I'm just—I guess I *am* surprised. I didn't think your people drank wine.'

He smiled. 'Believe me, Joanna,' he said, 'you are in for a number of surprises before the evening ends.'

He stepped hard on the accelerator and the car shot into the night.

CHAPTER THREE

EVERYONE Joanna knew had had the same reaction to the news that she was going to Casablanca.

'Oh,' they'd sighed, 'how incredibly romantic!'

Joanna, remembering the wonderful old Humphrey Bogart-Ingrid Bergman movie, had thought so too. But after a week she'd decided that things must have changed a lot since the days of Rick and Ilse. Casablanca was ancient and filled with history, it was beautiful and mysterious, but it was also the economic heart of Morocco which meant that in some ways it was not only prosaic, it was downright dull.

The man beside her, though, was quite another story. She gave him a surreptitious glance from beneath her lashes. There was nothing dull about him. She'd never met a man like him before, which was saying a great deal. The circles in which she travelled had more than their fair share of handsome, interesting men but even in those circles, this man would stand out.

Joanna's gaze flew over him, taking in the stern profile, the broad sweep of his shoulders, the well-groomed hands resting lightly on the steering wheel. He seemed so urbane, this Mr Hassan, so at home in his well-tailored suit, his pricey car, and yet she could easily imagine him in a very different setting.

Her lashes drooped a little. Yes, she thought, she could see him in her mind's eye, dressed in long, flowing robes, mounted on a prancing black stallion, racing the wind across the desert under a full moon.

'You're so quiet, Miss Bennett.'

Joanna's eyes flew open. They had stopped at a light and he was looking at her, a little smile on his lips. For some reason, the thought that he'd been watching her without her knowing made her uncomfortable. She sat up straighter, smoothed her hair back from her face, and gave him a polite smile in return.

'I was just enjoying our drive,' she said.

She glanced out of the window as the car started forward. They were passing the Place des Nations Unies, deserted at this hour except for a solitary pair of strollers, a man and woman dressed in traditional garb, she walking barely noticeable inches behind. Like a respectful servant, Joanna thought with a grimace, or a well-trained dog...

'She is not being obedient, Miss Bennett,' the man beside her said, 'she's simply gawking at the sights.'

Joanna swung towards him. He was looking straight ahead, intent on the road.

'I beg your pardon?'

'That couple.' He glanced at her, an insolent smile curled across his mouth. 'You were thinking the wife was following her husband out of custom, but I assure you, she wasn't.'

He was right, but what did that matter? Joanna gave him a frigid look.

'Do you make a habit of reading people's thoughts, Mr Hassan?'

'It isn't difficult to read yours. You seem convinced we classify our women as property in this part of the world.'

She smiled tightly. 'Your definition, not mine.'

He laughed. 'A diplomatic response, Joanna—but then, your father would not have sent you on such a delicate mission if he hadn't been certain of your ability to handle yourself well.'

Some of the tension flowed from Joanna's posture. He was right. This *had* been a delicate mission, and she'd carried it off successfully. Let the Hassans and Khalils of this world have their *baksheesh* and bribes. What did it matter to her? She'd set out to snatch success from the jaws of defeat and she'd done it, despite the arrogant high-handedness of the man next to her.

'You're quite right,' she said pleasantly, folding her hands neatly in her lap and watching as the dimly lit streets spun by, 'he wouldn't have.'

'He has no sons?'

'No.' Her smile grew saccharine sweet. 'I know you must think that makes him quite unfortunate, but——'

'I suspect it simply makes him all the fonder of you.' He glanced at her, then looked back to the road. 'You must be very important to Sam Bennett, not only as vice-president of Bennettco but as the jewel of his heart.'

Joanna looked at him. She was neither, she thought with a little pang, not the vice-president of Bennettco nor even the jewel of her father's heart. It was Bennettco itself that was his love, it always had been, but now that she'd pulled this off...

'Am I right, Joanna?'

She swallowed. 'Yes,' she said quickly, 'I'm as important to him as you are to Prince Khalil.'

His head swung towards her. 'As I...?'

'I mean, you must be very important to Khalil, for him to entrust you with negotiating such important matters.'

'Ah.' He smiled. 'Of course. You are wondering if my word is Khalil's bond.'

'No. I wasn't. It never occurred to me to doubt——'

'I promise you, he will abide by my judgement.' He looked towards her, and suddenly his smile fled. 'I will not repudiate anything I do this night.'

Joanna's brows rose a bit. 'I'm sure you won't,' she said politely.

The man wasn't just arrogant, he was contemptuous as well. '*I will not repudiate anything I do this night*'! It was almost laughable. How could he say that when he was only the Prince's minister?

Khalil would be even worse, Joanna thought with a sigh, rigid and imperious and completely egotistical. It was probably a good thing he hadn't agreed to meet with her. As it was, she'd had difficulty holding her temper with Hassan. Heaven only knew how she'd have been able to deal with someone even ruder.

But she didn't have to worry about that any more, she thought, permitting herself a little smile. She'd done the impossible, pulled the coup that would set her firmly on a path she'd always wanted, and if she'd have been happier managing it without pushing a bribe under Hassan's nose, well, so what? If that was how things were done here, who was she to ask questions? She had succeeded, and now she and Hassan were going to drink a toast to their agreement.

Joanna settled back in her seat. Where was he taking her, anyway? Somewhere far from the streets she knew, that was obvious. In fact, they'd left the streets behind completely. The car was racing along a straight, narrow road that disappeared into the night.

Perhaps he was taking her to some place less Western than the restaurant where they'd dined. Perhaps, for all his seeming urbanity, he'd been uncomfortable in its sophisticated setting.

'You've become quiet again, Joanna.' Hassan stepped down harder on the accelerator and the car seemed to leap forward. 'Have you nothing to say, now that you've got what you wanted from me?'

His tone was nonchalant but Joanna sensed the underlying derision in his words. She shifted into the corner of her seat and smiled politely.

'I think we've each gotten something from the other,' she said.

'Of course. You have my promise of co-operation and I——' He looked at her, his teeth showing in a swift smile. 'I have the bribe you offered me for it.'

It was what she had just been thinking but hearing it from the man on the receiving end made it different. Surely people who demanded you buy them off didn't go around admitting it, did they? And, just as surely, they didn't make it sound as if *you* were the one who'd done something vile—yet that was what his tone had clearly suggested.

Joanna caught her bottom lip between her teeth. Was he still smarting over the clumsy way she'd handled the bribe offer? She knew she hadn't done it with any subtlety, that she'd come within a breath of insulting him, something that was not done anywhere but especially not in this part of the world.

'Everyone benefits,' he said softly. 'Khalil is bought off, Bennettco turns a handsome profit—and Abu Al Zouad grows fatter.' He looked at her, his eyes unreadable in the darkness. 'All in all, a fine arrangement, yes?'

Joanna shifted uneasily. 'Look,' she said, 'I don't know what it is between your Prince and the Sultan, but——'

'Everyone benefits,' he said again, his tone hardening. 'Everyone—except my people.'

As if he or his mighty Prince really gave a damn, she thought angrily. But she bit back the words and offered ones that were only slightly more diplomatic instead.

'It's too late to have second thoughts, Mr Hassan. You gave me your word——'

'If you intend to speak to me of honour,' he said coldly, 'you are wasting your time.'

Their eyes met and held. All at once, Joanna wished she were anywhere but here, in this fast car tearing through the darkness to some unknown destination.

'I was only going to point out that we agreed on——'

'What would you have done if I'd turned down your bribe money?'

'Listen, Mr Hassan, if you've a problem with Prince Khalil's accepting money...' Joanna clamped her lips together. What was needed here was a touch of diplomacy, not anger. 'I wasn't suggesting that you were—that you should...' She shook her head. 'It's not my place to make judgements, but——'

'Of course it is. You and your estimable father both make judgements. You judged Abu Al Zouad worthy of Bennettco's largesse, you judged Prince Khalil a man to be easily bought off——'

'Easily?' His supercilious tone made Joanna bristle and she spoke sharply, before she could stop herself. 'Who are you kidding? I know how much is waiting for him in that Swiss bank account, remember?' Her eyes narrowed. 'Wait a minute. Is that what this is all about? Are you going to try and hold us up for more?'

'And what if I did? You'd pay it. You'd pay whatever you must to get what you want.' He shot her a look so deadly she pressed back in her seat. 'That's how people like you do things. Don't waste your breath denying it!'

Joanna stared at him. What was happening here? A little while ago, he'd been all silken cordiality, and now he was treating her with an abrasive scorn that bordered on insult. He was scaring her, too, although she'd be

damned if she'd ever let him know it. Well, not scaring
her, exactly, that was too strong a word, but it was hard
not to wish they were still seated in the civilised environs
of the Oasis Restaurant.

Was that why he'd dragged her to the middle of nowhere—so he could insult her? That was certainly how
it seemed. Even if he hadn't, even if he'd been deadly
serious about taking her somewhere for a glass of champagne, she had absolutely no interest in it now. All she
wanted was for him to turn the car around and take her
back to the city, to lights and traffic and people.

'I've changed my mind about having champagne,' she
said, swinging towards him. She waited for him to answer
but he didn't. After a moment, she cleared her throat.
'Mr Hassan?'

'I heard you. You've changed your mind about
drinking with me.'

'No, I mean, it's not that. I just—I—um—I mis-
judged the time earlier.' Damn! Why was she offering
an explanation? 'Please turn the car around.'

'I can't do that.'

Can't? *Can't*? Joanna stared at him. 'Why not?'

'We are expected,' he said.

'You mean, you made a reservation? Well, I can't
help——'

He swung to face her suddenly, and even in the
shadowy interior of the car, she could see the sharp anger
etched into his face.

'The sound of your voice annoys me,' he said coldly.
'Sit back, and be silent!'

Her mouth dropped open. 'What?' she said. '*What*?'
She stared at him, waiting for him to say something, to
apologise or offer some sort of explanation, but he
didn't. 'That's it,' she snapped. 'Dammit, Mr Hassan,
that's the final straw!'

'I don't like women to use vulgarities.'

'And I don't like men to behave like bullies! I'm telling you for the last time, turn this car around and take me back to Casablanca!'

He laughed in a way that made her heart leap into her throat.

'Is that a threat, Miss Bennett?'

'My father will be expecting me. If I'm not at the hotel soon——'

'How charming. Does he always wait up for your return at night?'

Her eyes flew to his face. What was that she heard in his voice? Disdain? Or was it something more?

'He'll be waiting to hear how our evening went,' she said quickly. 'And unless you want me to tell him that you——'

'Why would he do that?' He gave her a quick, terrible smile. 'Was there ever any doubt of your success?'

'Of course. There's always a chance of a slip-up when——'

'How could there have been a slip-up, once he put you in charge of dealing with the bandit Khalil?' The awful smile came again, clicking on, then off, like a light bulb. 'Surely he expected you'd get the agreement for him, one way or another.'

Joanna clasped her hands together in her lap. Something was happening here, something that was beyond her understanding. All she knew was that she didn't like it.

'If you're suggesting my father doesn't have every confidence in me,' she began, but the man beside her cut her short.

'Confidence?' The sound of his laughter was sharp. 'In what? You're no more a vice-president at Bennettco than that woman we passed in the street a while ago.'

'Of course I am!'

'What you are,' he snapped, 'is an empty-headed creature who knows nothing more important than the latest gossip!'

Colour rushed into Joanna's cheeks. 'How dare you?'

'What is the name of your secretary at Bennettco?'

'I don't have to answer your questions!'

'Do you even *have* an office there?' he demanded.

She swallowed. 'Not yet,' she said finally, 'but——'

'You are nothing,' he snarled, 'nothing! Your father insults me by sending you to me.'

'You've got this all wrong,' Joanna said quickly. 'I *am* his confidante. And his vice-president—well, I will be, when——'

'What you are,' he said grimly, 'is a Jezebel.'

She stared at him, her mouth hanging open. 'What?'

'I knew Bennett was desperate to hold on to his contract with that pig, Abu Al Zouad.' His eyes shot to her face. 'But even I never dreamed he'd offer up his daughter to get it!'

'Are you crazy? I told you, my father is ill. That's why he sent me to meet with you!'

'He sent you to do whatever had to be done to ensure success.' He threw her a look of such fury that Joanna felt herself blanch. 'If Khalil wouldn't accept one sort of bribe, surely he'd accept another.'

She felt the blood drain from her face. 'Are you saying my father... are you saying you think that I...?' She sprang towards him across the console and slammed her fist into his shoulder. 'You—you contemptible son of a bitch! I'd sooner sleep with a—a camel than——'

She cried out as the car swerved. The tyres squealed as they clawed at the verge; the brakes protested as he jammed them on, and then he swung towards her, his eyes filled with loathing.

'But it *would* be like sleeping with a camel, wouldn't it, Miss Bennett? Sleeping with a man like Khalil, I mean.'

'If you touch me,' Joanna said, trying to keep her voice from shaking, 'if you so much as put a finger on me, so help me, I'll——'

'You'll what?' His lips drew back from his teeth. 'Scream? Go right ahead, then. Scream. Scream until you can't scream any more. Who do you think will hear you?'

God. Oh, God! He was right. She looked around her wildly. There was darkness everywhere—everywhere except for his face, looming over hers, his eyes glinting with anger, his mouth hard and narrowed with scorn.

'My father,' she said hoarsely. 'My father will——'

'The scorpion of the desert is a greater worry to me than is your father.'

'Surely we can behave like civilised human beings and——?'

He laughed in her face. 'How can we, when I am the emissary of a savage?'

'I never said that!'

'No. You never did. But you surely thought it. What else would a greedy, tyrannical bandit be if not a savage?' His mouth thinned. 'But I ask you, who is the savage, Miss Bennett, the Hawk of the North—or a father who would offer his daughter to get what he wants?'

He caught her wrist as her hand flew towards his face. 'I've had enough, you—you self-centred son of a bitch! My father would no more——'

His face twisted. 'Perhaps I should have let it happen.' He leaned towards her, forcing her back in her seat. 'Maybe it wasn't your father who suggested you make this great sacrifice. Maybe it was *you* who wanted to share Khalil's bed—or did you think it would be sufficient to share mine?'

'I'd sooner die,' Joanna said, her voice rising unsteadily while she struggled uselessly to shove him off her. 'I swear, I'd sooner——'

His lips drew back from his teeth in a humourless smile. 'Just think what erotic delights a savage like me might have taught you. Enough, perhaps, to keep your useless New York friends tittering for an entire season!'

'You're disgusting! You—you make me sick to my stomach!'

His mouth dropped to hers like a stone, crushing the words on her lips. She struggled wildly, beating her free hand against his shoulder, trying to twist her face from his, but it was useless. He was all hard sinew and taut muscle that nothing would deter.

After a moment, he drew back.

'What's the matter?' he said coldly. 'Have you changed your mind about adding a little sweetening to Bennettco's bribe offer?'

Hatred darkened Joanna's eyes. 'What a fool I was to think I could deal with you in a civilised manner! You're just like your Prince, aren't you? When you can't get what you want, you just—you reach out and grab it!'

'What if I said you were wrong, Miss Bennett? What if I told you that I am not a man who takes?'

Anger made her reckless. 'I'd call you a liar,' she snapped.

To her surprise, he laughed. 'Which of us is the liar, Joanna? Or are you suggesting I not take what you are prepared to give?'

The look she gave him was pure defiance. 'I offered you nothing.'

For a long moment, their eyes held. Then he smiled, and the smile sent her heart into her throat.

'I never take that which has not been offered,' he said, very softly.

She cried out as he reached for her again but there was no way to escape him. He caught her face between his hands, holding it immobile, and bent his head to hers. She stiffened, holding her breath, preparing instinctively for the fury of his kiss, for whatever ugly show of strength and power lay ahead.

But there was no way to prepare for the reality of what happened. His lips were soft, moving against hers with slow persuasion, seeking response.

Not that it mattered. It was a useless effort. She would never, could never, respond to a man like him, a man who believed he could first terrorise a woman, then seduce her. His hands spread over her cheeks, his thumbs gliding slowly across the high arc of her cheekbones. His fingers threaded into her hair, slowly angling her head back so that his lips could descend upon hers again— and all at once, to Joanna's horror, something dark and primitive stirred deep within her soul, an excitement that made her pulse leap.

No. No, she didn't want this! But her body was quickening, her mouth was softening beneath his. Was it the way he was holding her, so that she was arched towards him, as if in supplication? Was it the heat of his body against hers?

The tip of his tongue skimmed across her mouth. She made a sound, a little moan that was barely perceptible, but he heard it. He whispered something incomprehensible against her mouth and his arms went around her and drew her close, so that her breasts were pressed against his chest.

Joanna felt the sudden erratic gallop of her heart as his mouth opened over hers. His tongue slipped between her lips, stroking against the tender flesh. Heat rose like a flame under her skin as he cupped her breast in his hand. She shuddered in his arms as his thumb moved against the hardening nipple.

'Yes,' he whispered, 'yes...'

How could this be happening? She hated him, for what he was and for the man he served—and yet, her hands were sliding up his chest, her palms were measuring the swift, sure beat of his heart as it leapt beneath her fingertips. Her head fell back; he kissed her throat and she made another soft sound that might have been surrender or despair...

He let her go with such abruptness that she fell back against the seat. Her eyes flew open; her gaze met his and they stared at each other. For an instant they seemed suspended in time, and then two circles of crimson rose in Joanna's cheeks.

Khalil smiled tightly. 'You see?' he said, almost lazily. He reached for the key and the engine roared to life. 'I never take what is not offered.'

Humiliation rose in her throat like bile. 'I get the message,' she said, fighting to keep her voice from shaking. 'I'm female, you're male, and I shouldn't have said anything to insult you or the mighty Khalil.'

'I'm happy to see you're not stupid.'

'Slow, maybe, but never stupid. Now, take me back to——'

'We are not returning to Casablanca, Joanna.'

She stared at him in disbelief. 'You can't possible think I'd still go anywhere with you after...'

Her heart rose into her throat. He *was* turning the car, but not back the way they'd come. Instead, they were jouncing across hard-packed dirt towards a long, looming shadow ahead.

'What is that?' she demanded, but the question was redundant, for in the headlights of the car she could now see what stood ahead of them.

It was a plane. A small, twin-engine plane, the same kind, she thought dizzily, as Bennettco owned. But this was not a Bennettco plane, not with that spread-winged, rapier-beaked bird painted on its fuselage.

Instinct made her cry out and swing towards him. She grabbed for the steering wheel but he caught her wrists easily with one hand and wrenched them down.

'Stop it,' he said, his voice taut with command.

The car slid to a stop. He yanked out the keys and threw the door open. Several robed figures approached, then dropped to their knees in the sand as Khalil stepped from the automobile.

'Is the plane ready for departure?' he demanded in English.

'It has been ready since we received your message, my lord,' one of the men answered without lifting his head.

Khalil hauled Joanna out after him. 'Come,' he said.

She didn't. She screamed instead, and he lifted her into his arms and strode towards the plane while her cries rose into the night with nothing but the wind to answer them. Khalil paused at the door and shoved her through. Then he climbed inside and pushed her unceremoniously into a seat.

'Let's go,' he snapped at the men scrambling up after him. 'Quickly!'

The little coterie bowed again, touching their hands to their foreheads. It was a gesture of homage that would, even moments before, have made Joanna laugh with scorn. Now, it made her dizzy with fear.

Suddenly, she understood.

'You're not the Prince's emissary,' she said, swinging towards him, 'you're—you're Khalil!'

He laughed. 'As I said, Joanna, you aren't a stupid woman.'

She leaped to her feet and spun towards his men. 'Do you understand what he's doing? He's kidnapping me! He'll lose his head for this. You'll all lose——' The plane's engines coughed to life and began to whine. Joanna turned back to Khalil. 'What do you want?' she pleaded. 'More money? You've only to ask my father. He'll give you whatever——' The plane began moving forward into the dark night and her voice rose in panic. 'Listen to me! Just take me back. No. You don't have to take me back. I can drive myself. Just give me the keys to the car and——'

Khalil's look silenced her.

'We've a three-hour flight ahead of us. I suggest you get some rest before we reach the northern hills.'

'You'll never get away with this! You can't just——'

Khalil put his hands on his hips and looked at her. His eyes were cold, empty of feeling. With a sinking heart, she thought what a fool she'd been not to have guessed his identity from the start.

'It is done,' he said. 'What will be, will be.'

Joanna stared at him, at that unyielding, harsh face, and then she turned away and looked blindly out of the porthole while the plane raced down the sand and rose into the night sky.

He was right. It was done. Now, she could only pray for deliverance.

CHAPTER FOUR

NOTHING made sense. Joanna sat stiffly in her seat, alone with her thoughts in the darkness of the plane, trying to come up with answers to questions that seemed as complex as the riddle of the Sphinx.

Why had Khalil played out the charade of letting her think he was someone else? He could have announced his identity when he'd discovered she was Joanna, not Joe.

Where was he taking her? This wasn't any quick trip around the block. She glanced at the luminescent face of her watch. They'd been in the air more than an hour now, and she'd yet to feel the tell-tale change in engine pitch and angle of flight that would mean they were readying to land. A little shudder went through her. No, she thought again, this wasn't a short hop by any means. Wherever Khalil was taking her, it was some distance from Casablanca.

And then there was the most devastating question of all, the one her frazzled brain kept avoiding.

Why had he taken her captive?

She had tiptoed around the issue half a dozen times at least, edging up to it as a doe might a clearing in the woods, getting just so close, then skittering off. She knew she had to deal with the question, and soon, for this flight could not last forever and Joanna knew herself well. Whatever lay ahead would only be the more terrifying if she weren't prepared for it mentally.

The plane bounced gently in an air pocket and she used the moment to try and see beyond the curtain that separated the tiny lounge area in which she was seated from the rest of the cabin. Khalil had gone to the front shortly after take-off, leaving her alone with a robed thug who sat in total silence. Did he speak English? She thought he must, but what was the difference? He was a brigand, the same as his chieftain, left to guard his prisoner. Where Khalil thought she might escape to was anybody's guess.

She closed her eyes. It was too late for that, too late for anything except standing up to whatever fate awaited her and showing this—this cut-throat marauder that Sam Bennett's daughter was no coward.

'Are you cold?'

Her eyes flew open. A man was standing over her, tall and fierce and incredibly masculine in flowing white robes. Joanna's throat constricted. It was Khalil.

'Are you cold, Joanna?'

'Cold?' she said foolishly, while she tried to reconcile the urbane man who'd sat beside her at dinner with this robed renegade.

'You were shivering.' His eyes, as frigid as winter ice, swept over her. 'But then you would be, wearing such a dress.' His tone oozed disdain. 'It hardly covers your body.'

Joanna felt heat flood her face. Her fingers itched with the desire to tug up the bodice of her dress, to try and tug down the emerald silk skirt, but she'd be damned if she'd give him that satisfaction. Instead, she folded her hands in her lap, her fingers laced together to keep them still, and looked straight at him.

'I am certain that Oscar de la Renta would be distressed to learn that you don't approve of his design, Your Highness, but then, the dress wasn't made for the approval of a back-country bandit.'

The insult struck home. She could see it in the swift narrowing of his eyes, but his only obvious reaction was a small, hard smile.

'I'm sure you're right, Joanna. The dress was meant for a finer purpose: to entice a man, to make him forget what he must remember and concentrate only on the female prize wrapped within it.'

Joanna smiled, too, very coldly.

'I am dressed for dinner at the Oasis. Had you told me we were going on a journey, I'd have worn something more suitable for travel.'

His smile broadened. 'Had I told you that, I somehow doubt you'd have come with me.'

It was impossible to carry off her end of the dialogue this time. He had struck too close to home, and she shuddered at the realisation.

'You *are* cold,' he said sharply. 'It is foolish to sit here and tremble when you have only to ask for a lap robe.'

It was hard to know whether to laugh or cry. A lap robe? Did he really think this was a flight on Royal Air Marroc to New York? Did he think she was wondering what would be served for dinner?

'Ahmed!' Khalil snapped his fingers and the man seated across the aisle sprang to his feet. There was a flurry of swift, incomprehensible words and then the man bowed and scurried off. 'Ahmed will find you a blanket, Joanna. If you wish anything else...'

'The only thing I want is my freedom.'

'If you wish anything else,' he said, as if she hadn't spoken, 'coffee, or perhaps tea——'

'Are you deaf or just a bastard? I said——'

She gasped as he bent and clasped her shoulders so tightly that she could feel the imprint of his fingers, the heat of his body.

'Watch your tongue! I have had enough of your mouth tonight.'

'Let go of me!'

'Perhaps you don't realise the seriousness of your situation, Joanna. Perhaps you think this is a game, that I have instructed my pilot to fly us in circles and then land at Nouasseur Airport before I return you to your hotel.'

It wasn't easy to look back at him without flinching, to force herself to meet that unyielding rock-like stare, but she did.

'What I think,' she said tightly, 'is that you've made one hell of a mistake, Khalil, and that there's still time to get out of it with your head still attached to your neck.'

He looked at her for what seemed a long time, in a silence filled only with the steady drone of the plane's engines, and then he smiled.

'How thoughtful, Joanna. Your concern for my welfare is touching.' He straightened and looked down at her. 'But you may be right. Perhaps I *have* made a mistake.'

A tiny flame of hope burst to life in her heart. 'If you take me back now,' she said quickly, 'I'll forget this ever happened.'

'Perhaps I should have accepted what you so graciously offered before I stole you.'

Joanna flew from her seat. 'How dare you say such things to me?'

'Highness?'

Khalil put his hand on her shoulders and propelled her back into her seat. He turned to Ahmed, who held a light blanket in his outstretched arms.

'Thank you, Ahmed. You may leave now.' Khalil dropped the blanket into Joanna's lap as Ahmed disappeared behind the curtain. 'Your temper should be enough to keep you warm, but if it isn't, use this.'

'Dammit!' Joanna shoved the blanket to the floor. 'Who in hell do you think you are?'

He bent, picked up the blanket, and dropped it in her lap again.

'I am the man who holds your destiny in his hands,' he said with a quick, chill smile. 'Now, cover yourself, before I do it for you.'

She snatched the blanket from him, draping it over herself so that it swathed her from throat to toe.

'What's the matter?' she said with saccharine sweetness. 'Are you afraid my father won't pay as much ransom if I come down with pneumonia and die?'

His thigh brushed hers as he sat down beside her, the softness of his robe a direct contrast to the muscled warmth of the leg beneath it.

'Such drama, Joanna. You're young and healthy and a long, long way from death.'

'But that is what you're after, isn't it?' The question she'd dreaded asking was out now, and she was glad. Still, it was hard to say the words. 'Ransom money, from my father?'

'Ransom money?' he repeated, his brows knotting together.

'Yes.' She made an impatient gesture. 'I don't know how you say it in your language—it's money paid to a kidnapper to——'

'I speak English as well as you do,' he said sharply. 'I know what the word means.'

'Well, then . . .'

'Is that what you think this is all about? Do you think me so corrupt that the money you offered me at the restaurant isn't enough to buy my co-operation?'

'What else am I to think?'

Khalil sat back, his arms folded over his chest. 'And just how much do you think you're worth?'

Joanna's jaw tightened. 'Don't play with me, Khalil. I don't like it!'

'Ah.' Amusement glinted in his eyes. 'You don't like it.'

'That's right, I don't. It's bad enough that you've kidnapped me——'

'And I don't like your choice of words.'

She stared at him in disbelief. 'What would you prefer me to call it? Shall I say that you've decided to take me on a sightseeing trip?'

His face turned cold and hard. 'What I do, I do because I must.'

Joanna sat forward, the blanket dropping unnoticed to her waist. 'All you had to do was say you wanted more money. My father would surely have been willing to——'

'Money!' His lip curled with disgust. 'You think there is a price for everything, you and your father. Well, this is what I think of your pathetic attempts to buy me!'

He dug the envelope she'd given him from his robe, folded it in half, and ripped it into pieces that floated into her lap like a paper sandstorm. For the first time, she permitted herself to admit that he might have kidnapped her for some darker, more devious reason.

'Then—then if it's not for the money...' She touched the tip of her tongue to her lips. 'I see. You want to hurt my father.'

Khalil's mouth narrowed. 'Is that what I want? It must be, if you say it is. After all, you know everything there is to know about me and my motives.'

'But you won't hurt him,' she said, leaning forward towards him. 'You'll just make him angry. And——'

'I don't give a damn what he is!' Khalil reached out quickly and caught her by the shoulders. 'He can be angry, hurt, he can slash his clothing and weep for all I care!'

'Then why—if you don't want money, if you don't care how my father takes the news of my kidn—of my abduction, what's the point? Why have you done this?'

A quick smile angled across his mouth.

'Ah, Joanna,' he said, very softly, 'I'm disappointed. You seem to know so much about the kind of man I am—surely you must have some idea.'

She stared at him, at those fathomless dark blue eyes. A tremor began deep in her muscles and she tensed her body against it, hating herself not only for her fear but for this show of weakness she must not let him see.

Before she'd left New York, the same people who'd teased her about her chances of running into the ghost of Humphrey Bogart had teased her with breathless rumours of a still-flourishing white slave trade, of harems hidden deep within the uncharted heart of the desert and the mountains that enclosed it.

'And what a prize you'd be,' a man at a charity ball had purred, 'with that pale skin, those green eyes, and all that gorgeous red hair!'

Everyone had laughed, even her—but now it didn't seem funny at all. Now, with Khalil's fingers imprinting themselves in her skin, she knew it was time to finally come face to face with the fear that had haunted her from the moment she'd found herself in this plane.

'My father won't let you get away with this,' she said in a low, taut voice.

'Your father will have no choice.'

'You underestimate him. He's a powerful man, Khalil. He'll find where you've taken me and——'

'He will know where I've taken you, Joanna. It will not be a secret.'

'He'll come after me,' she said, her voice rising, becoming just a little unsteady. 'And when he rescues me, he'll kill you!'

Khalil laughed, a soft, husky sound that made the hair rise on the nape of her neck.

'I am not so easy to kill. Abu Al Zouad will surely tell your father that.'

'How about my government? Do you think you can make a fool of it, too?'

'Your government?' His dark brows drew together. 'What part has it in this?'

She smiled piteously. 'I'm a US citizen. Perhaps, in your country, women are—are like cattle, to be bought and sold and—and disposed of at will, but in my country——'

'I know all about your country, enough to know your government won't give a damn about one headstrong woman who runs off——'

'I didn't run off! You——'

'—who runs off with a man on a romantic adventure.'

'Me, run off with you on a romantic adventure?' She laughed. 'No one would accept that! Anyway, my father will tell them the truth.'

'He'll tell them exactly what I authorise him to tell them,' Khalil said coldly.

'Don't be ridiculous! Why would he lie?'

'This thing is between your father, Abu Al Zouad, and me. No one else will be involved.'

'You're unbelievable,' Joanna said, 'absolutely unbelievable! Do you really imagine you can tell my father what to do? Maybe you should have spent more time in the West, Khalil. Maybe you'd have realised you're only

a man, not a—a tin god whose every insane wish has to
be obeyed!'

'I'm impressed,' he said, with a condescending little
smile, as if she were a pet he'd just found capable of
some clever and unexpected trick. 'Any other woman
would be begging for mercy, but not you.'

Joanna's chin lifted. 'That's right,' she said, determined not to let him see the depths of her fear, 'not me!
So if that's why you abducted me—so you could have
the pleasure of seeing me grovel and weep for mercy—
you're out of luck.'

'I'm sorry to disappoint you, Joanna, but my reasons
were hardly so petty.' He gave her a slow, lazy smile. 'I
took you because I can use you.'

Her eyes flashed to his. 'Use me?' she repeated. 'I
don't—I don't understand...'

His smile changed, took on a darkness that made her
breath catch, and his gaze moved over her lingeringly,
from her wide eyes to her parted lips, and finally to the
swift rise and fall of her breasts.

'Don't you?' he said softly.

'Khalil.' She swallowed, although the effort was almost
painful. 'Khalil, listen to me. You can't—you can't
just——'

'Shall I have you sold at the slave-market?' He took
her face in his hands and tilted it to his. 'You would
bring a king's ransom in the north, where eyes the colour
of jade and hair like the embers of a winter fire are very,
very rare.'

Oh, God, Joanna thought, oh, God...

'You wouldn't do that,' she said quickly. 'Selling me
would be——'

'It would be foolish.' He smiled again, a quick angling
of his lips that was somehow frighteningly intimate. 'For
only a fool would sell you, once he had you.'

'Abducting me is foolish, too!' She spoke quickly, desperately, determined to force him to listen to reason. 'You must know that you can't get away with——'

'What would you be like, I wonder, if I took you to my bed?'

Patches of scarlet flared in her cheeks, fury driving out the fear that had seconds before chilled her blood.

'I'd sooner die than go to your bed!'

He laughed softly. 'I don't think so, Joanna. I think you would come to it smiling.'

'Not in a million years!'

His fingers threaded into her hair; his thumbs stroked over her skin.

'How would your skin feel, against mine?' he said softly. 'Would it be hot, like fire? Or would it be cool, like moonlight against the desert sand?'

There it was again, that sense of something dark and primal stirring within her, like an unwanted whisper rising in the silence of the night.

'You'll never know,' she said quickly. 'I promise you that.'

Khalil's eyes darkened. He smiled, bent his head, brushed his lips against Joanna's. A tiny flicker of heat seemed to radiate from his mouth to hers.

'Your words are cool, but your lips are warm,' he murmured. Her breath caught as his hands slid to her midriff. She felt the light brush of his fingers just below her breasts. 'Fire and ice, Joanna. That is what you are. But I would melt that ice forever.' He pressed his mouth to her throat. 'I would turn you to hot flame that burns only for me,' he said, the words a heated whisper against her skin.

She wanted to tell him that it was he who'd burn, in the eternal fires of hell—but his arms were tightening around her, he was gathering her close, and before she could say anything he crushed her mouth under his.

He had spoken of turning her to flame but *he* was the flame, shimmering against her as he held her, his kiss branding her with heat. His tongue traced the seam of her lips, then slid against hers as her mouth opened to his, silk against silk.

Dear God, what was the matter with her? This man was everything she hated, he was her enemy, her abductor...

He felt the sudden tightening of her muscles and he reached between their bodies, caught her hands and held them fast.

'Don't fight me,' he whispered.

But she did, twisting her head away from his, panting beneath his weight. Still, he persisted, kissing her over and over until suddenly she went still and moaned his name.

'Yes,' he growled, the one word an affirmation of his triumph.

Joanna wrenched her hands from his and buried her fingers in his dark hair, drawing him down to her, giving herself up to the drowning sweetness of his kisses.

Khalil whispered something swift and fierce against her mouth. He drew her from her seat and into his lap, holding her tightly against him, his body hard beneath hers. His hand moved over her, following the curve of her hip, the thrust of her breast. Her head fell back and the dampness of wanting him bloomed like a velvet-petalled flower between her thighs. He bent and pressed his open mouth to the silk that covered her breast, and she cried out.

The sound rose between them, piercing the silence of the little cabin. Khalil drew back and Joanna did too.

They stared at each other and then, abruptly, he thrust her from him, shoving her back into her seat and rising to his feet in one swift motion.

'You see?' His eyes were like sapphire coals in his taut face; his voice was cold, tinged with barely controlled cruelty. 'I could have you now, if I wanted you. But I do not. I have never wanted any woman who offered her body in trade.'

Joanna sprang towards him, sputtering with fury, her hand upraised, but Khalil caught her wrist and twisted her arm behind her.

'I warn you,' he said through his teeth, 'you are done insulting me, you and your father both!'

'Whatever it is you're planning, Khalil, I promise you, you won't get away with it.'

He looked at her for a long moment, still holding her close to him, and then he laughed softly.

'It's dangerous to threaten me, Joanna. Surely you've learned that much by now.'

His gaze fell to her mouth. She tensed, waiting for him to gather her to him and kiss her again. This time, she was prepared to claw his face if she had to rather than let him draw her down into that silken darkness— but suddenly a voice called out from beyond the curtain.

Khalil's smile faded. 'We have arrived.'

She fell back as he let go of her. 'Where?' she asked, but he was already hurrying up the aisle towards the front of the plane.

She knelt in her seat and leaned towards the window. Some time during their confrontation, the plane had not only descended, it had landed. She pressed her nose to the glass. It was still night, yet she could see very clearly, thanks to a full moon and what at first seemed the light from at least a hundred lamps.

Her breath caught. Torches! Those were flaming torches, held aloft by a crowd of cheering men mounted on horseback.

With a little moan, she put her hands to her mouth and collapsed back into her seat.

They had arrived, all right—they'd arrived smack in the middle of the thirteenth century!

CHAPTER FIVE

IT WAS the sight of the horsemen that changed everything. Until now, Joanna had let herself half believe that if what was happening was not a dream, it was some sort of terrible prank, one that would end with the plane turning and heading back to Morocco.

But the line of horses standing just outside the plane, the robed men on their backs, the torches casting a glow as bright as daylight over the flat plateau on which they'd landed, finally forced her to acknowledge the truth.

Khalil had stolen her away from the world she knew. What happened to her next was not in the hands of fate but in the hands of this man, this bandit—and he didn't give a damn for the laws of his country or of civilisation.

'Joanna.'

She looked up. He was standing at the open door of the plane, his face like granite.

'Come,' he said.

Come. As if she were a slave, or a dog. Joanna's jaw clenched. That was what he wanted, to reduce her to some sub-human status, to stress his domination over her and make her cower beneath it. In some ways, he'd already succeeded. She had let him see her fear when he'd first abducted her, let him see it again when she'd pleaded with him to release her.

She drew a deep, deep breath. And her fear had been painfully obvious when he'd kissed her and she'd yielded herself so shamelessly in his arms. It was nothing but fear that had caused her to react to him that way. She knew it, and he did, too.

But his ugly scheme could only work if she let it—and she would not. She would never, ever let him see her fear again.

'Joanna!' Her head came up. He was waiting for her, his hands on his hips, his legs apart, looking as fierce as the predatory bird whose name he bore. 'Are you waiting for me to come and get you?'

She rose, head high, spine straight. He didn't move as she made her way slowly towards him, but she saw his gaze sweep over her, his eyes narrowing, his jaw tightening, and she knew he must be once again telling himself that only a woman who wanted to seduce a man would dress in such a way.

It was laughable, really. Her dress was fashionable and expensive, but it was basically modest and would not have raised an eyebrow anywhere but here or the Vatican. For a second, she wished she'd gone with her first instinct and worn a business suit, but then she thought no, let him have to look at her for the next hours—which was surely only as long as he would keep her here—let him look at her and be reminded constantly that she was of the West, that he could not treat her as he would one of his women, that she was Sam Bennett's daughter and he'd damned well better not forget it.

'You are not dressed properly.'

Joanna smiled coolly. He was as transparent as glass.

'I am dressed quite properly.' She gave him an assessing look, taking in the long, white robe he wore, and then she smiled again. 'It is you who are not dressed properly. Men stopped wearing skirts a long time ago.'

To her surprise, he laughed. 'Try telling that to some of my kinsmen.' With a swift movement, he shrugged off his white robe. Beneath it, he wore a white tunic and pale grey, clinging trousers tucked into high leather boots. 'You are not dressed for these mountains.' Briskly, as if she were a package that needed wrapping, Khalil dropped the robe over her shoulders and enfolded her in it. 'We have a climate like that of the desert. By day, it is warm—but when the sun drops from the sky the air turns cold.'

She wanted to protest, to tell him she didn't need anything from him, but it was too late. He had already drawn the robe snugly around her and anyway, he was right. There was a bone-numbing chill drifting in through the open door. Joanna drew the robe more closely around her. It was still warm from Khalil's body and held a faint, clean scent that she knew must be his. A tremor went through her again, although there was no reason for it.

'Thank you,' she said politely. 'Your concern for my welfare is touching. I'll be sure and mention it to my father so he'll know that my abductor was a gentle—hey! What are you doing? Put me down, dammit! I'm perfectly capable of walking.'

'In those shoes?' He laughed as he lifted her into his arms. 'It was the ancient Chinese who kept their women in servitude by making it impossible for them to walk very far, Joanna. My people expect their women to stride as well as a man.' He grinned down at her. 'If you were to sprain your ankle, how would you tend the goats and chickens tomorrow?'

Goats? Chickens? Was he serious?

'I won't be here tomorrow,' she said curtly.

'You will be here as long as I want you here,' he said, and stepped from the plane.

A full-throated cheer went up from Khalil's assembled warriors when they saw him. They edged their horses forward, their flaming torches held high. He stood still for a moment, smiling and accepting their welcome, and then one of the men looked at her and said something that made the others laugh. Khalil laughed, too, and then he began to speak.

Joanna knew he must be talking about her. His arms tightened around her and he held her out just a little, as if she were a display. The faces of his men snapped towards her and a few of them chuckled.

'Damn you,' she hissed, 'what are you saying about me?'

Khalil looked down at her. 'Hammad asked why I'd brought home such a lumpy package.' His teeth flashed in a quick grin. 'I suggested he remember the old saying about never judging a horse by the saddle blanket that covers it.'

Her face pinkened. 'It's a book one isn't supposed to judge in my country,' she said frigidly. 'And I would remind you that I am neither.'

His smile fled, and his face took on that stony determination she'd already come to know too well.

'No,' he said grimly, 'you are not. What you are is a guarantee that I will get what I want from Sam Bennett.'

So. It was ransom he wanted, after all. Despite all his cryptic word-games, it was money he would trade her for.

One of his men moved forward, leading a huge black stallion that tossed its head and whickered softly. Khalil lifted Joanna on to its back, then mounted behind her. She stiffened as his arms went around her.

'Yet another indignity you must suffer,' he said, his voice low, his breath warm against her ear as he gathered the reins into his hands. 'But only for a little while, Joanna. Soon, we will be at my home, and neither of us will have to tolerate the sight and touch of the other until morning.'

He murmured something to the horse. It pricked its ears and it began moving forward, its steps high and almost delicate. Khalil spoke again, and the animal began moving faster, until it seemed to be racing across the plateau with the wind. Khalil's arms tightened around her; there was no choice but to lean back and let his hard body support hers as they galloped into the night.

How long would it take to get his ransom demand to her father? And how long after that for the money to reach here?

Khalil's arm brushed lightly, impersonally, across her breast as he urged the horse on.

Not too long, she thought. Please, let it not take too long.

It couldn't possibly.

Her father would want her back, and quickly, no matter how outrageous the Prince's demands.

She had assumed the torchlight greeting had been ceremonial. It had been handsome, she'd thought grudgingly, even impressive, but a man who owned a private plane would not also be a man who travelled his country on the back of a horse.

But an hour or more of riding had changed Joanna's mind. There was nothing ceremonial about riding a horse in terrain such as this, she thought, wincing a little as she shifted her bottom and tried to find a spot that hadn't already become sensitised to the jouncing and bouncing of the saddle. The plane had landed on a plateau, but from what she'd seen so far that had probably been the only flat space in a hundred miles.

Ever since, they'd been climbing into the mountains, although calling these massive, rocky outcroppings 'mountains' was like calling the horse beneath her a pony. The resemblance was purely accidental. The moon had risen, casting a pale ivory light over the landscape, tipping the tall pines that clung to the steep slopes with silver.

How far up would they ride? It was probable that a bandit would want to have a hidden stronghold, but this was ridiculous! Only a mountain goat could possibly clamber up this high.

Suppose her father and the Sultan mounted a rescue mission? Could they make it? No. It was best not to think that way. She had to think positively, had to concentrate on how easily they'd find her. And they would. Of course they would. Khalil wasn't invincible and his hideout, no matter how it resembled the eyrie of a hawk, would not be impregnable.

Her father would come for her. He would find her. He would take her back to civilisation, and all this would just be a dream.

A dream. Joanna yawned. She was tired. Exhausted, really, and the slow, steady gait of the horse, the creak of leather, the jingle of the tiny bells that adorned the bridle, were all having a hypnotic effect. She yawned again, then blinked hard, trying to keep her eyes open. It would be so nice to rest for a few minutes.

Her head fell back, her cheek brushed lightly against a hard, warm surface. Quickly, she jerked upright.

'Joanna?'

'Yes?'

'Are you tired?'

'No. I'm not.'

'You must be.' Khalil lifted his hand to her cheek. 'Put your head against my shoulder, and sleep for a while.'

'Don't be ridiculous! I'd sooner——'

'Sleep with a camel. Yes, I know.' He laughed. 'Just pretend that's what I am, then, and put your head back and close your eyes.'

'Please,' she said coldly, 'spare me this attempt at solicitude. It doesn't become you.'

Khalil sighed. 'As you wish, Joanna.'

The horse plodded on, its movements slow and steady. Up, down, up, down...

Concentrate. Concentrate. Listen to the sounds, to the clatter of the horse's hooves, to the sigh of the wind through the trees.

Stay awake! Take deep breaths. Smell the fragrance of pine carried on the night wind, the scent of leather and horse...

'Dammit, woman, you're as stubborn as the wild horses of Chamoulya! Stop being such a little fool and get some rest.'

'I don't need rest. I don't need anything. And I especially don't need your help.'

'Fine. I'll remember that.' He jerked her head back against his shoulder. 'Now, shut up and stop fidgeting. You're making Najib nervous, and——'

'Najib?'

'My horse. And the last thing I want is for Najib to be nervous on the climb ahead.'

Najib, she thought giddily. She was making Najib nervous. By heaven, this man was crazy! He had kidnapped her, carried her off to God only knew where without so much as giving a damn if she turned to stone with fright, but he was worried that she was making his horse nervous.

Joanna's eyes flickered shut. Still, he was right. It would be stupid to upset the animal on a narrow mountain path. Closing her eyes didn't mean she'd sleep. She'd let her other senses take over. Yes. That was what she'd do, she'd—she'd think about the coolness of the night air—and the contrasting warmth of Khalil's arms, think about the softness of his robe on her skin and the contrasting hardness of his thighs, cradling her hips.

That was the word that best described him. He was hard. Powerful. That was how he felt, holding her—and yet she knew his hands were holding the reins lightly. Still, the black stallion responded readily to his slightest touch, to the press of his heel.

A woman would respond to him that way, too, Joanna thought drowsily; she would move eagerly to obey him, to pleasure him and to let him pleasure her...

A heat so intense it was frightening spread through her body. Her eyes flew open and she jerked upright in the saddle, steadying herself by clasping the pommel. Najib snorted and tossed his head, and Khalil caught her and pulled her back against him.

'Dammit!' he said tightly. 'What did I tell you about making the horse nervous?'

'I know what you said,' Joanna snapped, 'and frankly, I don't much care if I make your horse nervous or...'

A whimper slipped from her throat as she looked down. They were on a ledge that looked only slightly wider than a man's hand. Below, the earth dropped away, spinning into darkness.

'Exactly,' Khalil said gruffly.

Joanna didn't have to ask him what he meant. She turned her face away from the precipice.

'The stallion is sure-footed, Joanna. But I would prefer he have no distractions.'

She laughed uneasily. 'That's—that's fine with me. Tell him—tell him to pay no attention to me, please. No attention at all.'

Khalil laughed softly. 'I'll tell him. Now, why don't you shut your eyes again and sleep?'

'I wasn't sleeping,' she said. 'How could anyone sleep, on the back of this—this creature?'

'I'm sure it's a sacrifice when you're accustomed to riding in the back of a chauffeured limousine.'

She smiled smugly. 'No greater than the sacrifice one makes giving up the comfort of a private plane for the back of a horse.'

'The plane is necessary,' he said, so quickly that she knew she'd stung him. 'My responsibilities take me in many different directions.'

'Oh, I'm sure they do.' Her voice was like honey. 'They take you up mountains and down mountains—clearly, one needs a plane for that!'

He said nothing, but she had the satisfaction of seeing his jaw tighten. They rode on in silence while the moon dropped lower in the sky, and then, finally, Khalil lifted his hand and pointed into the distance.

'There it is,' he said quietly. 'Bab al Sama—Gate to the Sky. My home.'

Joanna sat up straighter and stared into the darkness. There were smudges against the horizon. What were they?

'Tents,' Khalil said, as if she'd asked the question aloud. 'Some of my people still cling to the old ways.'

Tents. Of course. His people lived outside the law. They'd want to be able to strike camp quickly.

But the tents were larger than she'd expected. They were, in fact, enormous. And what was that beyond them? Joanna caught her breath. It was a walled city, ancient and serene in the moonlight. A gateway loomed ahead and the horsemen filed through it, then stopped inside the courtyard of a stone building. The cluster of men dismounted, as did Khalil, and then he looked up at Joanna and lifted his arms to her.

'Come.'

Come. Joanna's chin lifted. There it was again, that single, imperious command. She tossed her head, deliberately turned away from him, and threw her leg over the saddle.

'Joanna!' Khalil's angry voice stopped her for an instant. He moved quickly, so that despite her efforts to avoid him she slid into his arms. 'You little fool! Didn't anyone ever teach you there's a right way and a wrong way to mount a horse?'

'I wasn't mounting him, I was getting off!' She put her hands on his shoulders. 'Put me down!'

'Horses are skittish creatures, Joanna. Surely, even you know that.' His eyes glared into hers. 'They're trained to accept a rider from the left side—but anyone coming at them from the right is asking for trouble.'

'I'll be sure and remember the next time,' she said with heavy sarcasm. 'Now, put me down!'

'With pleasure.' She gasped as he dropped her to her feet. 'Goodnight, Joanna. I suggest you get some rest. You've a long day ahead of you.'

She watched in disbelief as he turned on his heel and marched away from her.

'Goodnight?' she said. Her voice rose. 'What do you mean, goodnight? Where am I supposed to sleep, Khalil? Out here, with the horses?'

He spun towards her, and she saw the quick, humourless flash of his teeth.

'I think too much of them to subject them to an entire night in your company.'

'Damn you, Khalil! You can't just ...'

'*Mademoiselle*?'

Joanna turned quickly. A girl had come up silently behind her. She was slender, with long, dark hair and wide-set eyes.

'I am Rachelle, *mademoiselle*. I am to see to your comfort.'

Joanna's mouth narrowed as she looked at the girl. 'I suppose you usually see to the Prince's comfort.'

Rachelle's smooth brow furrowed. '*Mademoiselle*?'

Joanna sighed. It wasn't this child's fault that she had to play slave to a rogue. She forced a faint, weary smile to her lips.

'I could use some comfort. A basin of warm water, a cup of hot tea, and a soft, comfortable bed would be lovely.'

The girl smiled. 'It will be my pleasure, *mademoiselle*. If you will please follow me...?'

Warm water, tea, a comfortable bed—in the mountain hideaway of Khalil the bandit Prince? It was all out of the question and Joanna knew it, but she was too tired to care. A wash in a mountain stream, a cup of cold water, and a blanket spread on the floor were the best she could hope for, but after the last few hours even they would be welcome.

And tomorrow—tomorrow, her father would come for her. He wouldn't wait for Khalil's ransom demand. She was certain of it. Why would he waste time, and risk her life? By now, he would know that she was missing, and it wouldn't take any great effort to know what had happened to her. As for locating her—her father's resources were endless, his contacts enormous. He'd find her, and come after her, before the next setting of the sun.

Joanna's shoulders went back as she marched into the stone building on Rachelle's heels.

'You're the one who's going to need a good night's sleep, Your Highness,' she muttered. 'Because as of tomorrow, you're going to find yourself neck-deep in trouble!'

'*Mademoiselle*? Did you say something?'

Joanna cleared her throat. 'I said, I think I'd like a sandwich to go with that tea, Rachelle. Can you manage that, do you think?'

The girl stopped and turned to face her. 'Certainly. My lord has made it clear that I am to do whatever pleases you, *mademoiselle*. You have only to tell me, and I will obey.'

Joanna gave her a bright, beaming smile. 'How about giving me a map and a ticket out of here?'

Rachelle smiled uncertainly. 'I do not understand...'

'You know, point me towards the nearest highway and send me on my way.'

'*Mademoiselle* jokes,' the girl said, with another little smile.

Joanna sighed. '*Mademoiselle* is dead serious.' The only thing I really want is to get away from your lord and master.'

Rachelle ducked her head, as if Joanna's words had unsettled her. 'Here is your room,' she said, and opened the nearest door.

Joanna stepped inside the room. It was dimly lit, and what little light there was fell across a huge bed. An image flashed into her mind. She saw herself on that bed, locked in Khalil's arms, her mouth open to his, her breasts tightening under the slow, sweet stroke of his fingers...

'Stop it,' she hissed.

The girl looked at her. '*Mademoiselle*?'

Joanna puffed out her breath. She *did* need a night's rest. Hallucinations weren't her style, but she'd surely just had one. Any second now, a chorus line of pink elephants would probably come tap-dancing into view!

'I—uh—I think I'll pass on the tea and all the rest, Rachelle.' Joanna sank down wearily on the edge of the bed. 'Just turn out the lights and hang out the "do not disturb" sign.'

'I am afraid I do not understand...'

Joanna sighed. 'I just want to get to bed. It's very late, and I'm exhausted.'

'As you wish, *mademoiselle*.'

Sleep, Joanna thought as the girl moved silently around the room, sleep was precisely what she needed. It would clear her head, drive away the cobwebs. And, when she awoke, her father would probably be here, ready to take her home and make the almighty Khalil eat his every threatening, insolent word.

And that, she thought with grim satisfaction, would almost be enough to make this horrible night worthwhile.

CHAPTER SIX

JOANNA lay asleep in her bed, dreaming... Her father and a rotund little man sat in a pool of light, their heads bent over what looked like a game board while she sat in the darkened perimeter of the room, watching, when the silence was broken by the sound of hoofbeats. She looked up just in time to see a man on the back of a great ebony stallion bearing down on her.

Father, she cried. She wanted to run, but her legs wouldn't move. *Father*, she said again as the horseman leaned down, snatched her up, and tossed her across his saddle.

But her father didn't hear. He was intent on his opponent and on moving his playing piece around the board, and even though she called and called him he didn't——

'Good morning, *mademoiselle*.'

Joanna awoke instantly, her heart racing. The room was unfamiliar, grey and shadowed, and she stared blindly at the figure silhouetted against the drawn window curtains.

'Khalil?' she said shakily.

'It is Rachelle, *mademoiselle*.' The curtains whisked open and Joanna blinked in the golden sunlight that splashed across the bed.

'Rachelle.' Joanna expelled her breath. 'I—I was dreaming...' She sat up, her knees tenting the blanket, and pushed her hair back from her face. 'What time is it? It feels late.'

The serving girl smiled as she placed a small inlaid tray on the low table beside the bed.

'It is mid-morning, *mademoiselle*. I have brought you coffee and fruit.'

'Mid-morning? But I never sleep so...'

'My lord said to let you sleep.'

'Did he,' Joanna said, her voice flat.

The girl nodded. 'He said there was no reason to awaken you until he was ready to see you.'

Joanna snorted. 'That arrogant ass!'

Rachelle threw her a shocked look. 'We do not speak of our Prince that way, *mademoiselle*.'

'No? Well, maybe you should. Maybe you should start seeing him for the miserable donkey's *derrière* he really is!'

Rachelle's eyes widened. 'Please, *mademoiselle*. You must not say such things!'

Joanna sighed. What was the sense in taking out her frustration on a servant? The girl had no choice but to serve her master; hearing unkind things said about him clearly made her nervous. Perhaps she was afraid she'd be punished for permitting Joanna to make such remarks—the Jandaran version of guilt by association. It was the sort of thing that went on in dictatorships, wasn't it?

'Sorry,' Joanna said, with a little smile. 'I'm just feeling out of sorts this morning.'

Rachelle nodded. 'A bath will make you feel better. I have already run it. I added bath oil. I hope the scent is to your liking, *mademoiselle*. Is there something else I can get you?'

Yes, Joanna thought, you can get me my freedom. But she knew it was pointless to ask. The girl was obviously scared to death of Khalil, and desperate to avoid confrontation.

'No,' she said, after a moment, 'no, thanks. I can't think of anything more.'

'I will bring you some yogurt, *mademoiselle*, when you are finished bathing. Or would you prefer eggs?'

'I would prefer you call me Joanna. It makes me uncomfortable to have you address me so formally.'

Rachelle blushed. 'I am honoured.'

'For goodness' sake, you needn't be "honoured"! This is the millennium. Bowing and scraping went out with the Dark Ages.'

'Yes, Joanna.' Rachelle smiled sweetly. 'If you need me, you have only to ring the bell.'

She started towards the door, and suddenly Joanna's good intentions deserted her. She couldn't let the girl leave without at least trying to get through to her.

'Rachelle!' Joanna swung her legs to the floor. 'Rachelle, wait a minute.' The girl turned towards her. 'Prince Khalil brought me here against my will,' she said in a rush. 'He kidnapped me...'

Rachelle's eyes grew shuttered. 'I shall return,' she said, and the door swung shut after her.

Joanna sat staring at it for a long moment and then she muttered several short, impolite words she'd learned during the years she'd spent with Sam in his field operations and had never found suitable to use—until now. She sat up, threw back the blankets, and looked around the room.

It was handsome, she thought grudgingly. The tiled floor, the inlaid furniture, and the white walls on which hung old and beautiful Persian rugs were all pleasing to the eye.

But it was still a prison.

She rose from the bed, kicked aside her shoes, stubbing her toe in the process, and strode briskly to the adjoining bathroom. By now, she knew better than to expect to find a hole in the ground and a basin of cold water, but the tiled room and glass-enclosed shower still were enough to surprise her. Steam rose from a deep tub, and the scent of roses filled the air.

'His Almighty Highness likes to live well,' Joanna muttered as she yanked her slip over her head and tossed it on to the closed bathroom commode.

She glared at the tub, then turned her back on it, pulled open the door to the shower stall, and stepped inside. Khalil had given orders she was not to be disturbed this morning. Had he also given orders she was to be wooed with a scented bath? A shower, quick and modern, was more to her liking.

What insanity this was. First there'd been those silly men last night, riding up to greet Khalil with torches blazing in their hands, looking like nothing so much as a crowd of extras who'd wandered off a movie set, and now there was this silly girl, Rachelle, acting as if she either lived in mortal terror of offending her lord and master—or had been brainwashed to think of him as a tin god. Either way, it was ridiculous.

'Ridiculous,' Joanna said sharply, and she shut off the spray and stepped out on to the bath mat.

She dried off briskly, reached for her slip—and stopped. She'd slept in it last night rather than have to ring for Rachelle and ask for a nightgown or pyjamas. Now, the thought of putting on the wrinkled garment was not appealing. The thought of getting into the bit of emerald silk that lay on a chair in the bedroom wasn't appealing, either, but what choice did she have? Joanna's nostrils flared. Khalil hadn't exactly given her time to pack an overnight bag!

Well, she thought, wrapping the towel around herself, she could avoid wearing the slip, at least. The dress didn't really require more than panties and a bra, both of which...

She cried out as she stepped into the bedroom. A man was standing looking out of the window, his back to the room, but she knew instantly it was Khalil. No one else would have those broad shoulders, that tapered waist, those long, muscular legs. Yes, it was certainly Khalil, making himself at home.

'What do you think you're doing?' she demanded.

Khalil turned slowly and looked at her. Rachelle had said she'd drawn a bath for the woman. Why hadn't it occurred to him that he might well catch her as she emerged from that bath, looking scrubbed and innocent and beautiful when she was none of those things? No. He was wrong. She *was* beautiful, more beautiful now, without her make-up and jewellery, than she'd been last night.

He felt a tightening in his groin and it infuriated him. That he should be stirred by a woman like this was impossible. Despite her beauty, she was hardly a prize, not when she was nothing but the *baksheesh* meant to corrupt him.

'I asked you a question! What are you doing in my room?'

His dark brows rose a little. 'Rachelle told me you were awake, and so——'

'And so you thought you'd barge right in, without permission?'

'I knocked, several times, but you didn't answer.'

'I was in the shower!'

'Yes.' He leaned back against the wall and let his gaze drift over her. 'So I see.'

Joanna flushed. She felt as if he'd stripped away the towel and she was certain that was just the way he wanted her to feel. She ached to race back to the safety of the bathroom or to drag the blanket from the bed and enclose herself in it, but she'd be damned if she'd give him the satisfaction.

'Perhaps you can also see that I wasn't exactly expecting to receive visitors,' she said coldly.

'Rachelle said you were unhappy with her.'

'So?'

'So, she is very young, and very sensitive. And——'

'Let me get this straight. You came barging into my room because I hurt Rachelle's feelings?' Joanna laughed. 'You'll forgive me, Your Lordship——'

'That is not my title.'

'If you're waiting for me to apologise for upsetting your little slave, you're in for a long wait.'

'She is not my slave.' Khalil's eyes turned cool. 'We have no slaves, here in the northern hills.'

'Of course,' Joanna purred. 'I should have realised. The people here are all happy and content. The only slaves in Jandara are in the south, where the evil Abu Al Zouad rules.'

His eyes narrowed. The woman was impossible! How dared she speak to him with so little respect? How dared she stand before him as she did, flaunting her almost naked body?

'Don't you have a robe to put on?' he demanded.

She smiled sweetly. 'I'm afraid the hotel didn't supply one.'

'Rachelle was told to bring you anything you requested. If you had thought to ask——'

'The only thing I thought to ask for was my freedom,' Joanna said, lifting her chin in defiance. 'It was a request your little harem girl denied.'

'I shall see to it that you are given some proper clothing,' Khalil said stiffly.

'Meaning what? If you think I'm going to put on a robe that drapes me from chin to toe, if you think I'm going to wrap a scarf around my head and look out at the world through a veil——'

'Is that what you have seen Rachelle wearing?'

It wasn't, of course. The girl wore a soft, scoop-necked cotton blouse and a pretty skirt that fell to mid-calf; her hair hung loose and uncovered to her shoulders.

'Or is that description of your own invention, meant to shore up your belief that we are a backward people?' The flush that rose in her cheeks gave him a certain grim satisfaction. He shrugged his white robe from his shoulders and held it out to her. 'Here. Wear this until——'

'I don't want anything from you, Khalil!'

His mouth thinned. 'Put it on!'

Her eyes flashed as he stepped forward and draped the robe over her shoulders. His fingers brushed her bare skin; a tingle raced along her nerve endings, one that sent a tremor through her. Khalil frowned and stepped back quickly.

'I will see to the clothing.'

'Yes. So you said.' Joanna drew the robe around herself. 'But I'm more interested in what my father's had to say.'

His frown deepened. 'What do you mean?'

'Come on, Khalil, don't treat me like a fool! Surely you've contacted him with your ransom demands.'

He looked at her for a long moment, then turned and strolled to the window.

'I have, yes,' he said, his back to her.

'And?' Joanna took a step forward. 'What did he say? How soon will he meet them?'

'I cannot tell you that.'

'What do you mean, you can't tell me?' Joanna moved closer to him. 'I've every right to know how long I'm going to be your prisoner!'

He swung towards her, his face stony. 'You will be here until your father decides to be reasonable.'

'You mean, I'll be here until he can raise the money you've asked for my return!'

'I have not asked for money.'

'No.' Joanna's smile was chill. 'Of course you haven't. I keep forgetting—you're the Hawk of the North. It's Abu Al Zouad who's the villain in this piece.'

'Joke all you wish, Joanna. It will not change the truth.'

Her chin lifted. 'It certainly won't. Abu Al Zouad's supposed to be this—this monster, this evil emperor, but——'

'He is a man who has enslaved his people.'

'Don't be ridiculous! If there were slaves in Jandara, Bennettco wouldn't have——'

'There are all kinds of slavery,' Khalil said sharply. 'People who live in fear of displeasing their ruler may not be slaves in the classic sense, but they are slaves just the same.'

Joanna smiled coolly. 'I suppose *your* people do that ridiculous bowing to you out of love, not fear.'

It pleased her to see a wash of crimson rise across his high cheekbones.

'It is custom,' he said sternly, 'and foolish. I have tried to change it——'

'Yeah.' She laughed. 'I'll bet.'

'My people obey me out of respect. If they thought I was wrong, the elders would say so.'

'Remarkable! You've got yourself believing your own lies!'

'And what, precisely, is that supposed to mean?' he said, glaring at her.

'You know damned well what it means! You make yourself out to be this benevolent ruler, this wonderful good guy, but you're not! You're—you're——'

'A thief. A despot. A greedy pig who wants whatever he can get from Bennettco, or else I'll——' His brow furrowed. 'I never did ask, Joanna, what is it, exactly, that I'll do to the operation if I'm not properly bought off?'

'How should I know?' she cried angrily. 'Raid the camp. Harass the workers. Disrupt things any way you can. Does it matter?'

'And if I told you that you're wrong...?'

'Listen, Khalil, I'm not going to play this silly game! You want to pretend you're Lawrence of Arabia? Fine. Wear that foolish outfit. Ride that ridiculous horse. Stand around and look fierce while your people prostrate themselves before you. As for me, all I want——'

She cried out as he caught hold of her shoulders.

'All you want,' he said through his teeth, 'is to categorise me. And if I don't fit, you'll poke, prod, shove and squeeze until I do!'

'All I want,' Joanna said, her eyes snapping defiance, 'is to go back to Casablanca.'

'Nothing would suit me better! A scorpion would make a better guest than you!'

'I am not your guest!'

'Indeed you are not.' His lip curled with distaste. 'You are an unwelcome visitor.'

'Fine! Then put me on your plane and send me back!'

'I shall, the instant your father agrees to my conditions.'

'Well, then,' she said, tossing her head, 'tell your pilot to rev up those engines. Your money should be on its way.'

A furrow appeared between his dark eyebrows. 'Your father has yet to answer me, Joanna.'

She stared at him. 'I don't understand.'

'It is quite simple. He knows what I want for your return, but he has not offered a reply.'

Joanna's eyes searched his face. 'You mean, your messenger didn't wait for one.'

Khalil shook his head. 'I mean what I said.' His words were clipped and cold. 'Your father has not responded.'

'Well, how could he? If you asked some unholy sum of money, a million billion dollars or whatever, he'd have to find a way to——'

He gave her a thin smile. 'Is that what you think you're worth?'

'The question isn't what *I* think I'm worth,' she said coldly. 'It's what *you* think you can get for me.'

'I have asked a great deal,' he said, his eyes on her face.

Why did his answer make her heartbeat quicken? The words were simple, yet they seemed to hold a complexity of meaning. Joanna gave him what she hoped was an easygoing smile.

'Really.'

'A great, great deal,' he said softly.

'All right, tell me. How many dollars am I worth?'

'I didn't ask for dollars.'

'Swiss francs, then. Or Deutschmarks. Or——'

'I told you before, I want no money for you.'

Joanna's attempted nonchalance vanished. 'For God's sake,' she snapped, 'what did you ask from my father, then? Diamonds? Gold?'

Khalil's eyes met hers. 'I have demanded that your father withdraw from the contract with Abu Al Zouad.'

'What?'

'I said——'

'I heard you—but I don't believe you. All this talk about how you love your people and how they love you, and now you're trying to blackmail Bennettco into pulling out of a million-dollar deal that would pump money and jobs into your country?'

Khalil's eyes darkened. 'He is to withdraw from it and restructure it, so that the people benefit, not Abu.'

'Oh. Oh, of course. You want him to rewrite the contract——'

'Exactly.'

'—to rewrite it according to your dictates.'

'Yes.'

Joanna laughed. 'You're good at this, you know that? I mean, if I didn't know better, I'd almost believe you! Come on, Khalil. The only benefit you have in mind is for yourself.'

His expression hardened. 'Think what you will, Joanna. I have sent your father the terms of your release. Now, it is up to him to reply.'

'He will. He definitely will. And when he does——'

But Sam should have replied already, she thought with a start. He should have said, OK, I'll do whatever you want, just set my daughter free.

No. No, he couldn't do that. She wasn't looking at things clearly. Sam wasn't about to cave in, not without being certain Khalil would live up to his end of the deal. Kidnappers were not known for honouring their agreements; her father would want to do everything in his power to satisfy himself that he could trust Khalil to let her go before he said yes, otherwise he might put her in even greater jeopardy.

She looked up. Khalil was watching her closely. His expression was unreadable, but the little smile of triumph that had been on his lips moments ago was gone. In its place was a look that might almost have been sympathy.

'I cannot imagine your father will have trouble deciding which he prefers,' he said softly, 'his daughter or his contract with the sultan.'

Joanna flushed. The bastard wasn't feeling sympathy, he was just worried that her father might not give him what he'd asked for!

'My father's an astute businessman,' she said. 'Why should he trust you? He'll want some guarantee that you won't hurt me after he agrees to your demands.'

'My message made no mention of hurting you,' he said stiffly.

'Ah. I see. You simply told him you'd keep me as your guest forever if he didn't do what you wanted.'

Khalil began to grin. 'Something like that.'

Joanna's jaunty smile faded. 'What do you mean?'

He shrugged lazily. 'I suggested that if he did not want you back, we would accommodate you here.'

'Accommodate me?'

'You would learn to live among my people.' Still smiling, he strolled across the room to where her green silk dress lay across the chair. 'It will not be the life you know,' he said, picking up the dress. It slipped through his fingers, incongruously delicate and insubstantial, and fell back to the chair. 'But at least it would stop your complaining.'

'What are you talking about?'

'Our women lead busy lives. Only idle women have time to complain. You would start simply, tending the chickens and the goats, but if you showed you were interested in learning they would teach you to cook, to spin——'

'Never!' The word exploded from her lips. 'Never, do you hear me? I'd sooner—I'd sooner——'

'What would you sooner do?' He looked across the room at her, his eyes dark. 'Surely, you would have to do something. We are all productive here, everyone but the sick, the elderly, and the children.'

He started slowly towards her. Joanna's heart skipped a beat. She wanted to step back, to put as much distance as the confines of the room permitted between herself and the man pacing towards her, but she was determined to stand her ground.

'You fit none of those categories,' he said, stopping inches from her. He gave her a long, slow look, one that left a trail of heat across her skin and she thought suddenly that it was a good thing she hadn't fought him about giving her his robe, for if she had—if she had, he would surely see the quickening of her breath, the flush that she felt rising over her entire body, the terrible, hateful way her breasts were lifting and hardening as he looked at her.

'You are not elderly, or ill, or a child, Joanna,' he said softly. He reached his hand out to her and caught a strand of auburn hair between his fingers. 'I would have to find some other use for you, I'm afraid.'

'My father will come for me,' she said fiercely. 'And— and when he does——' Her breath caught as he put his arms around her.

'I think,' he said, his voice husky, 'I think I would not waste you on the goats, even if you wished it.'

'I would rather——' He put his lips to her hair and she swallowed hard. 'I would rather tend the goats than— than——'

'One of the laws we live by is that every person should do what he or she is best suited for.' He lowered his head and nuzzled the robe from the juncture of shoulder and throat. His mouth moved lightly against her skin. 'And you,' he said, his voice dropping to a whisper, 'you are surely best suited to be with a man, to sigh his name, and drive him to the point where his bones begin to melt.'

His teeth closed lightly on her flesh. Joanna gasped, and he touched his tongue to the pinpoint of pain, soothing it away.

'You smell of flowers,' he whispered, 'of flowers heated by the sun of the desert.'

Trembling, Joanna fought for control. 'I—I smell of soap,' she said as he pressed kisses across her shoulder. 'I—I didn't use Rachelle's precious bath oils to——'

'Then the scent in my nostrils is of you.' He threaded his hand into her hair, knotting it around his fist like a bright, gleaming band, so that she had no choice but to meet his eyes, eyes that had gone as dark as the sea at night. 'By Allah,' he whispered, 'it is a scent more sweet than any I have ever known.'

He bent and kissed her throat again. Joanna's eyes closed and she swayed in his arms, hating herself for whatever weakness it was that possessed her when he touched her, hating him even more for finding that weakness and exploiting it.

'The only name I'd ever call you is bastard,' she said unsteadily. 'And—and that would be only the beginning.'

Khalil laughed softly. 'Has no one ever taught you manners?'

'No one's ever tried to tell me how to live my life, if that's what you mean!'

She had meant to insult him, but her words only made him grin. 'Ah. We're back to that, are we? Khalil the dictator.'

'We never left it! You think—you think you can——'

'The first thing you must learn,' he said, 'is not to talk so much.'

His mouth dropped to hers. She had been expecting the kiss, steeling herself against it, and she went rigid at the first touch of his lips. But his kiss was like a whisper—gentle, almost soft—and it sent a swift *frisson* of pleasure shimmering through her blood.

Don't, she began to say. But the thought never became a word. Instead, it emerged a sigh against his mouth. Khalil's arms went around her and he gathered her so closely to him that Joanna couldn't tell whose heart it was she felt racing, whose skin it was she felt blazing with heat.

His teeth caught her bottom lip and he drew the soft flesh into the warmth of his mouth.

'Joanna,' he whispered.

He swept the robe from her shoulders and the lightly knotted towel fell to her waist. He drew back, just far enough so he could see her. Her skin was flushed, her breasts full and hardened with desire.

'How beautiful you are,' he said, his voice thick.

Joanna felt as if the room was spinning around her. 'Please,' she whispered, 'please...'

'What? What do you want me to do, Joanna?' He reached out blindly, his fingers trailing across her collarbone, and she caught her breath. 'This?' he said softly, his eyes on her face. He touched the rise of her breast, circling the aureole lightly. Joanna whimpered and now it was he who caught his breath. 'Or this?' he said, bending his head and putting his mouth to her flesh.

She moaned, would have fallen, but he caught her and gathered her fiercely to him, his hands cupping her bottom, lifting her into the hardness of his arousal.

'Joanna,' he whispered, his voice unsteady, and she moved blindly against him, exulting in the hard feel of him, her flesh on fire...

'No!' The strangled cry burst as much from her heart as from her throat. What was he doing to her? She wasn't the sort of woman who fell into bed with a stranger or with a man she loathed! Joanna slammed her hands against Khalil's chest and pushed him away.

'All right,' she said, her breathing swift, 'you've convinced me. You're bigger than I am, and stronger, and— and——' She closed her eyes, then opened them, determined to face her humiliation without flinching. 'And there's something you do that—that makes me—makes me receptive. But——'

'Receptive?' He laughed, and whatever unsteadiness she'd thought she'd heard in his voice was gone, replaced by smug satisfaction at her embarrassment. 'What you are, my charming Miss Bennett, is ready and willing.' Her hand flashed up but he caught it before she could slap him. 'But, of course, you'd have to be, wouldn't you, to have had any hope of carrying out your little scheme?'

'I hate you,' Joanna said through her teeth. 'Do you understand? I hate you, and I'd sooner die than——'

'Yes. So you said, several times.' His smile was chill. 'It must be difficult, trying to play the part of the seductress and the wounded innocent at the same time.'

'You'll pay for what you've done, when my father comes for me, I promise you that.'

'The sooner, the better,' Khalil said grimly, thrusting her from him. 'Rachelle will bring you clothing. Then she will show you the areas in which you will be free to walk.'

'Free? You don't know the meaning of the word!'

'Behave yourself and things will not be as difficult as you imagine,' he said, striding to the door.

'And if I don't?' She flung her defiance after him, some inner need more desperate than fear spurring her on. 'What then? Will you put me in chains?'

He turned and looked at her. 'Only a stupid man would resort to such measures, Joanna.' A quick smile flashed across his lips. 'Especially when there are ones that would please me far better.'

The door opened, then shut, and Joanna was alone.

CHAPTER SEVEN

'I HAVE brought you some lunch, Joanna.'

Joanna looked up as Rachelle entered the bedroom and set a tray on the table beside the window.

'You will like it, I think. There is *kofta* and *ommu-'ali*—little meatballs—and then some rice pudding, and——'

'Thank you, but I'm not hungry.'

The bright smile dimmed. 'But you haven't even looked at it!'

'I'm sure it's delicious. But I don't want it.'

'Joanna, please. You must eat.'

'Why?' Joanna's attempted good humour vanished in a haze of frustration and disappointment. 'Is that what the Prince said?'

Rachelle flushed. 'The Prince will be concerned about the welfare of his guest.'

'Ah. That's touching. Unfortunately for me, I am not exactly his guest.'

'He will be displeased with me.'

'Send him to me, then. I'll tell him you have nothing to do with my not eating. Perhaps he needs to be reminded that prisoners often lose their appetites—but then, what would a kidnapper and bandit know about such things?'

'Hush!' Rachelle's eyes were wide with shock. 'You must not say that of my lord!'

'Why? Will he have me beaten if I speak the truth? Will he have you beaten for listening to it?' Joanna got to her feet and stalked across the room. 'Why don't you

93

stop defending him? There's no one here but me—you can be honest for once. Your mighty Prince is nothing but a——'

Rachelle gasped, turned, and all but flew to the door.

'Rachelle!' Joanna's voice rose in dismay. 'Rachelle, wait, please! Don't go. I just wanted to——'

It was too late. The door swung shut, and she was alone again. She stared at it for a few seconds, and then she flung out her arms in frustration.

'How could you be so stupid, Joanna?' she demanded of the silent room.

She flung herself into a chair and stared blankly at the wall. She'd lost her temper with a slip of a girl who was too terrified of Khalil and the life-or-death power he held over her and the rest of his people ever to question what he did.

More importantly, she'd lost the chance to ask the only question that mattered. When would she be set free? Surely Khalil had heard from her father by now? Sam must be working as quickly as he could to meet the demands for her release, but——

A knock sounded at the door, as if in answer to Joanna's thoughts. She sprang to her feet, her heart pounding—but it was only Rachelle again, this time bearing an armful of what looked like bright lengths of fabric.

'I have brought you some things to wear,' she said, hurrying to the bed, her eyes downcast. Garments fell across the blankets, along with a pair of embroidered leather slippers. 'I hope they are to your liking, Joanna. If they are not——'

'Rachelle—I'm sorry if I insulted you before.'

The girl looked up. 'It was my lord you insulted, not me.'

'Yes.' Joanna sighed. 'And I suppose it's a capital offence to do that here, isn't it?'

Rachelle's brow furrowed. 'Capital offence? I do not
understand.'

Joanna smiled tightly. 'No, I'm sure you don't.'

'The clothing,' the girl said, gesturing to the bed. 'I
had to guess at the size, but——'

'I won't need it.'

Rachelle shrugged her shoulders. 'I thought you would
be more comfortable in these things than in the jellaba,
but if you prefer to wear it——'

'I won't be here long enough to bother changing what
I'm wearing.'

The girl's eyes met Joanna's, then skittered away. 'It
will not hurt to have these things,' she said.

'There's no point,' Joanna said firmly. 'Surely, by
now, Khalil has heard from my father, and...' She stared
at the other girl. 'He has, hasn't he?'

Rachelle seemed to hesitate. 'I do not know.'

'Khalil said he'd contacted him. Did he tell me the
truth?' Rachelle's face grew shuttered and Joanna's voice
sharpened with impatience. 'Come on, Rachelle, surely
you can answer a simple question. Does my father know
what's happened to me?'

The girl nodded. 'Yes.'

Yes. Yes. Sam knew she was being held prisoner, but
he hadn't yet arranged for her release ...

'I will take away the things I have brought, since you
do not wish to——'

'No!' Joanna shook her head and put her hand on
Rachelle's arm. 'No, leave them. On second thought, I
don't want to go on wearing this—this bathrobe of
Khalil's another minute.' She reached towards the bed,
then stopped abruptly. 'What,' she said disdainfully,
'is this?'

'A skirt.' The girl smiled hesitantly. 'And a blouse to go with it. If they please you, I will bring you other——'

'I have no intention of wearing anything like that!'

Rachelle looked bewildered. 'Are the sizes wrong? You are so slender, Joanna, that I was not certain——'

'I'm sure the size is fine.'

'The colours, then. I thought the shade of blue was very pretty, but perhaps you would prefer——'

'A skirt that length is a mark of subservience,' Joanna said, blithely ignoring the fact that New York women were probably that minute strolling Fifth Avenue in skirts even longer than the one that lay across the bed. Her eyes flashed to Rachelle's face. 'I mean no insult,' she said quickly. 'It's only that in my country, women don't dress that way.'

'Then you will go on wearing the jellaba?'

Suddenly, the weight of the jellaba seemed unbearable against her naked skin.

'No,' Joanna said quickly.

Rachelle looked bewildered. 'Then what will you wear?'

What, indeed? Joanna gave the first answer that came into her head.

'Trousers,' she said, taking an almost perverse delight in the shock she saw in Rachelle's eyes.

'Trousers? But——'

'I know. Women don't wear them in Jandara.' Her chin lifted. 'But I am not Jandaran, Rachelle. Be sure and give that message to your high and mighty Prince.'

It was a pointless gesture, Joanna knew. Even if, by some miracle, women's trousers could be found in Jandara, surely Khalil would never agree to permitting his hostage to wear something so Western.

An hour later, Rachelle appeared at the door carrying another armload of clothing.

'I hope these things suit you better,' she said, dumping everything on the bed.

Joanna waited until the girl left, and then she walked to the bed and poked at the garments lying across it. A smile curved across her lips. There were two pairs of trousers—soft, cotton ones—and a stack of shirts, as well.

She picked one up. This was men's clothing, not women's. Everything would be too large, but what did that matter? She wasn't trying to be a fashion plate and besides, getting such things past Khalil seemed like a victory. Perhaps Rachelle had taken pity on her; perhaps she'd got the items on her own, without seeking his permission.

Quickly, Joanna stripped off the jellaba. She pulled on a pair of trousers, then slipped a navy cotton T-shirt over her head.

It was Khalil's, she thought instantly, as the soft fabric brushed past her nose. The T-shirt, the trousers—they were all his. The garments were all clean and fresh, but they bore a scent compounded of the mountains and the wind and the stallion he rode... His scent.

A tremor went through her and she closed her eyes, remembering the endless ride to this mountain stronghold, remembering the feel of Khalil's arms as he'd held her before him on the saddle.

Joanna gave herself a little shake. Impatiently, she yanked the shirt down hard over her breasts. His scent, indeed! The T-shirt smelled of the soap it had been washed with and the sunshine that had dried it, nothing more. Honestly, if she didn't get out of this prison soon...

There was a light rap at the door. She spun towards it.

'Rachelle? Thanks for bringing me this stuff. It's just too bad it belongs to your almighty Prince, but——'

'I assure you, Joanna,' Khalil said with a cool smile, 'none of it is contaminated.'

Joanna's cheeks flamed. 'I thought you were Rachelle.'

He nodded as he shut the door after him. 'Obviously,' he said drily. His gaze flickered over her slowly, and then a smile curved across his lips. 'I am sorry I had nothing more to your liking.'

'This is fine,' she said stiffly.

His eyes darkened. 'I agree,' he said softly. 'That shirt has never looked quite as good on my body as it looks on yours.'

The colour in her face deepened. She was wearing no bra—she had none to wear—and she knew that he must be able to see the rounded outline of her breasts clearly beneath the soft cotton of the T-shirt, see the prominence of her nipples, which were hardening as he looked at her.

'Clothing is clothing,' she said, her voice chill. 'Nothing more.'

His smile tilted. 'Even when it belongs to the enemy?'

Joanna's chin lifted. 'If you've come here to taunt me——'

Khalil sighed. 'I came because Rachelle says you are distressed.'

She stared at him. 'Distressed? *Distressed*?' Joanna laughed. 'Don't be absurd! Why should I be distressed? After all, here I am, the guest of the great Hawk of the North, having an absolutely wonderful time——'

'I take it you are not pleased with out efforts at hospitality.'

'I just told you, I love it here! Especially the security. Armed guards at the door—how much safer could a guest feel?'

Khalil put his hands on his hips. 'Will you promise not to try and escape if I call off the guards?' He laughed at the look on her face. 'No. I didn't think so.'

'Would you really expect me to make such a promise?'

'I have not come here to debate, Joanna. Rachelle says——'

'Rachelle says! For God's sake, if you want to know what I think, why don't you ask me? I don't need Rachelle as my interpreter!'

A smile twisted at his lips. 'I agree. You have no difficulty speaking your mind.'

'So, what do you want to know?' She gave him a beaming smile. 'Is Room Service treating me OK? Do I like the accommodation? The view?' Her mouth narrowed. 'The shackles on the walls?'

He laughed. 'The only thing I see on the walls are paintings.'

'You know what I mean, Khalil! When are you going to let me out of this prison?'

Khalil's face darkened. 'Your freedom is in your father's hands, not mine.'

Joanna looked at him and tried to keep the sudden desperation she felt from showing in her eyes.

'Well?'

'Well, what?'

'Well, when is he coming for me?'

He hesitated. 'I do not know.'

'You do not know?' Joanna said, her voice mimicking his. 'How could that be? You said you'd contacted him.'

'Yes, of course.'

'And?'

'And he has not replied to my message.'

She shot him a cold look. 'That's very hard to believe!'

Khalil's mouth narrowed. 'I am not a liar, Joanna.'

Wasn't he? He had lied well enough to lure her into the desert and carry her here...

No. She'd lied the night they'd met, not he. He'd simply made the most of things. Besides, what would he gain by lying to her now? He had sent Sam a message and Sam—and Sam had not responded...

Sudden despair overwhelmed her. She felt the unwanted sting of tears in her eyes and she started to turn away, but before she could, Khalil stepped quickly forward and clasped her shoulders.

'Joanna?'

She looked up. There was an unreadable expression on his face, something that might almost approach concern. It startled her—until she realised he would have to have some interest in her emotional condition. The last thing he'd want on his hands was an hysterical captive.

'Don't worry, Khalil,' she said with a brittle smile. 'I've no intention of making a scene. I was only thinking that if you really did ask my father to withdraw from the mining deal, you have asked for a great deal.'

A muscle knotted in his cheek. 'Perhaps. But I promise you, I have not asked him for more than you are worth, Joanna.'

She felt a flush rise over her body. How did he manage to do this to her? When he looked at her like this, everything seemed to fade into the background—everything but him, and the awareness of him that he made her feel. It was perverse. It was impossible. And yet——

He bent his head and touched his mouth to hers. The kiss was soft, almost tender, and yet she felt the heat of it race through her blood and confuse her senses.

'Joanna,' he whispered, and his lips took hers again.

She swayed unsteadily and his hands clasped her more tightly, lifting her on tiptoe, moulding her body to his while their mouths clung together. It was Khalil who finally ended the kiss. When he did, Joanna stared at him, her lips parted, her breathing swift. She wanted to say something clever and sharp, something that would put what had just happened into chill perspective—but it was Khalil who did it instead.

'Your father is not a fool,' he said, with a little smile. 'He will do what any man in his right mind would do for you.'

Of course. Any man would meet the ransom demands of his daughter's kidnappers, and Sam was no exception.

Joanna forced a thin smile to her lips. 'You don't have to tell me that, Khalil. I know it. My father will pay what you ask—but you'll never have time to enjoy it. Not when you're going to be rotting in one of Abu's prisons.'

His hands fell away from her. 'Ah, Joanna, Joanna. Whenever I begin to wonder if your spirits are sagging, you say something sweet and loving and reassure me that you're the same soft-hearted creature you've always been!'

'That's the difference between us,' she said. 'You need reminding—but I never for a moment forget what an impossible bastard you are!'

His eyes went dark. 'You play with fire, Joanna.'

'What's the matter? Can't you handle the truth? Or do you expect me to bow and scrape and worship you adoringly, the way Rachelle does?'

To her surprise, he burst out laughing. 'You? Bowing and scraping? It is an interesting thought, Joanna, but I think the only things you will ever scrape will be the chicken coops.'

'What?' She moved after him as he turned and started for the door. 'Never,' she said, 'not in this lifetime...' the door opened '... or any other,' she finished, but it was too late. Khalil was gone.

After a moment, she sighed and walked to the window. Why had she wasted time letting him bait her? There were things she'd meant to ask him, things that would make whatever time she had to spend here more bearable.

There was an enclosed garden just outside, a handsome one, from what she could see of it. Would he permit her to walk in it? Surely, he didn't intend to keep her locked up in——?

A flash of colour caught her eye. Joanna leaned forward. A little girl dressed in jeans, sneakers, and a pale blue polo shirt was playing with a puppy. Despite her own worries, Joanna began to smile. There was something about children and small animals that never failed to move her.

The child laughed as she held out a bright yellow ball, then tossed it across the grass. The puppy wagged its tail furiously, charged after the ball, and brought it back. Joanna's smile broadened. The two were having a wonderful time, judging by the way the girl was laughing. The puppy looked as if it were laughing, too, with its pink tongue hanging out of its mouth.

Joanna tucked her hip on to the window sill and watched, chuckling softly as the game continued, until the ball bounced crazily on the cobblestoned pathway, tumbled into the dark green hedge that bordered it, and vanished.

The puppy searched, as did the little girl, but neither had seen where the ball had gone.

Joanna tapped the window pane. 'There,' she said, 'in the hedge.'

Neither the child nor the dog could hear her.

She tapped the window again. If the girl would just look up...

The child's face puckered. She plopped down in the grass, snatched the puppy to her breast, and began to sob. The puppy licked her face but the child only cried harder as she rocked the animal in her arms.

Joanna turned from the window, hurried to the door, and flung it open. The guard standing outside looked up, startled.

'Excuse me,' she said, brushing past him.

He called out after her, his equivalent, she was certain, of 'Hey, where do you think you're going?' but she was already halfway down the hall, heading towards an arched doorway that she knew must open on to the garden. She went straight through it, pausing only long enough to be sure the child was still sitting in the same place, holding her dog and weeping.

'Don't cry,' Joanna said when she reached her. The little girl looked up, her eyes widening with surprise. Joanna smiled and squatted down beside her. 'Do you understand me? You mustn't cry so hard. You'll make yourself sick.'

The child raised a tear-stained face. 'Who are you?' she said, in perfect English.

'My name is Joanna. And who are you?'

'I am Lilia.' The tears began rolling down her plump cheeks again. 'And I've lost my ball!'

Joanna took the girl's hands in hers. 'It's not the end of the world,' she said softly.

'It was a special ball. My father gave it to me, and——' The tears came faster and faster. 'And he's never coming back!'

Joanna rose to her feet. 'In that case,' she said, 'we'll just have to get that ball, won't we?'

She spotted not one guard but several hurrying towards her. Too bad, she thought defiantly, as she hurried towards the hedge that had swallowed the child's toy. When she reached it, she saw that the foliage was denser than it had seemed from her window. She hesitated, then shook her head over her foolishness. It was only a hedge, and the guards were almost upon her. Quickly, she plunged her hand deep into the bush's green heart.

'Joanna!'

The ball was here somewhere, dammit. If she could just——

'Joanna! Stop it! Do you hear me?'

There! She had it now. She winced as she felt something needle-sharp hit her hand, but what did it matter? Face flushed with triumph, she pulled the yellow ball from the tangle of branches and looked up into the dark, angry face of Khalil.

'Relax, Your Highness,' she said coolly. 'I'd love to escape, but I doubt if burrowing through some shrubbery will get me very far.'

'You fool.' He barked something at Lilia, who had followed after Joanna. The little girl wiped her eyes, dropped a curtsy, and ran off with the puppy at her heels.

Joanna's eyes flashed. 'You see? Everyone bows and scrapes to you, even a slip of a child who——'

Khalil grabbed the ball from her and tossed it aside. 'Would you risk everything for something as stupid as a child's toy?'

'I know a little girl's tears mean nothing to you, oh great one, but then, you're not exactly known for having a heart, are you?' Her chin tilted. 'What now? Do I get flogged? Put on bread and water?'

Khalil snatched her wrist. 'Look,' he growled, lifting her hand.

She looked. There was a single puncture mark in the flesh between her thumb and forefinger.

'So?' Joanna's mouth narrowed. 'Don't tell me all this rage is over my getting scratched by a thorn.'

'No thorn did that, you little idiot! Do you see any thorns on that bush?'

'So what? It's nothing but a little cut. What's the matter, Khalil? Are you afraid I'll sue you?'

'Damn you, Joanna.' He caught hold of her shoulders and shook her. 'Someone should teach you that a smart answer isn't always a wise answer!'

'It won't kill me,' she said coldly. 'I assure you, I've survived worse.'

'You fool,' he said sharply. 'When will you learn to shut up long enough to listen?'

'If you're finished, I'd like to return to my room.' Her teeth flashed in a tight smile. 'Even being locked inside those miserable four walls is preferable to standing here and dealing with you!'

A muscle knotted in Khalil's jaw. 'I couldn't agree more.'

'Well, then,' she said, and turned away from him. But she hadn't taken a step before he caught hold of her and swept her up in his arms.

'Put me down!' Joanna pounded her fist against his shoulder as he strode through the garden and into the coolness of the house. 'Are you deaf, Khalil? I said, put me down!'

'With pleasure,' he growled through his teeth. 'The instant I am done with you, I will do just that.'

'What do you mean?' She pounded on his shoulder again as he swept down the corridor past her room. 'Dammit, where are you taking me?'

He glanced down at her, his eyes shimmering like the heat waves on the desert.

'To my rooms,' he said, with a smile as cold as any she had ever imagined.

Before she could answer, he shouldered open a huge wooden door, then kicked it closed behind him.

Joanna glimpsed a high ceiling, a tapestried wall, and a massive, canopied bed—and then Khalil dumped her on to the mattress, put his hands on his hips, and glared down at her.

'Now, Joanna,' he said, 'let's get down to business.'

CHAPTER EIGHT

KHALIL was angry, angrier than he should have been, considering the circumstances, but what man wouldn't be angry when an educated, intelligent woman insisted on making a damned fool of herself?

'The woman is trying to escape, Highness,' one of his people had cried out, bursting into the library just as he'd begun a strategy session with his ministers.

His men had let her run when they'd realised she had made for the enclosed garden from which there was no escape.

'I'll get her,' Khalil had said, tight-lipped, but instead of chasing down a fleeing Joanna Bennett, he'd stumbled upon a foolish one, up to her silken elbows in a shrub she should have known better than to touch in the first place.

No. That was ridiculous. Even he had to admit that. How could she have known that the seemingly innocent shrub could conceal a venomous insect? It was obvious she hadn't been trying to run away, even though he knew she could hardly wait to see the last of him.

His teeth ground together. Then why was his temper so close to boiling point? He glared down at her. He knew she prided herself on maintaining self-control but in this moment she was as transparent as glass. Looking into her green eyes, he could see her indignation and anger giving way to something else. To fear—and to the bone-deep determination not to let him see that fear.

Instantly, he realised how his sharply spoken words must have sounded. His glare deepened. Did the woman really think him such a savage that he would take her in violence, in some barbaric, retaliatory rage? His nostrils flared with distaste. He would tell her that she was a fool, that he had never in his life forced a woman into his bed and that she was not a woman he would choose to have in his bed, even if she came willingly...

...But then he looked at the glossy auburn hair that lay tumbled over her shoulders, at the rapid rise and fall of her breasts beneath the ridiculously oversized T-shirt she'd insisted on wearing, and it was as if a fist knotted suddenly in his gut. His gaze fell to her mouth, soft as a flower and slightly parted, as if a breeze had disturbed its petals. Desire raged through him, as hot as the fire that sometimes followed a strike of summer lightning in the mountain forests, hardening his groin with a swiftness that stunned him.

What nonsense was this? He was not a boy, given to uncontrollable bursts of adolescent desire. And she was not a woman he would ever want. She was clever and beautiful, yes, but she was soft and spoiled, selfish and stubborn and altogether unyielding.

And yet, she had yielded to him, when he'd kissed her. Each time he had taken her in his arms to humble her, she had instead kindled a fire in his blood, then matched it with a scorching heat of her own.

His breathing quickened. What would happen if he came down on the bed beside her? It was what she expected, he knew, that he would take her now. What would she do if he did? Would she fight him? Or would she ignite with a quicksilver flame under his touch?

'Joanna,' he said, his voice a little thick, and instantly she rose up on her knees and bared her small, white teeth.

'Go on,' she taunted, 'do whatever you're going to do. It's all the excuse I need to claw out your eyes!'

So much for her igniting under his touch! Khalil burst out laughing.

'If you claw out my eyes,' he said reasonably, 'how will I attend to you properly?'

'You couldn't,' she said. 'I mean, you can't. There's nothing you could do that would make me...'

'Relax, Joanna.' The look he gave her was cool, almost disinterested. 'I assure you, I've no designs on your body.'

Her face coloured. 'Then why——?' Her voice rose as he strode into the adjoining bathroom. She could hear water running, cabinet doors opening and closing, and then he reappeared, bearing a small tray arrayed with a small basin, a bottle, cotton pads, and adhesive tape. Joanna's eyes lit with suspicion. 'What's all that for?' she demanded.

He sighed dramatically as he put the tray on the bedside table and rolled back his sleeves.

'I hate to disappoint you,' he said. 'I know you're convinced I'm about to subject you to some ancient and terrible ritual.' He dipped a cotton pad into the basin. 'But I'm not planning anything more exotic than cleaning your hand.'

She jerked her hand back as he reached for it but his fingers curled around her wrist like a vice.

'Come on, Khalil, give me a break! Surely, we're too old to play Doctor.' Her breath hissed through her teeth as he dabbed the pad against her skin. 'Hey! That hurts.'

'Not as much as it will if the bite isn't tended. Hold your arm to the light, please.'

'It's nothing,' she said impatiently. 'No one dies from——'

'You may be an expert on many things, Joanna, but you are hardly one on the flora and fauna of my country. The spider that bit you might well be poisonous.'

'Poisonous?' she said stupidly. 'Hey! Hey, what are you doing?'

'Drawing out the venom.' The breath caught in her throat as he lifted her hand to his mouth. A shudder went through her as she felt the tug of his lips, the light press of his teeth, and then he dropped her hand into her lap and strode into the bathroom. She heard water running in the sink and she closed her eyes, fighting for control, but she could still feel the imprint of his mouth, the heat of it...

'Joanna? Are you feeling faint?'

Her eyes flew open. 'I told you, it's just a bite. I'm not...' She frowned as he uncapped a bottle and dampened a cotton pad with its contents. Her breath hissed as he applied it to her skin. 'Ouch. That stings! What is it?'

'An ancient medication known only to shamans and holy men.' He looked up, and she could see laughter in his eyes. 'It is peroxide, Joanna. What did you think it was?'

'How should I know?' she said stiffly.

Khalil worked in silence for a moment, and then he looked at her again.

'My men think you were trying to escape.'

'I told you, I'd be delighted to escape,' she said with a quick, cool smile. 'But I'm not stupid enough to escape into your garden.'

He laughed softly. 'No. I did not think so.'

She watched as he bent his head and began dabbing at the tiny bite mark again.

'What were you doing, then?'

Joanna shrugged her shoulders. 'The little girl lost her ball. I saw where the ball landed but she didn't, and when she started to cry——'

'Her crying annoyed you?'

'Annoyed me? Of course not. I felt sorry for her. One minute she'd been laughing and the next——' She caught her breath as he ran a finger lightly over her skin.

'The bite will itch, for a day or two,' he said, 'but it will be fine after that.'

'Fine.' Her voice shook a little and he looked up, frowning.

'What is it, Joanna? Does it hurt when I touch you there?'

'No,' she said quickly. 'It doesn't hurt at all.'

What it did, she thought wildly, was send a wave of sensation along her nerve-endings. The feeling was—it was...

'That's great,' she said, snatching her hand away. 'Thank you. I'm sure I won't——'

Khalil clasped her hand in his again. 'I am not done,' he said. 'I want to put some ointment on your hand and then bandage it.'

'It's—it's not necessary. Really.'

'Just hold still, please. I'll try and be more gentle.' His hands moved on her lightly, without pressure. 'It will only take another minute.'

Joanna sat beside him, her spine rigid, as he smoothed a healing cream over her slightly reddened flesh. He would try and be more gentle, he'd said—but he was already being more gentle than she could ever have imagined. She had no doubt that those large, competent hands could tame the wildest desert horse; that they could also stroke her as if his fingers were satin and her skin silk came as a surprise. He was touching her with such care, as if she were too delicate for anything but the most careful caress.

Her breathing quickened. Khalil's head was bowed over her hand. She could see the way his dark hair curled lightly over the nape of his neck, as if it were kissing his tanned skin. The fingers of her free hand tightened against her palm. What would his hair feel like, if she were to touch it? And what would he do, if she reached out and lightly stroked that ebony silk?

Some time between the last time she'd seen him and now, he'd changed his clothes. Gone was the white jellaba; in its place was a very American blue denim shirt and jeans. It was amazing, she thought, how little he looked like a fierce mountain bandit and how much he looked like a man who could walk down a New York street without drawing attention to himself—except that he would always draw attention, wherever he went. He was too self-assured, too ruggedly handsome not to be noticed.

Joanna bit down lightly on her lip. Moments ago, he'd dumped her on this bed and stood over her, fury gleaming in his eyes, and she'd thought he was going to force her to submit to him. The thought had terrified her—and yet, if she were brutally honest, she'd had some other far, darker reaction deep within herself as she'd looked up at him.

What if she'd opened her arms to him? Would the fire of anger have left his eyes and been replaced, instead, by the shine of desire? Her lashes fell to her cheeks and she imagined the feel of his body against hers, the excitement of his possession . . .

Dear God! Joanna's eyes flew open. She really was going over the edge! She wasn't a woman who wanted to be taken against her will any more than he was a man who would take a woman in that fashion. Why would he, when surely any woman he wanted would come to him willingly, when any woman in her right mind would turn to flame in his arms . . . ?

'There,' he said briskly. He capped the bottle, put it on the tray, and rose to his feet. 'That should do it. The next time you want to do something heroic——'

Joanna blew out her breath. 'I wasn't being heroic. I told you, Lilia was crying, and I——'

There was a light knock on the door. 'My lord?' a little voice whispered, and Lilia stepped carefully into the room. She looked from Joanna to Khalil, who folded his arms over his chest in that arrogant posture Joanna had come to recognise. 'I am sorry, my lord,' the child said.

He nodded, his face stern. 'As well you should be.'

Joanna stood up. 'Khalil!'

'Will the lady be all right, my lord?'

'I'm fine,' Joanna said quickly.

Lilia nodded, but her attention was centred on Khalil. 'I really am sorry.' She sniffed, then wiped her hand under her nose. 'I didn't mean——'

'What you mean is, you didn't think.'

'Khalil,' Joanna said, 'for goodness' sake, tell the child that——'

'You have a place to play, Lilia. A safe place, with swings and toys—and with a nursemaid to watch over you.' Khalil's brows drew together. 'You ran away from Amara again, didn't you?'

The child hesitated. 'Well——'

'Tell me the truth, Lilia!'

'Amara fell asleep,' she said, hanging her head. 'She ate her lunch and then she ate most of a box of sweets and then she said she would just sit in the sun and rest...'

The child's mouth twitched. Joanna's eyes flashed to Khalil's face. Astonished, she watched his mouth begin to twitch, too, and then he squatted, held out his arms, and grinned.

'Come and give me a hug, you little devil,' he said. 'I haven't had one in days.'

Lilia laughed as he swung her into his arms. 'I love you, Uncle,' she said.

Uncle? *Uncle*?

He kissed the child on both cheeks, then set her on the floor and gave her a light pat on her bottom.

'Go on,' he said gently. 'Find your puppy and play some other game. I shall speak to Amara.'

'You won't be angry at her?'

He sighed. 'No.'

Lilia smiled. 'Thank you,' she said, and then she turned to Joanna. 'And thank you, for finding my ball.'

Joanna smiled, too. 'You're very welcome.' The child skipped out the door and Joanna cleared her throat. 'I didn't expect——' Khalil looked at her. 'I, um, I never imagined . . . I didn't know Lilia was your niece.'

'It's an honorary title,' he said.

'She's very fond of you.'

'Yes.' His expression was impassive. 'It is many years since any of us ate children for breakfast, Joanna.'

She flushed. 'I never meant to imply that you—that your people . . .'

'No.' His expression grew cold and forbidding. 'That's true enough. You never "imply". Why should you, when you are a veritable expert on our behaviour and customs?'

'Look, I suppose I deserved that. But you can't blame me for—for . . .' She sighed. 'She's a sweet little girl,' she said, after a minute.

Khalil nodded. 'I agree. She's the daughter of Amahl. He was one of my closest advisors.'

'I've never seen——'

'And you won't.' He snatched up the tray of first-aid equipment and stalked to the bathroom, Joanna trailing after him. 'Amahl was killed during a skirmish.' He yanked open the cabinet door and began slamming the first-aid equipment into it. 'Lilia was alone to start with—her mother died in childbirth—but after Amahl's death she had no one.'

Joanna could see the muscles knotting in his shoulders. Her throat tightened. She wanted to reach out, to touch him, to stroke away the tension that held him prisoner and tell him it was all right...

Prisoner? She was the prisoner, not he! She was——

Khalil swung around and faced her. 'Abu is evil, Joanna.' His voice was harsh. 'If your father signs this contract with him, it will ensure that he has enough money to buy the arms he needs to defeat us!'

She stared at him, her eyes wide. The bathroom was mirrored, and she could see their faces in its silvery walls. Khalil's and hers, their reflections seeming to slip into infinity.

What was reality and what was not?

'Abu is the Sultan of Jandara,' she whispered.

'He is a tyrant, and your father knows it.' Khalil reached out and clasped her shoulders. 'He knows it, and yet he would fatten Abu's coffers.'

'You're lying!'

'I told you, Joanna, I do not lie.'

Joanna drew a deep breath. 'I don't understand. How can he be the rightful leader of Jandara if——?'

'*I* am the rightful leader of Jandara! Abu snatched the throne from me when I was a boy.' His face darkened, and she gasped as his fingers bit into her flesh. 'My parents died in a plane crash when I was only a child. Abu and a council of elders were to rule until I came of age. Instead, he killed the elders he couldn't corrupt and seized absolute power.'

Joanna shook her head. 'If he did that, why did he let you live?'

Khalil smiled grimly. 'Perhaps because I would be more dangerous dead, as a martyr, than I am alive.'

'Then—then why haven't you done something? Why haven't you taken back the throne?'

'There is a war raging here, Joanna! You haven't seen it because it isn't the kind that's fought on great battlefields, or with planes and tanks. We meet the enemy when we can find him, we inflict damage—and wait for the day we can destroy him without destroying ourselves.' His mouth twisted. 'I cannot let my men offer their lives for me unless I am certain we can win.'

Joanna stared into Khalil's burning eyes. She wanted to believe him—but if she did, then her father would be the liar. He would be a man who had knowingly struck a deal with a tyrant...

Joanna drew a shaky breath. 'You talk about morality—and yet you deny me my freedom.' She ran the tip of her tongue over her lips. 'If you want me to believe you—if you're telling me the truth, let me go.'

Khalil's face darkened. 'It is out of the question.'

'You see? You make speeches about what is right, but...' She wrenched free of him. 'It's impossible. You stole me, Khalil. You've locked me away, kept me prisoner...'

He said a word under his breath, clasped her shoulders, and spun her towards him.

'I took you for a reason, Joanna. I had no choice.'

'Everyone has choices! Make the right one now. Let me go.'

Their eyes met and held. 'No,' he said. 'I cannot.'

'I'll tell my father what you said about Abu, I promise.'

Khalil shook his head. 'I have spoken, Joanna. I will not free you!'

Angry colour flashed across her cheeks. 'You—you pig-headed, insolent idiot! Why should I believe anything you say?'

'Stop it, Joanna!'

'I won't stop it! You're an arrogant, imperious bastard, and I can hardly wait to see you in chains!'

She cried out as his arms swept around her. 'If you won't keep quiet, I'll silence you myself,' he said, and kissed her.

Joanna twisted wildly in his arms. 'Damn you,' she hissed against his mouth. She bit down, hard enough to draw a bead of blood, but he only laughed and gathered her closer.

'Fight me,' he said, his arms holding her like bands of steel. 'What does it matter, Joanna? Soon you will be crying out my name, moving against me and pleading with me to end this war between us in the one way we both understand.'

'No,' she said, 'that's not true!'

But it was. He wanted her, and she wanted him, and whatever remained of reason fled in Khalil's impassioned kisses, kisses that demanded her submission yet promised his in return. Joanna gave a moaning sob. She wound her arms tightly around his neck and lifted herself to him, pressing her body to his, opening her mouth to the thrust of his tongue. He growled his triumph, lifted her into his arms, and carried her to his bed.

'Joanna,' he whispered.

She looked up as he lowered her to the mattress. He smiled a little, the triumphant smile of a man who knew what he wanted and was about to have it—and, with that smile, passion drained from her bones, leaving behind cold, harsh reason.

How could she let him do this to her? How could she *help* him to do this to her? He had stolen her! She was his prisoner, denied even the right to walk free in the sunshine, and he was telling her ugly lies about her own father and now here she was, in his bed, letting him use the weakness he'd found within her, use this terrible passion she had not even known existed, to make her not just his captive but his ally. She would become not only his hostage but her own, a hostage to her own sexuality.

'Let go of me!'

She slammed her hands against his shoulders and he drew back instantly.

'You're clever,' she said bitterly, 'oh, yes, you're very clever! I have to hand you that, Khalil.' She edged upwards against the pillows, her eyes locked with his. 'If you get me to sleep with you, you can't lose! You'll have me as a playmate so long as I'm here and as an insurance policy after I'm gone.'

He rose to his full height and stared at her. 'What the devil are you talking about?'

'I suppose you're right.' Joanna swung her legs to the floor and stood up. 'It would take a stronger woman than me to watch them hang the man she'd willingly gone to bed with!'

'That's nonsense!'

'Everything my father said about you is true, especially the part about you being a—a barbarian who wants to keep his stranglehold on his pathetic little fiefdom!'

She thought, for an instant, he would strike her. The bones of face showed white through his tan, and his eyes grew dark as stones. She could see him collecting himself, marshalling control of his emotions, and finally he spun on his heels, stalked to the door, and yanked it open. A man standing guard outside snapped to attention. Khalil spat a command at him, and the man nodded.

He looked at Joanna. 'Come,' he said, his voice hard as ice.

'You needn't throw me out.' She fought the desire to run and instead strolled casually to where he stood. 'I'm more than eager to leave.'

'I'm sure you are.' He put his hand in the small of her back and shoved her none too gently into the hall. 'My man will keep you company while you wait.'

'Charming. But what am I to wait for?'

Khalil smiled coldly. 'Smile, Joanna,' he said. 'Your days as a cloistered prisoner are about to come to an end.'

CHAPTER NINE

JOANNA stood in the corridor outside Khalil's bedroom and tried to look as if she found nothing unusual in being guarded by a man wearing a head-dress, a long robe, and a ferocious scowl.

Was she really going to be set free? It was dangerous to let herself believe she was—but what else could he have meant when he'd said she'd been a prisoner too long? Or something like that; she'd been so stunned by the suddenness of his declaration that she wasn't quite sure exactly what it was he'd said except to know that, for the first time since he'd carried her off, she felt a stir of hope.

It would be wonderful to be free, to be away from this awful place and this terrible man. He'd stolen her and now he was feeding her lies, keeping her locked up and under guard—she'd never forgive him for that or for the other indignities he'd heaped on her. Taking her in his arms, kissing her when the last thing she'd ever want were his kisses, sparking a wild passion in her blood that she'd never before known...

'Are you ready, Joanna?'

She spun around. Khalil stood in the open doorway, seeming to fill it. He wore an open-throated white shirt and black, snug-fitting trousers tucked into riding boots. A white cloak was thrown over his shoulders.

'Oh, yes,' she said with a dazzling smile. 'All I have to do is pack my suitcases and——'

'I have no time for games,' he growled.

'No. I'm sure you don't. I'm the only one around here with time on my hands.'

He smiled tightly. 'Perhaps we should discuss the goats and chickens again.'

'Perhaps we should discuss the fact that I'm not accustomed to sitting on my hands all day.'

'Had you shown me you could behave yourself, I intended to give you greater freedom.'

'Had I shown you I could...' Joanna tossed back her head. 'I'm not Lilia, Khalil. You can't make me do your bidding by promising me a reward.'

His eyes narrowed. 'Would you prefer that I threaten you?'

'I would prefer,' she said coldly, 'that you treat me with dignity.'

'You mean, you would prefer that I treat you as if we were in your world, that I dance attendance upon you and meet your every whim with a smile?'

'Is that how you think I live my life? Like some pampered princess in a fairy-tale?'

'Don't be silly. I know better.' Khalil folded his arms over his chest. 'You go to your office at Bennettco every day and put in long, gruelling hours, working side by side with your father.' He smiled grimly. 'That's what you wanted me to believe, isn't it?'

Joanna flushed. What was the sense in pretending? 'I would have gladly put in twenty-four-hour days at the office,' she said. 'But my father is as much of a male chauvinist as you are!'

'Another crime to add to my list.' Khalil turned as one of his men came hurrying down the hall. 'Ah,' he said, taking a silver-trimmed white cloak from his hands, 'you've brought it. Thank you, Ahmed.' He held it out to Joanna. 'Put this on.'

She eyed the garment with scorn. 'I'm not one of your women. You can't wrap me up like a Christmas package!'

Khalil sighed wearily. 'I would not dream of making a Christmas package of you. You are far too prickly a gift to give anyone.'

'Good. Then you can forget about me wearing that thing.'

He stepped forward and draped the cloak about her rigid figure, drawing the hood up and over her bright auburn hair.

'You will wear it,' he said.

Joanna glared at him. 'Why?'

Khalil put his hand in the small of her back and pushed her gently ahead of him along the corridor.

'For no more devious reason than your comfort. It's cool in the mountains this time of year.' He looked at her and shook his head. 'Why must you always search for hidden meanings?'

'Dammit!' She shrugged free of his hand and swung towards him, her mouth trembling with anger. 'Anyone listening to you would think you've treated me with honesty and respect from the moment we met!'

His eyes darkened. 'I've dealt with you as you deserved.'

'Would you respect me more if I'd spent my life herding goats?'

To her surprise, a grin spread across his face. 'Are we back to that? It might be a good idea for me to have you spend the day with the goat-herders!'

'I'd rather spend it with Lilia,' she snapped. 'That poor little girl seems almost as miserable as I am.'

Khalil's smile vanished. 'I try my best to make her happy,' he said stiffly.

'She's very lonely.'

'Do you think I don't know this?' His mouth tightened. 'I realise that she could use companionship—but it never occurred to me that you would enjoy spending time with her.'

'No. Why would it, considering that you're so certain you know all there is to know about me? You accused *me* of trying to categorise *you*, but you've done the same thing to me from the instant we met!'

'I know what I see.'

'Really. Then I suppose you know that I like children very much, that for a while, when I was at school, I thought of studying to be a teacher.'

'You?' He smiled again. 'A teacher?'

'That's right. Me, a teacher. And I'd have been a good one, too.'

'What stopped you, then?'

Joanna hesitated. 'My father didn't approve.'

'And you changed your course of study, because of that?' Khalil's smile was open this time, and genuine. 'That's hard to believe.'

'I changed it because...' She hesitated again, uncertain of why she was telling him something she'd never told anyone. 'I thought he disapproved of teaching because he wanted me to come into Bennettco.'

'But he didn't,' Khalil said softly.

Joanna shook her head. 'No. He—he just wanted me to—to——'

'He wanted you to be what I have accused you of being: a handsome accessory for a man to wear proudly on his arm.'

'Yes!'

Her head came up sharply; she was more than ready to tell him what she thought of such an attitude. But he wasn't looking at her with derision; what she saw in his eyes was nothing she understood.

'Perhaps we see only what we wish to see,' he said after a moment.

It was a strange thing for him to have said, Joanna thought. She wanted to ask him what he'd meant, but he put his arm lightly around her shoulders and they stepped out into bright sunshine. Ahead, two horses stood waiting in the cobblestoned courtyard. She recognised Najib instantly. The big stallion was pawing impatiently at the ground. But there was another horse standing beside him, a smaller, more delicate one, as white as Najib was black. Her bridle was hung with tiny silver bells, and her saddle was a masterwork of finely tooled leather.

'This is Sidana,' Khalil said, gently stroking the mare's long nose. He smiled. 'She is gentle, although even she may object if you mount from the wrong side. I promise you that she will take us safely to our destination and then back.'

Joanna looked at him. 'You're not setting me free, are you?' she said, with a sinking heart.

He shook his head. 'I am not.'

She nodded. 'I see.'

'No,' Khalil said fiercely, 'you do not see! But you will. After today, you will not believe the lies you have been told by your father.'

'What lies will I believe, then? Yours?'

The muscle in his jaw knotted with anger. 'Go on,' he said tightly, 'get on the horse.'

'This is pointless! If you really think I'm dumb enough to fall for some charade you've set up in my honour——'

'Get into the saddle, Joanna—or I'll lift you on to Najib's back and you will ride with me!'

Ride with him? Feel his arms around her, his heart beating against her back? Feel his breath warm at her temple, his thighs hard as they enclosed hers? Colour flamed in her cheeks.

'I'd sooner ride with the devil,' she muttered, and she grabbed for the pommel, stabbed her foot into the stirrup, and climbed into the saddle.

'All right?' She nodded and Khalil sprang on to Najib's back in one fluid motion. 'Hold the reins loosely but firmly, so the mare knows you're in command. You'll have no problem with her. She is sweet-tempered and obedient, and very well trained.'

'The perfect female,' Joanna said sweetly as they started from the courtyard. Behind them, two of Khalil's men and their horses fell into place at a slight distance.

Khalil laughed. 'I never thought of it that way, but now that you point it out, I suppose she is.'

'You still haven't told me where we're going.'

'You'll know the place when you see it.'

'I've no idea what that's supposed to mean.'

Khalil smiled. 'Why don't you relax, Joanna? You've complained about being cooped up—well, here's your chance to enjoy some fresh air and new sights. Look around you, and enjoy this beautiful day.'

He was right, she thought grudgingly. It was, indeed, a beautiful day. The dark green mountains pierced a sky so blue and so bright it almost hurt the eyes. It was spring, and wild flowers were beginning to carpet the gentler slopes, filling the air with their sweetness.

It was lovely here. Joanna thought of New York and Dallas, of crowded city streets thronged with people and automobiles. All of it seemed far, far away. How easy it would be to be happy in a place like this, she thought suddenly. Unbidden, her gaze flew to the man riding at her side.

What was wrong with her? Here she was, being taken out on a tether and thinking nonsensical thoughts, while somewhere her father must be agonising over her welfare.

'Listen,' she said, glaring at him, 'if you think taking me to some—some staged bit of theatre will turn my head around...'

'There is the stage, Joanna, and the players.' Khalil reached out and caught the reins of her horse. 'An hour from now, you can tell me what you think of the production.'

Before she could speak, he tapped his heels into Najib's flanks and both horses shot forward. Joanna clung to the mare's reins, too intent on what she saw to be afraid of the sudden swift motion.

They were entering a town, a real one, with houses and narrow streets. Not even Khalil could have had this place created overnight, she thought wildly as he brought their horses to a stop.

'Would you like to get down and walk around, Joanna?'

She started. Khalil had dismounted. He was standing beside the mare, looking up at her, his face as expressionless as a mask.

She nodded, too bemused to offer any objection when he held up his arms. She went into them readily, her hands light on his shoulders to steady herself, and he eased her gently to the ground.

'What is this place?' she asked.

'It is Adaba. Our central marketplace.' He took her arm and they set off along the narrow street, his two men trailing behind them. 'I thought you might like to see some of my downtrodden subjects with your own eyes.'

She wanted to make a clever retort but already her gaze was moving towards the market ahead. People were selling things and buying things, and she could hear bursts of chatter and laughter. It looked very much like the outdoor markets that flourished in lower Manhattan. People were busy. And happy. But—but...

'Observe the way my people cringe at the sight of me,' Khalil murmured.

In fact, most of the people didn't seem to notice him or, if they did, they paused in their transactions only long enough to smile and touch their foreheads.

'What did you do,' Joanna asked with a chill smile, 'tell them you'd chop off their heads if they threw themselves at your feet this one time?'

His hand tightened on her arm. 'Why be so uncreative, Joanna? Perhaps I threatened to skin them alive if they didn't behave.'

'No doubt!'

A woman came hurrying up to them. She touched her hand to her forehead but Khalil stopped her, put his arm around her shoulders, and kissed her cheek. The woman glanced shyly at Joanna and said something that made him laugh before she melted away into the crowd.

Joanna tried unsuccessfully to wrench her arm from his grasp. 'What's so funny?' she demanded. 'Or does the sight of a captive always rate a chuckle in this crowd?'

Khalil grinned. 'She wanted to assure me that even though your eyes are an interesting colour, she still prefers the blue of mine.'

'A fan,' Joanna said drily. 'How wonderful. Did she want your autograph, too?'

'Her name is Cheva. She was my nurse, when I was a boy. She loved my English mother very much, and it always pleased her that I inherited her——'

Joanna stared at him. 'Your mother was English?'

He laughed. 'Close your mouth, Joanna. It is a warm day, and there are flies about. She was, yes.' His arm slipped to her waist as he led her deeper into the crowded marketplace. 'She was an archaeologist, come to Jandara on a dig. I know you would like me to think my barbarian father abducted her, but the truth is they met at an official function, fell in love, and were married ten days later.'

'And were they happy?'

'The barbarian and the Englishwoman?'

'No,' Joanna said quickly, 'I didn't mean——'

'They were very happy. Is that so difficult to believe?'

Joanna looked at him. 'I—I'm confused,' she whispered. 'I don't—I don't really know what to believe.'

His arm tightened around her. 'Perhaps you will know, by the afternoon's end.'

When the sun began dropping in the sky, they made their way back to the horses. By then, Joanna's head was spinning. Nothing was as she'd expected—and yet, in her heart, she knew that everything was as she'd begun to suspect it might be.

She didn't speak the language of Khalil's people, but it didn't matter. Many of them spoke English, especially the younger ones.

'It is an important language, the language of nations, Prince Khalil says, so we learn it,' a horse trader told her earnestly. 'We start young, when we first enter school.'

'Ah,' said Joanna. 'Only boys learn a language, then?'

'Is that how it is in your country?' the young man said, frowning. 'That only boys may learn?'

She stared at him. 'No. Of course not. Boys and girls both learn what they wish.'

'Here, too.' He smiled. 'I am glad to hear that America believes in educating its women.'

Khalil laughed. 'I assure you,' he said, clapping the young man on the shoulder, 'it does!'

At a stall where fresh fruits lay heaped in abundance, a group of young women stood chatting.

'It must be difficult,' Joanna said to one of them, 'to raise a family here, so far from modern conveniences.'

The young woman nodded. 'It is not simple.'

Joanna's brows arched as she glanced at Khalil, who stood several feet away, lounging against a stall.

'Why don't you leave, then?' she said. Her voice fell in pitch. 'Is it because Prince Khalil will not permit it?'

The young woman repeated Joanna's words to her friends, who covered their mouths and laughed.

'We are free to leave, if we choose,' she said, turning back to Joanna. 'But only a fool would wish to live in the south, under the rule of Abu. Surely, you know this.'

Joanna stared at the woman. *I don't know what I know*, she wanted to say... But she only smiled.

'Thank you for talking with me,' she said.

She was silent when Khalil took her hand and drew her forward along the dusty street.

'Well, Joanna?' he asked softly. 'Have you seen reality?'

'It's been a long day, Khalil. I'm tired. Can we go back now, please?'

He looked at her, then nodded. 'As you wish.'

They made their way to where the horses waited. Joanna walked to the mare's side and put her hand on the animal's neck. She closed her eyes and pressed her forehead lightly against the coarse hair.

'Joanna.' Khalil's voice was gentle and so was the hand he placed on her shoulder. He said her name again but she didn't answer. After a moment, he spoke to his men. One of them reached for the mare's reins, and they led her away.

Khalil clasped Joanna's waist and lifted her on to the back of the stallion, then swung into the saddle behind her. His arms went around her as he gathered the reins into his hands, but she didn't protest. A terrible languor had crept over her.

The town fell behind them as they rode slowly towards the mountains. Finally, in a field of wild flowers, Khalil reined in the horse and slid to the ground. He looked at Joanna and held up his arms. She hesitated, then put her hands on his shoulders and dropped lightly to the ground.

'What is wrong, Joanna?'

She bowed her head, not wanting him to see the sudden dampness she knew must be glinting on her lashes, but he framed her face in his hands and lifted it to him.

'Is the truth so awful to see?' he said softly.

She shook her head again. Had she seen the truth, or had she seen illusion? It was becoming harder and harder to tell.

'Then why are you crying, Joanna?'

'I'm not,' she said, while one small tear coursed down her cheek.

He smiled a little and caught it on his fingertip. 'What is this, if not a tear?'

She sighed as she stepped away from him. Slowly, she bent and plucked a daisy from the chorus nodding at her ankles. She lowered her face to it, inhaling its sweetness, and then she stared blindly into the distance, where the mountains rose towards the sky. At last, she turned to Khalil and said what she had not even wanted to think.

'You told me the truth when you said the price of my freedom would be my father's willingness to give up his deal with Abu, didn't you?'

He nodded. 'Yes.'

Joanna swallowed hard. 'And he's refused to do it, hasn't he?'

Khalil nodded again. 'I'm sorry,' he said in a low voice. 'The only reality I wished you to see was that of my people.'

'There are many different realities, Khalil. Perhaps—perhaps it's time I finally faced my own.'

'Joanna.' She lifted her head and the hood of her cloak fell back, revealing her pale oval face and the long, fiery spill of her hair. 'I am certain he thinks I will change my mind and send you back to him.'

'And will you?' Her eyes caught his. 'Will you send me back, even though you haven't gotten what you wanted from Bennettco?'

Khalil came closer to her and cupped her face in his hands. 'How can I send you back?' he said fiercely. 'How can I do that, Joanna?'

He couldn't. She was his pawn, his bargaining chip—and, knowing that, believing she was in the hands of a man he thought a bandit and a barbarian, her father was still reluctant to do the one thing that would free her, to give up a fortune in the earth for his daughter's release.

No. No! It couldn't be! Khalil was lying. He was lying about everything.

'If there's a shred of decency in you, you'll free me,' she said.

His eyes darkened. 'I told you, I cannot.'

'You've lied to me! You haven't really contacted my father——'

'Joanna!' He took her by the shoulders. 'Listen to me.'

'My father loves me,' she said, her mouth trembling.

'In his way, I'm sure he does. But——'

'There is no "but", Khalil. Whatever you showed me today was—it was interesting, but——'

'Interesting? What do you mean, "interesting"?'

'I mean, it's interesting to—to see a little backwater town where—where people aren't living in poverty and misery, and I suppose—I suppose it must be quite a salve to your ego, hearing them talk about how wonderful you are, but that's not the whole story. There's more to it.'

'Joanna, dammit! If you won't listen to me, listen to yourself! What you're saying makes no sense.'

'No!' She flung her hands over her ears. 'I won't listen! I won't!'

'You will listen,' he said fiercely, catching her wrists and forcing her hands to her sides. 'You will, because—because...' He looked into her eyes, and then he pulled her into his arms and his mouth fell on hers.

'Don't!' Joanna pushed against his chest. 'I hate you, Khalil!'

'Liar,' he whispered, catching her mouth with his again.

'You think you can solve everything this way,' she said, twisting her face away from him. 'You think you can silence me and—and make me believe things that aren't true!'

Khalil's arms tightened around her. 'The only truth that matters is this one, this hunger that has been between us since the night we met.'

'Don't try and make it sound romantic! We met because you were determined to make it impossible for Bennettco to conduct legitimate business, and—and then you—you kidnapped me! You carried me off on your plane and——'

'And desired you, even then.' He laughed huskily. 'A hundred years ago, I would have carried you off on the back of my horse.'

'Exactly!' Joanna thrust her hands against his shoulders. 'Your ancestors were barbarians, and you——'

'My ancestors knew what they wanted and took it.' He caught her hands in his and held them against his heart. 'As I want you now—as you want me.'

'No! That's not true! I despise you, Khalil, I——'

He kissed her again, his mouth moving softly against hers.

'Despise me all you will,' he whispered, 'but do not deny me—or yourself.'

He was wrong. She was not denying anything. She didn't want this, didn't want his mouth on hers or his hand moving against her skin...

No. No, she didn't. She didn't...

Oh, God! With a desperate cry, Joanna threw her arms around Khalil's neck. He whispered her name and then his open mouth met hers in a wild kiss. His fingers speared into her hair as they sank to the ground and she fell back among the flowers, taking him with her. Khalil groaned and kissed her again and again, his mouth hot against hers.

It was as if Joanna were being swept along in a fever of desire. Her fingers flew to the neck of his jellaba, burrowed beneath his open-throated shirt. She had to touch his skin, had to feel its heat against hers or surely she would die.

Khalil lifted her to him, curving her soft body into the hardness of his. He kissed her deeply, crushing her mouth under his until she knew the taste of him would be a part of her forever.

He knelt and drew her up with him. 'Joanna,' he whispered as he slipped the white cloak and then her cotton shirt from her body. The air was cool against her skin, but his mouth and hands were hot. She caught her breath as he cupped her breasts and when he bent and kissed the nipples, she cried out in pleasure.

Khalil lowered her gently to the grass, then drew back.

'No,' she cried, reaching out to him—but he had only left her so he could strip off his jellaba and then his shirt. How beautiful he was! His skin was the colour of honey, his muscles hard and clearly defined. He was male perfection, and he was hers.

'Touch me,' he whispered, taking her hands in his and bringing them to his chest.

She gasped at the feel of his skin, hot from the sun and from desire.

'Joanna, my beautiful Joanna.' He came down beside her and stroked his fingers along her skin, over the curve of her breasts, down over the slight arch of her belly. 'How I want you,' he whispered, 'how I have wanted you from the moment I saw you.'

She reached up and clasped his head, brought his mouth to hers and kissed him, and then she smiled.

'How much do you want me?' she whispered.

A dark flush rose along his cheeks. He clasped her hand, brought it to his mouth and bit lightly at the soft skin below her thumb, then drew it slowly down his body, to where his aroused flesh pressed against his trousers. Her lashes fluttered to her cheeks as he cupped her hand over him. His erection seemed to pulse through the cloth, the heat of it burning her palm like flame.

'That much,' he said thickly. He bent to her and kissed her, his tongue moving within her mouth as she knew his body would soon move within hers.

A primitive rush of joy and desire swept through her. This was what she wanted, what she'd wanted from the start. Khalil, in her arms. Khalil, kissing her and touching her and bearing her down, down into the soft, sweet grass...

. . . Khalil, her captor. Her keeper. He had spoken of reality, and of truth, and yet wasn't that the one truth that mattered? She wasn't here of her own free will, she was here because one man refused to bargain for her freedom and another refused to grant it—and now she was in the arms of the man who'd caused the conflict, behaving as he'd predicted she would from the first night he'd met her.

With a cry, Joanna shoved free of Khalil's arms and scrambled to her feet, snatching up her cloak and whipping it around her, trembling with rage at him, at her father, but most of all, at herself. Khalil rose too, his eyes blurred with desire, and held out his hand.

'Joanna,' he whispered, 'what is it?'

'Who in hell do you think you are?' she said shakily. 'Treating me like—like one of your slave girls!'

His brows knotted together. 'What?'

'I've read a lot of stuff about women and—and this kind of sex,' she said, her words rushing together, 'about—about rape fantasies, but—but I never believed any of it, not for a minute, until——'

'Stop it!' Khalil's mouth twisted as he took a step towards her. 'You're talking nonsense.'

'I'm talking reality. Aren't you the one who's big on that?' Her breath was coming fast, in hard little gasps; she felt as if she'd been running for her life and it occurred to her that, in some strange way, she had been. 'I don't know how you set up today's performance in Adaba, my lord Khalil, but it doesn't matter. The point is, I've seen through it. Sam was right. You *are* a savage, and you always will be!'

He stepped forward swiftly and she flinched back, determined to show him no fear but unable to stop herself from reacting to the terrible darkness in his eyes.

'Get on the horse,' he said softly, in a voice that sent a shudder along her spine. 'Sit still and say nothing until we reach the palace.'

Joanna tossed her head. 'Certainly, my lord. Of course, my lord. Your every wish is my——'

She gasped as his hands closed on her shoulders.

'Push me, Joanna,' he growled. 'Push me, and you'll find out exactly how savage I can be.'

Her lips parted, preparatory to another quick rejoinder, but then she looked into his eyes and saw the coldness in them. The Hawk of the North, she thought, and a shudder went through her.

'That's right,' he said, very softly. 'I could do anything to you now, and no one—no one!—would ever call me to task for it. Now, turn around, get on the horse, and obey my every order. If you can do that, perhaps you'll get back to the palace safely.'

Joanna clamped her lips together defiantly, swung away from him, and did as he'd commanded. But as he swung into the saddle behind her and jabbed his heels hard into Najib's flanks, a little part of her wondered if she'd ever really be safe again.

CHAPTER TEN

JOANNA paced the confines of her room. Twenty paces to one wall, fifteen to the other, then back again. After a week, she knew the dimensions as well as she knew those of the garden, of the palace grounds, of Khalil's library. And she knew, too, that she would never again look at a caged beast without feeling a swift pang of compassion.

Not that she was being mistreated. Never that. If anything, the circumstances of her captivity had improved since that day in the meadow. Rachelle had brought her the news the following morning.

'You may walk with me where you wish, Joanna,' she'd said with a smile, 'and you may use my lord's library at will.'

Joanna's lips tightened. Perhaps Khalil had thought he could convince her he wasn't the savage she'd called him by allowing her to read his books and stroll the grounds. But he was wrong. She knew him for what he was, and nothing would ever change that now. The reality he'd wanted her to see wasn't in Adaba, it was here, in the way he kept her captive, in the way Rachelle turned pale each time Joanna dared to speak of her lord and master as the scoundrel he was.

Adaba! Joanna laughed bitterly. The dog and pony show that had been staged there only proved just how much power Khalil really wielded. Adaba had been a stage set! Oh, the thriving marketplace had probably been real enough—but the idiotically happy villagers had been straight out of Disneyworld!

137

Had Khalil bought their compliance with threats? Had
he bribed them with promises? Or were the people who'd
been so artfully displayed for her benefit simply among
the worshipful followers that inexplicably collected
around every tyrant the world had ever known, from
Attila the Hun straight through to Josef Stalin?

Joanna kicked her discarded shoes out of the way and
stalked the length of the room again, remembering how
she'd awakened here that first morning, coming hazily
out of a dream in which her father had been so busy
moving a piece around a game-board that he hadn't
noticed the horseman riding down on her.

'Stupid,' she muttered, flinging back her head. 'You
were so stupid, Joanna!'

Her father wasn't blind to what was happening to her.
He just didn't care!

No. No, that was putting things too harshly. Her father
cared. It was just that he wasn't worried about her being
held here. Why should he? He'd figured what she should
have realised all along, that although Khalil had not
hesitated to abduct her he wouldn't harm her, no matter
what he threatened. He needed her to get what he
wanted.

Sam had understood from day one. He had lots of
time to wheel and deal and see if he couldn't come up
with a way to secure her release without giving up the
lucrative contract he'd worked so hard to get. So what
if she'd been sitting here, docile as a clam, waiting to
be rescued while Khalil spun a web of confusion around
her!

Joanna spun towards the mirror on the far wall and
stared at her reflection. The woman in the mirror looked
well. Her cheeks had taken on a pink glow from the
hours she spent in the garden. The sun had burnished
her hair, and her eyes gleamed brightly.

'It is our mountain air that brings such a glow,' Rachelle had said just this morning.

Joanna smiled coldly. The girl was almost pitiably naïve. What her eyes glowed with was rage—and yet, for all her anger, she'd been able to do nothing to alter things.

But that was about to change. After days of scheming, she had finally come up with an idea that might work.

'With an idea that *will* work,' she whispered to her reflection.

God, it had to!

She took a deep breath. There was no reason to wait another minute. It was time.

Determinedly, she stabbed her feet into her shoes, then stalked to the mirror again. She peered into the glass and took half a dozen slow, deep breaths. Good. Now to relax her features. Yes. That was the way. She looked wistful, almost forlorn. Now a little tilt of the head. Not too much. Just enough to... OK. That was fine.

'It's now or never,' she said softly, and then she turned and walked to the door.

The guard in the corridor snapped to attention the instant the door swung open.

'*Ya?*'

Joanna gave him what she hoped was a tremulous smile. 'I should like to see the Prince.'

His brow furrowed and he shook his head.

'The Prince,' she said. 'Khalil.'

'Dee Prinz?'

'Khalil. Yes. I must speak with him.'

'Rachelle, *ya?*'

'No. I don't want to see Rachelle. I want to see your Prince.'

'Prinz. *Ya*. Rachelle.'

'Oh, for heaven's sake,' Joanna snapped, her modest smile gone in a flash, 'if everyone here speaks English, what stroke of bad luck put *you* at my door?'

She elbowed past the man before he had time to react and began marching down the corridor. His voice called after her, rising in intensity, and then she heard the thud of his footfalls following her. His hand closed none too gently on her shoulder.

'Let go of me, you ape,' she snarled. 'Let go, or I'll kick you in the——'

'What is going on here?'

Joanna and the guard both swung towards the sound of that steely voice. Khalil stood in the doorway of a room just beyond them, his hands on his hips, his expression grim.

The guard began babbling an explanation, but Joanna cut it short.

'Tell your Dobermann to let go of me,' she said.

Khalil's brows rose a little, but he barked out a command and the man released her.

'Now, Joanna, suppose you tell me what you are doing here.'

'I have to talk to you,' she said stiffly. 'I told this—this creature that, but he didn't understand me.'

'Mustafa is neither an ape, a dog, nor a creature. It is hardly his fault he doesn't speak your tongue. He was told to send for Rachelle if you needed something.'

'Rachelle can't help me. Only you can do that.'

'I am busy.'

'I'm sure you are. But——'

'Speak with Rachelle,' he said as he stepped back inside the room. 'She will convey your message to——'

'Wait!' Joanna sprang forward and thrust her hand against the door. The guard sprang forward too, clasping her arm and growling a warning, and almost too late she remembered that she'd come here with every intention of playing the reserved, unhappy maiden. 'Please,' she murmured softly, and turned her face up to Khalil's with a desperation that made her stomach threaten to give up her breakfast.

But it worked. She could see the faintest softening along the hard, set line of his mouth. He stared at her for a few seconds and then he waved his hand at Mustafa, who let her go instantly.

'I will give you five minutes, Joanna.'

She nodded as he opened the door and motioned her past him. She glanced around curiously. This was his den, she thought, or——

'This is my office.'

She swung around. Khalil was standing at the closed door, looking at her.

'I didn't realise I'd spoken aloud.'

'You didn't.' Frowning, he walked quickly to a handsome old desk that stood before the window. 'But I knew you must be wondering what possible use a savage could have for a room such as this, so I decided to save you the trouble of asking.'

'I didn't come here to quarrel, Khalil.'

'Why did you come here, then?' He pushed aside a stack of papers and leaned back against the desk, his eyes cool and steady on hers. 'If it is to ask if I have had any word from your father, I have not.'

'No.' She touched the tip of her tongue to her lips. 'No, I—I didn't come for that, either.'

'What is it, then?' He frowned, pushed back the sleeve of his shirt, and looked at his watch. 'I have much to do, and little time to spare.'

You arrogant s.o.b., Joanna thought. You impossible, imperious bastard...

'Well? What was so important that you saw it necessary to push past my man and disgrace him?'

She ached to tell him that it was she who had been disgraced, from the minute she'd walked into the Oasis Restaurant almost a week ago. But she had a plan, and she was going to make it work.

'I've been thinking about something we touched on the day you took me to Adaba——'

'Nothing that happened that day is worth discussion,' he said, his face hardening. He leaned away from the desk. 'Now, if that's all——'

'I told you that I was bored, sitting around and doing nothing,' Joanna said quickly. He looked at her, and she forced herself to smile politely. 'Surely, you can understand that.'

'I have granted you the freedom of the grounds,' he said. 'And the use of my library.'

'Oh, yes. You've been very generous.'

His eyes narrowed, and Joanna groaned inwardly. Don't overdo it, she told herself. The man may be arrogant, but he's not a fool.

'Then what more do you want of me?' His look hardened. 'If you have come to ask to spend time with Lilia, I must tell you that I have changed my mind about permitting it. I do not think you would be a good influence on her.'

Joanna's chin lifted. 'No,' she said evenly, 'of course not. She's much better off in your company.'

His eyes flashed to hers and she smiled pleasantly. After a moment, he nodded stiffly towards the shelves that lined the walls.

'There are more books here, but I doubt if they would be to your liking. However, if you wish, I will tell Rachelle to bring you——'

'Thank you. But I've enough to read. I need to do something active.'

'Rachelle takes you walking each afternoon.'

Like a pet dog on a leash, she thought. 'Yes,' she said evenly, 'she does. But I need more activity than that.'

His lips drew back from his teeth. 'I wish I could help you, but, unfortunately, we haven't much to offer in the way of parties or discos.'

'Exercise,' she said, hoping he couldn't hear the sharp edge of anger in her voice. She gave him another stiff smile. 'That's what I'm talking about. I'm not used to sitting around, Khalil. When my father and I are in New York, I work out at a gym.'

'I know this will astound you,' he said, his eyes cold, 'but somehow I've not got around to having a Nautilus machine installed.'

Oh, how pompous he was, how arrogant . . .

'I didn't think you would have,' she said pleasantly.

'Well, then——'

'When my father and I are on our ranch outside Dallas, I ride.'

'Ride?' he said, his brows angling up in his otherwise expressionless face.

'Yes. We have horses, and——'

'You?' He laughed. 'On a horse?'

'What's so funny?' she said, the carefully drawn smile slipping from her face.

Khalil shook his head. 'Nothing much. I was just remembering how you couldn't tell the front of my horse from the rear.'

'I was upset.'

'Not as upset as Najib,' he said, chuckling. 'He must have thought he was——'

'I don't give a damn what that miserable black beast thought!' Joanna slammed her hands on her hips. 'He's not a horse, he's—he's a creature come straight out of a nightmare.'

'Like his owner,' Khalil said, very pleasantly.

'Yes! Exactly like...' She stared at him, horrified. 'No,' she said quickly. 'No, I didn't mean——'

'Stop this farce, Joanna!' His smile vanished; the stony look settled on his face again and he rose to his full height and glared at her. 'I am not for a moment going to believe that you have suddenly turned into a sweet-tempered lamb when we both know that what you are is a sharp-toothed vixen. Tell me what it is you want, and be quick about it.'

Joanna nodded. 'All right. I was quite serious when I said I was going crazy with boredom and just as serious when I said I like to ride. Don't look at me that way, Khalil! I was too upset the night you brought me here to think straight, about getting on and off your horse or anything else.'

He nodded curtly. 'Perhaps.'

'It's the truth! I didn't have any trouble the other day, did I? I didn't need you to tell me how to handle the mare.'

He scowled. 'She is docile.'

'I can ride, I tell you. And I came here to ask you to let me ride an hour a day, to——'

'It is out of the question.'

'Why?' Joanna folded her hands in front of her so he wouldn't see them tremble. If he denied her this... 'Why?' she repeated. 'I do know how! If you don't believe me, you can take me out yourself the first time, you can watch me——'

'No.' He swung away from her so she couldn't see his face and walked around the desk. 'I'm much too busy to waste time in your company, Joanna.'

The sharp words knifed into her breast, although surely what she felt was anger at his insolence, not pain at his dismissal.

'I wouldn't expect you to.'

He looked at her and smiled. 'Do you really think me so stupid, that I would let you ride by yourself?'

'What I thought was that you could let me ride with an escort.'

'It's impossible.' He sat down behind the desk, bent over some papers, and began rifling through them. 'Now, if you're done——'

'Why is it impossible?'

Khalil looked up. 'Because I said it was.'

'You could let me ride the mare—heaven knows the only thing she'd do is plod along obediently beside my guard's horse.'

'Joanna——'

Desperation made her do what she'd promised herself she would never give him the satisfaction of doing. Her eyes grew shiny with unshed tears, her mouth trembled, and when she spoke, her voice did, too.

'Please,' she whispered, 'Khalil, please! I'll—I'll die if I have to sit around like a caged bird.'

Her words drifted away and she fell silent, hating herself for having thrown herself on his mercy, hating herself even more for the real wave of despair that suddenly threatened to overwhelm her. Why was looking at him, seeing that coldness in his eyes, so agonising?

She swung away. 'I'm sorry I've wasted your time.'

His chair scraped against the floor. She heard the sound of his footsteps coming towards her, felt the weight of his hands on her shoulders.

'Joanna.' He turned her towards him. 'Look at me.' When she did, he frowned down at her. 'Is it so terrible here for you?'

'Of course it is. How do you think it feels to be a captive?'

'Yes.' His voice was low. 'That is what you are, Joanna. My captive.'

Their eyes met. A soft sound rose in Joanna's throat as she looked into the dark blue depths of his eyes. He was right. She was his captive. She belonged to him.

There was a sudden tension in the room. Her heart began to race. She remembered how he'd kissed her in the meadow, how he'd drawn her down into the soft, sweet grass, how the heat of his mouth and the heat of the sun had seemed the same...

She stepped back before he could reach for her. 'I know what I am.' Her voice was cool and steady, although her heart was still pounding. 'And if you are half the great humanitarian you claim to be, I think it's time you considered my feelings and not just your own.'

Khalil's mouth thinned. 'Is that what you think this is about?'

'I've no wish to argue the issue, Khalil. I came to ask a favour of you. Will you let me ride, or won't you?'

Long seconds passed. Then he moved past her, marched to the door, and wrenched it open. The guard stepped forward, and Khalil barked a series of orders. When he finished, he looked at Joanna.

'It is done.'

She could hardly draw breath. 'You mean—you mean, you've given permission for me to ride?'

'Once daily, and only in the company of two of my men.' His face turned stern. 'I will be away the next few days, Joanna. My men will guard you well and keep you safe.'

'They'll make sure I don't run away, you mean.'

His expression didn't change. 'I must have your word that you will never try to slip away from them.' When she hesitated, he closed the slight distance between them and clasped her shoulders. 'Your word, Joanna! Or I will not permit you to ride.'

Joanna bit down lightly on her bottom lip. What did it matter if she lied? She wasn't his guest, she was here against her will!

'You have it,' she said.

She smiled faintly, then made her way past him and out of the door.

'Do you speak English?' Khalil heard her say to the guard, and when the man answered that he did, Joanna nodded. 'We will go to the stables,' she said, as if she had spent her entire life giving orders to men with fierce faces and flowing robes.

Despite himself, Khalil smiled as he walked slowly to the window. They were out in the sunshine now, Joanna and the guard. Another of his men joined them so that they flanked her. They were big men, better than six feet tall, and she was a woman of average height made smaller looking by fragile bone structure. Yet, in some strange way, she looked every bit their equal, if not physically then surely in determination.

And in courage. Sighing, he turned and sat down slowly at his desk. She was not quite what he'd thought she was, this Joanna Bennett. Khalil frowned and picked up his pen. It would be good when her fool of a father came to his senses and agreed to do that which had to be done. His people would be safe, Abu would take a step back, and Joanna—she would go back to the pretty world in which she belonged. He would forget her in an instant...

Certainly he would.

The pen dropped from his fingers. It seemed a long time until he picked it up again and bent over the papers strewn across his desk.

* * *

Joanna's guard seemed confused early the next morning when she opened her bedroom door and stepped out into the hall.

'I'm going horseback riding,' she said as she pushed past him and strode briskly down the corridor. She knew he couldn't understand her; knew too that she wasn't supposed to simply make her announcement and walk out, but it was all part of the painfully simple plan she'd hatched.

Pathetically simple was more like it, although now that she knew Khalil would be absent from the palace for a few days the odds of the plan working had improved. Still, everything would have to fall into place at once, if she were to make good her escape. It was why this initial attempt had to be done just this way.

Would the guard stop her?

He wouldn't, she thought with fierce exultation. He'd obviously been told she'd been granted a new privilege and now he was torn between that knowledge and whatever it was he was supposed to do next, perhaps notify the stable boy to saddle the mare, perhaps notify the men who were to accompany her that she was ready to ride.

At the door, she glanced over her shoulder. He'd finally started after her, but that was unimportant.

All that mattered was that he had let her get past him.

The next morning, she opened her door at the same hour. The guard was waiting, along with the men who'd ridden with her the prior day.

Joanna smiled. 'Good morning,' she said pleasantly. 'I was hoping Rachelle was here, with my breakfast.' She made a show of peering up and down the corridor. 'Not yet? Well, that's all right.' Still smiling, she stepped back into her room and shut the door.

At two in the afternoon, she repeated the performance of yesterday, pulling open the door, stepping past the surprised—and solitary—guard, and marching to the door. After a bewildered pause, he went trotting off in the other direction, looking, she was sure, for the men who were to ride with her.

She reached the stables first and caught the stable boy short. He was lying in an empty stall, dozing, and she had to clear her throat half a dozen times before he heard her.

Shamefaced, he sprang to his feet and said something in an apologetic tone.

Joanna smiled at him and pointed towards the mare. By the time the men who were to ride with her came scuttling into the stable, Sidana was saddled and ready.

The third day, she made her move in late morning. No one seemed too surprised this time; her erratic pattern had become the norm. That was what she'd counted on, and Khalil's absence only made things easier. Even if her guards had thought to report her, who would they have reported her to?

Besides, she was careful not to arouse suspicion. Each time, she waited politely for the men to catch up to her at the stables and once they were on their way, she made a point of not seeming to be anything but a clumsy rider.

At lunchtime that third day, she took the fresh grapes and nuts from her plate, along with the slices of bread that always accompanied her meal, and stashed them inside the deep pocket of the hooded robe Khalil had given her the day he'd taken her to Adaba.

'You ate well today, Joanna,' Rachelle said with a pleased smile, when she came to collect the lunch tray.

Joanna nodded. 'Everything was delicious. The grapes and nuts, especially, were wonderful!'

The girl's smile grew. 'I am glad you liked them. I shall make it a point to bring you more, for a snack.'

Joanna felt a twinge of guilt, but then she reminded herself that Rachelle, too, was her gaoler, the same as Khalil.

She smiled brightly. 'I'd like that.'

The snack went into the robe's pocket, too, along with the bread, cake, and raisins from dinner. It wasn't much, but it would have to do. She had no idea how long it would take her to reach the south, and freedom, but tomorrow she was going to make her break.

The next morning, well before breakfast, Joanna dressed, put on her hooded robe, then flung open her door. A guard she'd never before set eyes on stepped in front of her.

'Good morning,' she sang out and started past him.

The guard moved quickly into her path. He didn't have to speak. His body language said it all.

Joanna's heart pounded harder. 'Out of my way, please,' she said, dodging to the right. But he dodged, too, blocking the corridor. She faced him squarely, her back rigid with displeasure. 'I am going riding,' she said. When he didn't move, she repeated the words, more loudly and more slowly. 'I—am—going—riding. Do you hear me? Step aside, man!'

She thrust out her hand. It landed on his chest, a steel wall under the press of her palm, but he didn't move an inch. Joanna drew herself up.

'Get out of my way, you fool! I have the Prince's permission to ride. I'm going to the stables. Dammit, are you deaf?'

'What's the matter, Joanna?'

Joanna spun around. The child, Lilia, was standing behind her, her pretty face wearing a frown.

'Lilia.' Smiling, Joanna dropped to her knees and took the girl in her arms. 'How good to see you! I've missed you.'

Lilia smiled shyly. 'It is good to see you, too. I meant to ask Uncle Khalil if I might come to visit you, but he went away before I had the chance.' The little girl looked at the guard. 'Is Ali giving you trouble?'

It was hard not to laugh at the regal tone in the young voice. Joanna stood up, her hand on Lilia's shoulder, and nodded.

'Yes, he is. Your uncle gave permission for me to ride whenever I wished, but Ali doesn't seem aware of it.'

'Oh, you're just like me, Joanna,' Lilia said happily. 'I, too, like to ride just past dawn, when the earth smells sweet!' The girl stepped forward, a little figure accustomed to command. 'I will take care of Ali.'

Joanna held her breath while Lilia spoke. Ali's eyes darted to her. He didn't look happy, but, after a moment, he touched his hand to his forehead and stepped aside.

'Thank you,' Joanna said. Her knees felt weak with relief.

'May I ride with you?'

Joanna stared at the child. In her pleasure at seeing her, she'd all but forgotten her reason for this early morning ride. Now, guilt shot into her breast like a poisoned arrow.

'Oh, Lilia,' she said softly. 'I don't think——'

'Please?'

She glanced at the guard. The man was obviously uncertain of what to do next and suddenly she realised he'd yet to notify anyone that she was about to go riding.

Forgive me, Lilia, she thought.

'Yes, all right,' she said with a forced smile. She took the child's hand and they began walking, Lilia babbling happily and the guard trailing uncertainly in the rear. When they reached the stables, Lilia hesitated.

'I almost forgot,' she said. 'I may not ride without an escort. I will tell Ali to send for——'

'No,' Joanna said quickly. She bit her lip, then squatted down and framed the child's face in her hands. 'No,' she said softly, 'not yet. Why don't we have our horses saddled first? That way, we'll be ready to ride when the escort arrives.'

Lilia shrugged. 'As you wish, Joanna.'

The girl gave an order to the sleepy-eyed stable boy, who led out the white mare and a roan pony. The pony was saddled first, and then the boy turned to the mare. But he'd only got the bridle on when the guard, who'd grown increasingly restless, said something sharp-toned, spun on his heel, and trotted out of the door.

There was no time to spare. Joanna bent quickly, kissed Lilia's puzzled face.

'Forgive me, Lilia,' she whispered.

She straightened up, pushed the boy aside, and leaped on Sidana's back. Quickly, she gathered up the reins and kicked her heels hard into the mare's flanks. Before anyone had time to move, the horse was out of the door with Joanna bent low over its neck, riding hell-bent for freedom.

CHAPTER ELEVEN

By DUSK, Joanna was ready to admit what she'd known but refused to admit for hours. She was in trouble. She was hungry, thirsty, bone-weary from riding the mare without a saddle—and she was hopelessly, helplessly lost.

At first, she'd been so intent on making good her escape that she'd paid no attention to direction. All that had mattered was following the narrow dirt trail that led down the mountain to freedom.

She'd counted on the element of surprise to give her a decent head start and it had, at least five or six minutes. Eventually, though, she'd heard the pounding of hooves behind her. Glancing over her shoulder, she'd barely been able to make out the puffs of dust that marked the progress of the men riding after her. Even though she had the advantage, Joanna had known she could not outrun them for long.

Wildly, she'd glanced about, measuring her surroundings. There was a small copse of trees just off the trail. Desperate, she'd taken refuge in it only seconds before the riders had come thundering past. She'd been about to move out after them, seeing no choice but to play the risky game of following her followers, when she'd spied what had seemed to be a parallel path on the far side of the trees. Joanna had gritted her teeth and decided to go with the unknown.

For a while, her choice had seemed a good one. The path was narrower than the first and it twisted and turned like a snake, but it did lead down—only to suddenly peter out on the edge of a dizzying cliff.

A stone, dislodged by the mare's delicate hooves, had gone tumbling down into oblivion. Heart racing, Joanna had edged the animal away from the precipice but she hadn't gone all the way back up the trail for fear of losing too much time. Instead, she'd cut through the trees, pausing only long enough to dismount and rip the telltale bells from the mare's bridle. Then she'd ridden on until, at last, she'd come out in a narrow gorge.

Now, as the sun dropped a crimson mantle over the surrounding mountain peaks, Joanna was trying to decide what to do next. She stared up at the sky. If the setting sun were there, ahead of her, then east was directly behind her, and north and south were—they were...

A little sob of despair burst from her throat. What did it matter? The points of the compass didn't mean a damn if you were trapped in a cage and didn't know the way out.

An owl hooted mournfully in the trees. Joanna shuddered and burrowed more deeply into her jellaba. The night was cool, and steadily growing cooler. The mare was exhausted, head drooping, legs wobbly. She'd been wonderful and courageous, running like the wind after the first shock of being asked to do so, but for the past hour she'd moved at little more than a walk.

Except for the crescent moon hanging like a scimitar over the trees, the darkness was complete. The owl's cry came again and just after it came another cry, that of some small creature which had evidently met the owl and lost the encounter.

Joanna shuddered again. She had to do something, but what? Should she ride on, without any idea of where she was going? In the dark, the horse could easily misstep; they'd both end up at the bottom of some abyss, breakfast for the vultures she'd seen circling on the warm thermals of morning.

She could stop, give herself and her horse a rest. But if she did, she would lose whatever time she'd gained, perhaps give Khalil's men just the edge they needed to pick up her trail.

The mare lifted her head and snorted.

Joanna sat up straight, eyes wide as she peered into the darkness. Had the animal heard something?

Sidana snorted again and pawed the ground with a hoof. Joanna bent over her neck, patted it soothingly.

'What is it?' she whispered. 'Is there something out there?'

The horse took a tentative step forward. Joanna hesitated, and then she loosened her hold on the reins and gave the animal its head. Wherever the mare was leading had to be better than this.

Sidana's pace quickened. She was almost trotting now, and all at once Joanna understood. Ahead, just visible in the pale wash of moonlight, a spring bubbled from a rocky cairn and trickled into the trough-shaped depression it had worn into the rock over the centuries.

Joanna smiled. 'Good girl!'

She slid carefully to the ground, groaning. Muscles she hadn't known existed ached. She had not ridden bareback since a childhood summer spent on a Montana mining property.

The mare buried her nose in the shallow water and Joanna squatted beside her, sipping from her cupped hands, not caring that she and the horse were sharing their drink. Thirst had become a growing discomfort; she'd known it might be, but how could she have stolen a Thermos of fruit juice from her meal tray without drawing Rachelle's attention?

The horse, replete, lifted her head and whinnied softly.

'It does taste good, doesn't it?' Joanna murmured. 'I'm glad I gave you your head, girl, otherwise——'

What was that? Joanna stiffened. She could hear something. Voices. Male voices, low-pitched but carrying clearly on the still air, and now the sound of hooves and the creak of leather.

Khalil's men! They'd picked up her trail! Joanna snatched up the mare's trailing reins and led her back into the trees.

'Shh,' she whispered frantically, holding the animal's bridle with one hand and stroking its nose with the other, 'shh!'

She couldn't let them find her now, not after she'd come so far. Even if it took her until dawn to find the path that would lead her down the mountain, she wasn't going back, she couldn't go back, she——

There! She could see them now. They were heading for the spring. A dozen men, not any more than that—but—but——

But who were they? Surely, not Khalil's followers. She had never seen their faces before, and their clothing was all wrong.

The men dismounted, all but one obscenely fat man who she knew instinctively must be their leader and who barked out commands. One man scurried to the spring, dipped a cup into the water, hurried back and offered it with downcast eyes. The fat man drank thirstily, tossed the cup into the dirt, and slid clumsily from the saddle to the ground.

Joanna's gaze flew over the other men. They were heavily armed and had a grim, ugly look to them. And you didn't have to understand their words to shudder at their tone of voice.

The fat man snarled another command and one of the men bowed and answered. His answer meant nothing to

Joanna, except for the last words and the fearful respect that laced them.

'...Abu Al Zouad.'

Joanna's breath caught. Of course! The fat man was Abu Al Zouad! Her father had described him to her. Abu was a big man, he'd said, grossly overweight and clumsy, given to expensive Italian suits and too much gold jewellery.

What would he say now, if he saw him dressed in a greasy jellaba, his chest bristling with bandoliers of ammunition?

The men were clustered in little knots, smoking cigarettes and murmuring quietly to each other. Abu clapped his hands and they looked up as he began to speak. It was a long speech, and again incomprehensible to Joanna, except for two simple words that were repeated over and over.

Joanna Bennett.

Abu was talking about her! Had he come to free her? This looked more like a raiding party than a rescue mission, but Joanna wasn't a child. It wasn't only the good guys who wore white hats.

But why would her father authorise a risky attempt at rescue instead of negotiating for her freedom? Joanna blew out her breath. Perhaps—perhaps Khalil had not told her the truth? For all she knew, Sam might have made every possible effort to gain her release, only to be rebuffed by Khalil. In desperation, he might surely send men to find and free her.

It was reasonable, even logical—but if it were, what was keeping her from stepping out into the clearing and yelling, hey, here I am, Abu? Why was she still hiding, still praying that her horse would not suddenly whinny and give away her position?

Abu finished speaking. One of his men said something; she heard her name fall from his lips, and the others chuckled. Abu shook his head and pointed to himself, and their laughter grew.

There was something in the sound of the laughter, in the way her name had been used and in the way Abu had stabbed that pudgy finger at himself, that sent a chill along Joanna's spine.

She swallowed hard. The men were mounting up. In another moment, they'd ride out of here and she'd be alone again, and just as lost as she'd been before they arrived.

Now was the time to step forward, to call out Abu's name and identify herself. Determinedly, before she could lose courage, Joanna began rising slowly from her crouched position——

A hand clamped over her mouth and an arm, powerful and hard as steel, closed around her. Joanna cried out soundlessly and began to struggle, but she was helpless against the strength of the man holding her.

'Joanna!' Khalil's voice whispered into her ear. 'Stop it, Joanna! It's me.'

She almost sobbed with relief. She went still, and Khalil lowered her slowly to the ground, his arm remaining around her waist.

'You mustn't make a sound,' he said softly. 'Do you understand?'

She nodded and he took his hand from her lips. Beyond the trees, the little group of riders was just vanishing into the night.

She swung around and looked at Khalil. In the moonlight, she could see that he was unshaven, that there was a grim set to his mouth and that lines of weariness fanned out from his eyes, and yet she had never seen a man so beautiful. She had escaped his silken prison, she thought with a sudden catch in her breath, but how would she ever escape the memory of him?

The realisation was as stunning as it was bewildering. She whispered his name, but he shook his head, the stony expression on his face unchanging.

'There will be time for talk later.'

Najib stood just behind his master, ears pricked forward. Khalil took the animal's reins and set off through the trees, in the opposite direction from the spring with Joanna and her mare following after him.

A ten-minute walk brought them to what looked like a labyrinth of giant boulders and, at its end, the yawning, dark mouth of a cave.

Khalil tethered the horses in a blind passageway among the boulders, where no casual observer would see them, and then he took Joanna's hand and led her through the maze up into the cave.

'I played here often, as a boy,' he said, his voice echoing off the stone walls. 'It's deep enough for safety, and there's even a narrow cleft in the rocks at the cave's end that we can use to get out, if we should have to.'

Within minutes, he'd swept together a small pile of kindling and brush and lit a fire deep in the cave's interior. Joanna held her breath as he turned towards her. They had been alone before, but this time was different. She had been running away from him, it was true, but now, seeing him again, being so close to him, she felt— she felt——

'What the hell did you think you were doing?'

She blinked. Khalil's face was taut with barely contained fury.

'I don't—I don't know what you mean.'

'I don't know what you mean,' he mimicked. His mouth tightened. 'For a woman who always has a clever answer at her fingertips, that one is pathetic!'

Her spine stiffened. 'It is not!'

'If you behave like a fool, I'll treat you like one.'

She stared at him for a moment, and then she whirled around and started towards the mouth of the cave. His hand fell on her shoulder.

'Where do you think you're going?' he growled.

'Where I should have gone in the first place. With Abu. If you hadn't come along and ruined things——'

Khalil spun her towards him. 'You gave me your word, Joanna! But I should have known that such a simple pledge was beyond you.'

'What are you talking about?'

'You promised you would not ride alone!'

Joanna tossed her head. 'But I didn't promise I'd willingly remain your prisoner.'

'You little idiot! I'm not talking about escape. I'm talking about danger.'

'The danger of disobeying the rules of a petty dictator, you mean!'

'It is dangerous for anyone, but especially for a woman, to ride these mountains alone.'

'You never said that.'

'I didn't think I had to,' he said, glowering at her. 'Anyone with half a brain——'

'Stop it! I'm tired of your insults!'

'Then don't set yourself up for them. If you'd used your head, you'd have realised I gave you those instructions to keep you safe.'

'Oh, yes.' Joanna's voice shook, and she could feel the sting of tears in her eyes, although there was no reason to want to cry. 'Yes, you'd want me kept safe, wouldn't you? If I were hurt or damaged, what sort of bargaining chip would I be?'

His eyes narrowed. 'Bargaining chip?'

'What's the matter? Isn't your English good enough to understand a simple phrase? A bargaining chip is what a hostage is. It's——'

She cried out as he swept her into his arms and kissed her, his mouth taking hers with a passion so urgent it stole her breath away, and then he clasped her face in his hands and drew back just enough so he could look into her eyes.

'You cannot be so blind,' he whispered. 'Surely you see that you have become much more than my hostage.'

'No,' she said shakily, 'no, I don't see.'

He smiled, and suddenly his eyes were tender. 'Let me show you, then,' he said softly, and slowly, his head descended to hers.

He kissed her gently, his mouth moving softly against hers, his hands spreading under the hood and into her hair. A tremor went through her, but she didn't respond.

'Joanna,' he said, his lips still clinging to hers, 'Joanna, Joanna...'

And suddenly a wave of emotion, as unexpected and as fierce as a tidal wave, swept through her. She began to tremble.

'Khalil?' she whispered, and the question inherent in the single word was enough. He caught her in his arms and kissed her insistently. Her lips parted beneath his, her arms stole around his neck, and she clung to him and knew she would never, not in a thousand lifetimes, want to let him go.

'How did you find me?' she sighed, while he pressed little kisses to her temples and eyelids. 'And where did you come from? You were gone——'

'I was drawn away deliberately by Abu. It was a clever scheme, but there are few secrets that can be kept in this part of the world. I turned back when the information reached me, contacted my men, told them to put you under armed guard.'

'Abu was coming to free me, then?'

Khalil hesitated. 'It might be better to say that you were all the excuse he needed to ride against me.'

'But—what will happen when he reaches your village? Will your people be safe?'

He smiled grimly. 'He's riding into a trap. My men are waiting for him.'

'But how . . . ?'

'Joanna.' He stroked the hair back from her face. 'I don't want to talk about Abu now,' he whispered.

His mouth took hers again, this time in a deeper, more passionate kiss. Joanna moaned softly, and he lowered his head and put his mouth to her throat, as if to measure the racing pulse beating in its hollow.

She whispered his name as he eased the jellaba from her shoulders. His eyes burned into hers as he undid the buttons of her shirt. When it fell away, he drew back and looked at her with such hunger that she felt her breasts lift and harden under his gaze.

'You are so beautiful.' He reached out slowly and stroked his fingers across her nipples. 'You are more beautiful than any woman I have ever seen.'

'You're beautiful, too,' she whispered. The skin tightened across his cheekbones as she slid his jellaba from his shoulders. Her fingers trembled as she undid the buttons on his shirt. She slid her hands under the soft cotton, exulting in the feel of his silken skin, his taut muscles, and in the hiss of his breath when she touched him.

He caught her hand in his, carried it to his lips and pressed a kiss into her palm.

'I want to see all of you, Joanna.'

She stood still as he stripped away her shoes, her trousers, and, finally, her panties. Colour raced up under her skin as she watched him look at her, not from embarrassment but from the sweet pain of wanting him. Her body was already damp, ready for his, and although he had barely touched her so far, her blood was at a fever pitch.

'Now you,' she whispered.

She lifted her eyes to his as she reached out to his belt buckle. He made a sound in the back of his throat as she opened it. She swept her hand lightly down the length of his fly, her breath catching when she felt his arousal. His fingers curled around her wrist and he smiled tightly.

'Be careful,' he said. 'If you go on playing this game, the night may end before it begins.'

A smile curved across Joanna's mouth. 'Am I to obey you, my lord?'

He laughed as he caught her up in his arms, snatched up Najib's saddle blanket, and walked deeper into the cave, to where the fire's glow was only a soft reflection.

'We will obey each other on this night, my beloved.'

Slowly, he eased her down on the blanket, laid her back, and bent over her, his face shadowed and mysterious in the firelight.

'I wanted you from the moment I saw you,' he whispered.

Joanna laughed throatily. 'I thought you wanted to throttle me from the moment you saw me.'

Khalil chuckled. 'You are right. There have been times I didn't know which I wanted to do more.' His smile faded as he looked at her. 'But tonight—tonight,' he whispered, 'there is only one thing I wish to do tonight.'

He touched her with his fingertips, slowly following the curve of breast and belly, then moving lightly against her thighs. She whispered his name, held out her arms to him, but he ignored her, bending over her body so that he could trace the same path again, this time with his mouth. She moaned softly as his lips closed first on one breast, then on the other. When he drew back and bent again to kiss her thighs, her voice rose quavering into the silence of the cave. And when, finally, his mouth closed on the sweet centre of her, Joanna cried out his name in ecstasy.

The stars were still tumbling from the sky when he rose over her.

'Look at me,' he said. Joanna opened her eyes and he smiled down at her, a sweet, fierce smile of possession and dominance that made her heart seem to stop—but when he entered her, slowly, so slowly, with his eyes never leaving hers, she knew that her possession of him, her dominance of him, was as complete as his was of her.

She loved him, she adored him, and it stunned her that it had taken her so long to recognise the truth.

She wanted to tell him that, to whisper that he was the captor not of her body but of her heart and of her soul, but he was deep within her now and she was, oh, she was——

'Beloved,' he said fiercely, and kissed her deeply. Joanna cried out as she spun into the night sky, where she became a burst of quicksilver among the stars.

Joanna awoke once, during the night, drawn from sleep by the sweet touch of Khalil's mouth. Her awakening was slow and dreamlike, and after they'd made love she settled into his arms and fell back into deep sleep.

But when she awoke again, she was alert, uncertain as to what it was that had roused her. She lay very still, tension building in her muscles, and then she heard the faint whicker of a horse and she sighed with relief.

That was what had awakened her, the mare or Najib, offering gentle protests at having spent the night tethered.

Joanna smiled. She, too, had spent the night tethered, held closely in Khalil's arms—and it had been the most wonderful night of her life. She turned her face against his shoulder, inhaling the clean, masculine smell of his body, touching her lips lightly to his satiny skin, and gazed at his face.

How different he looked in sleep. The little lines that fanned out from his eyes were almost invisible, his mouth was soft, as if, in sleep, he could put aside, at least for a while, the burden of leadership he carried. She sighed and put her head against his chest, listening to the steady beat of his heart. And that burden had to be even heavier, knowing that part of his country had been stolen from him, that it was in the grip of an evil despot, for Joanna no longer had any doubts at all about Abu Al Zouad.

Her father had been wrong, whether through accident or design. Khalil was not the bandit. Abu was, and the sooner she was able to tell Sam that she knew the truth now, the better.

There it was, that sound again. Joanna sat up, tossing her hair back from her face. She was sure it was one of the horses, but what if the animal was whinnying a warning instead of protesting against inactivity?

She dropped a gentle kiss on Khalil's forehead, then rose to her feet, found her clothing, and dressed. It had been hard to see much last night, but she remembered that the cave entrance was on a slight elevation. Quietly, she made her way forward. Perhaps she could see what it was that——

A hand whipped across her mouth. Joanna gasped, kicked out sharply, and other hands caught hold of her and dragged her into the sunlight, where Abu and the rest of his men waited.

'Good morning, Miss Bennett.' Joanna glared at the fat man as he slid from his horse. He strolled towards her, smiling unpleasantly. 'I am His Excellency, Abu Al Zouad.' His smile became a grin, revealing a shiny, gold tooth. 'You don't look very happy to see me.'

Joanna's mind was spinning. Abu wasn't bothering to drop his voice. And now that she'd appeared, no one was paying any attention to the cave.

They had no idea Khalil was with her! He could escape through the rear of the cave. All she had to do was be certain he heard this fuss and awakened.

She bit down hard on the hand that covered her mouth. The man cursed, let her go, and lifted his hand to strike her.

'I wouldn't do that,' she said in her best Bennett voice. Whether he understood her English or not, her tone stopped him. He glanced at Abu, who motioned him away.

'Well, Miss Bennett. It is good to see that captivity has not dulled your spirit.'

Joanna's chin lifted. 'How did you find me?'

Abu smiled. 'My spies alerted me to your rather abrupt departure from the fortress of the bandit Khalil, and then it was simply a matter of following your trail— although I must admit, my scout stumbled upon your little hideaway quite by accident.' He moved closer to her. 'And now I have my prize.' Without warning, he reached out and ran his hand down her body. 'And what a prize it is, too!'

Joanna's blood went cold. She thought of Khalil's hesitation last night, when she'd asked him if Abu were coming to rescue her.

'It might be better to say that you were all the excuse he needed to ride against me,' he'd said.

Abu had no intention of taking her back to her father! He would kill her—after first taking his pleasure—and blame her death on Khalil.

Joanna slapped his hand away. 'I am not your prize!' The man nearest Abu snarled something and put his hand on the scabbard hanging from his belt. 'You have forgotten who I am,' she said, her voice so sharp and chill that only she knew she was really trembling with fear.

'I forget nothing,' Abu growled. 'You are a woman, stolen by a bandit. Whatever happens to you will be his doing, not mine.'

'And losing the reward for my return will be your doing—or are you so rich you can't use a million dollars in gold?'

'A million dollars? Your father did not say——'

Joanna drew herself fully erect. 'A million dollars, and the contract you want so badly with Bennettco. You will get neither, if I am not returned safely.'

'You are only a woman! You make no rules for Sam Bennett.'

'I am his daughter.'

'That is a guarantee of nothing.'

Joanna smiled tightly. 'Perhaps—and perhaps not.' With a last bit of bravado, she looked him straight in the eye. 'Are you willing to take that chance?'

She could almost see the wheels spinning in his ugly head, but her most desperate thoughts were deep within the cave. Had Khalil got away? Had he heard the noise, made good his escape? Had he——?

Her answer came in a sudden burst of sound, a blood-chilling yell that froze her with terror. It must have had the same effect on Abu's men, too, for when Khalil came bursting from the cave entrance there was time for him to lunge at Abu and almost curl his hands around the man's throat before anyone moved.

'Go on,' he yelled at Joanna as two men pulled him back and pinned him against the rocks, 'make a run for it! Dammit, woman, why are you standing there?'

Abu rubbed his dirty fingers over his throat. 'Well, well,' he said, very softly, 'this is indeed a morning of prizes—and of surprises.' He grinned, then pointed at one of his men. 'Kill the bandit!'

'No!' The word ripped from Joanna's throat. She stepped forward. 'No,' she said again, 'don't kill him.'

'We will spare you,' Abu said, as if it were an act of humanity that impelled him and not the threat Joanna had made. 'But I have waited too long for a reason the people will accept to kill the bandit.' He smiled. 'And now I have one. Kill him!'

'Very well.' Joanna's voice was cool. 'Kill him, if you like—but if you do, you are a fool.'

'Watch your tongue, woman!'

'He is not only your enemy, Abu, he is also my father's. He has dishonoured him—and me.' She took a breath. 'My father will surely want the pleasure of killing Khalil himself.'

Abu laughed. 'Westerners do not believe in taking blood for dishonour.'

'Do you think my father got where he is today by being soft-hearted?'

She looked over at Khalil, expecting to see a dark glint of admiration for her off-the-cuff cleverness in his eyes, needing to see it to give her the courage to go on. Her heart dropped like a stone. Khalil was watching her as if she were something that had just scurried out from under a rock. She turned away quickly, forcing herself to concentrate on Abu.

'My father will pay for having Khalil delivered into his hands,' she said coldly, 'and he will be grateful to you forever.'

'I think you say this to save the neck of the man who has become your lover.'

Joanna stared at him. 'No. No, I——'

'I think I am right, Miss Bennett.' He looked at one of the men holding Khalil. 'Go on,' he said, 'kill him!'.

'He took me,' Joanna blurted. 'He forced me! That's why I made such a desperate escape.' She knotted her hands into fists, marched up to Khalil and looked into his eyes, which were almost black with rage. My love, she thought, oh, my love!

Swiftly, before she lost courage, she drew saliva into her mouth and spat full into Khalil's face.

'He's a barbarian,' she said, swinging away so she didn't have to look at him, 'and I'll have no peace until my father takes my revenge.'

A heavy silence descended on the group, broken only by the laboured sound of Khalil's breathing, and then Abu nodded.

'Very well. We take him with us and——'

Cries filled the air. Joanna shrank back as Khalil's men came riding up the slope. Within minutes, it was over. Abu and his men were defeated.

With a little sob of joy, Joanna ran to Khalil and threw her arms around him, but he shoved her away.

'Don't touch me,' he said in a soft, dangerous whisper.

'Khalil. My love! I was bargaining for your life! Surely you didn't believe——'

'And now you are bargaining for your own!' He stepped forward, grasping her arms and yanking her close. 'Be grateful I am not the savage you think I am,' he growled. 'If I were, I would gladly slit your throat and leave you here for the vultures.' He flung her from him and strode to Najib, who stood waiting beside the white mare. 'Take her to the airstrip,' he snapped to one of his men, 'and have her flown to Casablanca. We have

Abu—Sam Bennett can have his daughter.' He leaped on to Najib's back, grasped the reins, and gave Joanna one last, terrible look. 'They deserve each other.'

He dug his heels hard into Najib's flanks. The horse rose on its hind legs, pawed the air, then spun away with its rider sitting proudly in the saddle.

It was the last Joanna saw of Khalil.

CHAPTER TWELVE

THE doorman pushed open the door and smiled as Joanna stepped from her taxi and made her way towards him.

'Evening, Miss Bennett,' he said. 'Hot enough to fry eggs on the pavement, isn't it?'

Joanna smiled back at him. 'Hello, Rogers. Yes, but New York in August is always pretty awful.'

The lift operator smiled, too, and offered a similar comment on the weather as the car rose to the twelfth floor, and Joanna said something clever in return, as she was expected to do.

It was a relief to stop all the smiling and stab her key into the lock of her apartment door. Smiling was the last thing she felt like doing lately. With a weary sigh, she stepped out of her high heels and dropped her handbag on a table in the foyer.

Sam kept saying she'd developed all the charm of a woman sucking on a lemon, and she supposed it was true—but in the three months she'd been back from Casablanca she hadn't found all that much to smile about.

Joanna popped off her earrings as she made her way towards her bedroom. She was vice-president of Bennettco now, she had an office of her own, a staff, and even her father's grudging respect.

So why wasn't it enough? she thought as she peeled off her dress and underthings.

She stepped into the blue tiled bathroom and turned on the shower. The water felt delicious but she couldn't luxuriate beneath it for long. In less than an hour, Sam was picking her up. They were going to another of the endless charity affairs he insisted they attend, this time at the Palace Hotel.

A mirthless smile angled across her lips as she stepped from the shower and towelled herself dry. The Palace. She had been to it before, knew that it dripped crystal chandeliers and carpeting deep enough to cushion the most delicate foot. But she remembered a real palace, one that boasted no such touches of elegance, yet had been more a palace than the hotel would ever be.

Damn, but she wished she hadn't seen that little squib in the paper at breakfast! 'Jandaran Prince Consolidates Hold on Kingdom, Seeks Financing for Mining Project', it had said, and she'd shoved the paper away without reading further, but it had been enough. A rush of memories had spoiled the day, although she couldn't imagine why. She didn't care what happened to Khalil. She had never loved him. How could she have, when they came from such different worlds? It was just that she'd been frightened, and despairing, and there was no point pretending he wasn't a handsome, virile male.

An image flashed into her mind as she reached for her mascara. She saw Khalil leaning over her, his eyes dark with desire. Joanna, he was whispering, Joanna, my beloved...

Her hand slipped and a dark smudge bloomed on her cheek. She wiped it off, then bent towards the mirror again and painted a smile on her lips. What had happened in Jandara was a closed chapter. No one even knew about her part in it, thanks to Sam.

'I didn't tell a soul,' he'd said, after she'd finally reached Casablanca.

'Not even the State Department?' she'd asked, remembering shadowy fragments of something Khalil had said the night he'd abducted her.

'Not even them. I was afraid I might compromise your safety. How could I know what an animal like Khalil might do if I called out the troops? That's why I couldn't give in to his demands. I figured once I did, the bastard might kill you. You understand, don't you?'

Joanna had assured him that she did. Sam hadn't been saying anything she hadn't thought of herself. Sending Abu after her had been the only way he'd thought he could rescue her. As for Abu—Sam had been duped, he'd said with feeling.

'The guy had me fooled. How could I have known what he really was like?'

Joanna slid open the wardrobe in her bedroom and took a sequinned blue gown from its hanger. The only fly in the ointment was that the proposed mining deal had gone down the tubes. Khalil had wasted no time making sure of that. Within twelve hours, Abu had been sentenced to life imprisonment, Khalil had been restored to the throne of Jandara, and the Bennett contract had been returned by messenger, accompanied by a terse note, signed by Khalil.

'We will develop the property ourselves.'

Sam had turned red with anger and cursed and then said hell, win some, lose some, what did it matter? He had his Jo back. That was all that counted.

Joanna whisked a brush through her hair. He was right. That was what counted, that she was back, and if sometimes, at night, she awoke from dreams she could not remember with tears on her cheeks, so what? She was getting ahead rapidly at Bennettco and that was what she wanted. It was all she wanted.

She glanced at the clock. It was time. Quickly she stuffed a comb, tissues and her lipstick into an evening bag, slipped on a pair of glittery high-heeled sandals, and made her way out of the door.

Sam was waiting at the kerb in his chauffeured Lincoln. 'Hello, babe,' he said when she stepped inside. 'Mmm, you look delicious.'

Joanna's eyebrows rose. 'What gives?'

He chuckled as the car eased into traffic. 'What do you mean, what gives? Can't I give my girl a compliment?'

'You're as transparent as glass, Father,' she said with a wry smile. 'Whenever you want something from me and you expect a refusal, you begin laying on compliments.'

He sat back and sighed. 'I was just thinking, on the way over here, what a terrible time that bastard put us through.'

Joanna's smile faded. 'Khalil?'

He smiled coldly. 'What other bastard do we know? To think he locked you up, treated you like dirt——'

'I really don't want to talk about him tonight, Father.'

'Did you know he's in town?'

She shrugged, trying for a casual tone. 'Is he?'

Sam grunted. 'Abu may have been a brute,' he said, 'but Khalil's no better.'

Joanna looked at him. 'You know that's not true!'

'You're not defending him, are you, Jo?'

Was she? Joanna shook her head. 'No,' she said quickly, 'of course not.'

'It burns my butt that the man treated you the way he did and gets rewarded for it,' Sam said testily. 'There he is, sitting in Abu's palace, snug as a quail in tall grass, counting up the coins in the national treasury.'

Joanna closed her eyes wearily. 'I doubt that.'

Sam chuckled. 'But we'll have the last laugh, kid. I've seen to that.'

Joanna turned towards her father. There was something in his tone that was unsettling.

'What do you mean?'

'We may have lost the mining deal—but so has Khalil!'

'He's not. He's going to put together a consortium himself.'

'He's going to try and milk a fat profit straight into his own pockets, you mean.'

'No,' Joanna said quickly. 'He'd never——'

'How do you think he'll like having the world hear he wanted the fortune tucked away in those mountains so badly he killed for it?' Sam said, his eyes glittering.

Joanna stared at her father. 'Killed who?'

'Abu. Who else?'

'But Khalil didn't kill him. He's in prison. And it isn't because of the fortune in those mountains, it's——'

'For God's sake, Jo!' Sam's voice lost its cheerful edge and took on a rapier sharpness. 'Who cares what the facts are? I'm telling you I've come up with a way to put a knife in that s.o.b.'s back for what he did to us!'

'Us? *Us*? He didn't do anything to us. I was the one he took, the one whose——'

'What? What were you going to say?'

She stared at him in bewilderment. She knew what she'd been going to say, that she was the one whose heart was broken. But it wasn't true. She was defending Khalil, yes, but not because she loved him. It was only because it would be wrong to lie about him, to raise doubts in the minds of his people.

'You can't do something so evil,' she said flatly.

Sam's face hardened. 'Listen to me, Joanna. Khalil's trying to put together this mining deal, sure. But when the banks and the power brokers know the truth about him, how he abducted you and how he treated you——'

'But they won't.' Joanna's eyes flashed with defiance. 'The story's mine, and I'm not going to tell it.'

Sam's mouth thinned with distaste. 'It's useless, treating you as if you understood business! You're not the son I wanted, and you never will be.'

Tears glinted on Joanna's lashes. 'Well,' she said, 'at least it's finally out in the open. I'm not, no, and——' The car jounced to a stop at the kerb. Joanna grabbed her evening bag from the seat. 'We can discuss this later, Father.'

'Jo. Wait!'

She snatched her hand from his and reached for the door, too angry and upset to wait for the chauffeur to open it. Sam cared about protocol, but it had never meant a damn to her.

'Joanna,' Sam said sharply, but she ignored him, swung open the door—and stepped straight into a bewildering sea of cameras and microphones.

'Miss Bennett!' Someone shoved a mike into her face. 'Is it true,' an eager voice asked, 'that you were abducted and held for ransom by the new ruler of Jandara?'

Joanna stiffened. 'Where did you——?'

'Is it true he abducted you because he'd demanded bribe money from your father's company and your father refused to pay it?'

She spun towards Sam, who had stepped out of the car after her. 'Did you do this?' she said in a low voice.

His eyes narrowed. 'We'll discuss this later, you said. I think we should stay with that idea.'

'Answer me! Did you set this up?'

'Do unto others as they do unto you, Jo,' Sam said out of the side of his mouth. 'Khalil's in New York, his hat in his hand. It's my turn now.'

Joanna's mouth trembled. 'You would lie about Khalil, let the media swarm over me, all to get even?'

Sam glared at her. 'Business is business, Joanna. How come you can't get that straight?' He pushed past her, making it look as if he were defending her against the press, and held up his hands. 'My daughter finds this too emotional a topic to talk about,' he said. 'I'll speak on her behalf.'

He launched into a tirade against Khalil, about his greed and his barbarism, about how he'd been angered by Bennettco's refusal to pay enough *baksheesh* and how he'd stolen Joanna in retaliation, then demanded a king's ransom for her return——

'No,' Joanna said.

The microphones and cameras swung towards her and Sam did too, his eyes stabbing her with a warning look.

'The only reason we've decided to come forward now,' he said, 'is because my daughter refuses to let Prince Khalil trick our bankers into investing in——'

'No!' Joanna's voice rose. 'It's not true!'

'Do you see what the bastard did?' Sam roared. 'She's still afraid to talk about how he imprisoned her, starved her, beat her——'

'It's a lie!' Joanna stepped past her father. 'Prince Khalil asked for no ransom, no bribes. He's a good, decent man, and my father's trying to blacken his name!'

There was a moment's silence, and then a voice rang out.

'Decent men don't abduct women.'

There was a titter of laughter. Joanna lifted her chin and stared directly into the glittering eyes of the video cameras.

'He didn't abduct me,' she said in a clear voice.

'Your father says he did. What's the story, Miss Bennett?'

What had Khalil said, the night he'd taken her? That he could tell the world she'd run off with him and be believed, that no one would doubt such a story. Joanna took a deep breath.

'I was with Khalil because I wanted to be with him,' she said. She heard her father growl a short, ugly word and her voice gathered strength. 'The Prince asked me to go away with him—and I did.'

A dozen questions filled the air, and finally one reporter's voice cut through the rest.

'So, you don't hate the Hawk of the North?'

Joanna's lips trembled. 'No,' she said, 'I don't hate him.'

'What, then?' someone called.

Joanna hesitated. 'I—I——'

'Well, Miss Bennett?' another voice insisted, 'how do you feel about him?'

Joanna stared at the assembled cameras. How did she feel about Khalil? What did she feel?

A woman reporter jostled aggressively past the others and stuck a microphone under her nose.

'Do you love him?' she said, her crimson lips parting in a smirk.

Joanna looked at the woman. The time for lies and deceit was past.

'Yes,' she whispered, 'I do.'

She heard Sam's groan, heard the babble of voices all trying to question her at once, and then she turned and fled into a taxi that had mercifully just disgorged its passengers.

Joanna stalked the length of the terrace that opened off her living-room. The night had proven even warmer than the afternoon; the long, white silk robe she wore was light against her skin but even so, she felt as if she were smothering.

But she knew it had little to do with the temperature. She was smothering of humiliation, and there was nothing she could do about it.

She groaned out loud and sank down on the edge of a *chaise longue*. How could she have made such an ass of herself?

I love him, she'd said—but she didn't. She *didn't* love Khalil, she never had.

So why had she said such a preposterous thing? Anger at Sam, yes, and pain at how he'd been prepared to use her, but still, why would she have made such an announcement?

She rose and walked slowly into the living-room, just as the clock on the mantel chimed the hour. Four a.m. If only it were dawn, she'd put on her running shoes, a T-shirt and shorts, and go for a long run through Central Park. Maybe that would help. Maybe——

The phone shrilled, as it had periodically through the night. Would it be the Press, which had found her despite her ex-directory listing, or Sam, who'd called three times to tell her she had ruined him? She snatched it up and barked a hello.

It was Sam, but the tone of his voice told her that his rage had given way to weariness.

'Will you at least apologise for making fools of me and of Bennettco, Jo?'

Joanna put a hand to her forehead. 'Of course. I never intended to embarrass you, Father.'

'How could you do it, then? My reputation and the company's are in shambles.'

She smiled. 'You've survived worse.'

Sam sighed gustily into the phone. 'I'm not saying you were right,' he said, 'but maybe my idea wasn't so hot.'

Joanna's smile broadened. 'Are *you* apologising to *me*, Father?'

'I've always walked a thin line between what's right and what's wrong and sometimes—sometimes, I lose my way.'

It was an admission she would never have expected, and it touched her.

'You're one tough lady, Joanna,' Sam said quietly.

'I love you, Father,' Joanna whispered.

'And I love you.' She heard him take a deep breath. 'Jo? I really did believe I'd endanger you by negotiating with Khalil. That's the only reason I didn't tear up that blasted contract. I want to be sure you know that. You mean the world to me.'

Tears stung her eyes. 'I know.'

'Well,' Sam said brusquely, 'it's late. You should get some sleep.' There was a silence. 'Goodnight, daughter.'

Daughter. He had never called her that before. Joanna's hand tightened on the phone.

'Goodnight, Daddy,' she said.

She hung up the phone and smiled. So, she thought, stretching her legs out in front of her, some good had come of this mess after all. She and her father might yet be friends——

She started as the doorbell rang. Who could it be, at this late hour? Who could the doorman have possibly admitted without calling her on the intercom first?

Joanna stood and walked slowly to the door. A reporter, she thought grimly, a reporter who'd sneaked in the back way.

The bell rang again, the sound persistent and jarring in the middle of the night silence.

'Go away,' she called.

Someone rapped sharply at the door.

'Do you hear me? If you don't get away from here this minute, I'll call the police!'

'You call them,' a man's voice growled, 'or your neighbours will, when I break this door down!'

Joanna fell back against the wall. 'Khalil?' she whispered.

'Do you hear me, Joanna? Open this door at once!'

'No,' she said, staring at the door as if it might fly off its hinges. 'Go away!'

'Very well, Joanna. We'll wait for someone to phone the police. They'll probably show up with a dozen reporters in tow, but that's fine with me. Jandara can use all the publicity it can get.'

She flew at the door, her fingers trembling as they raced across the locks, and then she threw the door open.

'How dare you do this?'

'This is America,' Khalil said with a cold smile. 'People can do anything they want in America. Didn't you tell me that once?'

'No! I certainly did not. I——'

Joanna fell silent. Khalil was dressed much as he had been the night they'd met, in a dark suit and white shirt, but somewhere along the way, he'd taken off his tie, undone the top buttons of his shirt, and slung his jacket over his shoulder. He looked handsome and wonderful, and the sight of him made her feel giddy.

She clutched her silk robe to her throat. 'You can't come in!'

He smiled, showing even, white teeth. 'Can't I?'

'No. This is my apartment, and——' The door slammed shut behind him as he pushed past her into the foyer. 'Damn you,' Joanna cried. 'Didn't you hear what I said? I don't want you here. Get out!'

Khalil shook his head. 'No.'

No. Just that one word, delivered in that insolent, imperious voice . . .

Joanna tossed her head. 'All right, then, wait here and get thrown out! The doorman's probably on the phone this very minute, calling the——'

'The doorman,' he said with a smug little smile, 'is chatting with my minister.' He folded his arms over his chest in that impossibly arrogant manner she detested. 'Did you know the man was born a stone's throw from Hassan's birthplace?'

Joanna's eyes narrowed. 'Hassan was born in Brooklyn?'

Khalil grinned. 'Well, perhaps he stretched things a bit. But it is true that Hassan has a cousin who was born in Brooklyn.'

Joanna lifted her chin in defiance. 'As far as I'm concerned, you and Hassan could have a string of cousins who——'

'We were at a dinner party all this evening, Joanna.'

'Isn't that wonderful,' she said sweetly. 'I'm delighted for you both.'

'I only just got back to my hotel, and I turned on— what do you call it?—the twenty-four-hour-a-day news channel——'

'I am certain there are lots of people who'd be interested in a minute-by-minute accounting of how you spent your evening, Khalil, but personally——'

'I saw your news conference.'

Joanna felt her face go white. 'What news conference?' she said with false bravado. 'I don't know what you're talking about.'

'That informative little gathering you arranged outside the Palace Hotel.' A cool smile curved over his lips. '*That* news conference.'

'It wasn't a news conference, it was a circus. Now, if you're quite finished——'

'What a clever pair you and your father are, Joanna.' She gaped at him. 'What?'

'Telling two such disparate but fascinating stories to the Press.' Khalil's eyes narrowed. 'What better way for Bennettco to garner publicity, hmm?'

'What better way for...' Joanna burst out laughing. 'Is that what you think? That Sam and I set that up?'

'Didn't you?'

'No, of course not. What would be the point?'

'How do I know? Perhaps the price of Bennettco's stock has fallen and you two decided front-page headlines would shore it up.'

Joanna shook her head in disbelief. 'My father would be proud of you, thinking of something like that.'

'You didn't arrange it, then?'

'Me? I had nothing to do with it. It was my father who...' She stopped in mid-sentence and colour spotted her cheeks. 'Look, if that's all you came here for——'

'Why?' He moved forward quickly, before she could back away, and took her by the shoulders. 'Why did he want you to pretend I had hurt you?' His eyes darkened. 'Heaven knows I would never do that.'

'I—I told Sam that. But—but he had some crazy idea that—that he could influence things in Jandara——'

'By destroying my reputation,' Khalil said, his voice flat.

'He knows it was wrong,' she said quickly. 'I swear to you——'

'But you wouldn't let him lie.'

Joanna's throat worked. 'I—I didn't think it was right.'

Khalil's hands spread across her shoulders. 'And so you told two hundred million people that you went away with me willingly.'

She felt the rush of crimson that flooded her cheeks. 'Please go now, Khalil.'

'Not yet, not until I have the answers I came for.'

'You have them. You wanted to know if my father and I——'

'I wanted to know why you told the entire population of the United States that you love me,' he said softly.

'It was—I mean, I thought it was——' She looked up at him helplessly. 'I couldn't think of anything else to say.'

He grinned. 'Really.'

'Yes. Really.' Joanna swallowed hard. 'I didn't mean it, if that's what you think.'

What he thought was that she was still the most beautiful woman in the world, and that he would surely have died if he had never looked at her wonderful face again. He smiled and traced the fullness of her bottom lip with his thumb. The last time he'd gazed into Joanna's eyes, his heart had been so filled with pain that he had been blind to everything but his own anguish.

But the passage of time had made him begin to wonder if he'd reacted too quickly that terrible morning three months before. He had dreamed of her for weeks, thought of her endlessly, and now he had come to the States on a mission for his country—but in the back of his mind, he knew he had come to find her, to find the truth...

...and there it was, shining along with the tears that had risen in her beautiful green eyes. He was certain of it, certain enough to do something he had never done before, put aside his pride—and offer up his heart.

'Didn't you?' he said softly.

Joanna swallowed again. 'Didn't I what?' she whispered.

'Didn't you mean it when you said you loved me?'

She closed her eyes. 'Khalil—please, don't do this——'

'I think the only time you lied about how you felt was that morning outside the cave.'

Her lashes flew up and she looked at him. 'You're wrong. I don't love you. I never——'

He lowered his head and gently brushed his lips over hers.

'How could I have been such a pig-headed fool? You told Abu you loathed me to save my life—didn't you, Joanna?'

Joanna stared into Khalil's wonderfully blue eyes. She could walk away from this with her pride intact. Well, sure, she could say, smiling, I did—but that doesn't mean I love you. I just did what I could to save your neck because it was the right thing to do...

'Joanna.' He cupped her face, tilted it to his, and when she looked into his eyes again, her heart soared. 'Beloved,' he whispered, 'will it be easier to tell me the truth if I tell it to you first?' Khalil kissed her again, his mouth soft and sweet against hers. 'I love you, Joanna. I love you with all my heart.'

Her breath caught. 'What?'

'Why do you think I kept you captive, even after I knew your father would never negotiate for your release?'

'Well, because—because——'

He smiled and put his arms around her. 'It was wrong, I know, but how could I let you go when I'd fallen in love with you? I kept hoping you would stop hating me, that you'd come to feel for me what I felt for you.'

Joanna felt as if her heart were going to burst with joy. 'Oh, my darling,' she whispered, 'my love——'

He drew her close and silenced her with a kiss. Then he sighed and brought her head to his chest.

'That night in the cave, I let myself believe you loved me, but the next morning——'

Joanna leaned back in his embrace and flung her arms around his neck. 'I do love you,' she said, laughing and weeping at the same time, 'I do!'

He kissed her again. After a long time, he lifted his head and smiled into her eyes.

'Lilia speaks of you. She is very happy. Her father was found alive, in one of Abu's dungeons.'

'That's wonderful!'

He grinned. 'Rachelle still speaks of you, too. She says she hopes some day you will see the error of your ways and admit what a wonderful person I really am.'

Joanna laughed. 'I'll do my best.' Her smile faded, and she touched the tip of her tongue to her lip. 'Khalil—about Lilia. I felt awful, involving her in my escape, but——'

'Do you still have it in your heart to be a teacher, beloved?'

She looked at him with a puzzled smile on her lips. 'What do you mean?'

'There is much to do in my country. Lilia, and all the children, are eager to learn.' Khalil kissed her tenderly. 'Do you think you could give up your job at Bennettco and come back to Jandara with me to teach them?'

Joanna's eyes shone. 'Is that all you want me to do?'

'What I want,' he said, holding her close, 'is for you to be my wife and my love, and to live with me in happiness forever.'

As the sun rose over the Manhattan rooftops, Joanna gave Khalil her promise in a way she knew he would surely understand.

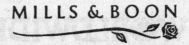

FOR BETTER FOR WORSE

They would each face life's bittersweet choices in their search for love...

Penny Jordan has created a masterpiece of raw emotion, with this dramatic novel which takes a fascinating and, at times, painfully telling look at three couples' hopes, dreams and desires.

A story of obsessions...
A story of choices...
A story of love.

AVAILABLE NOW

PRICED: £4.99

Next Month's Romances

Each month you can choose from a wide variety of romance with Mills & Boon. Below are the new titles to look out for next month, why not ask either Mills & Boon Reader Service or your Newsagent to reserve you a copy of the titles you want to buy – just tick the titles you would like and either post to Reader Service or take it to any Newsagent and ask them to order your books.

Please save me the following titles:		Please tick	✓
NO RISKS, NO PRIZES	Emma Darcy		
ANGEL OF DARKNESS	Lynne Graham		
BRITTLE BONDAGE	Anne Mather		
SENSE OF DESTINY	Patricia Wilson		
THE SUN AT MIDNIGHT	Sandra Field		
DUEL IN THE SUN	Sally Wentworth		
MYTHS OF THE MOON	Rosalie Ash		
MORE THAN LOVERS	Natalie Fox		
LEONIE'S LUCK	Emma Goldrick		
WILD INJUSTICE	Margaret Mayo		
A MAGICAL AFFAIR	Victoria Gordon		
SPANISH NIGHTS	Jennifer Taylor		
FORSAKING ALL REASON	Jenny Cartwright		
SECRET SURRENDER	Laura Martin		
SHADOWS OF YESTERDAY	Cathy Williams		
BOTH OF THEM	Rebecca Winters		

If you would like to order these books in addition to your regular subscription from Mills & Boon Reader Service please send £1.90 per title to: Mills & Boon Reader Service, Freepost, P.O. Box 236, Croydon, Surrey, CR9 9EL, quote your Subscriber No:................................... (if applicable) and complete the name and address details below. Alternatively, these books are available from many local Newsagents including W H Smith, J Menzies, Martins and other paperback stockists from 9 September 1994.

Name:..

Address:..

....Post Code:.........................

To Retailer: If you would like to stock M&B books please contact your regular book/magazine wholesaler for details.

You may be mailed with offers from other reputable companies as a result of this application. If you would rather not take advantage of these opportunities please tick box. ☐

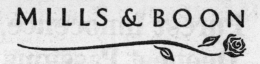

MILLS & BOON

Forthcoming Titles

FAVOURITES
Available in September

LOVE'S REWARD Robyn Donald
ROMANCE OF A LIFETIME Carole Mortimer

DUET
Available in August

The Roberta Leigh Duet **MAN ON THE MAKE**
 A MOST UNSUITABLE WIFE

The Penny Jordan Duet **BREAKING AWAY**
 RIVAL ATTRACTIONS

LOVE ON CALL
Available in September

STILL WATERS Kathleen Farrell
HEARTS AT SEA Clare Lavenham
WHISPER IN THE HEART Meredith Webber
DELUGE Stella Whitelaw

Available from W.H. Smith, John Menzies, Volume One, Forbuoys, Martins, Tesco, Asda, Safeway and other paperback stockists.

Also available from Mills & Boon Reader Service, Freepost, P.O. Box 236, Croydon, Surrey CR9 9EL.

Readers in South Africa - write to:
Book Services International Ltd, P.O. Box 41654, Craighall, Transvaal 2024.

Purest Innocence,
Deepest Passions
and Love's Choices…

Determined and ruthless, Comte Alexei Serivace would not be swayed from his cruel plan of revenge—a plan in which Hope Stanford was an unwilling pawn. Removed from her sheltered convent life, Hope quickly realised that she was no match for this arrogant sophisticate—but she didn't intend to be a pushover either.

Available now priced at £3.99

W⦿RLDWIDE